Brenda Jackson is a *New York Times* bestselling author of more than one hundred romance titles. Brenda lives in Jacksonville, Florida, and divides her time between family, writing and travelling. Email Brenda at authorbrendajackson@gmail.com or visit her on her website at brendajackson.net

Joanne Rock credits her decision to write romance after a book she picked up during a flight delay engrossed her so thoroughly that she didn't mind at all when her flight was delayed two more times. Giving her readers the chance to escape into another world has motivated her to write over eighty books for a variety of Mills & Boon series.

WHAT HAPPENS ON VACATION...

BRENDA JACKSON

THE RANCHER'S RECKONING

JOANNE ROCK

MILLS & BOON

First Published in Great Britain 2022
by Mills & Boon, an imprint of HarperCollins*Publishers* Ltd
1 London Bridge Street, London, SE1 9GF

www.harpercollins.co.uk

HarperCollins*Publishers*
1st Floor, Watermarque Building,
Ringsend Road, Dublin 4, Ireland

What Happens on Vacation... © 2022 Brenda Streater Jackson
The Rancher's Reckoning © 2022 Harlequin Books S.A.

Special thanks and acknowledgement are given to Joanne Rock for her contribution to the *Texas Cattleman's Club: Fathers and Sons* series.

ISBN: 978-0-263-30375-9

0322

MIX
Paper from
responsible sources
FSC™ C007454

This book is produced from independently certified FSC™ paper to ensure responsible forest management.

For more information visit: www.harpercollins.co.uk/green

Printed and Bound in Spain using 100% Renewable electricity at CPI Black Print, Barcelona

WHAT HAPPENS ON VACATION...

BRENDA JACKSON

To the man who will always and forever be the love of my life, Gerald Jackson Sr. My hero. My heart. My soul. My everything.

To my sons, Gerald Jr. and Brandon. You guys are the greatest and continue to make your parents proud.

To my readers who enjoy reading about the Westmorelands and their cousins, the Outlaws. This one is for you!

One

"**Y**ou're not coming home to Fairbanks during the monthlong summer break in the Senate, Jess?"

Senator Jessup Outlaw moved around his bedroom packing while talking to his oldest brother, Garth, on his cell. "No. I met up with Spencer last month when he was in DC on business. Reggie and I joined him one night for drinks." Spencer Westmoreland was their cousin from California who owned a huge vineyard near Napa Valley. Reginald Westmoreland was Spencer's brother and also a fellow senator.

"Spencer invited me to visit him and Chardonnay at the Russell Vineyards. Since many of you are busy right now and will be down there for the anniversary celebration at the end of the month anyway, I decided to accept his invitation."

"What about town hall meetings with your constituents?"

"I held several while home for Sloan's wedding, so I'm good there. Everyone needs a vacation, even senators."

Jess, as he was known to his family and friends, was thirty-eight and a senator for his state of Alaska. He also had four brothers and a sister who kept him busy. All Jess's siblings worked for the family-owned business, Outlaw Freight Lines. He'd worked there as a corporate attorney for over ten years before deciding on a career in politics. Garth had taken over as CEO a few years ago when their father, Bart, had retired, or more specifically, when the company's board had threatened to oust him.

Garth was the oldest sibling, with only a two-year difference in their ages. Garth and his wife, Regan, would soon be flying to Florida to visit his in-laws for the first time since the birth of their son, Garrison, who was born in the spring.

As of last year, Jess's brother Cash, who was two years younger, had made his home in Wyoming on the dude ranch he'd inherited. He was married to Brianna and they had twin sons, Cason and Cannon. Jess's brother Sloan was four years younger and the most recent Outlaw to marry this past June. Sloan and his wife, Leslie, had recently returned from a monthlong honeymoon.

Maverick, Jess's youngest brother, was seven years younger and was on a business trip to Ireland, while Jess's sister, Charm, who was eleven years younger, had made plans to visit the Westmoreland cousins in Atlanta. The only other family member left was their father, Bart. They'd talked a couple of weeks ago and Bart had mentioned that during August he and Charm's mother, Claudia, would be taking a trip to London.

"You're right. All of us have plans to arrive at the Russell Vineyards at the end of the month for the anniversary celebration, so I guess we'll see you then," Garth said.

Spencer and Chardonnay were hosting a seventy-fifth

wedding anniversary party for Chardonnay's grandparents, Daniel and Katherine Russell. It was always a fun time whenever the Westmorelands and Outlaws got together.

"Well, enjoy yourself and give Spencer and Chardonnay my regards."

"I will and I'll see everyone at the party."

A short while later, Jess had finished packing and glanced up at the television when a familiar face flashed across the screen. Grabbing the remote, he increased the volume to hear what the reporter was saying.

A week after illicit photos popped up on social media, actor Kemp Pierson and actress Maya Roadie still refuse to comment. It seems they really got into their roles while in New Zealand filming the movie Midnight Heat. *Apparently, they had their own midnight heat going on in spite of Kemp's serious relationship with actress Paige Novak. Ms. Novak, who just wrapped up filming in Japan, was unavailable for comment. In fact, nobody knows her whereabouts...*

Jess flipped off the television and shook his head. If the allegations against Kemp Pierson were true, then the man was an asshole. No one deserved that type of betrayal. Jess, of all people, should know. Thanks to Ava Sampson, he'd experienced a similar betrayal ten years ago, and he wouldn't wish that sort of heartbreak on his worst enemy.

It just so happened that Paige Novak was the sister of Pam Westmoreland, who was married to his cousin Dillon. Every so often, his and Paige's paths crossed at some Westmoreland family function. She was a very beautiful woman. A woman he'd been attracted to from the first. But he hadn't acted on that attraction because the timing hadn't been right. He'd needed to focus on his campaign. But he could now say that not hooking up with

Paige six years ago was a missed opportunity, one he'd come to regret.

If this vacation offered another such opportunity with a beautiful woman, he wouldn't miss it.

Paige Novak turned away from the window when she heard the knock on the door. After crossing the floor, she glanced out the peephole and smiled as she opened the door. "Chardonnay."

"Hi. I'm just checking to see if you want to join us for dinner."

Paige's smile widened. "I'd love to, and I appreciate you and Spencer letting me crash here for a while." This time last week she had been at the airport in Tokyo when she'd gotten a call from a good friend and neighbor letting her know the paparazzi were camped outside her door. It hadn't taken Paige long to find out why. The affair between Kemp and Maya had been all over social media.

"You don't have to thank us, Paige. You were overdue for a visit anyway," Chardonnay said.

Paige appreciated that, since she'd been at the vineyards a week already and had worried about overstaying her welcome. "I love it here," she said. "I was just looking at the view and thinking it's so beautiful and peaceful."

"Well, you can stay as long as you want. It's nice seeing the guest villas being used."

"Thanks, and I'd love to join everyone for dinner." She enjoyed Spencer's and Chardonnay's company, as well as that of their three children and Chardonnay's grandparents.

"Great. We'll be eating around five."

"Okay. I need to make a few calls. Nadia has been blowing up my phone for some reason, so I need to call her back."

After Chardonnay left, Paige tried calling her younger

sister, who had called four times while Paige had been taking a shower. She wondered what the urgency was. When
she got Nadia's voice mail, she figured her sister was in
a meeting and left a message for Nadia to call her back.

Paige decided to call her sister Jillian to see if perhaps
she knew why Nadia had been trying to reach her. Jillian,
who was two years older, was a neurosurgeon and working at a hospital in Florida. "Hi, Jill. Do you know why
Nadia has been blowing up my phone?"

"I have no idea," Jill said, sounding rushed. "You might
want to check with Pam. I'm due in surgery and will call
you back later."

"Okay."

Crossing the room, Paige then sat down on the sofa to
call her oldest sister, Pam, who had married Dillon Westmoreland thirteen years ago when Paige had been fifteen.
To Paige, Westmoreland Country—a rural area outside
Denver where thousands of acres were owned and occupied by the Westmoreland family—was more home to her
than the Novak Homestead she and her sisters still owned
in Gamble, Wyoming.

Paige had considered going home to Westmoreland
Country after leaving Tokyo, but had decided against it.
Pam had enough on her plate with a second set of triplets due to be born any day to Dillon's brother Bane and
his wife, Crystal. Pam and Dillon would look after the
first set of triplets—who would be barely six years old
when the new babies were born. Everyone in Westmoreland Country was excited about the births. The last thing
Paige wanted was to allow her issues with Kemp to cloud
everyone's happiness.

She speed-dialed Pam's number, and not surprisingly,
her sister picked up on the first ring. "Paige? The family
wants to make sure you're doing okay."

Paige smiled. She'd only called Pam twice since arriving in Napa Valley last week. Although Paige was twenty-eight, she knew her family still worried about her. "Tell everyone I'm doing fine."

"I wish I were there to give you a hug. I don't like that Kemp betrayed you and now the press will keep it front and center until one of you makes a statement about it."

Since Pam had once been an actress herself, she knew how the media worked. "I'm not keeping up with anything on television or social media, so I'm fine," Paige said. And she definitely had no plans to make a statement.

"Have you heard from Kemp?" Pam asked.

Kemp had called last week when the story first broke, and he hadn't bothered to deny the allegations. Instead, he'd said the affair meant nothing, that he and Maya had had a few drinks too many. He apologized for their reckless behavior and wanted to know where Paige was so he could send her flowers. Flowers! He honestly thought flowers would remedy what he'd done.

What bothered Paige more than anything was Kemp's attitude about the whole thing. He honestly expected her to accept his apology and for them to move on like nothing had happened. She had informed him that wouldn't be happening and for him to get on with life because she intended to get on with hers. He'd refused to accept she was breaking up with him and then had the audacity to get upset when she'd refused to tell him where she was.

"I blocked his number," Paige said.

"Well, just so you know, he's called here three times looking for you. Not that we care, but I think he got mad with us for not telling him where you are. I have a feeling he believes what Nadia said."

"Nadia?"

"Yes. Have you talked to her? Has she told you what she did?"

"No. I see I missed several of her calls, but when I called her back, it went to voice mail."

"She's probably in a meeting," Pam said. After graduating from college with an MBA, Nadia had moved back to Gamble, Wyoming, to manage the acting school Pam owned there.

"What did Nadia do, Pam?" Paige could just imagine. Of her sisters, Nadia was the youngest and was known to be outspoken.

"I'd rather Nadia told you herself, Paige."

Paige didn't like the sound of that and was about to say so when she saw another call coming in. It was Nadia. "Well, she'll get her chance, Pam. I have a call from Nadia. I'll talk to you later."

"Okay."

Paige then clicked to the incoming call. "Nadia, what's going on?"

"Have you listened to the news lately?" Nadia asked anxiously.

"No. Why?"

When Nadia paused, Paige then asked, "Nadia, what did you do?"

"Well, several reporters assumed since you weren't in LA or in Westmoreland Country that you were here in Gamble."

"Reporters showed up in Gamble?"

"Yes, and at the Novak Homestead."

"And?"

"And they were parked outside the house when I left for work. They surrounded me, put their mics in my face and tried to get me to tell them where you were."

Paige swallowed. She knew how insistent reporters could be. "Please tell me you didn't tell them."

"Of course I didn't tell them. But one particular reporter got on my last nerve, so I told him something else."

"What?"

"Well, that particular reporter, a real ass, suggested you were somewhere dealing with a broken heart and that maybe the incident had left you needing intervention."

Paige frowned. "That was a cruel thing to say."

"I thought so, too, which is why I said what I did."

"And just what did you say?"

"I told them that we didn't have to check on you because Kemp was the last man on your mind. That you've already moved on and are seeing someone else."

Paige shrugged. That wasn't true, but it didn't sound too bad. At least, she thought that until Nadia added...

"And that the two of you were involved in a hot, romantic entanglement."

"What! A hot, romantic entanglement? Honestly, Nadia," Paige said, wondering how Nadia came up with such a phrase. She had news for her sister. Paige had never been in a hot, romantic entanglement in her entire life. Even Kemp had left a lot to be desired in the romance department. Although Kemp assumed he was fantastic in bed and took her over the moon whenever they'd made love, in truth, she never even came close to reaching the stars.

"Well, that reporter pissed me off, Paige. You were getting ready to kick Kemp to the curb anyway."

Well, at least Nadia hadn't told *that* to the reporter. Paige had confided those plans to her sisters the last time they'd been together, during the holidays. After almost a year without developing feelings for Kemp, she'd planned to end things when they were back together after filming next month. Although she wasn't brokenhearted by Kemp's affair, she felt hurt and betrayed, nonetheless. He had disrespected her in the worst way a man could do to a woman.

"Now it's all over the media that you're dating someone else, and they're trying to find out where you are and who's your new guy. At least they don't know you're hiding out at Russell Vineyards."

Paige rubbed a frustrated hand down her face, wishing Nadia would have just ignored those reporters or given a "no comment."

"First of all, I'm not hiding out here, Nadia."

"Aren't you?"

"No. I'm visiting our cousins-in-law. My filming project is over, and I consider this a vacation."

"Vacation? Right. I bet you haven't left the vineyard to go into town to shop or anything. To me, that's hiding out."

Deciding to end the conversation with Nadia, she said, "I'm having dinner with Spencer, Chardonnay and the family in a few, and I need to get dressed. I'll talk with you later. 'Bye."

She quickly clicked off the phone. Nadia didn't understand that the media was a force to reckon with. Paige didn't see herself as hiding out. She was merely preserving her privacy for as long as she could. She would make an appearance when she was ready, and not because the media felt she should.

In less than an hour, Paige was walking out of the guest villa to head to the main house. The walk wasn't a long one and she enjoyed strolling around Russell Vineyards—three hundred acres of beautiful land in the Napa Valley.

When she got closer to the main house, she saw a car parked out front next to her rental and wondered if Spencer and Chardonnay were having guests for dinner. The door to the house opened, and Russell—Spencer and Chardonnay's sixteen-year-old son—came out to greet her with a huge smile on his face. Chardonnay had warned Paige that Russell was a huge fan, and his mom suspected he had a crush on her.

"Hi, Paige!" he said, coming down the steps to meet her.

"Hi, Russell. Where's Chablis and Daniel?" she asked. She thought Russell Spencer Westmoreland and his younger brother, Daniel Timberlain Westmoreland, were the spitting image of their father, Spencer; whereas their sister, Chablis, looked like her mother. All three—Russell, Daniel and Chablis—had inherited Chardonnay's family trait of beautiful gray eyes.

"Chablis is helping Mom and Grammy with dinner. How was your nap?"

Normally, she took an afternoon nap every day. "It was wonderful. Thanks for asking."

When they reached the door, Russell opened it and stood back as she entered. He had impeccable manners for someone his age.

When she stepped inside, a deep, husky voice said, "Hello, Paige."

She turned and her gaze connected to that of Jess Outlaw, a cousin to the Westmorelands. A smile touched her lips. "Jess."

When she'd seen the car outside, she hadn't known who would be visiting and had hoped it wasn't someone who would recognize her. The last thing she needed was word of her whereabouts getting leaked. But this was Jess and she'd gotten to know him over the years. He was someone she felt comfortable around. She recalled the first time they'd met, over six years ago, and how she had been attracted to him the moment their gazes had met.

There had been a sensual pull, which had been a first for her where a man was concerned. So much so that she'd felt bold enough to do a little flirting. But what woman wouldn't when Jess was tall, handsome and possessed a demanding presence? Definitely swoon-worthy. Regretfully, he hadn't reciprocated the interest.

Leaving Spencer's side, Jess crossed the floor and

reached out to give her a hug. "You're okay?" he asked her in a gentle, concerned voice.

She leaned back and smiled up at him. Obviously, he'd heard what was being splashed all over the media. "I'm fine. What brings you from the nation's capital, Senator?"

A warm smile touched his lips. "I'm here on vacation. Spencer invited me last month when he was in DC, and I decided to take him up on his invite."

"You're going to love it here."

"I do already."

At that moment Mrs. Katherine Russell, Chardonnay's grandmother, appeared in the kitchen doorway with a huge smile on her face. "Dinner is ready, everyone."

Jess offered Paige his arm, and she took it as he escorted her into the dining room.

Two

Jess tried not to stare across the dining room table at Paige. Had she felt the same electrical charge that had raced through him when he'd taken her arm? If she had felt anything, she was doing a good job of pretending she hadn't.

In his lifetime he had met numerous beautiful women, but he was convinced Paige was absolutely the most gorgeous. Everything about her was stunning. First there were her sable-brown eyes. Next were her lips. Their shape was perfect and he loved how they could ease into a sexy smile when she was amused or tilt at the corner when she had nothing to say. Every time he looked at them, he couldn't help wondering how they tasted. Just how sweet and delicious would they be in a kiss?

Then there were the rest of her features. High cheekbones and dimples that made her smile even more dynamic. A perfect nose and a glorious mane of dark brown hair. There was no doubt about it—Paige Novak was a knockout. He could see her beauty dazzling any television or movie screen.

He could clearly remember the first time he'd seen her—when he'd arrived in Denver to attend Bailey Westmoreland's wedding to a close Outlaw family friend, Walker Rafferty. Paige had been one of the bridesmaids, and he, like his brothers, had been a groomsman.

The Westmorelands had kicked off the wedding weekend with a huge family get-together two days before the event. Had it really been over six years ago? Due to being in the thick of his campaign for senator, he hadn't officially met the Westmorelands until a couple of months before the wedding. The Outlaws had been invited to join the Westmorelands for Christmas. It had been a time to get acquainted with the cousins he and his siblings hadn't known existed until a private investigator had shown up in Alaska telling them about the Westmorelands and how they shared the same great-grandfather Raphel Westmoreland.

Up until then, they hadn't known their grandfather had been adopted or that Raphel had died not knowing he'd fathered an illegitimate son. The Westmorelands had the proof, but to this day, Jess's father, Bart Outlaw, refused to accept the facts and claimed there was no Westmoreland blood in their veins. As far as Jess and his siblings were concerned, that was a damn sorry claim when the Westmoreland men and the Outlaw men could pass for brothers. Same thing with his sister, Charm, and the five Westmoreland-born women.

Paige hadn't made the trip home for the holidays that year since she'd been in a new version of *The Nutcracker* in Manhattan. The first time Jess had seen her had been that February at the wedding.

He recalled that day when he'd entered Dillon's home and his gaze had connected to hers. There had been instant attraction. When he'd inquired, he'd been told that she wasn't a Westmoreland cousin but one of Dillon's sisters-in-law. Jess had been glad to know they weren't related, especially when he couldn't keep his eyes off her. The short dress she'd been wearing had showcased a gorgeous pair of legs.

The one thing he recalled more than anything else was that she had flirted with him during those three days he'd been in Denver. He'd felt the magnetism whenever their gazes met or when they were within a few feet of each other. However, the attraction could not have come at a worse time due to his Senate campaign.

He would have to admit that Paige had affected him in an unusual way, and the thought of her had stayed with him for a long time. Now, while sitting across the table from her, he couldn't help but wonder—what might have happened if the timing hadn't been so lousy for him back then?

She seemed to be doing fine, just like she'd said when he'd asked. But she was an actress and was probably doing a good job of hiding her pain. There was no way she wasn't torn up over what that asshole of a boyfriend had done, and knowing her business was all over the media had to be another blow. At least she was smiling while Russell, Chablis and Daniel kept things lively.

A few years ago, Spencer had told Jess how he and Chardonnay had met. Spencer, a wealthy tycoon who enjoyed adding businesses to his portfolio, had set his sights on the Russell Vineyards, with plans to turn it into a resort. Spencer had heard of the Russells' financial problems and had intended to take over their property...until he'd seen Chardonnay. The rest, as they say, was history.

Anyone around the couple for any length of time knew how in love they were. Spencer still built his multimillion-dollar resort, but not on Russell land. Instead, it had been built on property he'd acquired ten miles from here. The five-star resort he called Windemere.

"How do you like being in politics, Jess?" Chardonnay's grandmother asked him, bringing him out of his reverie.

He smiled over at the older woman whom everyone called Grammy. "I enjoy it. Never a dull moment. I'm the new kid on the block and just getting my feet wet. However, I was lucky to get assigned to the education committee." He saw that Paige had stopped eating and was listening attentively.

She said, "I've heard about some of the bills your committee is proposing."

He lifted a brow. "You have?"

"Yes. The last time Reggie visited Westmoreland Country I happened to be home. He mentioned how when you arrived in DC, you hit the ground running. He likes the fact that the Westmorelands have two senators in the family."

The conversation then shifted to all the babies who had been born in the Westmoreland and Outlaw families in the past year. "Delaney gave birth to twin sons and I hear Sheriff Pete Higgins and his wife are expecting," Spencer said. Pete Higgins was a childhood friend of the Westmorelands.

"I heard that as well," Paige replied. "Everyone is excited about Bane and Crystal's second set of triplets. That's a first in the Westmoreland family. They are due to arrive any day now."

"I hear they're all boys," Chardonnay said.

"Yes," Paige said. "I talked to Crystal a few weeks ago and they were still deciding on names."

Chardonnay chuckled. "They said they wanted a large family, so they are definitely getting one."

"How's your mom?" Jess then asked Chardonnay.

"Mom is doing fine. Now that Dad has retired, they're doing a lot of traveling. I talked to her a few days ago when she called from Paris. They'll be arriving two weeks before the anniversary celebration to help out."

Then the topic shifted to the vineyards when Chardonnay's grandfather began explaining to Paige and Jess how the grapes that were planted in early spring were ready to be harvested and turned into wine during the summer months. And Chardonnay served an apple pie that Grammy had baked with glasses of wine from their vineyard.

"It's Russell's night to do dishes," Grammy said when the meal was over.

"But I want to walk Paige back to the villa, Grammy."

Spencer laughed. "I'm sure Paige has appreciated you walking her to the villa these past few days, Russell, but Jess is heading back that way and I'm sure he doesn't mind making sure she gets there safely."

Jess smiled. "Of course I don't mind." He glanced at his watch and saw it was close to eight already. They'd spent three hours eating and talking, but he had enjoyed everyone's company...especially that of Paige. He saw more laughter in her eyes now than he'd seen earlier, and that was good.

A short while later, he stood. "I'm ready to leave whenever you are."

"I'm ready now," she said, smiling over at him.

Both thanked everyone for dinner and then he escorted Paige out the door.

"It's such a beautiful night, isn't it, Jess?" Paige asked, looking up into the sky dotted with stars.

"Yes, it is. I can even smell the grapes. Can you?"

She sniffed the air and laughed. "Most definitely. Last

week I saw the equipment crush and ferment the grapes. It was fascinating to watch."

"I bet it was," he said as they strolled along the well-lit path.

"Over dinner you said you would be here awhile," she said when it got quiet between them.

"Yes, the entire month. The Outlaws are all traveling, so there's no one in Alaska. I'll see everyone when they come to the party."

"Do you have any big plans while you're here?" she asked, thinking this was the first time she ever recalled them being alone. All those times she'd seen him in Westmoreland Country, there had been others around.

He glanced over at her and smiled, showing that dimple in his bearded chin. Instantly, a spike of heat caught in the pit of her stomach. The same thing had happened the very first time he'd smiled at her six years ago. There had been a connection, she'd been certain of it, and she had made sure with her flirtation that he'd felt it. Obviously, she'd been wrong, since he'd never acted on it.

"No big plans other than to rest, relax and enjoy the scenery. And the foods in the area. One of the first things I plan to do is get a pizza."

"You like pizza?"

"I love pizza, and I heard there's this place not far from here called Phillippe's that serves the best," he said. "People say you can't come to Napa Valley without trying it, and that it tastes good no matter what kind of wine you drink with it."

She'd heard that, too, from her agent, Maxie, when she'd called to let her know where she was. "I love pizza, too."

She saw Jess was looking at her with a peculiar expression on his face. "Is something wrong?" she asked.

He shrugged massive shoulders. Paige thought the

slacks and button-up shirt looked good on him. She would have to admit that whenever she'd seen him over the years, whatever he'd been wearing had fit his body well. "I was just wondering about something," he said.

"About what?"

She saw the teasing glint in his dark eyes when he said, "While driving here from the airport, on the radio I heard what Nadia said to that reporter, and unless I'm missing something or someone, you don't appear to be engaging in a hot, romantic entanglement with anyone."

Paige laughed. "Nadia likes embellishing things. However, part of what she said was true."

"What part?"

"That Kemp and I are no longer together and that I have moved on."

"Does he know that?"

"He knows—trust me. I told him myself. However, I think he's convinced he can change my mind."

"Can he?"

Paige rolled her eyes. "Not in his lifetime or mine."

They walked for a while in silence before he asked, "How long do you plan to stay here?"

She shrugged. "I was going to leave next week. I don't start another film project for a few months, so this is a vacation for me. Spencer and Chardonnay would love for me to stay longer. I just might since I've seen Chardonnay's to-do list for her grandparents' anniversary party. It's rather long and I might help her shorten it some. That might mean I'll be here for the rest of the month, like you."

She didn't want him to get the impression *he* had anything to do with her decision to stay, so she quickly added, "This is a nice place, and Spencer, Chardonnay, the kids and the Russells make it easy to want to hang around. They take pampering to a whole new level."

"I'm glad. You need pampering."

"Thanks, Jess, but honestly, I'm fine. My only regret is that I misjudged Kemp's character," she added.

"It happens to the best of us—trust me."

She tilted her head to look at him. "Has it ever happened to you?"

"Yes. Ten years ago."

Ten years was a long time ago, but she knew heartbreak could last a lifetime for some people. Especially if they'd truly loved that person. She wondered if that was why he was still single, unlike his brothers, who seemed to be getting married every time she turned around. She couldn't help wondering what had happened.

Then, as if he knew her thoughts, he said, "Ava and I met in law school, and we began dating seriously. It was our plan—at least, I'd assumed it was—for us to start thinking about marriage once we graduated. We'd dated for almost a year and had gotten an apartment together. I had to leave school one week to return home due to a family crisis. I was only supposed to be gone two weeks, but came back early."

He didn't say anything for a minute. "I returned and walked in on Ava and another guy in bed. She said that after a few drinks one thing led to another."

Paige shook her head. "Blame it on the alcohol. Would you believe Kemp said the same thing about his affair with Maya? That they'd had one drink too many and things got out of hand."

Jess shoved his hands into his pockets as they continued walking. "The way I saw it then, and the way I see it now, is that we must not have meant a hell of a lot to Ava and Kemp for an overindulgence in liquor to cause them to be unfaithful to us."

"I agree."

They stopped walking when they came to her villa. "This is your guest villa, right?"

"Yes, this is it. Where's yours?"

"Down the path, about twenty feet away. I'm close by if you ever need me for anything."

"Thanks, Jess."

"Good night, Paige, and just remember one thing."

"What?"

"The man who doesn't appreciate you doesn't deserve you."

She nodded. "Thanks for saying that. Good night."

Paige opened the door and went inside. The first thing she did once she had closed the door behind her was draw in a deep breath. Why did Jess have to smell so good? She had picked up the scent of grapes, but she had also picked up the scent of man. The cologne he was wearing was the same one he'd worn the day they'd met and each time their paths crossed since. She didn't know of any other man who wore that particular fragrance. She recalled being so taken with it that she'd come close to asking him the name of it so she could buy Kemp a bottle for Christmas. Paige never did and now she was glad she hadn't. She honestly couldn't imagine that fragrance on any other man. It was uniquely Jess.

She entered the kitchen to make a cup of tea when her cell phone rang. She smiled, recognizing the ringtone. It was the theme music of a popular medical show. "You're up late, Jill."

"I'm on my way home after performing emergency surgery, and I wanted to check on you."

"I hope the surgery went okay," she said.

"It did. Aidan called as I was leaving the hospital to let me know he has dinner all prepared."

"Lucky you." Aidan Westmoreland was Jill's husband and also Dillon's cousin. Paige thought it was cute that two sisters had married cousins. "One day I hope to marry a guy like Aidan."

"And you will. I'm glad that Kemp's infidelity hasn't made you write off men forever."

"It didn't. Besides, you know my relationship with Kemp was coming to an end anyway."

"Yes, but he didn't know that. Having a man cheat on you has to be disappointing, Paige, and I regret you got tied up with a guy who didn't respect you or your feelings."

"I'm not lessening what he did by any means, but at least I wasn't in love with him to suffer a heartbreak along with disappointment. He was someone I thought I could trust."

"Well, I'm getting a kick out of seeing the media's reaction to that rumor Nadia's started."

Paige rolled her eyes. "I still can't believe Nadia did that. I'm hoping it will soon die down."

"Not sure that it will now that Kemp has made a statement."

Paige nearly dropped the teacup. "What? When?"

"A short while ago. I caught it right before leaving the hospital. When a reporter asked him about Nadia's claim that you'd moved on and were already seeing someone else, he said it wasn't true because you loved him and the two of you are still a couple."

She frowned. "Oh, he thinks I love him, does he? If he thought that, then why did he have an affair with Maya? And that part about us still being a couple is not true and he knows it. I ended things between us."

"Evidently, he didn't believe you. I hate to say it, but his statement makes you look like a woman who would put up with any bullshit a man throws her way in the name of love. Now that he's considered the Hottest Man Alive, he's convinced he's a prize."

"Kemp can believe whatever he wants," Paige said. "I blocked his calls. He can't reach me and doesn't know where I am." Deciding to change the subject, Paige said, "Guess who's here at Russell Vineyards vacationing?"

"Who?"

"Jess Outlaw."

"The Alaskan?"

Paige couldn't help but grin. Although Jess and his brothers were all eye candy, it had been Jess who had wowed her to the point that she had referred to him as The Alaskan whenever she mentioned him to her sisters. Charm had told them he'd been captain of the dogsled race team in high school and college. Jess Outlaw was so ruggedly built she could definitely see him doing that.

"Yes, The Alaskan. He's on a break from the Senate and will be here until the party."

"I remember when you had that crush on him."

Jill would remember that. "That was a long time ago, and it only lasted during the few days he was in Denver. Once he left, it was out of sight and out of mind."

"Well, I recall you flirted with him a lot."

Yes, she had, but he hadn't been interested. "Like I said, that was a long time ago and nothing came of it. I was twenty-two and didn't know better. Luckily for me, he was older and did know better and didn't take advantage of my naivete."

She and Jill talked for another half hour before they ended the call. As Paige sat down at the table with her tea, she hoped Jill was right, that one day she would find a man deserving of her love, someone she shared romantic chemistry with as well.

In two years, she would be thirty. She loved acting but didn't intend on making it her life's career. She'd even given serious thought to teaching drama at a university. What she needed to do more than thinking about men was get her personal life in order, and getting back with Kemp was not on the list, regardless of what he'd told the media.

Three

The villa was just as warm and cozy as his studio apartment in DC. It was definitely a lot larger. His brothers often teased him about the size of his apartment when he could certainly afford something more spacious. He was, after all, one of those Alaska Outlaws whose family owned a billion-dollar shipping company. However, he'd never been one to flash and flaunt and had known the moment he'd seen the studio apartment it was exactly what he needed.

He didn't require a lot of space. Just as long as he had a bed to sleep in, a bathroom and a desk to work at, he was fine. Since he'd signed up for one of those meal delivery services, his moderate kitchen served him well. And his place was walking distance to the Metro. Very few people living in and around Dupont Circle had a car. Everything was conveniently located.

What he liked about the two-bedroom guest villa was the decor, earth tones that blended with the environment.

The artwork depicted various locations at the vineyards, and the area rugs gave the place a homey appeal.

He flipped on the television to watch the ending of the baseball game before going into the bedroom to undress and put on something more comfortable. After changing into a pair of cutoff denims and a T-shirt, he walked to the kitchen to grab a beer out of the refrigerator. Spencer had stocked several bottles of his favorite brand.

Picking up the remote, he then flipped through channels to see if there was anything else worth watching when he came to one of those entertainment channels. He was about to turn the television off when he saw Paige's ex.

Jess turned up the volume in time to hear Kemp Pierson say, "Of course Paige isn't happy about what I did. I was wrong and I've apologized. We both agree what I did was a mistake, but not anything we can't work out."

Another reporter then asked, "And what about her sister's claim that Miss Novak has broken things off with you and has moved on?"

A smile spread across Pierson's lips as if such a thing was absurd. "Paige loves me, and regardless of what her sister is saying, there is no doubt in my mind that Paige has not moved on and the two of us will work things out." Pierson then pushed his way through a set of double glass doors.

One reporter looked at the camera and said, "Well, there you have it. According to Kemp Pierson, regardless of his affair with Maya Roadie, he and Miss Novak are still an item."

Jess frowned. Did Kemp Pierson honestly think he could betray Paige the way he had and then appear on national television and say she would forgive him because she loved him? What an ass.

He'd heard enough. He flipped off the television and went to the screened patio out back. The scent of grapes was even more potent here and he noticed his patio faced the one attached to Paige's villa.

After the first time they'd met, whenever his and Paige's paths crossed at any family functions, their encounters were brief and friendly. After he'd won the seat in the Senate and had more time, it was Paige who'd been focused on her career. More than once, he'd thought about giving her a call, but kept putting it off.

When he'd finally decided to get her phone number from Charm, his sister had mentioned that Paige was dating one of the sexiest actors in Hollywood and things looked serious. It was then that he'd realized not reciprocating her interest when they'd met had been a missed opportunity on his part.

His phone rang and he recognized the ringtone. It was his brother Sloan. Clicking on, he said, "Yes, Sloan?"

"Have you heard that BS about Paige and that guy she's been dating?"

Jess took a sip of his beer. Over the years, his brothers and sister had made more frequent visits to Westmoreland Country than he had, so they'd gotten to know Paige well. "Yes, I heard. What of it?"

"The man messed around on her. She deserved better than that."

Jess agreed and that was the same thing he'd told Paige. "Yes, she did."

"Well, I hope what Nadia told that reporter is true, and Paige has met another guy and is somewhere enjoying her time with him."

"Why?" he asked, deciding not to mention that Paige was here at the Russell Vineyards, and she wasn't with a man. It was up to her to share her business.

"You've never met Kemp Pierson, but I have. One of my companies invested in a couple of his movies." Sloan's words reminded Jess that in addition to being an executive in their family's shipping business, Sloan had a stake in several other business ventures, including a film production company in LA. "He's arrogant, self-centered and egotistical. I heard he's even worse now since being voted the Hottest Man Alive by that magazine."

"Well, undoubtedly Paige loved him." According to what Pierson had just said in the interview, she still loved him. He sounded pretty damn sure of it.

"And that's what I don't get. Paige is a beautiful woman and can definitely do better."

"Better than the hottest man alive?" he asked, just to see what Sloan would say.

"Looks aren't everything, Jess. None of the Westmorelands like him either. The few times she's brought him to Westmoreland Country, Derringer claims he acted so condescending and patronizing, they counted the hours until he left. Zane even thought they might have one of those contract relationships for publicity. We all agreed that was a possibility."

Jess lifted a brow. "What's a contract relationship?"

"When a couple pretends they're together. Their agents draw up a contract for the charade. It benefits them both."

Hope sprang up inside Jess. "So, all of you think that's what they had? One of those contract deals?"

"We did, but not anymore. Zane asked her about it, and after she had a good laugh, she assured him that was not true. She and Zane have a close relationship, and she would have leveled with him. Even if she'd signed a contract not to tell."

Jess ignored the disappointment he felt. Wanting to change the subject, he asked Sloan how he and Leslie had enjoyed the road-trip part of their honeymoon. The newlyweds had driven from Alaska to the Lower 48 through Canada. When they had reached New York, they'd boarded a private jet to Belize.

"It was great and the road trip was something we've wanted to do since our college days," Sloan said, adding that he and Leslie would be joining everyone for the Russells' anniversary party.

After ending the call with Sloan, Jess finished off his beer and saw the lights go out in Paige's villa. He hoped she got a good night's sleep, and he looked forward to seeing her again tomorrow.

He wouldn't question why.

Leaving the villa, Paige glanced up at the sky. It was a great day for an early morning jog. A few years ago, to get in the role of a movie about a competitive runner, she had to get in shape for the part by jogging three to five miles a day. Now she made jogging a part of her regular fitness routine. She'd found a couple of paths around the vineyards, and one led to a huge clearing and lake. After jogging for a while, she slowed down to a walk as she took in the picturesque view.

"Good morning, Paige. You're into jogging, too, I see."

She quickly turned to find Jess standing there. Why did the man have to be so darn attractive even while covered in sweat? And his body. OMG! He was standing there shirtless, wearing a pair of running shorts, and every single muscle was hard, solid and well-defined. Her gaze automatically latched on to his broad shoulders, muscular chest and corded forearms. Even his thighs were exquisitely taut.

He'd been running awhile, if his sweat was anything to go by. Her gaze followed one particular drop as it slowly ran down his chest, then moved past his navel to disappear beneath the waistband of his shorts. Dang, but she envied that drop of sweat.

"Paige?"

When he said her name, she realized that not only had

she not responded to his comment, but he'd probably noticed her ogling his body. Looking back up to his face, she said, "This morning I'm doing more walking than jogging, Jess. Seems like you've been at it awhile."

"I have," he said, wiping sweat off his forehead. "I got up before sunrise. Normally I jog five miles a day, but since I registered for this year's Rock 'n' Roll marathon in DC, which is in three months, I figure I better get my body in better shape. Now I'm up to seven miles a day."

She honestly couldn't imagine his body in any better shape than it was now. Even his running shorts were perfect for his lean, muscular hips.

"What about you? When did you get into jogging?" he asked.

His question popped into her thoughts, and it was a good thing. She needed to stay focused. "I started jogging for a part in a movie and decided to keep it up. Some days are more challenging than others."

"I feel you."

If only he knew how often she had dreamed of him doing that very thing. He would feel her all over, first with his hands and then his mouth. It was a good thing he couldn't read her mind.

"I'll let you get back to your walk. I need to go shower before I head over to Bruno's for breakfast."

"Bruno's?"

"Yes. It's in town, and according to Spencer and Chardonnay, it's one of the best places for chicken and waffles. Mrs. Russell offered to make me some, but I refused to let her go to the trouble. Besides, I want to check out the area." He paused a moment and said, "I would invite you to join me, but I know you're hanging low for a while."

Yes, she was. "Well, enjoy your breakfast. I'll see you later at dinner."

"And enjoy the rest of your walk, Paige."

And then he was jogging off, and she stood there watching him until he faded from sight. Her heart was still beating fast, overworked at seeing such male fineness. Not all men who thought they had a fabulous-looking body really did, but Jess Outlaw did. Definitely.

An hour later, she had returned to the guest villa. Chardonnay called to see if Paige wanted to join her for breakfast. Her grandparents were out riding the vineyard in one of the golf carts, Spencer had gone to his office at the Windemere Resort, and now that Russell was driving, the kids had gone into town to meet up with friends. School started back in a couple of weeks, and the three were determined to enjoy the remaining days of summer. Chardonnay figured now was a good time to go over the list of things she still needed to do for the anniversary party.

Paige told Chardonnay she could be there after taking a shower. She was headed to the bedroom when her phone rang. "Yes, Nadia?"

"Is it true The Alaskan is there with you?"

Evidently, Nadia had talked to Jill. "Yes, and do you have to shout in my ear?" Paige asked, noting the excitement in her sister's voice. "And to set the record straight, Jess is vacationing here at Russell Vineyards, but he's not *with* me." She felt she needed to clarify that.

"I think that's great."

Paige put her sister on speakerphone as she began undressing for her shower. "And why do you think it's great?"

"Because next to Jess, Kemp is lacking in so many ways."

Paige would agree. "And what does that have to do with anything?"

"Because if anyone saw you and Jess together, they would assume he's the guy who replaced Kemp."

Paige stopped undressing, knowing how her sister's

mind worked. "First of all, Jess didn't replace Kemp, and I don't want anyone getting that assumption. Jess and I just happen to be here at the same time on vacation. We are not together that way, and it wouldn't be fair to him for anyone to assume that we are. For all I know, he might have a girlfriend."

"He doesn't. I talked to Maverick and—"

"Whoa. You talked to Maverick?"

"Yes. He called from Ireland last night after meeting a couple vacationing there from Gamble. I recalled the guy graduated from high school with Jillian. Isn't it a small world?"

Seeing her sister was digressing, Paige asked, "Okay, but what made you ask Maverick if Jess had a girlfriend?"

"I asked out of curiosity when he mentioned Jess was vacationing at the Russell Vineyards."

So, Nadia had gotten word about Jess being there from Maverick and not Jill. "And?"

"And I got a great idea, Paige."

Paige knew her sister like a book. "Whatever crazy idea is going through your head, please get rid of it."

"Just hear me out, Paige, please."

Paige released a frustrated sigh. "What is it?"

"I'm sure you've heard Kemp's comment by now. He acts like he has you wrapped around his finger, not to mention he's calling me a liar."

"It was a lie," Paige reminded her sister.

"Yes, but he doesn't know that. A man who is too sure of himself irks the hell out of me, Paige. Besides, we both know you and Kemp haven't slept together in six months, and even then he was shitty in bed."

There were times Paige regretted Nadia and Jill were her confidantes. She could trust them not to share anything she told them, but sometimes she wanted to handle her personal business herself. There was no need to repeat that the reason she and Kemp hadn't shared a bed was because they'd been on the other sides of the world filming. And there was nothing she could add about Kemp's performance in bed because he definitely lacked there and she'd told her sisters that on several occasions.

"Don't worry about what Kemp is saying, Nadia. He'll be the one with egg on his face when we don't get back together," Paige said.

"But what's wrong with him thinking you've already kicked him to the curb for someone else, Paige? You need to do something to deflate his overblown ego."

"The only thing I need to do is ignore Kemp like I'm doing now."

"What you're doing is hiding out, acting like you're too pitiful and embarrassed to show your face because of what he did. You were the victim and not the perpetrator. Kemp's not hiding out. He's in front of the cameras saying you'll get over anything he's done because you love him."

Paige could tell Nadia was really worked up. "I couldn't care less what Kemp says."

"Well, you should care. You have a lot of fans, Paige. Some are young, impressionable women who look up to you. What type of message are you sending by letting Kemp treat you so shabbily? You're basically telling them to take anything a man dishes out and hide out somewhere in shame. No man should get away with what Kemp did."

Paige appreciated her sister getting upset on her behalf, but at that moment she really didn't want to discuss with Nadia something that really wasn't Nadia's business. "Look, Nadia, I need to shower and get dressed."

"Why? All you're doing is hiding out, so why do you care about how you look?"

Paige tilted her head back. Did Nadia honestly see her as a pitiful coward just because she had backed away from a confrontation with the media? "We'll talk later, Nadia. Goodbye."

"'Bye, Paige."

She clicked off the line and tried not to focus on the disappointment she'd heard in Nadia's voice.

"Thanks for offering to help me with the anniversary party," Chardonnay said, handing Paige a list. "Since I know you still want to keep a low profile, the things I put on your list are things you won't have to leave the vineyard to do."

Hiding out...hanging low...keeping a low profile...

She had heard all three terms used today to define her existence. Was she really sending the wrong message to her young female fans like Nadia had claimed? Shouldn't how she handled Kemp be her business and not anyone else's? Didn't she have the right to avoid the media if she wanted to? But then, she knew, as an actress, the media thought it was their business to share whatever went on in her life. She resented Kemp for placing her in such a predicament.

"Paige, are you okay?" Chardonnay asked, placing a gentle hand on hers.

Paige blinked. "Yes, I'm fine. Why do you ask?"

"Because I asked you a question three times and you didn't say anything. It was as if your thoughts were a million miles away."

"Sorry about that. I was just thinking about something my sister said." She smiled over at Chardonnay as she tried perking up a bit. "I'm glad to help you and I will get started today."

"Thanks, and you're sure you're okay?"

"Yes. I've just got a lot on my mind."

Chardonnay nodded. "I caught the comment that Kemp made on television earlier."

Paige released a frustrated sigh. "I didn't see it, but I heard about it. Nadia is upset with me because she thinks I should do something rather than hang out here hiding, as she put it."

Chardonnay nodded again. "Are you not going to make a comment of your own?"

"I don't want to. I wish the media would move on to some other scandal."

"Do you think they will?"

Paige shook her head. "No. At least, not anytime soon. I have a feeling they will milk it for all it's worth."

Chardonnay was quiet for a moment. "I have a feeling whatever decision you make will be the right one, Paige."

Paige wished she had the same feeling, but she didn't.

Four

Later that day, Jess sat in the same spot on the patio where he'd sat the night before and again sipped his beer. He was on his laptop, checking to see what, if anything, was occurring in Washington. Since most politicians had left for the recess, nothing was happening, but he looked anyway.

He heard a sound and glanced over to see Paige walk off her patio onto the courtyard that connected the four villas. He had strolled the area the first day and liked how the courtyard jutted out into several paths. One path led to a huge guest swimming pool and another to a small pond with a fountain. He'd also stumbled upon a glass-enclosed summerhouse that wasn't far away. He'd nearly missed the summerhouse because it was tucked amid vines, ferns and a cluster of oak trees and palms. It had reminded him of a lovers' hideaway.

Paige appeared deep in her thoughts and hadn't even looked his way. He started to make his presence known, but then decided not to in case she wanted a moment of privacy. That was fine with him since he preferred sitting here watching her as the midday sun highlighted her features.

God, she was beautiful. When he'd seen her that morning while out jogging, her hair had been pulled up in a knot. It still was, but now several loose tendrils had fallen around her face. She had changed and was now wearing a pretty printed sundress that showcased her toned arms and legs. When she sat down on the bench that faced the pond, he could see the sadness in her eyes and it tugged at his heart.

He knew Pierson's statement to those reporters had made headlines. He'd made it seem like all that stuff Nadia said about Paige moving on was utter nonsense.

Jess pinched the bridge of his nose, thinking, not for the first time, that the man was an asshole. A part of Jess wished Paige would prove the bastard wrong just for the hell of it. But then, what she did or didn't do was her business and not his.

After closing his laptop, he grabbed it and the empty beer bottle and went inside. He even milled around a few minutes in the kitchen, hoping that when he returned to the patio Paige would be gone. However, when he went back out twenty minutes later, she was still there, sitting in the same spot and with the same gloomy look on her face.

Something tugged deep inside him. Opening the patio door, he then walked along the courtyard toward her. She was so deep in thought that she didn't hear his approach. When she did hear him, she jerked around with her hand braced over her heart.

"Sorry, I didn't mean to scare you, Paige."

"Jess. I thought you had gone into town and wouldn't be back for a while."

There was no need to tell her that staying away had

been his original plan, but he'd sat in that restaurant thinking about her. Specifically, just how sexy she'd looked out jogging that morning. After seeing those tabloid headlines, he'd also thought about the hell her ex was putting her through.

"I decided to come back and check email," he said. "Although I'm on vacation, I'm curious to see what's going on in Washington. It's a bad habit of mine, and one I should break."

"Yes, you should. Vacations are time for fun."

He leaned against a tree and shoved his hands into the pockets of his jeans. "True, but habits, good or bad, are hard to break. Any bad habits you want to break?" He saw how her body tensed with his question. She obviously had loved the douchebag to be hurting so badly. But then, hadn't it been the same for him when Ava had dumped him for her ex? He knew Paige's pain because he'd felt it himself.

"Yes, there is a habit I wish I could break. It's one I started when I became an actress."

"Oh, and what habit is that?"

"Being a conformist. In my former life I was a rebel."

He mulled over her response as he recalled how Dillon had once shared that when he and Pam first met, she'd been engaged to marry another man. A man who Pam's three younger sisters—Jill, Paige and Nadia—had disliked immensely, and the three had rebelled. They'd deliberately annoyed Pam's fiancé to drive him away. Jess had found the tale amusing, an example of the rebellious side of a younger Paige.

"Can I ask you something, Paige?"

"Yes."

"Why did you stop being a rebel?"

She didn't say anything at first and then, "Hollywood is no place for rebels if you want to succeed in the industry.

Your image is all they care about. You have a PR person who instructs you on every answer and usually your words are scripted. After a while you forget how to speak up for yourself because doing so can be fatal to your career."

"And is that what's happened to you? You gave in to the Hollywood establishment?"

"Yes, pretty much, so I guess it's not really a bad habit but a way of life I've accepted." She then added, "I talked to Maxie, my agent, just before coming out here. She feels it's time for me to make a statement."

"And what does she want you to say?" he asked, as if he had every right to know.

Releasing what he detected as a frustrated sigh, she said, "She feels I should follow Kemp's lead and admit that, although I needed time alone for the past weeks to sort out a few things, Kemp and I are still a couple. She doesn't think the timing is right for me to admit that we've broken up."

Timing. That was the one word Jess was coming to detest. "Why does she feel that way, considering what he's done?"

"Mainly because Kemp is Hottest Man Alive and being the woman by his side will enhance my career."

He frowned. "Does your career mean more to you than your pride?" he asked, trying to keep his anger in check.

His tone made her switch her gaze from the pond to him. The moment their gazes met, he felt connected to her. And what was really weird was that he felt it on a deep level. Why? He'd never felt that sort of bond with any woman. At least, not since Ava.

She broke eye contact with him, and he wondered if she'd felt the same connection or if he was just imagining the whole thing. Moments later, she looked back at him and said, "No, but Maxie thinks I should agree to work things out with Kemp."

He didn't say anything for a minute. Then he asked her, "Forget about what your agent wants. What is it that you want, Paige?"

"Honestly?"

He nodded. "Yes, honestly."

A rebellious smile touched her lips and she said, "What I really want, Jess, is to do just what Nadia told the media I'm doing. I'd like nothing better than to make a statement that I've moved on and that Kemp and I are not together and that I am seeing someone else."

"If that's what you want to do, then do it."

Jess's words made Paige's lips twitch in amusement. "News flash, Jess Outlaw. Wanting to do it and actually doing it are two different things."

"Why?"

She studied him as he leaned against the tree with his hands shoved into the pockets of his jeans. She also took note of the rolled-up shirtsleeves that showed a nice set of forearms. When did a man's forearms become such a turn-on for her? Then there were his dark eyes, which were studying her intently and waiting on her response.

"First of all, doing something like that is career suicide. Even so, a part of me would risk it. But the main holdback is because such a guy doesn't exist. There is no man I'm having a 'hot, romantic entanglement' with."

"And what if there was a guy and you were seen with him?" he asked.

She leaned back on her arms as a whimsical smile touched her lips. "Then Kemp would have egg all over his face for being cocky enough to claim that I hadn't moved on. He would really look stupid."

Jess moved away from the tree and came to stand in front of her. He stood so close his jeans touched the material of her dress. Was she imagining things or was heat radiating off him to her? Or was it coming off her to him? Just moments ago, she had imagined a similar heat when their gazes connected, and for a quick moment she was bounced back in time to when they had first met. She could truthfully say that was the first time she'd experienced instant attraction to a man. And with him standing so close, she was realizing the attraction on her part was still there. Possibly even stronger.

"I have another question for you, Paige."

She unconsciously licked her lips, thinking about his. They went well with his stunning eyes, sexy dimple and fabulous forearms…especially the one with the tattoo of a willow ptarmigan, which she knew was the state bird of Alaska. "And what question is that?"

"Are you opposed to making your ex look stupid?"

His question caught her off guard. She laughed because it had made her day. "Trust me—not in the least. However, hiring a man to pretend to be my new boo would mean contacting one of those escort agencies. Since you never know who will sell your secret for a price, I'd rather not."

"I'd rather you didn't as well," he said, smiling. "Not when I know a guy who would do it at no cost."

She lifted a brow. "You do? Who?"

"Me."

Jess took a step back and prepared himself for all the questions he figured were coming. His hands were still tucked in his pockets, otherwise he would have been tempted to pull her up from the bench and wrap his arms around her. And it would not have stopped there. He truly was attracted to her, even when he knew the last thing she needed right now was a man lusting after her. But it just couldn't be helped. He was lusting.

"You?"

Her question meant she'd finally picked up her dropped jaw. "Yes, me. Is there any reason I wouldn't work?"

Her gaze roamed all over him. Maybe he was imagining it, but he swore he could feel the heat in her eyes move over his lips, eyes and forearms. Then her gaze connected with his and she said, "No, but..."

Not giving her a chance to complete whatever it was she was about to say, he quickly said, "Good, because I'm applying for the job."

She blinked. "You're joking, right?"

"No. Why should I be joking?"

Then she tilted her head to the side and gave him a speculating glare. "Did Nadia put you up to this, Jess?"

He raised a brow. "I haven't spoken to Nadia. Why would you think she put me up to it?"

She continued to hold his gaze as if she expected to catch him in a lie or something. "Because when I spoke with her this morning, she suggested the same thing after finding out you were here from Maverick last night. Of course, I told her that I couldn't ask you to do such a thing."

"Why not?"

She gave him one of those "duh" looks, as if his question was absurd. "First of all, Jess, it would involve pretending to be romantically involved with me. Your name will become connected to mine in the media."

He shrugged. "I don't have a problem with that."

"Why wouldn't you?"

"Why would I?"

He could tell his counterquestion threw her for a minute. She quickly recovered and said, "I think the answer to that would be obvious. For all I know, you might be serious about someone."

"I'm not."

Paige licked her bottom lip and his stomach clenched

watching the movement of her tongue. She was thinking and he was lusting. It was a good thing her concentration was on his face and not below the belt or she would see the evidence of his desire for her. Thinking it might be a good time to sit down, he eased to the bench beside her. She quickly scooted over as if to make sure there was a lot of space between them. He was about to tell her that he didn't bite and decided not to. He would definitely want to take a delicious bite of her.

"Well?" he said.

"Well, I can still see where it might cause you unnecessary problems. You're a senator and are expected to retain a stellar reputation."

He tilted his head and grinned. "And you honestly think my reputation will get tarnished getting linked to yours, Paige?"

"Maybe not tarnished but blasted when our connection appears in the news. The media will beat it to death."

"Let them. It wouldn't bother me. You're a single woman and I'm a single man and we're both here on vacation. What happens on vacation is nobody's business."

"The media will make it their business—trust me."

"Then let them. The way I see it, my name linked to yours just might benefit me."

She lifted a brow. "In what way?"

"I'm a young senator and any publicity is good because it gets a camera or mic in my face and I can control the narrative. If nothing else, I'll get national exposure. It will make for interesting conversation back home with my constituents who think, at thirty-eight, I need more of a social life anyway."

Of course, all he'd just said was a bunch of BS. He wasn't looking for publicity, nor did he relish the thought of a camera or mic in his face, and it definitely wasn't a big deal for him to get national exposure. He'd only said those things as a way to convince her that his reputation wouldn't be tarnished if linked to hers.

"I hear what you're saying, Jess, but I'm not sure we can pull off such a thing."

"Sure we can. I would love nothing more than to see egg all over Kemp Pierson's face."

Paige stood and began pacing. Watching her legs in motion was just as affecting as seeing the movement of her tongue on her lips.

She suddenly stopped and looked at him. "I think we need to talk about it some more, Jess."

"We can do that. In fact, I have an idea," he said.

"What?"

"I didn't get a chance to go by Phillippe's Pizza, but Spencer said they deliver. How about we do wine and pizza for dinner in my villa and talk more about it then?"

She held his gaze, and he knew what she needed. Standing, he opened his arms and she walked right into them, and he held her. The air was filled with the scent of grapes, but at that moment he was filled with the scent of her.

More than anything, he wanted to kiss her, but the timing wasn't right. Would it ever be right for them? One day he wouldn't worry about timing where she was concerned. But not today. What she needed today was a hug.

Moments passed before she finally lifted her head from his chest and leaned back to look up at him. She took a deep breath and slowly let it out. "Thanks, Jess. I needed that."

He smiled down at her. "You can get a hug from me anytime." He truly meant it. "So are we on for pizza and wine later?"

She flashed him a smile, one he thought was hot as hell. "Yes, Jess. We're on."

Five

Paige stepped out of the villa and glanced up into the sky. Although the sun had gone down, the area surrounded by oak trees still reflected the daylight hours. That was the one thing she loved about California. It was still awake while most parts of the country had bedded for the night.

As she walked the path to Jess's villa, she was reminded of the English countryside with unspoiled meadows and valleys. The four guest villas were situated in such a way that they had privacy due to large trees, yet at the same time the windows had views of the lush greenery of the fields.

As she walked, one thought kept going through her mind—her and Jess's earlier conversation. He could definitely give Kemp serious competition. Whereas Kemp had that proverbial handsome Hollywood look, Jess was effortlessly gorgeous with his strong, masculine features and his tall stature. He didn't need that actor appeal because his all-American look worked for him just fine. He didn't have to work hard for his easy charm and masculine charisma because for Jess those things came naturally.

Knowing how Kemp was convinced his dashing good looks were everything, she wondered how he would react if she appeared in public with Jess by her side. Not only would he have egg on his face, he would see he wasn't the only man alive with hot looks.

Kemp was counting on them working things out and getting back together, although she had told him otherwise. What irritated her more than anything was that he felt entitled to a comeback. So did Maxie. Her agent had called again an hour ago to suggest Paige agree to a press conference, and then asked if Paige wanted her to write out the statement. A statement that pretty much backed up what Kemp had said.

It had taken everything within Paige not to tell Maxie where she could take that statement and shove it. Instead, she'd said she hadn't made up her mind yet. Before hanging up the phone, Maxie had reminded her what she stood to lose if she didn't go along with Kemp. She hadn't bothered telling Maxie what she stood to lose if she did. Namely her self-respect. Nadia had the right idea after all, and now was the time for Paige to take a stand.

The one thing she still wasn't sure about was Jess's involvement. The paparazzi could be intense and brutal at times in their pursuit of a story. She was certain he got coverage in Washington, but media coverage of politicians wasn't the same as media coverage of Hollywood celebrities. Was Jess really ready to find out the difference? She needed to be absolutely sure he knew what he was getting into.

Then there was the fact that after all these years she was still attracted to him. If she hadn't been certain of that before, then their time spent together by the pond had definitely made it real to her. Even while having a serious discussion with him, her mind managed to conjure up sexy ideas where he played the leading man in a hot love scene with her as the leading lady.

But she accepted that Jess wasn't interested in her. For that reason, him playing the role of her lover could lead to problems, more on her end than his. Especially if she was to forget it was only acting.

She reached his villa and had lifted her hand to knock when the door was snatched open. "I saw you coming up," he said, moving aside to let her in.

"Oh." He must have been looking out the window.

She entered and glanced around. "Nice place, Jess."

"I think so, too. I'm sure yours is just as nice."

"Even nicer," she said, laughing. "I've got a better view of the vineyards from my kitchen window."

"Well, I happen to like that my back window faces the pond," he said, grinning. "I've ordered the pizza and it's on its way." He looked at his watch. "It should be here in ten minutes."

"Need my help with anything?" she said, following him to the kitchen.

"No, but you can keep me company while I get things set up. Just grab a chair at the island. If you like, you can go ahead and pour the wine," he said, pulling dishes from the cabinets.

"All right," she said, noticing there were several bottles on the island top. "Which one will we open first?"

He turned and raised a brow. "You plan on going through all three?"

"Why not?" she said, chuckling, while lifting a bottle to read the label. "I don't have a job to go to tomorrow. Do you?"

"Nope. We're on vacation and anything can happen," he said, placing a plate of cupcakes on the counter.

"Where did those come from?" she asked excitedly, grabbing for one.

He quickly slid the plate out of her reach. "This is dessert that Grammy Russell made for us when I told her we were making it a pizza-and-wine evening. As you know, dessert is eaten *after* the main meal, Paige."

She tapped her chin a few times. "You sure?"

He smiled. "Positive. Now tell me which wine we'll drink first."

"This one," she said, handing him the bottle to open. "It was the year Pam was born, so I figure it has to be good."

"That will work," he said, opening the bottle and handing it back to her. At that moment there was a knock at the door. "I believe our pizza has arrived."

With slices on their plates, Jess slid in the seat across from Paige at the island. She had poured glasses of wine, and he took a sip to sample her choice. "Hmm. This *is* good."

She took a sip for her herself and smiled. "It is. I've liked every single glass of wine that has come from this vineyard."

"So have I."

He watched her bite into her pizza, and when she closed her eyes and moaned, the sound was a total turn-on. She sounded like a woman satisfied and he wondered what type of moan she made when caught in the throes of an orgasm. "It's delicious?"

"Too delicious," she said. "It's living up to every claim Maxie told me about a pizza from Phillippe."

Adjusting his position in his chair, he said, "You and your sisters are close."

It was a statement more than a question since he knew they were. However, he figured holding a conversation with her was better than getting turned on while watching her eat.

"Yes, we're very close. We have the same father, but Pam has a different mother. Her mother died when she was three, and Dad married my mother, Alma, when Pam was ten. That's when Jillian, Nadia and I came along. Pam is twelve years older than Jill, fourteen years older than me and sixteen years older than Nadia. While growing up, we were one big happy family. Pam has always been the older sister we adored." She paused. "Jill, Nadia and I cried a river of tears when she left for college."

"Did she go far away?" he asked.

Paige chuckled. "You would have thought she had moved to Mars from the way we carried on. She'd gotten a scholarship to attend UCLA to pursue an acting career. Then a year later, our life changed. Mom got sick and died."

She had stopped eating as if she was recalling that sad period in her life. "Jillian was eight, I was six, and Nadia was four. Pam had talked about dropping out of college to help Dad with us, but he wouldn't let her. But she came home every chance she got. Then a few years later, Dad got sick and died."

"How old were you then?" Jess asked, watching her take a sip of her wine and getting turned on by the way her lips fit on the glass.

"It was a few days before my fifteenth birthday. Pam had come home before Dad died and promised him that she would take care of us and keep us together, and she did. Even when she married Dillon, she took us with her to Westmoreland Country. I think that's why she and Dillon got along so well when they met. They'd both made sacrifices for their families."

After biting into another slice of pizza, she said, "I love

how close you and your siblings are, Jess, given all of you have different mothers. I find that amazing."

"All of us, except for Charm, were raised by Bart since we were babies. How Dad managed to get custody of his sons always baffled us while growing up, but the older we got, we knew. I love the old man to death, but he's such a manipulator. Granted, some of our mothers were gold diggers, but in the end, the only thing they got from Bart was a hard way to go."

She nodded. "What about your own mom? Do you remember her?"

He didn't say anything for a minute. His mother was what she was until the day she died. Hell, even after she died. "My mother, Joyce, was the first official gold digger. I don't remember her from my earlier years because she and Dad got a divorce within the first year of marriage. Bart didn't have to take her to court for custody, but he did so anyway to prove a point."

He took a sip of wine. "I was born with a price on my head. She'd asked for a million dollars for me the moment she'd discovered she was pregnant, and he'd agreed. However, she got greedy and asked for twice that much after I was born and that pissed him off. By the time it was over, Dad's team of attorneys made sure she got half of what she'd originally asked for."

"I guess it doesn't pay to be greedy."

"No, especially when you're dealing with Bart Outlaw. But that didn't stop Joyce from taking him to court several times, but she never could get more. She died of cancer a few years ago and planned this elaborate New Orleans funeral for herself, and she made sure Dad got the bill. The cost was close to a million dollars."

"You're kidding, right?"

"No. Bart outright refused to pay and told the funeral directors they could cremate her and toss her ashes in the Mississippi River, for all he cared. I refused to let that happen, so I paid for it out of my trust fund. She was my mother even though she never tried cultivating a relationship with me no matter how many times I reached out to her."

"What sort of funeral costs close to a million dollars?"

"It was one of those New Orleans jazzy funerals done in grand style with a parade, several marching bands, a procession of umbrellas and a horse-drawn carriage motorcade. My brothers and I had never seen anything like it before. It might have been expensive, but it was also an experience. There's nothing like a New Orleans funeral."

"Is that where she was from?"

"Yes. Born and raised. That's probably why I love Cajun and Creole cuisines so much. It's in my blood."

She smiled, nodding. "It's in my blood, too. My mom was born in Louisiana, but left in her teens when her parents divorced. She loved cooking foods with a New Orleans flair. Did your father attend your mother's funeral?"

"No. The only Outlaws who attended were me, my brothers and Charm."

He noticed she didn't ask him about Charm, and he figured that since the two were friends, Paige knew that Charm's mother had been the one woman Bart hadn't married but not for lack of trying. Hell, he was still trying.

They had finished the pizza, were enjoying the cupcakes and had knocked off the first bottle of wine when she looked over at him and said in a teasing voice, "Any chance we're going to get around to discussing the reason I'm here before the sun comes up in the morning? I hadn't counted on a sleepover."

He knew her comment had been meant as a joke, and he bit back saying that he had no problem if she spent the night. Instead, he broke eye contact with her to look out the window to see it had gotten dark outside. "I guess it's time, but I really enjoyed just sitting here conversing with you, Paige."

Resting her elbows on the island's top, she looked at him and said, "And I enjoyed talking with you, too. But now it's time to get down to business."

Yes, it was. Easing out of the chair, he came around and took her hand. "I think we'll be more comfortable in the living room."

Tingling sensations rushed through Paige at the feel of her hand in Jess's as he walked her from the kitchen to the living room. Once there, he led her over to the sofa and then took the wing-back chair across from her. When he smiled, she nearly melted. That dimple in his chin was going to be her downfall.

Needing to break eye contact with him, she looked toward the kitchen. "We forgot the glasses and the wine."

"No problem. I'll get them."

When he walked to the kitchen, she was fixated on his every movement, especially those masculine thighs in a pair of jeans and the shape of his tush... OMG! She swore her heart took a thump with every step he took. When, with an agility that had her exhaling a deep breath, he leaned over the island to grab the wine bottle and both glasses in one smooth sweep.

As he returned, she noticed their gazes were locked. It was only when he set the wine and glasses on the coffee table in front of her that she broke eye contact with him. She was beginning to think all that sexual chemistry she'd felt earlier today hadn't been one-sided after all.

He eased back in his chair, glanced over at her and smiled. That sexy smile caused a rush of sensual heat to flow through her. "What are you thinking, Paige?"

He honestly didn't want to know her real thoughts right now, so she stated the other thoughts on her mind. "I'm having misgivings about getting you involved, Jess. I'm thinking about just calling a press conference and telling the media that Kemp and I aren't together, and that I have moved on."

He nodded. "And when they ask about Nadia's claim that you've taken up with someone else, what will you say?"

For a moment she felt like she was being coached by an attorney, but then, he *was* an attorney. At least, that had been his profession before entering politics. She nibbled on her bottom lip. "I won't confirm or deny anything."

"By not confirming it, you're basically denying it."

A part of her knew what he said was true, but why did he have to point it out? Drawing in a deep breath, she said, "I'm trying to give you an out, Jess."

"Why?"

"I just don't want you to feel compelled as a family friend to help me out just so I can retain my dignity."

Paige saw his gaze narrow. "First of all, regardless of what you decide to do, there is no threat to your dignity—trust me. You are one hell of a classy woman, Paige. You've handled yourself admirably through this entire thing. As far as I'm concerned, Kemp Pierson is the one looking like an ass. Some women would have been petty or vindictive. Instead, you've kept a low profile for almost two weeks. But…"

She raised a brow. "But what?"

"But the way you want to handle it is making it seem you really aren't moving on. It appears that a part of you wants to leave the door open to take Pierson back."

"That's not true!"

"Are you sure?"

"Of course I'm sure."

"Then prove it. The only way you can is to make it seem you're now interested in someone else. That will seal the deal. There's no reason anyone should question our story. We've known each other for some time. I'm not married, nor am I in a serious relationship with any woman, and you're single and not in a serious relationship either. I'm confident I could play the part of your love interest with no problem, Paige."

Jess leaned forward and asked, "Why are you so against giving me a try?"

His question, spoken in a warm, deep, masculine voice, counteracted the sensuous chills flowing through her. Paige was certain her heart skipped a beat, maybe two, as his penetrating dark eyes held hers. "I'm not against it, Jess. I'm just not as certain as you that we could pull it off."

"I suggest we give it a try and see what happens."

That was what she was afraid of. Giving it a try and *nothing* happening. He wouldn't be any more interested in her now than he had been six years ago. But what he'd said was true. The only way anyone would actually think she had moved on was for her to be seen with someone else.

"Okay, Jess, if you're positive that you really want to do this."

"I'm positive I want to do this, Paige," he said.

She heard so much conviction in his voice that she was tempted to ask why, but then she knew. Jess was a thoughtful guy who did good things for people. That was obvious, with him footing the bill for his mother's funeral when his father would not. Granted, the woman was his mother, but it wasn't as if they'd had a close relationship. That hadn't mattered. He'd done what he thought was the right thing to do. A part of her didn't want to be another "do good" project for him. But it seemed that she would be.

"Fine," she said. "I hope you don't live to regret it, Jess."

A smile spread over his lips. "I can assure you that I won't."

Six

The next morning Jess stepped out of the shower eager to get dressed and take Paige to breakfast. Last night, while finishing up the second bottle of wine, they made their plans. First on the list was to go to breakfast at a restaurant located in Windemere.

They didn't expect to see any members of the press, just people with cell phones who would take pictures to spread across social media. Proof of a Paige Novak sighting would pinpoint her location and the media would be out in full force during dinner. And he and Paige would be ready when they dined later at Sedrick's.

They had agreed to put their plan into motion only after talking it over with Spencer and Chardonnay. Once the media got wind of Paige's location, there was a possibility they would camp out near the vineyards, convinced they had a story.

That discussion with Spencer and Chardonnay had come sooner than they'd expected. While walking Paige back to her villa last night, they'd run into the couple, out for a late-night stroll. From Chardonnay's swollen lips, Jess surmised they'd been out doing more than that, but he had kept those thoughts to himself.

Both Spencer and Chardonnay had seen Kemp's interview and thought the plan was a good idea. Neither was worried about the vineyards being bombarded with media. Like his relatives in Westmoreland Country, Spencer was friends with the local sheriff, and the man would know how to handle trespassers.

As Jess continued to get dressed, he again thought how differently things might have gone if the timing had been right when he and Paige had met six years ago. A lot of what-ifs were filling his head.

What if when Paige had flirted with him that night, he'd flirted back? *What if* his mind hadn't been consumed with his campaign and he had given Paige his full attention? It suddenly occurred to him that after six years those what-ifs no longer existed. He was no longer consumed with his campaign and she wasn't in a relationship with Kemp Pierson.

Now he was dealing with *why not?*

Jess kept smiling while getting dressed. A pretend courtship with Paige would be easy. For him, there would be no pretense about it. He intended to wine and dine her, and what better place than here at the vineyards while they were both on vacation? To Paige, this might be an act, but for him, starting today, it would be the real thing. He'd been given a second chance and he intended to give it his best shot.

The phone rang and he knew it was a call from Garth. Another thing that he and Paige agreed to do was let the family know what was going on. Most would figure things out anyway since they knew he and Paige weren't romantically involved. That might be the case for his other brothers, but not so much with Garth.

One night while he was home, over drinks, he'd mentioned his interest in Paige to Garth and that he viewed their first meeting as a missed opportunity. Garth had told him that no opportunity was missed with the right strategic planning.

Garth and Regan were still in Florida. Since it had been late on the East Coast by the time Paige had left last night, he'd texted Garth and asked that he call him this morning. "Hello?"

"Yes, Jess, I got your message. What's up?"

It didn't take Jess long to sum up what he and Paige had decided to do and why. "I've always regretted not striking up a relationship with Paige, Garth—now is my chance," he ended his spiel by saying.

"My only warning, Jess, is for you to keep in mind that she's on the rebound, and most rebound relationships don't last."

Jess rubbed his hand down his face. He, of all people, knew that. All he had to do was remember Ava's betrayal. When they'd met, she'd been broken up with her boyfriend for six months. The same boyfriend he had caught her in bed with less than a year later. "I won't forget what happened with Ava, Garth, but this time I plan to be prepared."

"Prepared how?"

"You're not the only one who knows something about strategic planning. Paige isn't looking to get into another serious relationship, and I can respect that. However, I plan to leave a lasting impression on her so when she is ready, she'll know I'm not a bad prospect."

"Sounds like you've pretty much thought this through."

"I have."

"Then I wish you the best, Jess."

"Thanks, Garth."

A short while later, Jess left the guest villa determined that some very interesting things would be happening on his vacation.

"So, there you have it. That's my and Jess's plan," Paige said to Jill and Nadia. She had arranged a group call with them to tell them what was going on.

She could hear clapping in the background and knew it was from Nadia. "I'm glad the real Paige Novak has returned," Nadia said. "The one with a backbone."

Paige rolled her eyes. "My not making a comment before has nothing to do with not having a backbone, Nadia. It's just how things are done in Hollywood if you want to succeed. It's knowing when to pick your battles."

"Well, I just think having your boyfriend mess around on you, admitting he did and pretending it's no big deal is a battle I'll fight any day. There's such a thing as respect."

She knew Nadia was upset on her behalf and she also knew her sister was right. Paige noticed Jill hadn't said anything. "So, what do you think about my and Jess's plan, Jill?"

"I agree with what Nadia said, but not everybody reacts to a given situation the same way. You know how I reacted when I thought Aidan had cheated on me. I didn't confront him or go into a battle mode. I retreated. He would never have discovered why I broke things off with him if you hadn't told him, Paige."

"Which is why I did," Paige said.

"And I thank you for doing so. Because of my past, I can understand why you haven't gone to battle with Kemp, especially when you'd planned to break up with him anyway. However, Kemp didn't know of those plans, so humiliating you publicly and then brushing it off like you'd take him back regardless of his behavior is pretty darn arrogant on his part. I wouldn't let him off easy and you'll be getting him where it will hurt. His pride. But be careful. It's my impression that Kemp is a man who likes having the upper hand. We all know he thinks a lot of himself. More than he should. The only thing that worries me is that he's not ready to let you just walk out of his life for another man."

"He has no choice. Jess and I plan to be convincing."

"That might be the case," Jill continued, "but you heard what your agent told you. Your breakup with Kemp might have an adverse effect on your career. Are you prepared for that?"

Paige nibbled on her bottom lip. She had thought about her career when she'd gone to bed and couldn't sleep. There was a time when her career had meant everything to her because following in Pam's footsteps had always been her dream. But now she was feeling more negatives about being an actress than positives. "Yes, I'm prepared for it."

"Of course she's prepared for it," Nadia said. "Nobody screws over a Novak and comes out smelling like a rose. I'm glad it was Paige and not me, or Kemp would be missing both balls by now."

Ouch. Paige fought back a grin. Nadia intended to be a renegade until the bitter end. She couldn't wait to meet the man her sister would one day fall in love with. The poor guy better walk the straight and narrow or he wouldn't have a chance. "I hate to end this call, but I need to finish dressing. Jess and I are going to breakfast."

"Um, now, that's something else you need to be careful about, Paige," Jill interjected.

"What?"

"You and Jess pretending. What happens if pretending becomes reality? You were all into The Alaskan a few years ago."

"Yes, but need I remind you that he wasn't into me."

"That might have been the case then, but now the two of you will be spending a lot of time together. People change, things happen."

"I agree with Jill," Nadia piped in to say. "Normally what happens on vacation stays on vacation, but in your and Jess's case, the media is going to let all of us know practically everything you're doing."

"And it will all be an act for their benefit while we're here. The last thing I want is to get seriously involved with any guy right now and that includes Jess. I need space to get myself together."

After ending the call with her sisters, Paige dressed, deciding to wear one of her new sundresses and a pair of sandals, both purchased while she'd been filming in Japan. She stared at her reflection in the vanity mirror, pleased with the results. With just eyeliner and a touch of lipstick, she was good to go. She smiled when she tossed her head, making her hair fall in waves around her shoulders.

Although getting to sleep last night had been hard, after making an important decision regarding her career, she had awakened this morning feeling good. The best she'd felt since the story about Kemp and Maya had broken. Moving on had never felt so great, and she was doing so with Jess.

Well, not exactly, she thought, recalling Jill's warning. She had to remember that no matter what, she and Jess would only be playacting.

When she heard the knock at the door, anticipation ran through her. Grabbing her purse off the bed, she headed for the door. She opened it and saw Jess standing there, all six foot two of him, and immediately thought—not for the first time—that Jess Outlaw was one hot man. Why did he have to look so good? And why did his jeans and shirt fit so perfectly? Just seeing him gave her a tingling sensation all the way to her toes.

And why did he have to flash her such a sexy smile? Dimple in his chin and all.

"Good morning, Paige. Are you ready?"

"Good morning, Jess. Yes, I'm ready."

If only he knew just how ready she was.

Seven

When Jess walked Paige over to the car, it took all his willpower to act unaffected.

The moment she had opened her door, his gaze had taken in her outfit, and then those long, gorgeous legs in a pair of sandals. Her sundress was an array of colors in a soft flowery print. Thin straps covered her toned shoulders and the neckline scooped in a way that hugged her breasts. And the top portion of the dress was backless. When had he started noticing women's clothes? Down to every single detail? Probably when he'd noticed how well Paige wore hers.

"Thanks," she said, when he opened the car door for her.

His gaze sharpened when he saw a flash of thigh as she eased down onto the leather seat. If that sight had nearly knocked the breath out of his lungs, he didn't want to think what effect seeing more would cause. She glanced up at him, probably wondering why he was still standing there and hadn't closed the door. Giving him a warm, questioning smile, she asked, "Is anything wrong?"

He blinked, glad she didn't have a clue about the desire he was feeling. "No. I was just thinking about something," he said, quickly closing the door and walking around the back of the car to get in. No way he could walk around the front, where she might see the state of his arousal.

When he got into the car, her scent filled his nostrils. He glanced over at her as he settled in the seat behind the steering wheel. "You look nice, Paige." That was an understatement. She looked stunning.

"Thanks, and you look nice yourself, Jess. Are you nervous about breakfast?"

"No." There was no need to tell her the reason he wasn't nervous was because he intended to be himself, a man who not only would enjoy her company but who would also enjoy *her* if given the chance. "Are you nervous?"

She shook her head, making the hair framing her face move silkily around her shoulders. "Nope. I'm just treating this as an acting job."

For some reason, he didn't like the sound of that. He merely nodded, started the ignition and backed out of the driveway. "I talked to Garth and told him of our plan. He will tell the others as needed."

Nodding, she said, "And I talked to Pam last night and Jill and Nadia this morning."

"No one tried talking you out of it?"

She chuckled. "No. They didn't like Kemp much anyway and now they like him even less."

There was no need to mention that his siblings who'd met Kemp Pierson hadn't liked him much either. It really hadn't mattered what they liked as long as Paige had been happy. Obviously, she had been, since she and Kemp had been together for almost a year.

"What about Garth?"

Now it was his turn to chuckle. "You know Garth. He has strategic planning down to an art form and thinks it will work. Of course, he said that we have to be convincing." He decided not to tell her what else Garth had said.

"I agree. However, I know how reporters' minds work, so how will we handle it if one comes right out and asks if we've been involved in a 'hot, romantic entanglement'? You just got here a couple of days ago, which could be easily tracked, so how can we be engaged in something like that already?"

Didn't she know it wasn't uncommon for a romantic relationship to follow after a breakup like hers? But then, like Garth had warned, most of those rebounds didn't last.

"Anything is possible, Paige. We can certainly give off enough chemistry to convince people there's a strong attraction between us." He decided to switch subjects so she wouldn't ask any more questions that he really didn't want to answer. "This is beautiful country, isn't it?"

The sun was out, and the sky was blue. The road they were traveling was high in the valley, and below, as far as the eye could see, were rows and rows of vineyards. Even from their distance, he could see ripe grapes.

"Yes, it is beautiful."

She was beautiful, he thought, glancing over at her. "Tell me about the movie you just completed in Japan. How did it go?"

Paige glanced over at him and smiled. "I think it wrapped up well—at least, my director said it did. He was easy to work with."

He nodded. "Anyone else in it that I might have heard of?"

She answered him but he didn't recognize any names. He wasn't into movies, but he would admit to having watched every single one she'd been in.

"You were the lead, right?" he asked.

"Yes. My first time. One of the reasons Maxie wants

me to stay with Kemp is because some big-time producer wants Kemp and I to make a movie together."

"Could you do that after what he did?"

She shrugged. "Yes. We're professionals. Of course my agent prefers we be more than that. It gives the media a lot to talk about. Are the kisses the real thing? And how far did we actually go in the love scenes? That sort of thing."

He wondered how she managed to live that way, having her business out there for everyone to see. But then, there were a number of politicians who lived the same way. He wasn't one of them and didn't plan to be. When he could get away from Washington, he usually did, by hightailing it back to Alaska.

"Do you still go dogsledding?" she asked.

Jess wondered how she knew he'd been into that. He didn't recall ever mentioning it to her. His expression must have given him away since she said, "Charm told me. I asked her about it when I saw a photo of you that time I visited her."

He'd heard about her visit. He'd been away in DC at the time. She had been filming in Vancouver and caught a flight to visit Charm in Fairbanks. From there she'd flown to visit Bailey and Walker on Kodiak Island.

"Yes, I still do go dogsledding, whenever I can. There's nothing else like it."

When she made a face, he chuckled and said, "Don't tell me you can't handle cold weather."

"After having spent most of my life in Wyoming and Denver, I have no choice, but when I think of doing something like bundling up to ride on a dogsled, it doesn't sound like anything I'd do."

"Hey, don't knock it until you try it. I have a feeling you just might like it."

"Why would you say that?" she asked.

"I say it because you come across as someone who isn't afraid to try something new and different, Paige."

He hoped like hell that was true, he thought as they entered the Windemere Resort. He was about to start throwing her all kinds of curveballs with the faith that one would eventually land right in her lap.

The notion that no one would recognize her vanished from Paige's mind the moment they walked into the restaurant and headed over to the counter to be seated. The hostess's eyes widened, and her mouth formed an O.

Before she could speak, Jess, who'd been standing by Paige's side, said, "Good morning. We would like a table for two in an area where we can see the lake, please."

The young woman, who looked to be in her early twenties, blinked again before giving Jess an astonished smile.

"Certainly, sir." Then she looked back at Paige. "You're Paige Novak, the actress, right?"

Paige smiled. "Yes." The woman might be looking at her, but she was also giving Jess the eye. Paige couldn't much blame her.

"I've seen all your movies and even watched you on that soap, *Touch the Heart*. Since they didn't kill you off, I'm hoping that means you might be coming back."

Paige's smile widened. "There's always that possibility."

The woman, whose name tag said Tobi, nodded and then glanced back over at Jess. He must have smiled at her because Tobi looked like she would melt in a puddle in front of them.

"Do you have any tables available?" Paige asked.

"Yes. Right this way."

They followed Tobi, and warmth raced through Paige when she felt Jess's palm at the center of her back. The restaurant was crowded, but she didn't have to look around to know that once again she'd been recognized. Soft murmurs flowed around them with a few gasps, and she could hear the clicking of cell phones letting her know photos of her and Jess were being taken.

Tobi led them to a table in the back next to a window. Jess pulled out the chair for her and suddenly she realized Kemp hadn't ever done anything so courteous. It hadn't bothered her because she could certainly pull out her own chair, but the gesture from Jess reminded her that with some men, especially those with Westmoreland blood flowing through their veins, manners were ingrained. Kemp, on the other hand, didn't have a chivalrous bone in his body.

"Your server will be here in a minute," Tobi said, handing them menus. Before walking off, she asked, "You've been here at the resort all this time?"

Paige had anticipated that question from someone today and gave her the response she, Jess, Spencer and Chardonnay had agreed on. "No, I'm on vacation visiting friends, Spencer and Chardonnay Westmoreland, at the Russell Vineyards."

Tobi blinked again. There was no doubt in Paige's mind that, as an employee of the resort, Tobi knew who owned the place. "The Westmorelands?"

"Yes."

Then, as if Tobi didn't want word to get back to the resort owner that she'd been taking up too much of Paige's time, she said, "Welcome to Windemere."

"Thank you."

When Tobi walked off, Paige glanced over at Jess and smiled. "So far, so good."

So far, so good was an understatement, Jess thought a short while later. Their server placed their breakfast plates in front of them, and he didn't need to look around to know photos were being taken. The clicking sound was all over the restaurant.

"Everything looks delicious, doesn't it?" she said, glancing up to find him staring at her. Hell, everyone snapping their photo would have captured him staring at her like a besotted fool. But then, that was a good thing. He wanted everyone to know just how taken he was with her. Truly.

He nodded. "Yes, everything does," he said, as he picked up his coffee cup, breaking eye contact.

She took a bite of bacon and gave him a dreamy smile. One he wished he could kiss right off her face, only to have it come back to kiss again. "The bacon is crisp, just the way I like it."

"Mine is cooked just the way I like it, too."

The couple sitting at the table next to theirs kept glancing over at them, and it was obvious the woman was trying to eavesdrop on their conversation.

"Did I tell you how beautiful you look this morning, Paige?"

"Yes, you did, and I'm looking forward to dining with you at Sedrick's tonight." There—she'd deliberately given the eavesdropping woman information that hopefully would be shared with the media.

"I'm glad we hooked up while on vacation," he said.

"So am I, Jess."

Not to be caught in lies unnecessarily, they had decided to be truthful about their relationship as much as possible. They would merely say that since the two of them were vacationing together with relatives and friends, they'd decided to spend time together. Their body language, facial expressions and physical responses would denote to any onlookers just how much and to what degree they enjoyed spending time together.

Jess figured that would be a piece of cake for him

because every part of his body yearned for Paige. He wanted to touch her, taste her. More importantly, a part of him wanted to protect her from the Kemp Piersons of the world.

"When I talked to Pam last night, she mentioned that Crystal had delivered her triplets. Mom, babies and Daddy Bane are doing great," she said, breaking into his thoughts.

He nodded, smiling. "That's good to hear. More Westmorelands."

Jess and Paige then talked about the names Bane and Crystal had decided on for their sons. At least, she talked. He listened while watching her closely. He actually found the movement of her mouth fascinating. The same thing had happened last night when she'd been eating pizza. He'd never thought of a woman eating as erotic, but sharing a meal with Paige had definitely made him reach that conclusion.

"Other than dogsledding, what else do you like to do, Jess?"

He lifted his eyes to Paige and instantly his arousal shot up another notch. "I like playing cards."

"Oh? What do you play?"

"Mostly poker."

"A true Westmoreland. They all like playing poker. In fact, that's how it goes whenever they get together."

"I know. I've been part of their poker games before," he said, grinning.

"That's how I learned to play," she said. "Zane, Canyon and Jason taught me, but I'm far from being a card shark."

He was about to suggest they play a game of poker while they were here. Just the two of them. Hmm…strip poker would be nice.

"Anything else you like to do?" she asked.

He shrugged. "I like to dabble in paint every once in a while."

Her eyes widened in surprise. "You're an artist?"

"I wouldn't claim that, but I'm not so bad. It's a way for me to relax."

"Do you have anything that you've done that you're proud to display?"

"Display?" He chuckled. "No farther than my phone, trust me." He pulled out his phone from his back pocket. After clicking it on, he scrolled through several photos until he came to one particular picture. "I usually paint scenes and not people, but Dad commissioned me to do a painting of a person," he said, handing her the phone.

He watched her study the image. "You did a great job. She's beautiful. Who is she?"

"Claudia Dermotte, Charm's mother."

"She doesn't look old enough to have a daughter Charm's age."

"That's what most people say. She could be Charm's sister instead of her mother. She was only twenty-one when Charm was born, a lot younger than Bart. But then, most of his wives were. Claudia is the love of Bart's life and the one woman who refused to marry him and the only one he can't control."

Jess and his brothers thought that was an understatement. Bart loved Claudia, and they figured she loved him, too, but she refused to put up with Bart's arrogant attitude. That was one reason he was always on good behavior around her. Um…maybe *good* was pushing it too much. *Acceptable* behavior was probably a better word.

"I'm surprised you haven't seen her before," Jess said.

Paige continued to study the image. "No, I've never seen or met Charm's mother. I didn't attend any Outlaw weddings due to being out of the country on film shoots, and I don't recall seeing her at Bailey and Walker's wedding."

"You wouldn't have. I'm sure you've heard that Bart is in denial as far as our relations to the Westmorelands are concerned. No one knows why. He's even approached a Westmoreland thinking it was his own son. That happened at Garth's rehearsal dinner—he tapped Riley on the shoulder thinking it was Garth. If anyone can find out why he feels that way, Claudia will be the one."

Paige glanced back at his cell phone. "Well, this is a beautiful painting and you're not giving yourself enough credit. You're truly gifted."

"One day I'd like to paint you, Paige," he said casually.

"You would?" she asked as her lips quirked in a smile.

"Yes."

"Then we're going to make sure that happens one of these days, Jess."

He nodded. Whether she knew it or not, he intended to make it happen.

Eight

"The Windemere Resort is amazing."

Paige looked at Jess, totally in agreement with what he said. "No matter how many times I come here, I can't get over how beautiful it is," she said as they walked the grounds. It was a gorgeous day, and although the sun was shining brightly, Napa Valley sat between two mountains that pretty much shielded the valley from the heat. That was also the reason for the cool nights.

"And I heard Spencer designed the resort himself," she added.

The moment they ended breakfast and left the restaurant and began walking around the resort, it was obvious that more people had recognized her. A text from Nadia just moments ago had informed them that Paige's appearance with a very handsome man was all over social media with pictures. Everyone was scrambling to determine Jess's identity.

Jess had a firm grip on her hand. They appeared as if

they were any other normal couple spending time at the resort. More than once, Jess had touched the bare skin at the center of her back. He'd also brushed his thumb over her knuckles a few times and placed his arm around her shoulders. If she didn't know better, she would think he couldn't keep from touching her, but she knew he was just trying to display tenderness, affection and even possessiveness to anyone watching them. And there was no doubt in her mind they were being watched and filmed. People were whipping out their cameras left and right, although no one had approached them.

Paige glanced at her watch. They had been at the resort for four hours and it was time to head back to the vineyards if they wanted to rest up for dinner. By then, the media would be out in full force, and she and Jess needed to be ready.

"It's time to head back," she said.

"All right. What do you plan to do until dinner?"

She shrugged. "Take a nap, and then when I wake up I'll work on my hair."

He glanced at her head. "What's wrong with your hair?"

"I want to fix it differently tonight. I really want to look pretty."

He gave her a disbelieving look before saying, "You're always pretty, Paige. I think you're beautiful."

Appreciating the compliment, she reached up and cupped his cheek, smiling at him. "That's a nice thing to say, Jess." At that very moment, a woman snapped a picture.

Grinning at her, Jess whispered, "I recall a time cell phones didn't come with cameras."

"The good old days?" Paige asked, chuckling.

"Yes, the good old days. I think our work for today is finished." As he still held tight to her hand, they walked toward the parking lot to leave.

* * *

Less than a half hour later, Paige was back at her villa and Jess was headed to the guest pool for a swim when her phone rang. It was Nadia.

"You again?"

Nadia laughed. "Sister-girl, you and Jess are blowing up the internet. The media did their research, and Jess has been identified. Pictures are all over the place of him as a dogsledder and he looks hot. They even found a calendar a few years ago that he did for some charity in Alaska where he was Mr. December, and trust me, December never looked so good. The women are going crazy."

Paige shook her head. "At least they don't think I went from a prince to a toad."

"Far from it. Some think he's hotter than Kemp. You should read their comments."

"I'll pass since you're reading them for me anyway."

"And I'm enjoying doing so. Right now the one with the most 'likes' is the one with your hand on his cheek. Dang it, Paige, that picture is so romantic. I could feel the chemistry between the two of you."

Paige rolled her eyes. "You could not."

"I could, too. You guys are laying it on thick."

Were they? Of course they wanted to come across as a couple who enjoyed being together. That way everyone could see Jess as someone who would make moving on easy.

And honestly, he was. She was comfortable with Jess. Conversation between them flowed easily. He'd told her about his dogsledding days and she'd told him how hard it had been to get a part in any movie because she was an unknown.

"Tonight, we're going to dinner. Since we dropped the name of the restaurant several times today, I expect the media will be there waiting."

"Are the two of you ready for that?"

"Yes." She liked Jess a lot and there was no doubt everyone would be able to see it. Everyone other than Jess himself.

"I need to take a nap before getting ready."

"You and your naps. Okay, I'll keep you updated about what's happening on social media."

After ending the call with Nadia, Paige couldn't help checking to see any pictures. The first one she saw was the one where her hand was on Jess's cheek as they stared at each other. Nadia was right. It did look romantic. Just seeing the way he was looking at her had heat churning in her stomach. He had definitely gotten into the role of a man who desired a woman. She could see it in his eyes.

She then studied her own eyes and saw how intense they were as she looked at him. She didn't just look like a woman who desired a man, but a woman who was falling in love.

Paige blinked, knowing that just wasn't true, and figured that she was more tired than she'd thought. Her brain was turning to mush. She definitely needed a nap. She came to another "liked" photo and threw her hand over her mouth to stop screaming out in laughter. Someone had taken a photo, a pretty darn good one, of Jess's denim-clad ass. The post said, "I've never seen anything so yummy. Have you?"

Her phone suddenly rang, and she saw it was a call from Maxie. She took a deep breath, knowing her agent was probably not happy with her.

She clicked on. "Yes, Maxie?"

"I hope you know you've ruined your chances of ever getting another decent part in any movie production. Kemp Pierson is the hottest thing in Hollywood and it's unfortunate you couldn't appreciate that fact."

Paige frowned, fed up with Maxie's attitude. "What I

couldn't appreciate is him messing around with Maya and thinking I'd forgive him, like it was nothing. What's even more disappointing is that you think I should go back to him for the sake of my career, Maxie."

"Some women have done worse, Paige. This is Hollywood. Kemp holds the title of Hottest Man Alive, and you were the woman by his side. People expect him to act indecent once in a while, and they expect you to get over it."

Paige's frown deepened. If she didn't know any better, she would think Kemp's affair with Maya had been part of some script for publicity. Had it? "Maybe that's the problem. If that's what people truly expect, well, I have news for them. I have moved on and I really like the guy I'm with now. He's kind and—"

"He's not Kemp Pierson."

"Thank God for that. Goodbye, Maxie."

Paige ended the call, then threw her head back to draw in a deep breath. Maxie had been her agent for five years and her contract was up for renewal. Maybe it was time to end things if the woman felt it was okay for Paige to lower her standards just because of Kemp's popularity. But then, she had a feeling she wouldn't have to bother. Maxie would probably be dropping her.

Just like she'd told Jill, she was prepared for the consequences.

Jess glanced at his watch as he made his way down the path to Paige's door. Hopefully, she wouldn't mind that he was a few minutes early. Adrenaline was flowing through his veins and it couldn't be helped. He wanted to see her again. He *needed* to see her again.

Upon returning to the villa after breakfast, he had changed clothes and gone swimming to work off his sexual frustration. He doubted Paige realized just what being around her had done to his libido. Spending most of the morning with her had reminded him that he still had one.

Since becoming a senator, he'd never lost sight of the reason he'd been sent to Washington, and he'd kept himself busy. He had dated a few women, but he knew he would not get serious about any of them. Whenever he'd needed a date to an event, Charm would fly in, and he'd been satisfied with that arrangement. No wonder his constituents had suggested he get a social life. And now, after spending the last couple of days with Paige, he would have to agree with them.

Jess knocked on the door, and it didn't take long for Paige to answer it. The moment he saw her he was glad his legs were planted firmly on the ground, otherwise he might have dropped to his knees. She was that gorgeous.

"Come in. I just need to grab my purse."

He entered, and by the time he could breathe again, she was back.

"How do I look?" she said, twirling around. Just like this morning, he noticed everything about her outfit. How the dress stopped above the knee...way above the knee... and fit her body, every single delectable curve, like it was hand painted on her. He was tempted to reach out and touch it to make sure it wasn't.

And then her hair... When she had twirled around, it had moved as if in slow motion, the waves fanning around her face. Knowing she was waiting for his response, he finally said, "You look magnificent, gorgeous, beautiful, stun—"

She threw up her hand and laughed. "No need to get carried away, Jess."

Was that what she thought? He was getting carried away? If she did, then she hadn't seen anything yet. And the sad thing was that this was not a ruse to him. This was the real thing, and he was as serious as he could get.

"I will say, Jess Outlaw, that you look rather dashing yourself. I love a man who wears a suit well, and trust me, you look good."

"Thanks. Luckily, I brought one with me for the anniversary party."

"Have you seen the comments being made about us on social media? Namely the ones about you?" she asked.

"No, but my brothers and Charm have. They called to tease me."

"Having regrets?"

He saw the concern in her features and shook his head. "Not a single one. My siblings wouldn't be who they are if they didn't rag me about anything. They know I'll take it in stride. In fact, Maverick told me to tell you that he would have loved to have flown here to be your love interest. He thinks I'm nothing but a stuffed shirt."

She leaned close and said, "I'd rather be with you than Maverick. He would have dumped me the second a woman with big boobs caught his eye."

Jess laughed. Although that did sound like something his baby brother would do, he couldn't imagine anyone dumping her. Even Kemp wasn't dumping her; he just wanted to have his cake and eat it, too.

"Is there anything we need to go over beforehand? The media can be fierce."

"I'm good. I've dealt with them before. My campaign in Alaska was anything but smooth." Jess offered her his arm. "Are you ready to go?"

She smiled at him and took it. "Yes, I'm ready."

Nine

Sedrick's was situated on a grassy slope in the heart of Napa Valley. The huge European-style structure was built of stone and brick and seemed to stand like an elite beacon. Lights surrounded the establishment and Paige noted most of the cars in the parking lot were expensive, which pretty much defined the restaurant's clientele. This was a Thursday night, and if the full parking lot was anything to go by, the place was packed.

Jess had told her on the drive over that he'd made reservations and would be using Spencer and Chardonnay's private room. On their first date, Spencer had brought Chardonnay here, and eventually he'd struck a deal with the owner to have that private room always available for whenever he and Chardonnay returned here to dine. Paige had never heard of anyone owning a room in a restaurant, but somehow Spencer, being the astute businessman that he was, had become a silent partner with that benefit.

She glanced over at Jess and recalled the moment she'd

opened her door for him. His gaze had roamed her from head to toe, and she'd sworn she'd seen deep male appreciation in his eyes. Desire was something most men couldn't hide. Seeing that look had sent heat rolling around in her stomach, and she had even felt the tips of her nipples harden against the fabric of her dress. She had to remind herself she had recognized desire in his eyes six years ago, too, but he hadn't acted on it then, and chances were, he wouldn't do so now.

A valet quickly moved forward to greet them and his smile widened when he saw her. Opening her car door, he said, "Welcome to Sedrick's, Miss Novak."

"Thank you."

Jess came around the car to stand by her side as he handed the attendant the keys. No sooner had they rounded the corner to the restaurant's entrance than reporters appeared, swarming around them with their cameras flashing.

"Is it true you've been hiding out here in Napa Valley all this time, Miss Novak?" a reporter asked as flashbulbs fired off in her and Jess's faces. The feel of his hand at the center of her back gave her comfort.

She smiled at the reporter. "Hiding out? That's definitely not true. As you know, I just finished filming in Japan and decided to take a vacation and visit my cousins-in-law, the Westmorelands, at Russell Vineyards for a bit of rest and relaxation."

"And why weren't you available to make a statement?" another reporter asked.

Paige smiled. "There was nothing for me to say. I'd spoken with Kemp. He knows I've moved on and I wish him the best."

"So, the two of you are no longer together?"

She was about to reiterate when Jess surprised her by

saying, "As Paige stated, she has moved on, and I'm more than happy to help her do so."

With Jess's statement, the reporters' attention was now on him. "Senator Outlaw, are you and Miss Novak involved in a 'hot, romantic entanglement' as her sister claims? And if so, does it not bother you that Miss Novak jumped into a relationship with you so soon after ending one with Kemp Pierson?"

Jess chuckled. "I refuse to comment on the first question, and as far as the second question goes, the answer is no. The timing of Paige's breakup with Pierson doesn't bother me. In fact, I feel that now is the perfect time for me to do what I didn't do a few years ago when I first met Paige."

"And what was that?" a couple of reporters asked at once.

"Make sure she knows just how taken I am with her," Jess said. Paige stood beside him and smiled, thinking the reporters were eating up the fake story Jess was weaving.

"And why didn't you make your move then?" a female reporter asked.

"At the time, I was knee-deep in my campaign and was only focused on that. I've run into Paige over the years, but she was either filming or I was getting settled in Washington as a senator. When I was finally ready to make my move, she had become involved with someone."

Paige noted Jess refused to mention Kemp by name. He paused. "All that is behind us, and this is the perfect time for me and Paige to enjoy each other's company without any distractions."

"What about the comment Kemp Pierson made about the two of you still being together, Miss Novak?"

Paige eased closer to Jess's side, and he slid what appeared to be a possessive arm around her waist. "As I've stated, Kemp and I are *not* together, and he knows that.

As you can see, I'm here with Jess, and there's no other person I'd rather spend my vacation with."

She glanced up at Jess and noted the intense way he was staring at her. A very sensuous look. Suddenly, it was as if all the reporters faded to the background, and Jess began lowering his head to hers.

He was going to kiss her.

They hadn't discussed the possibility of sharing a kiss, but it would make sense, to substantiate all they'd said tonight. She turned into Jess's arms, and when his mouth connected to hers, she ignored the multitude of bulbs flashing to capture their kiss. If ever there was a kiss designed to render a person senseless, this one was it.

This wasn't a regular kiss—it was hungry, seductive and possessive—and she returned it in kind, not caring about the photographers or reporters or those dining in the restaurant who could probably see them. Nothing mattered to Paige but this, the feel of Jess's lips on hers and the taste of his tongue in her mouth.

Although they had given the reporters more than enough coverage tonight, Paige wasn't ready to end the kiss and would still be in Jess's arms if one of the reporters hadn't said, "Kemp Pierson is going to blow a fuse when he sees that Paige has moved on."

"But then, what did he expect after being unfaithful to her?" another reporter asked.

Paige drew her mouth away from Jess. If he kissed like this with an audience, how would he kiss in private? Tasting him on her lips, she turned to the reporters. Before she could say anything, one asked, "What about what the senator said? Will you let him show you how taken he is with you?"

Paige chuckled. "Most definitely."

"And what do the two of you anticipate happening while vacationing here in Napa Valley?"

Paige glanced up at Jess and smiled sweetly before saying, "You know the saying—what happens on vacation..."

She left the sentence hanging, and Paige thought that was a perfect way to end their time with the reporters. "Jess and I will be going inside to enjoy our dinner. Good night, everyone."

With his arm still placed possessively around her waist, Jess escorted her into the restaurant.

Jess kept his hand at the center of Paige's back as the maître d' escorted them through the mass of well-dressed patrons. A number stared at them with huge grins on their faces. There was no doubt in his mind some had probably witnessed his and Paige's first kiss. Granted, he wished it hadn't been done to put on a show. Even so, he still got the Paige-effect from mingling his tongue with hers, and parts of his body were still raging with need for another kiss. The next one would be private and just as potent.

They continued following the maître d' until they reached a private room in the back. The man opened the door to a space with brick walls, dark wooden beams, cast-iron chandeliers and a beautiful table set for two. The size of the room was no larger than one's dining room, but the entire area held an ambience of romance.

After being seated and given menus and the wine list, they were told that only wine from the Russell Vineyards could be served in this room. The maître d' then informed them their waitress would arrive soon to take their dinner order and wine selection.

The second they were alone, Paige smiled and said, "I think the interview with those reporters went great. You're the one who should be the actor, Jess. What you said sounded so believable, and I can't wait to see how those reporters will spin things."

He returned her smile. Eventually she would figure

out nothing had been playacting on his part. What he'd told those reporters had been the truth. He figured he had caught her off guard with that kiss and his possessiveness, but he had been acting on male instincts and nothing more. A lot could happen on vacation and he intended to make sure theirs was one neither of them would forget.

They studied their menus and wine list and agreed on what they would have. The door opened and a waitress came in and they gave the woman their order. She was back within minutes to pour their wine and leave a basket of bread on the table.

"I like this room," he said, once they were alone again. "I see why it has sentimental significance for Spencer and Chardonnay."

She nodded. "It is nice, and the view from that window is awesome." Buttering one of the breads from the basket, she asked, "Is there any place that has sentimental significance for you?"

That one was easy. "Yes, in fact, there is such a place," he said.

"Where?"

"The Westmoreland House that Dillon built on his property."

She smiled at his mention of a place so special to her family. "When Pam and Dillon married, it was important for his family to know she wasn't taking him away from them, that they would always remain a big part of the family, so she implemented a huge dinner in their home once a month and all the family was invited. At the time, Dillon was the only one who was married."

She took another sip of her wine, and from her expression, Jess could tell she liked it. "Anyway," she continued, "the once-a-month dinners became twice-a-month dinners when more Westmoreland men got married and everyone began having children. Dillon has a huge house, but pretty soon the dining room couldn't accommodate everyone, so he and Pam came up with the idea to build the Westmoreland House on his property. It has a humongous kitchen, where all the wives can help with the cooking, and a dining area that seats over two hundred. It's plenty big enough when the Atlanta, Montana and Texas Westmorelands come to visit. And now the Outlaws. Of course, the men insisted the Westmoreland House have a man cave where they can play poker. Which made the women insist on having a theater room to watch movies. And they even added a game room for the teens and a playroom for the little ones. Everyone is happy."

After biting into her bread, Paige asked, "Why would the Westmoreland House be of any sentimental significance to you, Jess?"

He took a sip of his own wine before saying, "Because it was there, where Pam and Dillon hosted that holiday dinner and invited the Outlaws, that I saw you for the first time."

Paige tilted her head and gazed at Jess. Why would he say such a thing now when no reporters were around? They were alone. And why was he looking at her like that over the rim of his wineglass? Perhaps they'd taken their playacting a little too far... He had to have been joking, although he looked serious. A part of her refused to go there.

"Did you know Russell will start taking classes at the Napa Valley Wine Academy this fall?"

In a way, Paige was grateful for the transition in conversation. "While in high school?"

"Yes. It's part of a dual enrollment program. He's decided to follow his father into finance. But unlike Spencer, who got his MBA from the University of Southern California, Russell wants to be a Harvard man."

"Well, I can certainly see him working by his father's

side as he gets older. More than once, Spencer has stated he's building his empire to pass on to his children."

Then they began discussing various other subjects and he mentioned that his cousin Delaney and her husband, Jamal, had issued a personal invitation to the Outlaws to visit them in the Middle East.

"Do you plan to go?" she asked him.

"I'm thinking about it. Reggie, Olivia and their kids are there now. I understand Reggie and Delaney were besties while growing up."

She nodded. Senator Reginald Westmoreland, or Reggie, as everyone called him, was one of Jess's Westmoreland cousins. "Yes, that's what I heard as well." Was she imagining things or was Jess staring at her mouth? Did he find her lips as fascinating as she found his?

"Paige?"

She blinked and shifted her gaze from his mouth to his eyes. "Yes?"

"I was asking you a question."

Oops. "Sorry, my mind was elsewhere. Could you repeat it?"

"Sure. I asked if I could paint a portrait of you while you're here."

Paige couldn't imagine sitting before him, quiet and unmoving, staring at him without drooling. Luckily, she was spared from giving Jess an answer when the waitress arrived with their food.

Ten

Paige still hadn't given him an answer to his question, Jess thought, when he brought the car to a stop in front of the main house at Russell Vineyards. Over dinner she had kept the conversation lively, but hadn't gone back to him painting her. Why?

There hadn't been any reporters waiting on them when they'd left the restaurant. Evidently, they had given the media enough information before going inside. He could just imagine the stories that would appear when they logged on later.

"Thank you for such a lovely evening, Jess."

"You're welcome. It's still early yet. How about us killing that last bottle of wine from the other night?" He figured they could handle it since they'd only had a glass at dinner. They had ordered coffee with their dessert.

Jess couldn't help getting turned on whenever Paige began nibbling on her lips, like she was doing now. They were lips he wanted to taste again. "And you never gave me an answer to my question about painting you."

"I wouldn't want you to go to any trouble."

"No trouble at all. Like I told you earlier today, I prefer painting scenery, but you will be a beautiful subject with the vineyards as the backdrop. In fact, I saw the perfect spot while out jogging this morning."

"You did?"

"Yes. The moment I saw it, I knew I had to paint you there. It would be a great addition for my home in DC."

He saw her brow lift. "You would hang it in your home?"

"Of course. Then whenever I look at it, I will have memories of my time with you."

"Oh."

She began nibbling her bottom lip, a gesture he'd come to realize meant she was thinking hard. Good. He added, "I've enjoyed spending time with you these past couple of days, getting to know you, Paige. Over the next weeks, I hope to get to know even more about you."

She glanced over at him. "I've enjoyed spending time with you as well, and look forward to getting to know you better," she said softly. "But…"

He studied her features. "But what?"

She looked away, tracing the edge of the leather seat with her fingertips. When she didn't say anything and refused to look at him, he gently caught her wrist in his hand. When she glanced up at him, the look he saw in her eyes made his heart ache. "Tell me, Paige. But what?"

"But I'm not sure where all this will end or what you expect of our time together, Jess. There is chemistry between us and it's strong. I can feel it. At first, I thought it was one-sided, but I'm not sure that it is."

Jess decided to be honest with her. "It's not one-sided.

I can feel it as well. But then, I think that's understandable. You are a very beautiful woman."

"Thank you, and you're a very handsome man. However, I feel as if my life is pretty messy right now."

He could understand her still having feelings for Kemp, no matter what he'd done. When you loved someone and they betrayed you, you hurt, but the love didn't go away immediately. He understood that. It had taken him a while to get over Ava, but he had gotten over her. The same would happen with Paige...with the right person in her life.

"Since we need to spend time together for the media, Paige, then let me help you get your life un-messy," he said, tucking a strand of hair behind her ear. "All I want is to help you get through a rough time, Paige. I'm honestly not expecting anything."

That wasn't totally true. What he did expect was to leave an impression on her. A positive impression, and just like he'd told Garth, hopefully, when she was ready to move on and indulge in a serious relationship, she would recall that he was a pretty likable guy, a man who would appreciate the woman she was. Over the course of the following weeks, he was going to do whatever it took to make sure of it.

She nodded. "Okay."

He raised a questioning brow. "Okay what?"

"I could definitely enjoy having my life un-rattled, Jess."

He tilted his head and looked at her. "When was the last time you had some real honest-to-goodness fun, Paige?"

The fact that she had to think hard about his question let him know it had been too long.

"I honestly can't remember," she murmured softly.

"Then let's make this a fun vacation."

A slow smile touched her lips. "I'd like that, and since I'm not a good planner of fun stuff, I'll leave it up to you."

He was not sure that was such a good idea when even now he loved the scent of her and wanted to breathe her all in. A part of him wanted to pull her into his lap to taste her lips again. He doubted she had any idea just how much he wanted her. How much he intended to leave an impression on her, both mentally and physically.

"I have no problem doing that," he said, still holding her wrist and loving the feel of her skin in his hand. "So, what about that third bottle of wine?"

"Wine sounds great. And, Jess?"

"Yes?"

"I'm not that twenty-two-year-old girl anymore," she said.

He released a gusty breath. Was there a specific reason she was telling him that? He could definitely see that she had matured into an even more gorgeous woman. "And I will enjoy getting to know the older woman you've become, Paige."

It was a nice night, although being smack in the middle of two mountains made the temperature cool. However, as they walked toward Jess's villa, the cool air wasn't the main thing on Paige's mind. He was.

Although she had told him that she wasn't ready for a serious relationship, she had no qualms about indulging in a nonserious one. She definitely didn't have a problem enjoying her time with him. She wondered how Jess would react if he knew the one thing that had remained constant over the years was that he was still her fantasy man.

And what if, while getting to know each other, all that sexual chemistry got out of hand? Was a vacation fling— if it came to that—so bad? She couldn't forget that the only reason he was spending time with her was to help her out with the media. At the end of the month, he would go back to DC and she would return to Hollywood.

Six years ago, she'd been fresh out of college and ready to take on the world. She knew, without a doubt, that even if Jess had responded to all that flirting that she'd done, it would only have resulted in an affair. She would not have wanted anything more than that.

Did she want anything more now? She drew in a deep breath, knowing she wasn't sure. What she did know was that she would love more kisses like the one Jess had laid on her earlier tonight—the one that made her nipples hard just remembering it. With Kemp, she'd never come close to feeling the heat that one kiss with Jess had caused.

And then there was his touch. He'd slid his hand in hers the moment she'd gotten out of the car, and he was still holding it as they walked the path leading to his villa. She was amazed how easy it was for her body to react to him. How deep her attraction went. She could just imagine getting naked and being naughty with him. That kind of thought was territory she'd never moved into with another man, but she could definitely see going there with Jess. There was something about him that made her think things, want things and need things... How was that possible?

"You've gotten quiet, Paige."

She glanced over at him. "I was just thinking."

"About what?"

No way she would tell him what her true thoughts had been, so she said, "I was wondering if I should be concerned with what you might put on that 'fun' list. I guess now is a good time to let you know I'm not into mountain climbing."

He chuckled and the sound stirred something within her. "You're not?"

"No. Bailey tried teaching me and gave up."

Jess nodded. "Okay, then maybe you need to tell me some things we could do that might interest you," he said. "At breakfast you mentioned that you like horseback riding and skiing. There's no snow here, so skiing won't make the list."

"Phooey."

She heard his chuckle. It was rich and sexy. Just like the man himself. She was tempted to say he could add anything involving his mouth, tongue and hands to the list.

"Hopefully we'll come up with a few more things over wine."

"That sounds good to me." She glanced over at him. "So, when do you want to paint me?" Now that he had suggested it, she rather liked the idea.

"I'll be glad to show you the exact spot I have in mind tomorrow. I suggest we go jogging together. Afterward, we can go somewhere for breakfast and then make a stop to purchase paint supplies."

She liked that he was planning her into his day. "I'd like that."

"Here we are," he said, upon reaching his villa. After opening the door, he flipped on a light and then stood back to let her enter.

"Thanks," she said, walking to the living room. "I need to get out of these," she added, kicking off her three-inch heels.

"Your feet hurt?"

"They always do with new shoes that I haven't quite broken in." She glanced around and then asked, "Are we doing it in the living room or the kitchen?" Too late she realized how that sounded and quickly said, "What I meant was—"

"I know what you meant," he said, removing his dinner jacket to hang it neatly on the coat tree while flashing that dimple in his chin when his lips began twitching.

Paige hoped he never stopped doing that. Smiling at her. Showing that dimple.

"I prefer the living room, if that's okay," Jess said in a husky voice.

"That's fine with me," she said, trying not to blush. "If you want to grab the glasses from the cabinet, then I'll grab the wine."

Heaven help me, Jess thought, loosening his tie while following Paige into the kitchen.

Those legs, bare feet or in heels, were such a gorgeous pair in that damn sexy dress on such a delectable little body—she was almost giving him heart failure. And then there was that ass. He had no choice but to look when he had to walk around the island to grab the wineglasses out of the cabinet. He had intended to take things slow with Paige, but damn, she made him want to speed things up a bit.

"Ready?" she asked, after he rinsed out the glasses. He hadn't known she was still there. He'd assumed she had grabbed the wine bottle and headed to the living room.

"Yes," he said, moving around the island to walk beside her to the other room.

He watched as Paige placed the wine on the coffee table, before sitting down on the sofa and tucking her legs beneath her. He exhaled deeply, trying to recall the last time he'd been faced with such temptation. Of course she would choose that moment to look at him, raise a questioning brow and ask, "What's wrong?"

Too late. He'd been caught staring. "Nothing. I was just thinking about something." He poured their wine, and then, fighting for control, he took a sip. "You want to tell me some of the things you'd like for us to do together for fun, Paige?"

She took a sip of her own wine and said, "Other than the mountain climbing thing, I'm open to just about anything."

He nodded, wondering if she knew what "just about anything" could entail in his book. "What about riding in a hot-air balloon over the valley?"

Paige giggled and he loved the sound of her laugh. "I've never done that before, but it sounds like fun. Please add it to the list."

"What about bike riding?"

"Wow," she said, brushing her hair back from her face. "I haven't done that in years. I'd love to. And don't forget horseback riding. And swimming. I love swimming."

Jess smiled. "Okay, we have a few things on the list. We'll start with those."

"Sounds good to me."

"And I figure if we spend a couple of hours each day painting, preferably in the evenings, I should be able to finish in a week or less."

"That soon?" she asked, shifting positions on the sofa to untuck her legs. Jess watched as she smoothed her hand down one leg and then the other, kneading the muscles there.

"Are you okay?" he asked.

"Yes, I'm fine. My legs got a cramp. It happens sometimes when I sit in that position too long."

"Maybe I can help," he said, crossing the room to sit on the sofa. "Scoot sideways," he said. After she followed his instructions, he reached out and pulled her legs into his lap.

"I'll massage the cramp away," he said, gently rubbing the palm of his hand into the muscles of her legs and then slowly moving downward toward her feet. He hadn't seen her coral nail polish before now. He liked it.

"That feels good," she said softly. She had closed her eyes.

"I'm glad you're enjoying it."

"I've enjoyed everything about tonight, Jess."

That was good to hear, he thought, because he'd enjoyed everything about tonight as well. He especially liked this, massaging inch after inch of one leg and then the other, the feel of her satiny smooth skin.

Jess trailed his gaze upward to her face and studied her features. With her eyes closed she looked peaceful. Not for the first time, he wondered how any man could be unfaithful to such a gorgeous creature. "You okay?" he asked huskily.

"Yes," she responded, curving her lips in a smile, without opening her eyes. "Your hands feel nice, Jess."

His gaze moved from her face downward to her chest. Her arms were folded under her breasts, lifting them provocatively against the neckline of her dress. He licked his lips and imagined skimming the nipples with his fingertips before taking them into his mouth. Feeling his control slipping, and knowing his lusty thoughts would only get him in trouble, he returned his gaze to her face.

Her eyes were open, and she was staring at him. There was no way she hadn't noticed the attention he'd given her breasts. And she'd probably seen when he'd licked his lips while looking at them. Their gazes held for a long moment, and sexual chemistry flowed between them, sucking them in. There was no way she couldn't feel his erection growing beneath her leg.

She finally broke the silence, and with her eyes still glued to his, she whispered, "Do you know what else I enjoyed about tonight, Jess?" Her voice was so soft that it stroked his insides. All the way to his groin.

"No, Paige, what else did you enjoy about tonight?" he asked, not caring if she saw the intense heat in his gaze.

"Our kiss."

Damn. He could recall the way her lips had fit to

his, how easy it had been for his tongue to slide into her mouth, wrap around hers. He could even recall the breathy moan she'd made when he had deepened the hottest kiss he'd ever shared with a woman. Neither he nor Paige had cared that they'd had an audience.

Now they were in his villa. Alone.

More than anything, he wanted to feast on her mouth. Her eyes were pinned to his, and he felt a need so intense, it made him intoxicated. Not able to resist any longer, he pulled her into his arms and covered her mouth with his.

Eleven

The moment Paige knew the kiss was coming, she opened her mouth so Jess's tongue could easily slide inside. Even with an audience, his mouth had held nothing back. It had taken hers, making every cell in her body respond to the way their tongues had tangled.

With this kiss, he was taking it up a notch—maybe two.

Suddenly, he broke off the kiss and rested his forehead against hers as they both breathed in. Moments later, he leaned back and stared at her. Chemistry floated all around them, making the air crackle and pop with sexual energy. She felt it and wanted nothing more than to rejoin their mouths again in deep, heated bliss.

"I need to get you home, Paige," he finally said.

She blinked. Did he just say he needed to get her home and not that he intended to sweep her into his arms and head for his bedroom? She tilted her head and could see desire in his eyes the way she knew it was in hers. Even now, anticipation thickened the air, so what was going on?

As if he knew her thoughts, he said, "When we make love, I want you to be ready, and I don't want to rush things with you, Paige."

Holy crap. He didn't want to rush things? He couldn't rush a woman whose body felt like a massive sensual throb. A woman who needed sexual relief. And as far as readiness went, the buildup had started the moment he'd arrived on her doorstep for dinner. Just seeing him at the door had stirred something within her. Then later that kiss had ignited the fire. Being in his presence, sitting across from him at dinner, seeing his smile and hearing his sexy voice had kept the fire roaring. Then his touch on her legs, followed by their second kiss, had set the fire ablaze. Now he wanted to put it out?

"The last thing I want to do is to come across as a sex-crazed guy, Paige," he said, his words intruding into her thoughts.

She nibbled on her bottom lip. If he had any idea how long it had been since the last time she'd had sex, he would know *sex-crazed* sounded pretty darn good to her right now. Before she could respond, he eased her legs off his lap to stand. Shoving his hand into his pocket, he said, "I doubt you know how hard this is for me."

If his erection was anything to go by, yes, it obviously was hard. Literally. "You don't think I'm ready for you?" Even now, he'd made her panties wet.

"I want you ready both physically and mentally. I admit that in my younger days I was into one-nighters and wham-bam-thank-you-ma'am sex, but not now and definitely not with you."

She frowned. Why was he making this such a big deal? She wasn't asking for a ring on her finger or a declaration of undying love. "I'm not looking for anything serious," she said, in case he assumed that.

"I know you aren't, and you shouldn't this soon anyway. I won't take advantage of your vulnerability."

Paige squared her shoulders. "How noble. And this nobility will last how long, exactly?" she asked, trying to keep the disappointment out of her voice.

"Not sure. I haven't been with a woman in almost a year, Paige. As a result, my sexual hunger is at an all-time high. You are a very desirable woman who has filled my mind with lusty thoughts. However, when it comes to you, I refuse to think with the wrong head."

He hadn't been with a woman in almost a year? With his looks, there was no way women hadn't come on to him. So why had he denied himself sexual pleasure?

As if he read the question in her eyes, he said, "I haven't had the time."

It had been six months for her. No wonder they were like a spontaneous combustion. The very idea relit her fire.

Standing, she eased close to him and wrapped her arms around his neck. Before she could open her mouth to comment, he said, "Don't tempt me, Paige. I've made my decision about tonight. You need to sleep on what I said, and if tomorrow you're ready to take me on, just let me know."

And then he swept her into his arms.

"We'll grab your shoes on the way out. I'm taking you home."

He was actually taking her home. "I can walk, Jess."

"I'd rather carry you there." He didn't say anything for a moment, and then he added, "Be forewarned, Paige. Once I'm certain that you're ready to take me on, our 'hot, romantic entanglement' will begin, and I won't hold anything back."

Not to be outdone, she said, "And be forewarned, Jess. I don't plan to hold anything back either."

Jess needed a drink. He'd just returned from carrying Paige home, literally, and now he was trying to convince himself he had done the right thing by waiting. Even now, he was tempted to walk back down the path, knock on her door and tell her he'd changed his mind. However, what held him back was knowing his actions tonight were part of his strategic planning.

She might not think one night would make all the difference in the world, but it did. He needed to show her that she meant more to him than being a one-night stand. Hell, she was more than a casual fling, but she'd have to realize that for herself. Of course, with a little help from him.

Like before, whenever she came and left, her scent lingered. At her door he'd told her to get a good night's sleep. Now chances were, he wouldn't. He glanced at their wineglasses that had been left on the coffee table. The wine bottle was half-full. Instead of drinking and talking, they'd been kissing. He wouldn't complain about that.

Now he needed a drink, but something stronger than wine. Spencer had mentioned he'd put a bottle of cognac, Jess's drink of choice, in the cabinet over the refrigerator. He appreciated his cousin for doing so because tonight he definitely needed it. He left the wine bottle on the coffee table with hopes he and Paige would eventually finish it. Grabbing their glasses, he then took them to the kitchen to rinse out and place in the dishwasher.

He found the bottle of cognac just where Spencer said it would be, and after grabbing a glass, he headed to the patio. Tonight, he needed to sit, drink, plan and strategize.

Dinner had been delicious and intimate. That private

room had been perfect, and sitting across from Paige, seeing how her beautiful features had reflected in the moonlight and listening to her hold a conversation with both intelligence and insight had been enlightening. She might travel the globe a lot, but she kept up with the national news. All of their conversations during dinner had been interesting.

Jess glanced over at the villa where Paige was staying. A couple of her lights were still on; he'd flipped all his out. He much preferred the darkness, the peace and quiet. He'd taken a few sips of cognac before leaning back in the chair to close his eyes. It had been a long day, but a productive one. He hoped like hell that Kemp Pierson had egg all over his face tomorrow.

He opened his eyes when he heard a sound. Straining to see in the dark, he could make out Paige in the moonlight and in the lights lining the path. He sat up straight in his chair. Where in the hell was she going? It was past midnight. He studied her attire, saw the bathing robe and then figured she was going for a swim. At this hour? Why wasn't she in bed?

Why aren't you? he asked himself as he watched her stroll up the path. She didn't even glance over at his place, probably figuring, since all the lights were out in his villa, that he'd gone to bed. Although he knew Russell Vineyards was pretty safe twenty-four hours a day, and the pool was well lit, he still didn't like the idea of her going there alone. What if she slipped and bumped her head? What if she got another cramp in her legs while swimming? What if…?

Jess rubbed his hand down his face. What if he stopped coming up with these crazy scenarios that likely wouldn't happen? When Paige took a turn and was no longer within his sight, he stood, deciding he would check on her to make sure she was okay. There was no way he could sleep until he knew for certain she was fine.

Paige glided through the Olympic-size pool, doing laps. The water was warm and wonderful over her skin. Tonight, she had felt undeniably hot for Jess, to the point where she'd decided to go swimming to cool off and work off sexual frustrations.

"...I haven't been with a woman in almost a year, Paige. As a result, my sexual hunger is at an all-time high..."

Jess's words kept flowing through her mind as she stroked her way through the water. *Almost a year?* He definitely had to be ready for sex, yet he'd refused to make love to her until he was certain she was ready to take him on. She couldn't wait until she saw him tomorrow. She'd show him what readiness looked like.

Paige continued swimming, thinking about the articles about her and Jess that would hit in the morning. Kemp and Maxie would be pissed, but she didn't care. How Kemp dealt with the true status of their relationship was his problem, not hers.

Jess was her problem.

She had wanted him tonight more than she'd ever wanted a man before. He had stroked something within her that she hadn't known was there. Real passion. She would listen to Jill tell her and Nadia just how wonderful making love was, and Paige had known she'd been missing out on something. Nadia hadn't contributed to the conversation one way or the other since she thought no man alive was worth sharing her bed until she got good and ready, and she wasn't ready.

Paige, on the other hand, had had her first sexual encounter in college. Alvin Lanford had been such a big disappointment, and so had the next guy, Marion Bovina. She had decided she'd had it with the bedroom until Kemp. She'd expected him to rock her world. Um, not at all. She had begun thinking that maybe the problem was her and not her bed partners.

However, she would have to say, neither Alvin, Marion or Kemp had turned her on with a mere kiss the way Jess had. If he'd continued kissing her, she would have climaxed right then and there. Every part of her had felt alive, rejuvenated in a way that tingled. And for her that wasn't normal.

The only other time she had reacted that way to a man had been six years ago, and that man had been Jess. He hadn't touched her, hadn't even kissed her then, but her entire being had reacted the moment he had walked into the Westmoreland House. The moment their gazes had connected, she had felt a throbbing heat from the top of her head to the bottoms of her feet.

She swam back and forth doing more laps, trying to push everything and everyone from her mind. She wasn't sure how much longer she swam or how much longer she planned to keep swimming. It was getting late and Jess had put a lot on their agenda for tomorrow. She needed to get out and go to bed. Maybe now she would be able to sleep.

She swam to the pool's edge and got out of the water. Using the towel she'd brought with her, she began drying off. Suddenly, she heard a sound. Jerking around, she was surprised to see Jess.

Drawing in a deep breath from the fright he'd given her, she asked, "Jess, what are you doing here? Why aren't you in bed?"

"I could ask you the same thing, Paige," he said, coming closer to stand right in front of her. He was wearing the same clothes—dark slacks, white shirt but minus the tie. And from the look of things, his erection was making itself known. There were some things a man couldn't hide.

"I couldn't sleep," she finally said.

"Neither could I. I was sitting out on my patio when I saw you leave the villa. I could tell by your outfit this was where you were headed."

She tilted her head to look up at him. "So, you followed me."

"Yes. I wanted to make sure you were okay."

She had been okay until she'd seen him just now. With him standing in front of her, all those sexual frustrations she had swum away were back in full force. "You didn't have to follow me. I felt safe coming here alone." Then she recalled what he'd said and asked, "You've been here the entire time? Watching me swim?" If that was true, no wonder he was aroused. Her skimpy two-piece bathing suit left little to the imagination. She might as well be swimming in a bra and thong.

"Yes," he said, shoving his hands into the pockets of his slacks. She wondered if he knew doing that made the huge bulge pressing against his zipper more pronounced. "You're an excellent swimmer."

"Then I guess it's a good thing I decided not to ditch my bathing suit and swim nude."

He reached out and tucked a wet strand of hair behind her ear. "Yes, that was a good thing. But then again, I would not have minded seeing you swim naked, Paige."

Paige looked into the penetrating dark eyes staring back at her. "What time is it, Jess?"

He glanced at his watch, then back at her, and said, "It's close to one in the morning."

She nodded. That meant it was a brand-new day. Making up her mind about what she wanted and how she intended to get it, she tossed the towel aside and began stripping out of her bathing suit top.

"What do you think you're doing, Paige?" Jess asked in an incredulous tone.

"What does it look like?" she asked, removing her bikini bottoms and then stepping back so he could take in the view. "You said you wouldn't mind seeing me swim naked, and I'm ready to take you on, Jess Outlaw."

She quickly turned and got back in the pool.

Twelve

Desire slammed through Jess with a force that nearly knocked him to his knees. In the moonlight, Paige's naked body was total perfection as she stroked through the water. As she swam from one end of the pool to the other, his gaze followed her. It roamed over her ass each time it protruded gracefully to the top, and over her breasts that poked out of the water when she switched to the backstroke. He was mesmerized.

"Hey, aren't you going to join me?" she asked, pushing wet hair back from her face and treading water in the center of the pool. "Swimming is on my list of fun things. We might as well kick things off with a bang."

Bang? Why had she said that? Lust took over his senses. Desire consumed him. His libido reached an "I need her now" level, and his arousal reached a state of no return. By the time they parted ways at the end of the month, their sexual needs, wants and desire would be fulfilled.

After quickly removing his shirt, Jess's hands went to his zipper, inching it down. Then he slid his pants, along with his briefs, down his legs. He knew Paige was watching him, and he was glad that he was the man she wanted. Reaching down, he grabbed his wallet from his pants to retrieve a condom. It had been in his wallet a long time, so he checked to make sure it hadn't reached the expiration date. It hadn't, thank God.

He watched her as he sheathed himself before easing his nude body into the pool. If there was any uncertainty in her mind about his intentions, all doubt should now be gone.

"Come here, Paige."

She smiled and shook her head. "If you want me, Jess, you have to come and get me." She then swam to the far end of the pool, away from him.

Oh, so now she wanted to play hard to get? He had no problem going after her. Maybe now was a good time to tell her that not only had he been captain of his dogsled team, but he'd also been captain of his college swim team.

He glided through the water like a swimmer going for the gold, and it didn't take long to reach her. When she saw him getting close, she laughed and swam to the other side. Without missing a stroke or losing speed, he did a freestyle flip turn and caught her by the ankles. The capture was swift. The minute he touched her, even more desire rammed through him, to the point where water couldn't cool him down.

"I got you," he said, pulling her toward him and swimming with her in his arms to the edge of the pool.

When they reached the shallow end, her feet touched the bottom, and she circled her arms around his neck. "No, Jess, I got you and I'm ready for you." Then she leaned in and took his mouth.

Jess didn't resist, and their tongues mated as they

feasted on each other's mouths like this would be the last time they could. She then wrapped her legs around his hips. He cupped her backside and eased inside her.

Knowing he was inside her body nearly pushed him over the edge, but he was determined to hang on. He had never made love to a woman in a swimming pool, but damn, he was going to make love to her here. After breaking off the kiss, he licked the side of her face when she leaned back against the edge of the pool, pressing their bodies more tightly together.

"I would have preferred our first time being in a bed, Paige," he whispered before licking the side of her neck.

The sound of her chuckle spiked his arousal again. "This is more fun and a new adventure for me. I've never made love in a pool before," she said.

"Neither have I," he said, taking her mouth again. The heat was on, and he was taking full advantage, no longer able to keep his desire in check. When she began kissing him back while moving her hips in earnest, he thrust hard into her. Then harder. He tried to tell himself to slow down, but he couldn't. Her moans and the way she moved her hips to their rhythm drove him on.

Determined not to be denied the taste of her breasts, he released her mouth to take hold of one nipple and suck hard, loving the taste. After a while he was convinced that he was addicted to her nipples.

"Jess!"

The sound of her screaming his name while grinding her hips against him pushed him totally over the edge. He could feel his neck enlarge as he was hit with a full-blown orgasm, the likes of which he had never experienced before. The intensity ripped from the top of his head to the bottoms of his feet planted solidly on the bottom of the pool.

He had been mesmerized by the beauty of her naked

body moving through the water, but now he was totally captivated by this, the way her inner muscles clenched him as another orgasm tore through him and, from the reaction of her body, a second one consumed her as well.

"Paige!"

It seemed to take forever for the effects of their orgasms to pass. When his heartbeat had returned to normal, he pulled her close, knowing what they'd shared was an experience he would never forget. Even now, his greedy erection wanted to go for thirds when her inner muscles tightened on him again. That was the only condom he had with him, so he needed to get out of here so as not to put her at risk.

"We need another condom or two," he said, climbing out of the pool with her body still wrapped around him.

"Even three, four or more," she added excitedly.

He laughed. "I have more at my villa. We'll shower and then make love in a bed. Your villa or mine?"

She smiled, and unable to resist her lips, he kissed her. When he released her mouth, he put her on her feet.

"Doesn't matter to me," she said, sliding back into her bathing suit. "You've never been to my place, so the first time we try out a bed, it should be mine."

He chuckled. "Is that some kind of a rule?"

"Yes. It's the 'When on Vacation Rule Number Three.'"

He slid into his slacks and left off his shirt. Leaning in close, he brushed a kiss across her lips. "You need to tell me what rules one and two are later."

"Okay. Let the fun begin, and remember, what happens on vacation…"

"…stays on vacation," he said, pulling her close to his side as they headed back down the path.

Jess and Paige entered her villa and stripped naked. They rushed to the shower, and the moment they stepped inside, he pulled her into his arms and kissed her.

She would have thought they would be tired of locking lips, since they'd done it a lot of times tonight. Even when walking from the pool to their villas, they'd stopped every so often for their tongues to tangle. One time it had been so heated she thought he would haul her off to the nearest bench. He hadn't. But he had told her over and over again just how good her mouth tasted and how much he enjoyed savoring it.

When he released her mouth now, Paige couldn't help moaning her objection. She was still in awe of the feelings surging through her. Thanks to Jess, not only had she experienced her first orgasm, a second had followed close behind. She no longer wondered if she was one of those women unable to enjoy sex. Jess had definitely proved that notion wrong.

"Ready for our shower?" he asked in a husky voice against her moist lips.

"Yes, and, Jess?"

"Yes, baby?"

He licked around the corners of her lips, which made it hard for her to think straight. When she didn't say anything, he said, "You were saying, baby?"

Fighting back emotions stirring inside her, she said, "I have no problem with you being a sex-crazed guy. Right now, that's the kind of guy I need."

He stopped licking her lips to look at her. He had to be wondering why she'd said that. However, instead of asking her about it, he said, "I warned you earlier that I wouldn't be holding anything back. And, Paige, I meant it."

She doubted any guy had ever gone full speed ahead with her, and she couldn't wait to see what that entailed. From the penetrating look in his eyes, he didn't intend to give her any mercy. That thought made what little control she had left dissolve.

"Then bring it on, Jess," she whispered.

"Trust me—I will." Reaching up, he turned on the water and it sprayed over their bodies. Grabbing the tube of her shower gel, he squirted some into the palms of his hands and worked it into a lather before spreading it over her body. He lathered her chest, lingering on her breasts before moving to her stomach and legs and then upward to the juncture of her thighs. The moment he touched her there, she couldn't help but moan.

"You like my touch or the fragrance?" he asked as the scent of honeysuckle surrounded them.

"Both, but your touch takes top billing," she said, standing under the spray as she watched him cover the same paths on his own body. "I could have lathered you down," she said.

He shook his head. "No, Paige, you couldn't. I would not have lasted one second with your hands on me."

Before she could say anything else, he pulled her with him directly under the water to rinse the foam from their bodies. The warm water flowing over them felt divine. They were standing so close she could feel his erection.

"Now that we've gotten rid of that chlorine, let's concentrate on doing other things," he said, reaching out and pushing wet strands of hair from her face. "Have you ever made out in a shower before?"

His question made her blink. "Wh-what?"

He smiled. "Shower sex. I guess that means no. In that case, I'm going to make your first time one you won't ever forget."

The next thing Paige knew, Jess had dropped to his knees, buried his head between her legs and thrust his tongue inside her. The touch of his tongue on her clit made her weak in the knees, but his firm hands on her thighs kept her upright.

"Jess."

Her entire body nearly exploded when she saw, as

well as felt, just what he was doing to her. Feelings she thought she was incapable of, especially to this degree, overwhelmed her. His tongue made her body writhe mercilessly against his mouth.

"What are you doing to me?" she asked.

He pulled his mouth away just long enough to look up at her and say, "Getting a good taste of you." Then he was back at it at full force, making her finally realize what all the hoopla was about.

She couldn't stop herself from gripping his shoulders hard when the sound of licking pushed her over the edge, making her hips tremble. She screamed his name. "Jess!"

He refused to let go until the last spasm left her body. Then he rose up, gathered her into his arms and whispered, "I've branded you with my tongue, Paige."

In all honesty, he'd done more than that, but she was too weak to tell him that, or anything else, for that matter. She whispered his name again. "Jess."

"I'm here, baby. Are you ready to dry off and get in bed?" he asked her while using the water nozzle to rinse them off again.

She nodded, and then he swept her into his arms and carried her out of the shower.

After drying them both off, Jess swept Paige back into his arms and left the bathroom to carry her to the bed. He had told her that he had branded her with his tongue. What he didn't say was that her flavor was now embedded in his taste buds, just like her scent was ingrained in his nostrils, for all eternity.

Not that he was counting, but he knew so far he'd given her three orgasms. He had felt them, tasted them and enjoyed them as much as she had. The only reason he hadn't made love to her in the shower was because he hadn't had a condom with him. The next time, he would.

He glanced around her villa's bedroom, seeing how much it resembled his. However, he noticed the primary baths were different. This villa had both a huge Jacuzzi tub *and* a walk-in shower. Whereas his only had a walk-in shower. However, he would say the shower in his villa was three times the size of hers. The next time they showered together they would use his. He imagined everything they could do within those four walls.

"You want me to get your nightgown?" he asked, when he noticed it thrown over the back of a chair.

"No, I want to sleep naked tonight," she said, easing under the covers. She smiled over at him. "Now you'll have to sleep naked, too."

Was that her way of inviting him to spend the night? Hell, he hoped so, because he didn't want to leave. "I don't have a problem with that. Let me lock up and I'll be back."

"Okay."

What he also needed to do was grab all those condoms he'd stuffed in the pockets of his slacks when they'd made a pit stop at his villa. With just a towel around his middle, he walked out of the bedroom and picked up their clothes from where they'd stripped out of them. After checking to make sure all the doors were secure, he went back into the bedroom. Glancing over at the bed, he saw Paige had dozed off. That was fine. She needed her rest and there was always morning.

After placing all the condom packets on the nightstand, he put his slacks on the same chair where she'd laid her nightgown. He then took her wet bathing suit into the bathroom and placed it in the sink. Going back into the bedroom, he then flipped off the light and eased in bed beside her. When he gently pulled her into his arms, she mumbled a few words in her sleep, but didn't wake up. He studied her face. Her lips were swollen from his kisses.

It had been a while since he'd gone to bed with a

woman sleeping in his arms. She looked beautiful, peaceful. Like her, he should be exhausted. It would be daybreak in a few hours. But he couldn't sleep because their lovemaking had filled his body with combustible energy.

Never had he wanted a woman more and never had he been as satisfied after making love. But for him it wasn't just sex. He couldn't help but admire her for the recent decisions she had made. There was no doubt siding against her agent and standing up for herself wouldn't win her any brownie points in Hollywood. From the sound of it, Kemp was Hollywood's golden boy. Still, someone needed to school him on how to respect a woman, especially when that woman was supposed to matter to him. That was just common decency. Something Pierson evidently didn't have. What an ass.

Paige shifted positions, which brought them chest to chest. He could feel her breasts pressed against him and, instinctively, he entwined their legs. Not that he thought she was going anywhere, but he'd discovered how much he liked their bodies to be connected. Besides, just in case she woke up during the night, he wanted to be as close as he could get to her. He had wanted Paige the first time he'd seen her. It had taken six years, with regrets for him and a heartbreak for her before they finally got the timing right.

Whether she realized it or not, he'd done more than brand her. He'd staked a claim. By the time their vacation came to an end, she would know the place she had in his life.

Thirteen

The ringing of the phone caused Paige to open her eyes. She would recognize that ringtone anywhere. Why was Nadia calling her before daybreak? She opened her eyes to reach for her cell phone when she realized her legs were entwined with someone else's. That was when she recalled everything that had happened last night, at the pool and in the shower. She then recalled getting into bed naked after inviting Jess to join her. Obviously, he had.

"Here you are," a deep, husky voice said, close to her ear. She was then handed her cell phone. She looked into Jess's face and saw the morning stubble. She liked the unshaven look on him.

"Thanks." She then clicked on. "Nadia, why are you calling me so early?"

"Stop whining, Paige. It's after seven here, which means it's after six there. Most people are up and moving around."

Paige yawned. "Whatever. What do you want?"

"To tell you what the media is saying about you and Jess. Put me on speakerphone so Jess can hear, too."

Paige raised a brow and glanced over at Jess. He'd been staring at her, and their gazes connected. Immediately, her body responded like it had been a physical caress. Unable to look away, she then asked Nadia, "What makes you think Jess is here?" and put Nadia on speakerphone anyway.

"Honey, after seeing that kiss that has been seen around the world, I can't imagine him being anywhere else." Then, as if Nadia had known for certain Jess was there, she called out, "Good morning, Jess."

He smiled, and at Paige's nod, he said, "Good morning to you, too, Nadia. Now, what were you saying about my and Paige's kiss?" he asked, pulling himself up in bed and bringing Paige with him. The moment he touched her, frissons of heat raced through her body. That had never happened with a man's touch before. Only his.

"I said, your interview last night is all over social media. I even understand YouTube crashed from the number of people viewing the video of the two of you kissing. What you said, Jess, about letting Paige know just how taken you are with her, was so romantic, and then to follow it up with one of those tongue—"

"Thanks for calling to let us know our interview went over well, Nadia," Paige interrupted her sister to say. The last thing she needed was for anyone, especially Nadia, to describe the kind of kiss Paige and Jess had shared in front of those reporters. She knew just how magnificent it had been.

"Has Pierson made a statement yet?" Jess asked.

"Not yet. He's probably somewhere wiping mess off his face. Everyone expects him to say something since Paige pretty much contradicted his claim that the two of them were still together. You and Paige looked good together,

Jess, like you belong to each other. Several papers said that as well. Twitter users think you using this time to go after Paige is so romantic, Jess, and the hashtag #Jessie'sGirl is trending. Also, #ReclaimingJessTime. There are some articles and posts suggesting you should be a top contender for Hottest Man Alive for next year, Jess," Nadia said.

Paige glanced over at Jess, and, amazingly, he only shrugged, like the thought of such a thing was of no significance to him. When Kemp had gotten the news that he was being considered for the title, he had danced around her bedroom for a full hour. Then he had called his agent to make sure all the proper interviews would be set up and necessary contacts made.

"If I didn't know better, I'd think the two of you aren't playacting and that Jess meant everything he said about being taken with you from the first and that the two of you are now making a go of it," Nadia said. "And that kiss. You can't convince me it wasn't real. Paige, you were as caught up as—"

"Thanks for the update, Nadia," Paige interrupted again. "I need to get up and get dressed now."

"Are you going to tell me why Jess is there with you this early?"

"No."

"Jess, will you tell me?" Nadia asked.

Jess chuckled and then asked, "How much is it worth to you?"

Paige gave Jess a warning look before throwing her hand over her eyes and grinning. Her sister was too much, and she didn't need Jess to encourage her. "Love you, Nadia. 'Bye." Paige then clicked off the phone and handed it back to Jess to place on the nightstand before she eased back down in bed.

After replacing the phone, Jess turned back to her and stretched his naked body alongside hers. If it was his intent for her to feel his erection, then he'd accomplished that feat. It felt hard, massive and definitely ready. "Good morning, Paige," he said in a deep voice while gazing at her with those penetrating eyes.

Why did he have to look at her like that? Doing so only made her remember their night in the pool and then later what he'd done to her in the shower. The memories were so vivid she could feel herself getting hot between the legs. "Good morning, Jess."

"Are you ready for our day to begin?" he asked.

Paige wasn't imagining it. His erection was getting even larger against her hip bone. "Yes, we're going jogging this morning and then breakfast, and later I will go with you to buy your paints," she said.

"Right."

"Just so you know, I'm having lunch with Chardonnay at the main house to follow up on my assignment."

"Your assignment?"

She swallowed. Was she mistaken or was his face moving closer to hers? "Yes. I told you I offered my help with her grandparents' anniversary party. My job is to follow up with those who haven't sent back their RSVPs. Most are those who might have forgotten. I'm calling them with a friendly reminder. That shouldn't take but a couple of hours."

"I see."

His face was now so close to hers that she could interpret the desire in his eyes and feel his breath on her lips. "What about you?"

"What about me?"

She groaned when he snaked out his tongue to lick one corner of her lips and then the other. His action nearly made her cry out his name. "What about me, Paige?"

She drew in a deep breath. "What will you be doing while I'm spending my time with Chardonnay?"

"I can use that time to make calls to set up some of our fun activities for the week. Hopefully, if I'm able to find all the supplies I need at the store this morning, we can have our first portrait session this evening."

"That sounds good." She was tempted to tell him his body close to hers felt good, too.

He shifted in bed again and his body moved even closer, nearly on top of hers. "But you know what I want to do now, Paige?"

She had an idea, but preferred that he tell her. "What?"

"This."

He took her mouth, showing her that he craved her taste as much as she craved his. Each and every time their tongues tangled, erotic sensations captivated her. No other man's kiss had the ability to do that. If this was what a "hot, romantic entanglement" entailed, then she was more than all in as long as Jess was involved.

He finally released her mouth and threw back the bedcovers to gaze at her naked body. Watching him look at her with such intensity and desire was one of the most erotic moments she'd ever experienced.

"Now I get to make love to you in a bed, sweetheart," he whispered in a low voice.

Reaching up to the nightstand, he grabbed a condom, and while she watched, he sheathed his huge erection. *Lordy.* She was amazed at how such a large penis could fit into such a small condom. But it had.

He looked at her and smiled before straddling her with a pair of muscled thighs. Then he closed his mouth over hers, kissing her with more deliberation than before. She heard her own moans, which meant he heard them as well.

Jess slowly broke off the kiss and eased back to stare down at her breasts, at the hardened tips of her nipples. She drew in a quick breath, marveling at how aroused she got just from knowing he was paying attention to a certain part of her body…and licking his lips while doing so.

Shifting, he lowered his head to her chest. Before she could pull in another breath, he had cupped her breasts in his hands and was devouring her nipples while gently kneading the firm mounds.

Her nipples throbbed mercilessly beneath the onslaught of his mouth, and she was convinced at that moment that her breasts were specifically made just for him.

Sensations swept through Jess as he sucked hard on Paige's nipples. Never in his life had he wanted to taste a woman so badly—to the point where he was filled with a sexual need so intense that her moans were nearly pushing him off the edge.

Trying to regain control, he eased back from her breasts and trailed kisses down her stomach and licked around her navel. Her taste was addictive. It unleashed an urgency within him to brand her again. Just in case he hadn't made his point last night.

Moving his lips farther south, he captured her womanly core, locking his mouth on her while tightening his hold on her hips. There was no doubt about it—he was definitely captivated by her taste. He was as hooked as any man could get. That had to be the reason a primitive urge had taken over his body as he greedily displayed, with his tongue, just how obsessed he was. Her moans were getting louder, and when her thighs began shaking, he knew what was coming. She was.

He barely had time to tighten his hold on her hips when she released a deep, wrenching scream that shook the rafters. However, he refused to let up. He continued to stroke her with his tongue while she writhed. He'd never known a woman who was as passionate, responsive and receptive as Paige.

When the last spasm left her body, he eased up to straddle her and waited for her to open her eyes to look at him. His loins were about to explode with the need to get inside her, but he needed her to look at him. He needed the connection to her. So he held on to what little control he had until her eyes flickered open and met his gaze.

At that moment whatever he was going to say was lost as emotion caught hold of his senses. It left him speechless.

"Jess?"

Instead of answering her, he leaned in and took her mouth with a hunger he felt in every part of him. He finally released her mouth, mentally accepting all he was feeling. He lifted her hips and slowly eased into her. He watched her reaction as he did so, loving the sounds she made, which meant her body was ready again.

Slowly, with a measured pace, he pushed inside until he'd reached the hilt and couldn't go any more. As he drew in a deep breath, their scents were absorbed in his nostrils and total sexual awareness consumed him. Then he began moving, stroking the full length of himself in and out. Her response was immediate. Their limbs interlocked as he continued thrusting at a pace that was as deep and overpowering as it could get.

They were sharing perfect harmony. When she closed her eyes and moaned, thrashing her head from side to side, he increased the pace with every downward thrust. Over and over again. He felt it when her inner muscles took hold of him, clenched him, clamped down hard, but he kept going, refusing to let up.

Her movements matched his rhythm. His moans matched hers, and he was driven to reclaim her mouth, mate with it while the lower part of him mated with her. Her taste fired his need, took control of his senses and pushed him over the edge. But he was determined to take her with him when he went.

The magnitude of his thrusts increased. He released her mouth and threw back his head as the veins in his neck nearly popped from pleasure. That was when he felt her body begin shattering beneath him, and it drove his to do likewise.

"Jess!"

The moment she screamed his name, he felt like everything was ripped out of him, pushing him into a universe of sensual bliss. He couldn't stop coming. It was as if his release was a nonending flow just for her. Gripping her hips, he continued to thrust hard, letting it rip, giving them both what they needed and wanted.

And at that moment he knew what it meant to not just have sex but to make love. He'd known it last night in the pool, and what they'd just shared reaffirmed that belief. Paige Novak had taken him to a place he thought he could never go again, and he knew there was no turning back.

Paige looked at herself in the vanity mirror, not believing how long she and Jess had spent in bed that morning. He had left an hour ago to go jogging without her. She'd been too exhausted. Instead, she had stayed in bed to rest up before her meeting with Chardonnay. That meant his painting would be delayed a day, but what they'd shared this morning—practically all morning—had been worth it.

She wasn't sure how many times they'd made love. More specifically, how many times he'd made her come. All she could say was it had been more than she'd ever done before, because until him, she hadn't done a single one. If her face was glowing, it was because Jess had given her something no other man had—total, absolute and complete sexual fulfillment.

Paige had, however, noticed several passion marks on certain parts of her body. Thankfully, none in places that could be seen by others. Jess had left a number of marks on the areas close to the juncture of her legs. Her body ached in certain places, but that didn't bother her. Instead, it was a wonderful reminder of what they had shared.

She had finally gotten up to get ready and was about to blow-dry her hair when her cell phone rang. It was Jill. She wondered if Nadia had told Jill about Jess spending the night. It didn't matter if she had.

Paige clicked on the phone. "Yes, Jill?"

"Don't 'yes, Jill' me. Everybody is talking about that kiss."

Deciding to play dumb, Paige said, "What kiss?"

"You know what kiss. And just so you know, according to the media, Kemp is scheduled to make a statement later today."

Paige rolled her eyes to the ceiling. "I honestly don't know what kind of statement he can make, unless it's to admit he screwed up and that we've both moved on."

"Well, all I've got to say is that you and Jess have played your roles well. A lot of people believe your story."

Jill's words made Paige realize Jill hadn't talked to Nadia. "Have you spoken to Nadia today?" she asked.

"No. I see I missed a couple of her calls, but when I called her back, she was in a meeting. I figured she was calling to let me know about all the media buzz, so I checked for myself. Like I said, you and Jess have outdone yourselves."

Paige nibbled on her bottom lip before coming out and saying, "Jess spent the night, Jill. That kiss was real."

There was a pause, and then Jill said, "Seriously?"

"Yes, seriously."

"And what he told those reporters about letting you know how taken he is with you—that's real, too?"

"No, not that part. Just the kiss."

"Um, are you sure?"

"Yes. After that kiss we needed to explore all that sexual chemistry we're transmitting, but it's not that he is taken with me. We're both horny."

Jill burst out laughing. "That's too much information, Paige."

"Well, it's true. Our relationship is based on sexual pleasure and nothing else."

"Wow. And how do you feel, being the object of Jess Outlaw's attraction and receiving all that sexual pleasure?"

Paige couldn't help but smile. "Wonderful. Over the moon, thrilled with every part of my body."

"My goodness. So what's the rest of your plan? You've started something and you better believe the media will keep up."

"Let them. Jess and I planned to do a lot of fun stuff on vacation, not for the media but for us. We figured we might as well enjoy our time here. We're going up in a hot-air balloon, bike riding, horseback riding and a lot of other stuff. Did you know he likes to paint?"

"No, I didn't know that."

"I didn't either. He showed me a picture that he did of Charm's mother, and he's good. He wants to paint me while I'm here. He intends to hang it in his place in DC."

"Seriously?"

"Yes."

"Um…"

"Okay, Jill, what's that *um* for?"

"I'm just wondering why Jess would want to hang a portrait of you in his home."

Paige rolled her eyes. "It will not be of me per se. It will be a painting of Napa Valley. He's using the vineyards as the backdrop."

"I don't care what you say, Paige. You'll be the main focus of that picture. No man hangs a woman's picture in his home unless she means something to him."

Paige shook her head. "You've been watching too many romantic movies, Jill."

"I think you need to keep your eyes open, Paige, for signs that Jess may honestly like you."

"He does like me. If I thought otherwise, I wouldn't be indulging in a vacation affair with him. But neither of us is looking for a long-term commitment. After Kemp, the last thing I want is to jump back into a serious relationship with anyone."

Jill didn't say anything for a moment. "When Aidan and I first got involved, it was not supposed to be serious either, but..."

"But you ended up falling in love with him—I know."

"If you know it happened to me, then you should know it could happen to you, Paige."

There was no need to tell her sister that it had already started happening. She'd been falling for Jess for a while, and at some point, either last night in that pool or in the shower or in bed this morning, she'd accepted it to be true. It really didn't matter. The important thing was that neither she nor Jess was ready for that kind of a commitment. Her life was in Hollywood and his was in Washington. All they had and would ever have was what they were sharing now. Even so, she wasn't opposed to an occasional hookup whenever she saw him at family functions.

"Paige?"

"Yes?" Then, remembering what Jill had said, her response was "Jess and I know falling in love is not in the plan, Jill." She was speaking for him now and not for herself since it was too late for her. Jess didn't love her, and she accepted that.

"Still, my advice to you is to be careful and guard your

heart. Westmoreland blood runs through Jess's veins, and take it from one who knows. A Westmoreland man is capable of capturing your heart even if you don't want it seized."

Knowing she needed to end her call with Jill before she spilled her guts and told her sister how she really felt, she said, "Thanks for the warning, and I will be careful."

There was no need to promise to guard her heart. It was too late for that.

Fourteen

"You don't seem bothered by the comment Pierson has released, Paige," Jess said, glancing over at her as they walked from the main house back to their villas.

Paige's tasks for Chardonnay hadn't taken up as much time as she'd assumed they would, and they had gone into town to purchase the paint supplies he would need. After returning to the vineyards, they'd even gone walking and he'd shown her the area he had selected for the backdrop. She had agreed it was nice.

She looked up at him now. "Why would I be bothered? I can't control what Kemp says while he's trying to save face. He's the one who will look like a fool when the two of us don't get back together, Jess."

Jess didn't say anything as they continued walking. Paige hadn't seen Pierson's interview with the press a few hours ago, but he had. The man seemed pretty damn cocky, too sure of himself...and of her. He'd basically said he wasn't concerned about her starting a relationship with anyone because, in the end, he would be the man in her life.

"He's saying the two of you will eventually get back together. That you're just going through a moment," he told her.

Her chuckle should have been reassuring, but he honestly believed the man had gotten into his head that what he'd said was true.

"One thing I've learned about Kemp is that he's all into himself. Like I said, we won't be getting back together for any reason."

He heard what she was saying, and he hoped like hell she meant it. Why did it mean a lot to him that she did?

Jess suddenly knew the answer. He had fallen in love with her. Absolutely and irrevocably.

When had it happened? He wasn't sure. Could have been the first time he'd seen her six years ago. But he could say he'd first realized it while making love to her. Now there was no doubt. He was certain. As certain as she sounded about the end of her relationship with Pierson.

He looked down at their joined hands. He had taken hold of hers the moment they'd left the main house after dinner to walk to the villas. He liked touching her, and with her hand in his, they were a united force. He felt good about that.

"How's the guest list coming?" he asked.

"Great. Like I figured, most of the people planned to come—they just hadn't taken the time to mail back their replies. There were a few who weren't home, so I left a message. I will follow up with them by the end of the week."

After a pause, she asked, "So what's on our agenda for tomorrow? My entire day is clear."

He glanced over at her. As usual, she looked beautiful in her yellow sundress. He'd noted she had worn flats. He hadn't realized just how short she was; however, in bed their bodies fit perfectly.

"I figured we could go jogging in the morning, then have breakfast with the family." He chuckled. "You heard Grammy Russell. She's making her red wine pancakes. I haven't had them before, but they sound delicious."

Paige smiled. "They are."

Unable to resist, he wrapped his arms around her shoulders and gently pulled her closer to him as they walked. This was much better. He liked the feel of their hips brushing as they continued their stroll.

"And then we have an appointment to go up in a hot-air balloon that includes lunch at one." He paused. "Then tomorrow night we're going dancing."

She looked up at him. "Dancing?"

"Yes. Spencer mentioned early today that there's a nice nightclub at his resort that's perfect for dinner and dancing, with a live band. How does that sound?"

A huge smile spread across her face. "Wonderful."

He doubted she knew how hearing her excitement made him feel. Although when they'd gone into town for the painting supplies they had encountered reporters, that had been before Pierson's press statement. It had been easy to say "no comment" or "Jess and I are enjoying our vacation" and leave it at that. Tomorrow the press would expect her to address what Pierson had said. Would she?

He had received a number of calls from his siblings. Like Nadia, they'd told him about the public's reaction to that kiss he and Paige had shared. All of his siblings believed it had been for show except for Garth and Maverick. Maverick claimed he knew a real kiss when he saw one.

They came to the fork in the road. One led to her villa and the other to his.

"It's still early," he said, turning her in his arms.

She looked up at him. "Yes, it is. We never did finish up that last bottle of wine, did we?"

"No, we didn't," he said, his gaze on her face before he cupped her chin with his hand.

"Do you feel like having company?" she asked.

If only she knew how much. "Yes. You're welcome to my villa at any time, Paige."

"And you to mine, but tonight I want to do yours."

And he wanted to do her. "Then let's go to mine, sweetheart."

They were out of their clothes the moment the door closed behind them. Very similar to the night after their swim. The only difference was that tonight they were wearing more clothes and undressing took longer. But it was time well spent. All Paige had to do was glance over to see Jess's naked body to know he was ready for her. Of course, it had taken him less time to undress, but from the way he was watching her, she could tell that he had enjoyed watching…especially when she had stepped out of her panties.

"Come here, Paige," he said in a voice that seemed to caress her skin. She recalled him making that same request last night in the pool. She hadn't gone to him then and wouldn't be going to him now. She rather enjoyed him coming after her.

She shook her head. "If you want me, Jess, then you come and get me," she said, walking backward toward the bedroom.

He nodded while his gaze roamed all over her. "I have no problem doing that."

"Then do it."

When he moved toward her, she took off and had nearly made it to the bedroom when he caught her from behind and whisked her off her feet and into his arms. Wrapping her arms around his neck, she smiled up at him. "You got me."

"And I intend to keep you," he said, dumping her in the middle of the bed and then joining her there.

It was on the tip of her tongue to say that she would love keeping him, but she refused to say that. She knew the score. She was one of his "do good" projects, and he was merely helping her out as a friend. But what if...?

She wiped that possibility from her mind. If anything, Kemp had shown her that long-distance relationships didn't work. All those months apart while filming had only deteriorated their relationship. And she would admit the distance between them hadn't been the only thing lacking with her and Kemp. The lack of sexual chemistry had been the main culprit. However, she had no such issue with Jess. All he had to do was look at her and she was turned on. Like she was now.

Not waiting for him to kiss her, she leaned in and kissed him. Jess was the only man Paige was convinced she could never get enough of kissing. His tongue was made to give pleasure, and it did so with such vigor and hunger, it caused her to moan. She was convinced she could reach a climax just from kissing him, especially if he continued to take her mouth the way he was doing now.

Jess held her in his arms so tightly that she could feel them skin to skin, flesh to flesh, with the tips of her nipples pressing against his chest. There was no way she could miss the feel of his engorged sex pressing hard against her thigh. He broke off the kiss, and the look in his eyes increased her desire for him.

Paige watched as he reached to the nightstand and opened the drawer to grab a condom packet, then ripped it open with his teeth. The hunger she saw in his gaze nearly undid her. He made quick work of sheathing himself, and then he was there, straddling her, and she automatically widened her legs for him. Cupping her hips tightly, while still holding her gaze, he entered her, filling her totally and completely. To her way of thinking, their bodies fit well together. Perfectly.

"Paige?"

She swallowed at the intense desire she saw in his eyes. "Yes?"

He opened his mouth as if he was about to say something and then he closed it. Instead, he began moving, making slow, long strokes at first, and then increasing the pace. He continued to hold her gaze, and she wondered what he'd been about to say. But at that moment words didn't matter—feelings did. And from the way he was staring down at her with heavy-lidded eyes, she was experiencing all kinds of feelings.

She grabbed hold of the strong forearms planted on both sides of her. Throbbing desire overtook her, and the feel of flesh sliding against flesh had purring sounds coming from her throat.

Her hands wrapped around his magnificent back and she felt the muscles bunch beneath her fingers with his every thrust. She decided that he wasn't the only one who could work muscles, and she began working hers, clenching him hard with her inner muscles, refusing to release him when he tried pulling back.

"Give it to me, Jess. All of it. All of you."

The lush shape of his mouth eased into a smile. "Are you sure you want all of me, Paige?" he asked with so much passion she could actually hear it.

"I'm positive."

He then leaned in and kissed her, taking her mouth with an urgency she felt all the way to her toes. This kiss was taking her on a high she'd never been on before and she intended to savor it. He sucked hard on her tongue as his thrusts went deeper, and she literally lost it. Her body jerked at the same time his did, and they both convulsed with desire.

He kept thrusting as sexual fulfillment ripped through every part of her body. When he broke off their kiss, she screamed his name at the same time he hollered hers.

"Jess!"

"Paige!"

They both surrendered to the pleasure overtaking them. She called out his name again, drowning in the essence that was Jess. The taste, scent and feel of him were so sinfully erotic it took her breath away.

It did something else, too. It made her realize just how much she loved him. Not just for this, but also for the man that he was. She had dated enough to compare, and she concluded Jess was in a class by himself.

She settled into his arms as he held her, her cheek against his, and although he had no idea, her heart now belonged to him.

"That was some ride," Paige said the next day as Jess placed his arm around her shoulders, leading her away from the area where the colorful hot-air balloon had landed. "It was fun."

"I'm glad you thought so." He had enjoyed being with her as they glided across the valley, more than fifty feet in the air. Feeling her excitement the moment they'd boarded had been a high for him by itself. Then, standing beside her as they prepared for liftoff, he hadn't been able to stop his gaze from roaming over her in a pair of skinny jeans and a cute sleeveless top.

Every time he looked at her, he had remembered last night. She had spent the night in his villa, and that morning they had gone jogging and showered together. He doubted he would ever forget all the things they'd done in that shower. His shower was larger than hers and had a bench that he'd put to good use, making love to her while water streamed down on them.

"Jess?"

"Yes?"

"Do you want to stop somewhere to grab something to eat? We have a few hours before we start the painting session."

He had made dinner reservations for them at one of the restaurants in town before a movie. Tomorrow they would go bicycling in the countryside. Today he'd begin painting her and he was looking forward to it after getting all the art supplies he needed.

"What do you have a taste for?" he asked her.

She looked up at him. "Chardonnay told me about a place not far from here that sells the best hamburgers and fries. What do you think about that?"

His arm tightened around her shoulders, drawing her body closer to his. "That sounds great. Let's go."

Less than an hour later, they were sitting outside at a café that overlooked the valley while enjoying the best hamburger he'd ever eaten. Even the fries and strawberry milkshake were awesome. When he finished the first hamburger and ordered a second, Paige's eyes had widened. He had laughed and told her that he was a man who had a big appetite after all. Whether it was eating a meal or making love to her. His words had made her blush.

Jess liked seeing her blush. She'd done it a lot last night, and he'd said some pretty risqué things just to see that color come into her cheeks. It was obvious other men hadn't told her what they wanted to do to her, and how they would be doing it. He also liked surprising her and had done so with several positions she hadn't known were possible. He appreciated that she'd been open to new things.

There was so much sexual chemistry surrounding

them. Did she feel it, too? He'd gotten turned on just watching her eat her burger and fries. And then the way she was sucking on her straw reminded him of when she had…

His phone rang and he released an annoyed sigh. The ringtone indicated it was his office back in Washington. They wouldn't be calling unless it was important. "Excuse me—I need to get this," he said to Paige, and then walked over to an area that would provide better phone reception. "This is Senator Outlaw."

"Senator Outlaw, this is Ron Overstreet. I just wanted to give you a heads-up that the Senate majority leader has indicated he might call everyone back to Washington to vote on an important bill next week."

Jess knew exactly what bill would be voted on, and it was important that his party seized the opportunity to make sure it passed. That meant everyone needed to be there for the vote. He glanced to where Paige was sitting as she sipped through her straw, gazing over the valley. The thought of leaving her, even for just a day or so, had him missing her already. "That's not a problem, Ron. Just keep me informed so I can make the necessary arrangements."

"Yes, sir."

When he returned to the table, Paige glanced over at him. "Everything's okay?"

"It depends on how you look at it." He then told her he might be needed back in Washington next week.

She nodded. "Duty calls. How long will you be gone, or will you even return here before the party?"

Was that disappointment he heard in her voice? He hoped so. That would mean she didn't want him to leave any more than he wanted to go. "No more than a day or so. Once the vote is taken, I'll be back. We still have a lot of fun things to do."

"When will you be leaving?"

"Not sure. Probably the middle of next week, if the majority leader can round up everyone by then. We're on vacation and everyone is in different places. Some of my fellow senators even made plans to leave the country, like Reggie. He's visiting Delaney in the Middle East. It won't be easy to get everyone back. However, we all know how important it is for this bill to pass."

She smiled over at him. "I'm going to miss you even if you're only going to be gone for a day or so."

"And I'm definitely going to miss you," he said, taking her hand and bringing it to his lips. "That means we need to have as much fun as we can before I leave."

Around them, they could hear the clicking of cell phones, which meant their picture was being taken. Jess didn't mind. He liked being photographed with her. "Are you ready for your painting session today?"

"Yes, but you haven't told me what to wear or if there is a particular color that will blend better with the background."

While still holding her hand, he leaned closer and whispered, "I would love painting you wearing nothing at all, Paige."

She threw her head back and laughed. "That wouldn't go over well if you still plan to hang it in your living room."

He smiled. "Art is art. However, I never said I would hang the picture of you in my living room. It's been my intention all along to hang it in my bedroom."

Jess saw surprise light her eyes. "Your bedroom?"

"Yes." There, he'd given her something else to think about. Before she could ask him about it, he released her hand and said, "It's time to leave."

Holding hands, they were walking toward their parked car when suddenly they were surrounded by a number of reporters. They were not surprised their location had been leaked when several people at the café had been taking pictures with their cell phones.

"Miss Novak, are you going to refute what Kemp Pierson said yesterday?"

Jess wrapped his arm around Paige's waist, as she smiled at the reporters. "Jess and I have been so busy enjoying our vacation that I have no idea what Kemp said," she said.

"He's saying that no matter what you've told us, it's all been a misunderstanding. Once he completes the filming of his movie and the two of you get a chance to talk, everything will be worked out."

Jess didn't say anything, but wondered how in the hell Pierson thought betraying Paige had been a "misunderstanding." He glanced over at Paige. Retaining her smile, she tilted her head as if giving the reporter her complete attention. She moved closer to Jess, and he tightened his arm around her even more when she said, "Regardless of what Kemp says, I think I've made it clear that I've moved on and therefore I really don't have any more to add. Good day, everyone."

Jess opened the car door. Ignoring the reporters throwing out more questions, she waved at them before he closed the door. One reporter then asked Jess, as he walked around the car to get in on the other side, "Senator Outlaw, do you feel like you're caught in the middle of a Kemp-Paige affair?"

Jess stopped. "No, not at all. I'm not caught in the middle. You all heard Paige. She has moved on, and it's unfortunate Kemp Pierson isn't doing the same thing." He was tempted to add "What man would continue to claim a woman who'd made it clear on more than one occasion that she didn't want him?"

He didn't know Kemp, had never met the guy, although he'd seen one or two of his movies. Jess always thought he was a good actor but was beginning to wonder about his attitude. When a woman made it plain that she had moved on, then a man was expected to move on. Then again, the man had made a costly mistake. If he loved Paige, then he would fight for her.

Was that what Pierson was doing? Fighting for Paige and hoping she would eventually forgive him? They *had* been together for almost a year, so there had been an investment in the relationship on both of their parts. Could the man truly regret betraying her? And if given the chance to wear down Paige's defenses, would she forgive him?

Ignoring other questions being thrown at him, Jess got in the car and drove off.

"Tilt your chin up just a little, Paige."

Following Jess's instructions, she did just what she was told as he stood behind an easel. She was convinced an artist's cape had never looked as good on any man. His expression was serious, his concentration intense as he painted her. She recalled what he'd said at lunch. He would hang the portrait up in his bedroom. Was he serious? Why would he do something like that? She had been about to ask when he suggested they leave the café. They were then overtaken by reporters, and she had given them the same response she'd been giving since Kemp's statement.

Paige figured a lot of people were probably wondering why Kemp was so determined to get her back. What Kemp was doing was changing the narrative. At least, he was trying to change it. Instead of people seeing him as the man who'd betrayed her, he was trying to get them to see him as the man determined to win back her love. Kemp didn't want her love, and she knew it was nothing more than a publicity stunt cooked up by his publicist. He was capable of turning any negative into a positive. Well, she intended to be his one failure.

"Whatever thoughts are making your brows wrinkle, Paige, get rid of them. Think of something pleasant," Jess said. His words made her blink, as she did as he instructed. Thinking of something pleasant meant thinking about him.

When they'd returned for lunch, they'd made time for a "quickie" in her villa. She had wanted more, but hadn't wanted to appear greedy. They only had two weeks left before their vacation ended and she wanted to stock up on all the memories of Jess that she could. Today had been her first quickie, but she didn't intend for it to be her last. It had been short but so darn enjoyable. He had cut through the foreplay and gone straight to the heart of the matter, and she had loved it.

"Did I tell you how much I like your outfit?"

Jess's words made her smile. "Thank you."

"That's it," he said in a husky voice, watching her before looking back at the canvas. "That's the smile I want to capture. The one I want to see every morning when I wake up and glance at your portrait."

Immediately, her full attention was on what he'd just said. "Why?"

He looked over the canvas at her. "Why what?"

"Why would you want to see my portrait every morning when you wake up?"

"Because I honestly can't think of seeing anything more beautiful."

His words made a lump form in her throat. "No more talking. I want to capture as much of the daylight as possible."

She didn't say anything else. Instead, she stared at him, giving him the expression he'd asked for. He'd told her to wear a blue dress. Not too dark and not too light. He wanted her hair down, flowing around her shoulders, and he wanted her to wear as little makeup as possible. She'd given him all he'd asked for, and when he'd seen her, he had said she looked perfect. Luckily, there was a bench for her to sit on, one that Spencer's men had placed there.

As she gazed at Jess, she focused on his mouth, that delicious mouth she loved whenever it connected to hers. Then, as he continued with swipes of his paintbrush, she saw how she was the focus of those deep, dark eyes. They had been at it for almost an hour, and she wondered how much longer today's painting session would take. She hadn't drooled yet, but if he continued to stand there while she visualized all that sexy, masculine body had done to her, she—

"Are you okay, Paige?"

She blinked. Her wanton thoughts had nearly overtaken her senses just now. She figured since he had asked her a question, it was okay to answer. "Yes. Why do you ask?"

"You look a little flushed."

Was that his way of saying she appeared hot? If only he knew. "How much longer?"

He tilted his head and looked at her. "Getting tired?"

She decided to go for total honesty. "No. I'm getting aroused sitting here looking at you, Jess."

Paige saw the way her words made his eyes darken, and then she watched as he placed the brush down and removed his cape before moving around the easel toward her. It was as if he was slowly stalking his prey and she couldn't move. She had no problem being an easy capture.

He offered his hand, and she took it. Then he drew her up close, and not for the first time, she thought they were a perfect fit. "You ever made love outdoors in the open?"

She shook her head. "No," she said, ensnarled by the look of passion in his eyes.

"Then let me show you how it's done." He swept her into his arms.

Fifteen

Paige sat in the huge Jacuzzi tub and soaked in the warm bubbly water. It had been another fun day. Over the past week they had gone horseback riding, had played strip poker a number of times—with her always losing—had helped pick grapes and had attended a wine tasting. And every day Jess would paint her. After that first day, she knew how each session would end. Jess said he was almost finished, but he refused to let her see any of it until it was completed. All he ever said was that, like he'd known, she was a beautiful subject.

That morning she had awakened in Jess's arms, and after making love they had showered together. After getting dressed, they had left her villa to drive to Windemere for breakfast and bike rentals. She didn't see as many reporters out and about. Since Kemp hadn't made any more comments, maybe they were no longer news. At least, she and Kemp weren't, but it seemed she and Jess were. Die-hard romantics were still posting photos of them being seen together.

After breakfast, she and Jess had gotten on the bikes and ridden through several vineyards of Napa Valley. The terrain and scenery had been beautiful. They had taken a packed lunch—compliments of Grammy Russell—and had stopped to eat in front of a huge lake. She hadn't been on a bike in years and had enjoyed seeing the beauty of the land.

When they had returned to Russell Vineyards, they had showered and taken a short nap before going to play a game of tennis with Spencer and Chardonnay. It had been the battle of the sexes, and although the guys had won, Paige had totally enjoyed herself.

She and Jess had decided to make it an eat-in night where he would do all the cooking. Together they had gone to a grocery store in town to get all the ingredients he needed. There was an outdoor grill between the two villas, and they decided to use it.

But now she needed to soak. He had prepared the bath for her before getting a phone call. She wondered if it was the dreaded call to let him know he needed to return to Washington. She would miss him, but he'd said he'd only be gone for a couple of days and would return.

Paige definitely had something to do until he got back, like finally getting into that book she'd packed. She could envision herself hanging out by the pool and reading. It had been years since she'd taken time out for herself. It felt good to slow down and enjoy life, and thanks to Jess, she was doing that. Tomorrow they would be taking a wine-tasting class at the resort, and she was looking forward to it.

She tilted her head when Jess walked into the bathroom. She studied his features and knew, as she'd suspected, he had gotten the dreaded call. Funny how after having spent only weeks together she was able to read his expressions. He might have to leave, but she would definitely give him a good reason to rush back.

"Join me," she invited when he handed her a glass of wine. "This tub is big enough for the both of us."

He stood there for a minute as if thinking about her invitation. Then he sat on the edge of the tub to remove his shoes and socks. She drew in a deep breath as she watched him, and again her brain registered just how handsome he was. She recalled what Nadia had said some social media users were buzzing about. Jess Outlaw was a hottie, through and through. She would have to agree. There was more hotness in Jess's little finger than Kemp had in his entire body.

He stood, and she thought even now, while standing beside the tub fully dressed in a pair of jeans and a T-shirt, he looked gorgeous. Seeing him made her mouth water. That was why she decided at that moment to take a sip of her wine.

"And you're sure there is room in there for me?" he asked, glancing down at her. Bubbles totally covered her body, practically to her chin. He had prepared her bath and had gotten a little heavy-handed with her foaming bubble bath. Not only were there bubbles all over the place, the scent of honeysuckle filled the air.

"I'm positive, Jess."

"In that case…" His hands went first to his shirt and pulled it over his head before moving to the waist of his jeans to slowly ease down the zipper.

She watched his every movement. One thing she liked about her "hot, romantic entanglement" with Jess was how he turned each moment into a memorable experience. One that was fun in a way she'd never experienced before. And she was glad she was sharing it all with him.

She would need these memories at the end of their vacation when he went his way and she went hers.

Looking up at him beneath her long lashes, she couldn't help the purr that flowed from her lips when he removed his jeans and briefs and stood there naked, displaying all his masculine and magnificent glory. The woman in her couldn't help appreciating the size of his manhood. She recalled the times she had fondled it, tasted it, kissed it.

"I need to pour my own glass of wine before I join you," he said, his words, along with his warm smile, awakening an achy hunger she felt all the way to her womb.

"Don't bother," she said, holding up her glass. "We can share."

His smile widened even more. "I'm fine with that," he murmured.

And then, after sheathing himself with a condom, he lifted one leg and then the other to join her in the tub. "Did I do this?" he asked, indicating all the bubbles, as he eased down in the water.

"Yes," she said, chuckling. "You were only supposed to put in one capful, but I think you put in four."

"Oh, well, I guess we'll both be squeaky clean in the end," he said, easing closer to her. "I like all this room we have in here. More room to play."

She thought so, too, and handed him her wineglass. He took it and placed it to his mouth for a sip. "I can't say enough how good Russell wines are."

"I can't either. I've already made plans to ship bottles to my home in California. Guess what all my friends are getting this Christmas?"

He then placed the wineglass to her lips for her to take a sip. Their gazes held. He hadn't mentioned what his phone call had been about and she figured he would verify her suspicions later. In the meantime, she wanted to enjoy every moment she could spend with him.

When he placed the wineglass aside, she knew he was ready to get down to business. He wrapped his arms around her, easing her close. So close that her nipples pressed against his chest, and she could feel his hardness between her legs. The water hadn't affected his length. If anything, his erection seemed to have lengthened to reach her.

They leaned in for a kiss at the same time, and the minute their tongues connected, the flames between them were already out of control. His tongue made all kinds of erotic movements in her mouth as he continued to stoke the passion blazing between them. This was the kind of kiss a woman could get addicted to, the kind that could leave its mark.

A part of her wanted to claim his mouth and tongue as hers, but she knew she couldn't do that. A "hot, romantic entanglement" was not meant to last. It was just for the moment, so she was definitely enjoying every second. Deciding to give just as much as she was getting, she gripped Jess's shoulders and slanted her mouth, needing as much of the wildness of his taste as she could get.

When he deepened the pressure, she couldn't help but moan. Suddenly, he broke off the kiss and she saw fiery desire in his eyes. "Turn your back to me, Paige."

Paige did what he asked, trying not to swish any water on the floor from the tub. He fit his body snugly behind her and used his hand to open her womanly folds before entering her. And then he began riding her, thrusting in and out, splashing water all over the place. But she didn't care. All that mattered was Jess and his ability to pleasure her so immensely.

When she began screaming his name, he tilted her head back toward him and covered her mouth to kiss the scream. Their tongues tangled again until he pulled his mouth away to holler out her name. Then he was kissing her again while turning her around in his arms, bracing her back against the tub, making sure she felt every stroke of his tongue.

Paige knew the one thing that was happening on this vacation was that Jess was branding her as his. Not a single place on her body was left unmarked. That might not have been his intention, but it was happening regardless.

"I'll be leaving Wednesday to return to Washington for a couple of days, Paige."

She opened her eyes and looked up at Jess. They had gotten out of the tub hours ago. After making love in bed, she was cuddled close to him and had been about to fall asleep. "I figured as much, although I was hoping otherwise," she said softly. "I'm going to miss you."

"I'll miss you, too. We'll have three days before then, and I'll be back in two."

She nodded. "And I'll look forward to your return." And she meant it. It would be crazy to tell him how she felt about him, though she would admit that tonight, while making love, she'd been tempted to. But she hadn't. She would keep her feelings to herself.

"Ready for dinner?"

Paige smiled at him. "Yes, since you are doing the heavy cooking. I'm just making the salad."

He chuckled. "There is nothing heavy about throwing a couple of steaks, potatoes and corn on the grill."

"If you say so."

He pulled up in bed and pulled her up with him. "You've never grilled before?"

She shook her head. "With all those male Westmorelands around who swore they were an ace when it came to grilling, there was no need. But just so you know, I'm starving. Thanks to you, I've worked up an appetite."

An hour later, they had gotten dressed and were outside. Jess had thrown on a couple of steaks and she'd come outside to keep him company. Later tonight they would go swimming again.

"I got a call from Pam. She said Crystal is doing fine with the babies and Bane is a big help."

"I bet he is. Now he has five sons and one daughter."

She glanced over at Jess. "What about you? Do you think you'd ever settle down, marry one day and have children?"

She might have been mistaken, but there was a look in his eyes that stirred emotions within her. Emotions that seemed to be flowing between them. She drew in a slow breath and figured she had only imagined such a thing.

"Yes, I plan to marry one day, and I do want kids. I'm not getting any younger. What about you? Marriage and kids in your future? Or are you planning to make your career in Hollywood your life?"

She took a sip of her wine as she thought about his question. "I don't plan to make Hollywood my life. In fact, lately, I've been thinking about getting out of acting and into teaching."

Paige could tell by his expression that her statement surprised him. "Why? You're good at what you do."

She smiled. "Thanks, but there are times I want the old Paige back."

"The one who was a rebel instead of a conformist?"

She was glad he had actually been listening to her that day. "It's not that I want to be a rebel, Jess. I just want to be me. Like I told you, Hollywood expects you to be who they want you to be. Pam tried to warn me, but I thought I was ready and could take them on and still be myself."

"And now?"

"And now I'm tired of thinking my image is all that matters, and that I should meekly go along with having my words scripted. Not sure I'm going to last in Hollywood, Jess." There was no need to tell him about that call she had gotten from Maxie, where this big producer had threatened to pass on her being in a movie for which she had been a top contender. Needless to say, her agent was not too happy with her now, especially with how Paige was handling the Kemp issue.

She paused and then added, "So to answer your question, yes. One day I want to get married and have children."

What she didn't say was that she would marry him in a heartbeat and have his babies. In just the short time she'd spent with him, she could see Jess being both husband and father material. He was thoughtful, kind, considerate and dedicated to those things he believed in. He was a good senator, and she could see great things in his political future.

"I think these are ready to come off the grill now," he said, breaking into her thoughts. She glanced over at the steaks. They liked theirs the same way, well done, and he was right. They were ready, and they smelled delicious.

"Are we playing cards after we eat?" she asked him.

"Yes. Strip poker. You game?"

She threw her head back and laughed. "Yes, Jess Outlaw, I'm game."

Sixteen

"I hate that you'll be gone by the time I get there, Jess, but I'll be glad to keep Paige company until you get back."

Jess paused while tugging on his slacks. He had placed Maverick's call on speakerphone as he got dressed. Now he wished modern technology was such that he could reach into his phone and pull his brother through it. He knew Maverick's comment was meant to get a rise out of him, so he would oblige his baby brother. "Cross the line with her, Maverick, and I'll kick your ass."

Maverick laughed. "Why, if I didn't know better, Jessup, I'd think you were jealous. But that's not possible since all you and Paige are doing is role-playing, or am I thinking wrong?"

"Think whatever you want, just remember what I said. And why are you coming to Russell Vineyards now when the party isn't for another week and a half?"

"I finished up the business I had in Ireland and returned to Alaska to find everyone was gone. I thought about flying to Wyoming to pay Cash, Brianna and the twins a visit, but decided not to wear out my welcome since I was there just last month. So I decided to fly to Napa Valley to hang out with you and Paige. Too bad you won't be there most of the time."

"I'll only be gone a couple of days, so don't do anything that will get you in trouble."

Maverick chuckled. "So warns the man whose face is all over social media. Do you know a group of women are trying to get your name added to the list of contenders for next year's Hottest Man Alive? I bet Kemp doesn't like that. I heard he'd planned on holding the title two years in a row."

Jess honestly didn't care anything about Kemp Pierson. He was glad the media was convinced Paige had moved on even if Pierson wasn't. A short while later, Jess had ended the call. After telling Paige he would be leaving today to return to DC, they had worked in all the fun they could within those three days. Thankfully, he had finished his painting of her.

He glanced at his watch. He would be leaving for the airport soon. They had spent last night together in his villa and had showered together this morning. She had left so he could pack and said she would grab breakfast for them to share before he left.

Jess didn't ever recall regretting leaving a woman, but he regretted leaving Paige. It didn't matter that he would be seeing her again in a couple of days. He had gotten used to spending time with her. Every waking moment. In and out of bed. He had gotten to know her, and she had gotten to know him. He'd never shared any details of his relationship with his mother to any woman, but he had shared them with Paige. He'd even talked with Paige about the bill he was flying back to Washington to vote on and why it was so important that it passed. She had listened, asked questions and genuinely seemed interested in what he had told her.

He heard the knock on his door. Upon leaving the bedroom, he moved through the living room to open it. Seeing Paige standing there with bags in her hands and a huge smile on her face made him miss her already. He had even thought of asking her to go to Washington with him, but knew she had promised to take on a couple more duties to assist Chardonnay with the anniversary party.

He stood back, let her in and then watched as she sashayed her delectable backside in a pair of shorts into his kitchen and placed the bags on the counter. By the time she had turned around, he was there, standing in front of her.

"Jess! Goodness. I didn't hear you move from the door."

He didn't respond. Instead, he pulled her into his arms and held her. "I'm going to miss you."

She pushed back to look up at him. "I'm going to miss you, too. Terribly."

Hearing her say that gave him hope. Hell, it gave him more than hope. It gave him enough motivation to say, "I think we need to have a long, hard talk when I get back. A talk about us, Paige, and where we want to go from here."

He held his breath, hoping she didn't say they didn't need to talk because they wouldn't be going any place from there. But she didn't say that. Instead, she said, "I will be looking forward to having that talk with you, Jess."

He released the breath he'd been holding and pulled her back in his arms, capturing her mouth with his.

"Have you heard from Jess?" Chardonnay asked Paige a few days later as they went over the final list of attendees. The caterers had to be notified of the exact number of those attending.

"No, but I did catch the news. It seems the senators are

practically spending their nights at the capital, determined to push the bill through."

Chardonnay nodded. "That's what I heard as well."

They looked up when there was a knock on the door. "Janice, our housekeeper, is off today, and the kids started back to school this week. Spencer is out of town and everyone else is out in the vineyards, so I guess I need to get that," Chardonnay said, grinning.

When Chardonnay left the kitchen, Paige decided to pour another cup of coffee. She missed Jess like crazy and he'd only been gone for three days. A day longer than either of them had expected. That first day he had texted her a few times, but she hadn't heard from him since. She knew how busy he was.

He'd said they would talk when he got back and that the conversation would be about them. Was she crazy to hope he wanted more from their relationship than what they were sharing on vacation? That he would want forever like she did? Did he feel they had shared something special over the past two weeks? Something that was too meaningful to walk away from?

She had just refilled her cup when she heard Chardonnay return. "Paige, you have a visitor."

Paige's back was to Chardonnay, and when she turned around, she knew both surprise and shock covered her features. "Kemp? What are you doing here?"

The man who stepped forward looked nothing like the savvy, handsome Ralph Lauren model he used to be. Instead, the dark eyes—known to make his fans drool—looked tired. His clothes, which usually looked immaculate, appeared to have been slept in.

"Over the past twenty-eight hours I've been on six different flights to get here, Paige. We need to talk."

Before she could say anything, Chardonnay said, "I need to take care of a few things upstairs."

Paige watched her friend leave and then narrowed her gaze at Kemp, wondering what lie he'd told to get past the vineyards' security. "There's nothing we need to talk about."

"Please, Paige. I really want you to hear me out. I flew all the way from New Zealand to come talk to you. At least please listen to what I have to say."

At the sound of voices out back, she figured Chardonnay's grandparents were returning. Letting out a deep breath, Paige said, "Fine. We can go to the villa where I'm staying. It's only a short walk from here."

"Thank you."

Jess glanced at his watch as the plane landed. The vote in the Senate had taken a lot longer than he had anticipated, with both sides trying to argue the point. In the end, the bill had passed. Everyone had reason to celebrate and some had done so. He had caught the first plane out of DC to return here.

He missed Paige like crazy and couldn't wait to see her again. He had called ahead for a rental car, and it should be ready. He thought about calling Paige to let her know he was flying back today but decided to surprise her. He couldn't wait to hold her in his arms again, make love to her, but more importantly, he wanted to talk to her, tell her how he felt.

A short while later, he was tossing his luggage into the trunk of his rental car when his phone rang. Recognizing the ringtone, he clicked on. "What's up, Maverick?"

"Are you still in Washington?"

"No. My plane landed in California fifteen minutes ago and I'm loading up my bags in the rental. Are you at the vineyards?"

"Not yet. I met this flight attendant at the airport, and she invited me to hang out with her for a couple of days."

"Flight attendant? I thought you were flying your Cessna here."

All of the Outlaws, including Charm, had their pilot licenses. In addition to the huge company jet, they each owned a Cessna. Due to Alaska's very limited road system, one of the most common ways of getting around was by aircraft. Locals liked to say that more Alaskans owned personal planes than cars. Not to give the impression of being the rich kid on the hill, Jess kept his Cessna back in Fairbanks and only used it whenever he went home.

"I did. I met her at the airport when we were both claiming our rental cars. She was staying at a hotel in town and invited me to join her for a night, and I took her up on it. One night turned into two, but what can I say?"

His youngest brother really couldn't say anything. It was no secret in the family that Maverick kept his pants unzipped more than he kept them zipped. "I'm still at the hotel, but will drive over to the vineyards in an hour."

"I'll probably get there right ahead of you and will see you when you arrive." Then he thought of something. "On second thought, Maverick, just catch me sometime tomorrow."

"Tomorrow?"

"Yes, tomorrow."

He didn't want Maverick to interrupt the quality time he intended to share with Paige. More than anything, Jess wanted to see her, and the first place he intended to go when he arrived was her villa.

"So what do you want to talk to me about, Kemp?" Paige asked the moment the door closed behind them.

"I owe you an apology about that situation with Maya."

"That situation with Maya…" Funny how he'd phrased that. "You've apologized already."

"Yet you won't accept my apology."

She placed her hand on her hip. "Yes, I've accepted your apology, but that doesn't mean we will get back together. You destroyed my trust in you, Kemp, and I refuse to be with someone I can't trust."

"Would you feel better if I told you that we found out how it got leaked to the press?" Before she could answer, he said, "One of the maids at the hotel was paid a lot of money to get those pictures."

Paige rolled her eyes. "And you're shifting blame on the maid for your failure to keep your pants zipped?"

He rubbed his hands down his face. "I just wanted you to know how those pictures got out there."

"Honestly, Kemp, do you think it matters? You betrayed my trust. That's what matters."

"And what about you and that senator? You couldn't wait to hook up with him."

"Don't bring Jess into this like I did something behind your back. I told you when you called from New Zealand that I was ending our relationship, that I was moving on, and I suggested you do the same."

He lifted his chin. "No woman has ever broken up with me before."

"Then consider me your first."

"I need us to get back together for my next movie, Paige. The investors aren't happy about the negative publicity I'm getting. Our agents are working out a deal. Just pretend we're back together until filming is over. That shouldn't be hard to do. It's not like you're really serious about that Outlaw guy anyway."

She lifted a brow. "And why wouldn't I be serious?"

"Too soon. There's no way you've gotten over me."

That hit a nerve. "For your information, Kemp, I got over you months ago. In fact, I had planned to break up with you next month when you finished filming and returned to LA. Things weren't working out with us."

Anger flared in his features. "You were planning on dumping me? Yet you're upset because I slept with Maya?"

"One has nothing to do with the other. You should have been committed to me and our relationship until we ended things, just like I was. You didn't know what I intended to do, yet you slept with Maya anyway. I might forgive, but I won't forget. With that said, I want you to leave."

"Leave? I just got here. I'm tired and need a shower. Can I shower and then crash here for a few hours, Paige? I'm so tired I can't think straight. I promise to leave after getting a few hours of sleep."

Shower? Grab a few hours of sleep? Here? He has to be kidding. "No! Absolutely not!"

"Please, Paige. I'm about to fall on my face."

She drew in a deep breath. He did look as if he would fall on his face any minute. "Where's Marv?" Marv was Kemp's bodyguard and he rarely traveled without the man.

"He's at the hotel. I told him I needed to talk to you privately and had him drop me off. I'll call Marv to come back and get me when I'm ready to leave, but I desperately need to at least shower and grab a few hours of sleep."

Paige released a frustrated breath and glanced at her watch. "Fine. I will give you three hours, Kemp, and then I want you gone. I'm leaving."

"Leaving for where?"

"That's not your concern. Just be gone in three hours." She then walked out of the villa.

She was about to head down the path to the main house, but then she figured Chardonnay had probably left to go get the kids from school. And this was the time of day that Grammy and Grampa Russell settled in for a nap.

Paige could walk down to the pool and hang out there, but three hours was a long time to wait for Kemp to leave. Her conversation with him had been downright exhausting and now she felt tired. She then remembered Jess telling her where he kept the key to his villa, in case she ever needed to get inside for something while he was gone.

She headed for Jess's villa. Before she took her nap, she would call Maxie. How dare her agent work with Kemp's agent on anything before discussing it with her? Locating the door key under the mat where Jess had said it would be, she opened the door to his villa. She went inside after placing the key back where she'd found it.

Seventeen

Jess pulled into the grounds of Russell Vineyards and brought the car to a stop in front of the main house. Spencer was out of town on a business trip, and since it was close to dinnertime, he figured everyone was inside preparing for the meal. The first thing he intended to do was see his woman.

His woman.

He smiled as he got out of the car. Yes, Paige was his, and when they had their talk, hopefully she would agree with that assessment. Without even bothering to get his luggage out of the truck, he quickly walked down the path to her villa. He'd discovered she liked taking a nap around this time every day and hoped she didn't mind being interrupted from her sleep.

The first thing he intended to do was kiss her. Then he would make love to her. And later they would go out to eat and then return to his place or hers and talk before making love again…and again…and again. Like he'd told his brother, he didn't want to be interrupted tonight.

Jess even thought about borrowing Maverick's Cessna so he could fly her to Alaska, that part of the north where it snowed all year round. He would love surprising her and taking her on a dogsled ride. Maybe sometime after the party.

The thought of being alone with her in a cabin high up in the mountains of Alaska had him smiling. He would even take her to his home in Fairbanks. The thought of that made him smile even more. He had it bad. He was in love, and after ten years, it felt good.

He finally reached her door and knocked. When he didn't hear a sound, he knocked again since she was probably napping. When he still didn't hear anything, he decided, quite disappointedly, to just let her sleep. He would go back to the car and get his luggage, go to his villa and unpack while waiting for her to wake up.

He was about to turn to leave when the door was snatched open. He blinked. Standing in the doorway was a half-dressed man wearing only his briefs and a damn sleepy look on his face. He recognized the man immediately. Kemp Pierson. What the hell?

Jess frowned. "Where's Paige?"

Instead of answering him, the man rubbed a hand down his face before looking at him with a smug smile on his lips. "Paige is in bed. Asleep."

The man's words were like a slap. It hit so hard he took a step back. "In bed?"

Kemp Pierson crossed his arms over his chest. "That's what I said. I'm surprised at you, Senator. You're older than I am, so you should know never to mess with a woman on the rebound. In the end, she's going to get back with the dude her heart belongs to. Sorry. Better luck next time. Now, if you don't mind, your timing is lousy. But for me it's perfect since I'm going to wake up Paige so we can get it on again." He then slammed the door in Jess's face.

Jess just stood there, anger boiling through him. He raised his hand to knock on the door; he had something to say to Paige, but then he decided not to bother. She'd made her choice. What had happened to what she'd told him about moving on? All the man had to do was reappear and she'd taken Kemp back after what he'd done?

Sucking up his pride, Jess turned and headed back down the path. Jess kept walking until he reached his rental car and got inside. There was nothing for him here. He would go back to the airport for a flight home to Fairbanks. Forget the anniversary party. He wanted to be as far from here as he could get.

He was halfway to the airport when his phone rang. It was Maverick. At first he wasn't going to answer, but then knew he needed to. Chances were, Maverick had arrived at the villa and discovered he wasn't there.

"Yes, Maverick?"

"I thought you said you would be here. Chardonnay said she hadn't seen you, although she saw a rental car parked in front of the house earlier. Why did you leave?"

He didn't say anything for a full minute. "Have you seen Paige?"

"No. Why?"

"When you do see her, try asking her why I left."

"Oh. Did the two of you have a disagreement about something?"

"Yes, I guess you can say that. As soon as I got back, I went straight to her villa, and a half-naked Kemp Pierson answered the door."

"What!"

"You heard me. The man was dressed only in his briefs

and proceeded to tell me that he and Paige had gotten back together."

"He told you? What did Paige say?"

"I didn't talk to Paige. She was in bed asleep."

"And you believed him?"

"Look, Maverick, I don't want to talk about this. I'm on my way back to the airport."

"Why?"

"I decided to fly home to Alaska after all. You're welcome to use the villa I was using since I don't plan to return, not even for the party. I'll call Spencer and Chardonnay tomorrow and give them my regrets."

"You're quitting just like that? Without hearing Paige's side of things? That's crazy, man. What if Kemp Pierson was lying? Paige isn't Ava."

Jess rolled his eyes, remembering how Pierson had said his timing was lousy. It seemed that was the story of his life. "Look, Maverick, I don't need advice from you. The key to the villa is under the mat." He then clicked off the phone.

"...You're quitting just like that? Without hearing Paige's side of things? What if Kemp Pierson was lying? Paige isn't Ava..."

As Jess continued to drive, Maverick's words kept ringing in his ears, and no matter what he did, he couldn't get them out. What if Pierson was lying? The man had certainly done nothing but lie during this entire ordeal, especially when claiming he and Paige would get back together. Had that been a self-assured man or an overconfident one? Or maybe one who enjoyed weaving his own tales?

Deep down Jess knew Paige was nothing like Ava, who had dumped him when her ex-boyfriend had come back into the picture. But what reason would Pierson have to be at her villa wearing nothing but his briefs, opening her door, if they weren't back together?

The only person who could answer those questions was Paige. She owed him an explanation, and dammit, he intended to get one. Making a U-turn at the next traffic light, he headed back to Russell Vineyards.

Paige came awake from her nap when she heard the sound of the villa door opening. It took her a minute to remember where she was. In Jess's villa, lying across his bed. She pulled herself up and remembered that episode with Kemp and glanced at her watch. His three hours were up, and he should be gone by now.

A huge smile covered her entire face when she heard the sound of movement in the living room. Jess was back! She quickly got off the bed and rushed out of the bedroom. "Jess!"

She frowned when the man who turned to look at her was Maverick. Feeling disappointed, she said, "Oh, hi, Maverick. I thought you were Jess."

He leaned back against the door. "Why would you think I was Jess?"

She tilted her head to look at him, thinking he'd asked an odd question. "Because this is the villa Jess is using."

"And why aren't you at your own villa?"

She wondered what had gotten into Maverick. Usually he was the fun-loving, playful Outlaw. For some reason, he seemed awful serious today. "Because, if you must know, Kemp showed up."

Maverick crossed his arms over his chest. "Did he? And?"

And? What on earth was wrong with Maverick? Why was he looking at her funny? "And he wanted to talk, and we did."

"That doesn't explain why he's in your villa and you're here."

Paige was getting a little annoyed with Maverick's questions and his attitude. "Okay, Maverick, what's going on?"

He rubbed his hand down his face before crossing the room to stand in front of her. "Evidently, Jess got played."

"Played?"

"Yes. By Kemp Pierson."

Paige lifted a brow. "What do you mean?"

"Jess arrived a half hour ago and went straight to your place. Pierson answered the door wearing only his briefs and claimed the two of you had gotten together and that you were in the bedroom asleep."

"What! And Jess believed him?"

"Evidently, Pierson put on a convincing act because, yes, Jess believed him."

"The man is an actor, for heaven's sake." Now it was Paige who rubbed her hand down her face. "Where is Jess now?"

"On his way to Alaska."

Paige's jaw almost dropped to the floor. "You mean to tell me that Jess came back here, believed what Kemp said without talking to me and is now on his way to Alaska?"

"Yes."

Anger flared inside Paige. "Well, he undoubtedly doesn't think a lot about my character if he thinks I'd spend two weeks in his bed and then share a bed with Kemp when he shows up," she said, not caring if she was giving Maverick too much information.

Maverick shrugged. "He probably was quick to think that way because of what Ava did to him. Did he tell you about her?"

"Yes, he told me how she betrayed him with some guy."

"Did Jess tell you that guy had been her old boyfriend?"

Paige paused. "No, he didn't tell me that. But it doesn't matter. I am not Ava."

"Well, you were on the rebound when Jess got involved with you, and so was Ava."

Paige glared at Maverick. "I'm not on the rebound. A woman can only be on the rebound if she's still emotionally attached to her ex."

"And you're not?"

"Heck no. I planned to break up with Kemp anyway. I was just waiting until we both finished our film projects to do it."

Maverick nodded. "I take it that Jess didn't know that."

"I saw no reason to tell him before telling Kemp. The only reason I'm even telling you is because I told Kemp earlier."

"Why is Kemp at your place?"

"When he got here, he was tired after six flights. After our talk, he asked if he could take a shower at the villa and grab a few hours of sleep. After seeing how exhausted he was, I told him that was fine and he needed to be gone in three hours. He said he would be and that his bodyguard would be coming back to pick him up. He should be gone by now."

"Not sure that he is."

Paige frowned. "Hell, he better be," she said, moving around Maverick and leaving Jess's villa. She didn't care that Maverick was right on her heels as she marched down the path to her own villa. After slinging the door open, she found Kemp sitting on the sofa, drinking a glass of wine and watching television.

He had the audacity to smile when he saw her. "Hey, baby. I was wondering when you were coming back." He then frowned when he saw Maverick and asked, "Who the hell is he?"

Without answering his question, Paige crossed the

room and stood in front of him. "How dare you give Jess the impression that you and I were back together?"

Kemp shrugged nonchalantly. "He believed it, so what does that tell you about him?"

Refusing to entertain his question with an answer, she said, "Leave, Kemp. Your three hours were up a while ago."

"Leave? Why should I leave now that you and the senator are no longer together? We need to sit down, talk and work out our problem." He glared over at Maverick and then looked back at her and said, "Privately. I had Marv bring my luggage since I'll be staying awhile. Our fans are counting on us working through this, sweetheart." He glared at Maverick again. "And you haven't said who this guy is."

"Don't worry about who I am, asshole," Maverick said with a lethal tone in his voice, moving around Paige.

Paige touched Maverick's arm. "I got this, Maverick." She then turned to Kemp. "Your things are here?" she asked coolly.

He smiled. "Yes. I've unpacked most of them. And this is some pretty good wine," he said, holding up his glass. "I can't wait to meet your cousins-in-law who own this vineyard."

Paige fumed. As far as she was concerned, Kemp was an overconfident ass. He honestly thought he was staying. Without saying anything, she went into the bedroom and headed straight for the closet where she figured Kemp had hung his designer suits and hand-tailored shirts. Grabbing them in one huge sweep, she marched back to the living room, right past him and opened the door.

That got Kemp off the sofa real quick. "What do you think you're doing?"

Instead of answering, she tossed out the armload of clothing. And like she figured he would do, he rushed out past her to gather his expensive clothing off the ground. By then she had gathered the rest of his stuff and dumped them on the pile with the rest.

Down on his knees gathering his clothing, Kemp stared up at her in shocked disbelief. Maverick was laughing while taking photos of the entire thing with his cell phone. Unbeknownst to the three of them, Jess had walked up the path and was a witness to it all.

Eighteen

Jess would have thought the entire thing comical if Paige didn't have some explaining to do. At least, he thought she did, until she screamed at Pierson, saying, "How dare you insinuate to my boyfriend that you and I were sleeping together? I wouldn't waste my time sleeping with you again, especially now that I know what it's like to be made love to by a man who knows what the hell he's doing."

Something bloomed to life inside Jess. Had Paige just referred to him as her boyfriend and insinuated that Pierson was lousy in bed? All in the same breath? And from what she'd just said, Kemp had lied about them being together in her villa.

Before Pierson could say anything, Paige kept on talking. "Like I told you, I had planned to break up with you anyway, but you convinced yourself I still wanted you. What part of the words *I have moved on* didn't you understand? We are through, Kemp. I told you that three weeks ago. If you needed to hear it in person rather than on the phone, now you've heard it. Leave!"

Something must have given his presence away. Suddenly, Paige glanced over to where Jess was standing, and the glare she gave him was just as fierce as the one she'd been giving Pierson. Then she looked beyond him and her eyes widened. He turned around and saw the photographer at the same time bulbs from the man's camera flashed several times.

"No! No! Stop! I didn't want you to take any pictures now," Pierson bellowed out to the photographer, who only grinned while taking a few more shots before he dashed off to a parked car.

Paige glared back at Kemp Pierson. "You invited a photographer here to take pictures?"

Pierson glared back at her. "Yes, I invited him. He was to take photos showing we were back together."

Placing her hands on her hips, Paige scowled down at Pierson. "We are not together. I have moved on, and I suggest you do the same, Kemp."

Jess felt the intensity of her anger with him when she cut her scowl from Pierson and leveled it on him before walking around Maverick to go inside her villa and slam the door shut.

Maverick was rolling with laughter while Kemp Pierson was still on his knees in the grass trying to pick up all his belongings, mumbling about how much all the stuff cost. Suddenly, Paige's door flew open, and she tossed out Pierson's designer luggage.

"Wait, Paige. Baby. Can we talk? I didn't mean to make you mad," Pierson said, pleadingly.

She slammed the door shut, and that made Maverick laugh even more. Jess had seen and heard enough. He strolled up the walk to where Pierson was trying to put his clothes into his luggage. "When you finish with that, do as Paige said and leave."

Jess turned and moved toward Paige's door, but Maverick put a hand on his arm to stop him. "I wouldn't tangle with her right now if I were you, Jess. Give her time to calm down. She's pretty pissed at you for believing what that asshole said. She's hurt that you didn't trust her. The only thing you have in your favor is that you didn't fly home to Alaska, which hopefully means you thought about it and began doubting Pierson's story."

Maverick was right. He had begun doubting Pierson's story. "Where was she when Pierson was at her place?"

Maverick grinned. "She was at yours. In *your* bed taking a nap. Imagine what I thought when I walked into your place and this very attractive, sexy woman, with a mane of thick brown hair and drowsy sable eyes, sauntered out of your bedroom looking gorgeous as sin and delectable as any meal I could claim to have ever eaten."

Jess glared at his brother. "I imagine you were thinking she was off-limits and that your brother was a damn lucky fellow."

"I wouldn't count yourself lucky, Jess. Not until Paige forgives you." Maverick then put his cell phone in his pocket. "Had I known Pierson hired a photographer for this show, I wouldn't have bothered getting my own flicks."

Jess looked at Pierson, who was still on his knees in the grass gathering up his belongings, and shook his head. "Damn. How much stuff did he bring?"

"From the looks of it, a lot. Probably planned a lot of photo ops. Obviously, he honestly thought he could sweet-talk Paige into letting him stay awhile," Maverick said, chuckling. "Even I know a man should never be overconfident when it comes to a woman."

Jess eyed his brother. "If anyone should know, you would."

Maverick smiled. "Of course." He then glanced at his watch. "I suggest, while Paige is cooling off, that we go to your place for a beer, Jess."

Paige had stepped out of the shower and dried herself off when her phone rang. The ringtone indicated it was Nadia. Grabbing her phone, she clicked on, placing her sister on speakerphone when she slid into her caftan. "Yes, Nadia?"

"I can't believe you tossed Kemp and all his stuff out the door," Nadia said, laughing.

Paige lifted a brow. "How do you know about that?"

"Girl, it's all over social media, with pictures of Kemp on his knees in the grass gathering all his stuff. The tagline says 'When A Woman Tells You That She's Moved On, Believe Her.' The Twitter hashtag is #KempOutJessIn."

Paige rolled her eyes. "Whatever."

"So, what happened to bring out the wicked witch in you?"

Knowing Nadia would harass her until she told her, Paige sat on the edge of the bed and told Nadia everything, starting with when Kemp had shown up in Chardonnay's kitchen.

"And he made it seem as if the two of you were in bed together when Jess returned? But actually you were at Jess's villa in his bed?"

"Yes. All Jess had to do was to leave my place and go to his villa to find me and see Kemp was lying. Instead, he left to return to the airport to fly home to Alaska."

"Yes, but he did come back after he thought things through," Nadia rationalized.

Paige frowned. "He should not have left in the first

place. Jess, of all people, should not have believed Kemp. I told everyone, including Jess, that I had moved on, and he should have believed me."

"Well, I'm sure Kemp was pretty convincing."

Paige rolled her eyes again. "Of course he was convincing. The man is an actor. Jess should have seen through the lie. He should have trusted me, and he didn't."

"Well, it sounds like you and Jess need to talk."

"I don't want to be bothered by Jess, Kemp or anyone else right now. I'm still mad."

"Well, don't overdo your madness and let a good man get away."

"A man who doesn't trust me."

"Where were Spencer and Chardonnay when all this action was going down?" Nadia asked.

"Spencer is out of town, and Chardonnay's parents arrived in town and she and her family were having dinner. She didn't know what had gone on until Kemp's bodyguard arrived to pick him up. That's when I told her the entire story, and like you, she had a good laugh."

"Well, everyone is laughing at those pictures. If nothing else, I think you got your point across to Kemp. And the no-nonsense women of the world applaud you."

After her call with Nadia, Paige got other calls—Jill, Pam and several members of the Westmoreland family. Even Delaney called from the Middle East. It seemed the incident had made world news. Spencer even called from Seattle to make sure she was all right and said he would find out how Kemp, his bodyguard and the photographer got on the grounds of Russell Vineyards. He wasn't happy about that. Paige had a feeling a few heads would be rolling.

Chardonnay was kind enough to send dinner to her by Russell. After eating, Paige sat at the table and drank a glass of wine. That photographer had taken those pictures mere hours ago, yet he'd wasted no time putting them out there. Kemp's plan to have a photo op showing them back together had backfired on him. It served him right.

Her thoughts then fell to Jess. She should have appreciated that he had come back and hadn't flown to Alaska, but then, why should she? He should have trusted her. He should have known she would choose him over Kemp any day.

But then, why would he think that way when he had no idea how she felt about him? He had no idea that their "hot, romantic entanglement" had turned into something she wanted to last forever. But still...

She glanced over at her door when she heard a knock. She had a feeling it was Jess. Should she answer it or not? She was still pissed. But in his defense—and she would admit he did have a defense—he was clueless about how she truly felt. They hadn't had that talk they were supposed to have when he got back. So for that reason, she would at least listen to what he had to say.

Moving from the kitchen table, she walked over to the door and looked out the peephole to make sure it was Jess and not Kemp returning. She honestly hoped he got the picture this time.

It was Jess, and as if he'd known she was looking at him, he stared back. She felt a deep stirring in the pit of her stomach. Frustration and desire were doing a serious dance inside her right now. Taking a deep breath, she braced herself and opened the door. He had showered and changed out of the slacks and shirt he'd been wearing earlier and was now dressed in a pair of jeans and a pullover sleeveless muscle shirt that showed off those forearms and shoulders she liked so much.

Forcing that thought from her mind, she tried to keep her face void of expression when she said, "Jess, what are you doing here?"

"It's time for us to have that talk, don't you think?"

At that moment she honestly didn't want to think *or* talk. He was staring at her with more than an assessing gaze. His close scrutiny made her feel downright carnal. How could a mere look from Jess do more than a touch from Kemp ever could?

Even now, he had every hormone in her body sizzling. The intensity of his gaze caused her entire body to react, which prompted her to say, "You believed I could leave your bed and then sleep with Kemp, all in the same week."

The reminder of what he'd thought gave her a chill, but even that wasn't strong enough to quench the heat she felt with his dark eyes staring at her. "I'm sorry about that, Paige. May I come in so we can talk about it?"

She wasn't sure she wanted to accept his apology. She should close the door on him to let him know he was no more welcome into her space than Kemp. But she knew that wasn't true. It was this thing between her and Jess that had been there from the first, and they both knew it. Was she willing to turn her back on it now? No, but she wasn't about to make things easy for him. She would listen to what he had to say and then decide what direction she would take.

Instead of answering him, she took a step back. The moment he entered and closed the door behind him, she visualized all the other times he had walked into this villa. She was convinced that over the past two weeks they had made love nearly everywhere in her villa and his. And she had not one regret about it.

When he turned to face her, she asked, "So why are you here and not in Alaska, since you intended to put as much distance between us as you could, Jess?"

Jess shoved his hands in his pockets and met her gaze. He hoped she would listen to what he had to say. He loved her, and more than anything, he wanted to convince her of how much. "I came back because I realized I let my emotions overrule my common sense."

Paige shrugged. "Well, I'm not sure returning here did any good."

"I want to think the opposite. Can we sit down and talk?"

She didn't say anything for a minute. "Okay then, let's talk."

He followed her to the living room and watched her ease down on the sofa as he sat in the wing-back chair facing her. She was watching him expectantly. What could he say to make her understand just how he'd felt at the thought of her reuniting with Kemp?

"I told you about my last serious girlfriend, Ava. What I didn't tell you was the guy I found her sleeping with was her ex-boyfriend. She had broken up with him less than a year before she and I got together."

She waved her hand dismissively. "I know that. Maverick told me earlier. What I don't understand, Jess, is what that has to do with me."

Could she not see the connection? "When I got here and Pierson told me the two of you had gotten back together, for me it felt like déjà vu. He sounded believable and I panicked when I should not have. It was only when I was halfway to the airport that something Maverick said made sense."

"What did Maverick say?"

"He reminded me that you weren't anything like Ava."

"So, it took another man to tell you what, as far as I'm concerned, you should have known?"

She was right. "I would have figured it out on my own, Paige—I had fallen in love with you so hard that I couldn't think straight."

She sat up straight in her seat. "What did you say?"

He had no problem repeating what he'd said. "I said I had fallen in love with you so hard that I couldn't think straight."

She tilted her head and looked at him. "You love me?"

"Yes."

"Since when?"

"Probably since the first time I saw you. If you recall, I told you the Westmoreland House held sentimental significance for me because of you. I'm convinced that's when I fell in love with you."

While she looked like she was in shock, he continued, "For years I saw the night I met you as a missed opportunity. When Dillon introduced us and I saw that flirty little gleam in your eye, I knew I had to put the brakes on or I'd be in trouble. That night I made a decision to choose a career in politics over starting something with you that I couldn't finish. A part of me has regretted it ever since."

"What are you saying?"

"I'm saying what I told those reporters that night at Sedrick's was true, Paige. What I've tried to do these past weeks was to let you know just how taken I am with you. The only reason I didn't let you know six years ago was the timing. Like I told those reporters, I was knee-deep in my campaign and intent on staying focused."

"But what about the other times, after you won your Senate seat?" she asked.

"I thought the time would be right, but you were either off filming or I was trying to get settled in Washington. When I had finally made up my mind to make my move, that's when I heard you'd become involved with Kemp Pierson and everybody was saying it was serious."

"It should have been, but it wasn't," she said softly.

"My time spent with you here was meant to recapture that missed opportunity, but what I really wanted to do,

Paige, was to capture your heart the same way you had captured mine."

When she didn't say anything, just stared at him, he continued, "I didn't expect to pull things off in four weeks or less. I was planning to part ways with you at the end of our vacation, but I had hoped spending time with me would be so enjoyable that we could continue seeing each other."

"You never told me any of this, Jess."

"No. I never told you because I didn't want to rush you. I was operating on the assumption that you were trying to get over a broken heart. A woman on the rebound."

She let out a frustrated sigh. "If I hear that word *rebound* one more time I will scream. Like I told Maverick, I'm not, and never was, a woman on the rebound. I was never emotionally attached to Kemp after we broke up because I had planned to call it quits between us anyway. I was just waiting until we both finished our film projects to do it."

"So, in other words," Jess said, "Kemp's affair gave you an excuse to do what you'd planned to do anyway, which was to end things between the two of you."

"Yes, but regardless, he should have remained faithful to me until we mutually ended things. He didn't, and I had every right to feel betrayed."

"I agree."

She paused and then said, "I wish we would have had this talk sooner, Jess. Then you would have known that I fell in love with you that night six years ago as well. I told myself I was just attracted to you and the attraction would fade, but I would dream about you often. Things didn't go well for me and Kemp on so many levels. He was so full of himself, so overconfident in his abilities, that he never noticed how unhappy I'd become."

Jess leaned forward in his seat. "What are you saying, Paige?"

"I'm saying that I love you, too. I am at a point in my life where my career doesn't mean as much as it once did. If you recall, I even told you I was thinking about leaving Hollywood. I want to teach drama at one of the universities."

He captured her hands in his, not believing their talk had brought them to this point. Now, like her, he wished they would have had it sooner. She loved him and he loved her. "You do know there are performing arts departments at Howard University, Georgetown and George Washington University."

She smiled at him. "Any reason you mention those three that are located in DC?"

"Yes." He stood and pulled her from her seat and into his arms. Looking down at her, he said, "I just happen to know someone who would love seeing you more often."

She wrapped her arms around his neck. "How often?"

"How about every night and every morning? I love you, Paige."

"And I love you."

He then captured her mouth before sweeping her up and heading for the bedroom.

Epilogue

"For a while I thought I would have to send a search party out for you two," Maverick said, grinning at Jess and Paige when they walked into the anniversary party. It was obvious his gaze was drawn to the huge diamond on the third finger of Paige's left hand. He lifted a brow. "Is there something I need to know?"

A huge smile covered Paige's face. The day after their "talk," Jess had convinced her to fly with him to Alaska, high in the mountains near the Yukon and Arctic Ocean. A friend of his was the sheriff of this small town where it snowed all year round. His purpose for taking her there was for her first dogsledding experience. He had borrowed Maverick's plane to fly them there.

Jess pulled her closer in his arms and smiled at his younger brother. "Yes. We had a great time in the mountains, Paige loves dogsledding and I brought your Cessna back in one piece."

Maverick frowned. "Cut the BS, please. That diamond

on Paige's hand is almost blinding me. Do you want to tell me about it?"

Paige giggled and held out her hand. "We're engaged!"

Maverick lifted a brow. "Engaged?"

"Yes. We're getting married on Paige's birthday in late November," Jess said.

"November? That's three months from now," Maverick said.

Paige smiled. "Yes, three months, five days and approximately thirty-nine hours, but who's counting?"

Maverick laughed. "Damn, just what happened on that mountain, so I'll know never to take a woman there?"

Paige gave her future brother-in-law a cheeky grin. "Don't you know what happens on vacation…"

"…stays on vacation," Jess finished. "We will talk more later—it's time for us to mingle."

And they did. The Westmorelands and Outlaws were there in full force, and news spread quickly of an upcoming wedding in three months. Another Novak was marrying a Westmoreland cousin. Everyone was excited and happy for the couple.

"So, are you moving to Hollywood or is Paige moving to DC?" Dare Westmoreland wanted to know. Dare and his wife, Shelly, lived near Atlanta, where Dare was the sheriff of College Park, Georgia.

"We'll be living in both places until Paige finishes all her film projects. Then she's moving to DC," Jess said, smiling down at his fiancée.

"That's wonderful," Shelly said. She then glanced beyond them to see more guests arriving. A huge smile touched her face. "I see our son is getting a lot of attention."

Everyone followed Shelly's gaze and settled on AJ Westmoreland, Dare and Shelly's oldest son, who was the spitting image of a younger Dare. In other words, he was handsome as sin.

"That's AJ?" Paige asked, surprised. "Or should I say Alisdare," she added, since everyone had gotten word that nowadays he preferred being called by his birth name. "I haven't seen him in years. Last time was when he graduated from high school, and we all went to the graduation."

"Alisdare finished college with a bachelor's degree from the University of Maryland and a master's from Harvard, both in criminology," Dare said proudly. "Earlier this year, he was hired by the FBI. He wants to work a few years as an agent before joining his cousins at the Westmoreland Security Firm." The Westmoreland Security Firm was run by Dare's cousins, Cole and Quade Westmoreland. Cole, who was a former Texas Ranger, and Quade, who'd worked for PSF, a special unit of the Secret Service protecting the president, had started a network of security companies that was in thirty of the fifty states.

The seventy-fifth wedding anniversary party for Daniel and Katherine Russell was well attended and turned out to be the fabulous affair Chardonnay had wanted it to be. Pam and Dillon didn't make the event. They were busy back in Denver helping out Bane and Crystal with their two sets of triplets. Pam and Dillon had been the first Paige and Jess had called to give them their good news.

It took a while before Jess and Paige had a moment alone. He pulled her into his arms as they stood outside and gazed up into the sky.

"It's a beautiful night, isn't it?" she said.

Jess turned to Paige. "As beautiful as the woman I intend to marry. I love you, Paige."

Paige smiled up at him. "And I love you, Jess."

When he pulled her into his arms, Jess knew this had ended up being the best vacation ever.

* * * * *

THE RANCHER'S
RECKONING

JOANNE ROCK

To my mother. I love you, Mom.

One

Please respond. I think you might be the father of the late Arielle Martin's six-month-old baby.

Seated at the oak desk in her room at a bed-and-breakfast in Royal, Texas, investigative journalist Sierra Morgan reread the text she'd just composed.

Blunt?

Absolutely. And considering the negative stereotypes of journalists as relentless sensationalists who would do anything for a story, Sierra hated that this text played a little too close to that depressing portrayal. But she couldn't imagine any story more worthy of closure than that of a fatherless six-month-old.

Forcing herself to take an extra moment before clicking Send on the text, Sierra idly spun a yellowed globe from the early 1900s, her gaze moving over the stack of old leather-bound novels that served as a makeshift pedestal. She'd been staying at the Cimarron Rose for months to solve the mystery paternity of baby Micah, who'd been found abandoned in the parking lot of the Royal Memorial Hospital.

Sierra had just arrived in town to do a story for *America* magazine on the ten-year anniversary of the Texas Cattleman's Club allowing women into their ranks. She'd filed her story after the gala celebrating the TCC milestone, and freelanced several articles for the local *Royal Gazette*, but she hadn't been able to tear herself away from baby Micah's story. Yes, she was dogged and relentless and all those other things that made up a good reporter.

Better people thought that than the truth—that baby Micah tugged at her heartstrings for far more personal reasons.

She'd figured out who the baby's mother was soon enough once Micah's aunt woke up in the hospital after an untimely collapse. But even then, Eve Martin hadn't been able to shed any light on the mystery of Micah's father, because Eve's sister, Arielle, had died of a heart attack before naming the daddy. Since then, Sierra had been pursuing leads for five months with Arielle Martin's diary as her guide.

Now, Sierra spun in the desk chair, the afternoon light slanting through a window overlooking the lawn. A vintage map of the world sprawled above the four-poster bed, and a huge repurposed suitcase served as a chest at the foot of it. While she cooled her heels in Texas, somewhere on the other side of the globe, rancher Colt Black was revamping a French winery, ignoring all her more subtly worded texts and voice mails.

She truly believed she'd finally cracked the mystery of Micah's parentage. But she needed Colt Black to answer her in order to confirm it.

Grip tightening on her phone, she returned her gaze to the least tactful lines she'd ever composed.

Blunt and relentless? Color her guilty.

She jabbed the send button.

Because she knew how it felt to grow up with the knowledge that you'd been abandoned as a child. That was a lifelong wound she wouldn't wish on anyone, and Sierra felt deeply protective of the sweet six-month-old she'd visited many, many times since his arrival in Royal.

One way or another, Colt Black would have to answer her now.

Had a homecoming ever felt so hollow?

Colt Black didn't even look out the window of the luxury SUV he'd hired at the airport as they drove through downtown Royal. He'd been away from Texas for fifteen months. Just twenty-four hours ago he would have guessed he'd feel some gladness to return to the Lone Star state after being in the Occitanie region of southwest France for over a year.

Not now.

He withdrew his cell phone from the pocket of his sports jacket to re-read the series of texts from the journalist Sierra Morgan. He'd never heard of the woman until he'd researched her last night after that final, devastating message.

Please respond. I think you might be the father of the late Arielle Martin's six-month old baby.

The words still made his chest seize up even on the hundredth read. Yes, he'd ignored all her other texts and voice mails leading up until that last bombshell. But that had been when he'd thought she was just a reporter sniffing out gossip for more articles for the local paper, the *Royal Gazette*.

Once Arielle Martin's name came up, however, he'd dropped everything else. Literally. He'd been in the winery's tasting room shortly before midnight, testing a competing vintage from a neighboring winemaker, when he'd read the words that gutted him.

Had he fathered a child without knowing?

Immediately, he'd gone back to read Sierra Morgan's other texts more carefully, only to discover Arielle had died one month after giving birth. And that her child—quite possibly *his* child, even though he'd only been with Arielle for one night—had been without a parent ever since. That had been five months ago.

If this child was his?

Colt wouldn't ever forgive himself.

Glancing up from his phone, he pocketed the device again as he saw the bed-and-breakfast come into view. The unassuming Cimarron Rose had been a Royal fixture for years, long before Natalie Valentine took it over and turned the downstairs into a bridal shop. In one of the journalist's messages, she had told him she had taken a room here, and she'd listed all her contact information for him to get in touch. Of course, he hadn't. Last night he'd been too devastated to call her for more details. Instead, he'd booked the first flight out to discover the truth for himself.

So here he was, showing up at her door unannounced at—he checked his watch, too jet-lagged to remember the local hour after crossing so many time zones—ten o'clock in the morning.

The SUV rolled to a stop on the gravel drive that wound under a porte cochere. The bright red roof and ivory exterior of the main building had a hospitable air with a wide porch and hanging ferns between every column. After paying the driver, Colt approached the wide front entrance, where the door had been left ajar, perhaps to let the mild breeze inside.

"Hello?" he said through the screen, rapping his knuckles lightly on the wooden door frame.

The scent of coffee and cinnamon preceded the sound of muted footsteps and a feminine voice.

"Come in," called a woman before she came into view. "Natalie's out, but I'm—"

A petite blonde beauty stopped as she opened the door wider and met his gaze.

Wide, moss green eyes stared up at him. Tousled, flaxen hair spilled over the shoulders of her black T-shirt with a picture of a coffee cup and the words Caffeinated Writer in swirling script. She wore a pair of pink-striped pajama pants with the tee and a pair of gray flannel slippers on her feet.

"You must be Sierra," he managed to say at last, suddenly aware of the moments that had passed while he took a far too detailed inventory of the woman. "I'm Colt Black."

She blinked at him, seeming to awaken from her own perusal. No doubt she was surprised. "You're *here.*"

She probably thought him the world's biggest dead-beat for not replying to her messages before. Or were her reporter instincts too busy salivating over the possibility of a local scoop?

"And well overdue, at that," he said dryly. Then, nodding at the screen door, he tugged it toward him, determined to keep his cool until he took her measure. "May I?"

Belatedly, she backed up a step to clear the way.

"Of course. Yes. I've been anxious to speak with you. Obviously. I just wasn't expecting you so soon after—" Her green gaze stuck to him while he stepped onto the dark welcome mat and set his leather overnight bag on a wooden hall bench. She seemed to regroup, and he suspected she made an effort to restrain the questions plainly written in her gaze. Instead, she asked, "Would you like some coffee? Tea?"

Sierra gestured to a small breakfast bar laden with pastries, a coffee machine, a kettle and a basket of tea bags. She retrieved her own mug, positioning it like a barrier between them, then took a careful sip while eyeing him over the rim.

"No, thank you. I'm wound up enough as it is between not sleeping and your text." He couldn't help the bite in his tone.

One eyebrow arched. "The fate of an infant seemed too important to waste any more time mincing words." Her green eyes blazed.

But was that defensiveness of the baby she felt? Or did that inner fire stem from a drive to nail down a story? If he didn't want to be the subject of her next feature, he needed to be on guard.

"You certainly came right to the point." He ground his teeth together as he peered around the front parlor room devoid of any guests save her. "Care to share what led you to me? And if I'm the subject of an article? I know you write for *America* magazine."

"Not currently, I don't." She shook her head. Then, gaze narrowing, she continued. "And although I freelance for the local paper, I'm not writing any more about Micah out of respect for Eve Martin and her nephew."

"There've already been stories about the baby." He'd Googled his way across the Atlantic. "So excuse me if I find that hard to believe."

"I wrote initially to drum up more leads to the father. But now I won't write anything else until I can report a happy ending, and only then with the father's permission. Today I'm interested in resolving a human drama because I was there when Micah was found."

Was she personally invested? The hint of accusation made him defensive.

"Well, I'm here now," he reminded her, needing to figure out if the child was his. "I'm ready to meet the boy. Talk to Arielle's family. Put the wheels in motion for an expedited DNA test—"

He had a to-do list a mile long, but Sierra settled a hand on his forearm, startling him to silence with the unexpected touch.

"No one will be more supportive of moving quickly on this than me, but we should probably share what we know before you meet Micah." She seemed to realize she'd left her hand on his arm because she yanked it away quickly. Then she nodded toward a back door visible through a bright yellow-and-white kitchen. "Can we talk outside? I could use some air."

"Anywhere is fine," he said more tersely than he'd intended. "I just need answers. The sooner the better."

Bristling, she straightened her shoulders and set her coffee mug back on the buffet table.

"I have been trying to talk to you for *weeks*," she informed him levelly, folding her arms. "Before that, I spent months following leads from Arielle Martin's diary to locate Micah's father. So believe me, I am ready for answers, too."

It was on the tip of his tongue to say she should have tried harder to reach him. That if she'd sent that last text message two weeks ago, he would have been here that much sooner. But since he wouldn't even know that Arielle had given birth to a child without the woman standing before him, Colt reined himself in.

"Of course, you're right." His heart slammed in his chest, the angst of the last twenty hours wrecking his head. "Excuse my lack of manners, Miss Morgan. I'm furious with myself at the possibility that I left Arielle with no support…"

There were no words that could adequately describe his regret if that turned out to be the case. Accountability and responsibility could have been the Black family motto, drilled into him from an early age. The only thing that came a close second in importance was family itself. And that might be another institution Colt had denigrated by leaving the States fifteen months ago.

"I imagine it's a lot to process. Which is why I would have preferred to be less blunt in my text." Her tone was softer as she pivoted on her heel and started toward the kitchen. "Come on. Let's get some air. And please, call me Sierra."

Colt followed her through the kitchen, a flyer for a local Wine and Roses Festival snagging his gaze for an instant and capturing his professional interest as a

newly minted French vintner. But with any luck he'd
be back overseas before the event anyhow. He kept
pace with Sierra down the back steps of the bed-and-
breakfast onto a shaded lawn where an oak tree spread
thick boughs over much of the space. A wrought iron
bench sat between pink and purple azalea bushes already in bloom.

Sierra's slippers scuffed quietly against the flag-
stones as she moved toward the bench, her long blond
hair blowing lightly against the middle of her back.

"Thank you." He waited for her to sit and then took
the opposite end of the bench for himself. In the light
breeze, he thought he caught a hint of her scent vying
with the green shoots of a fresh Texas spring. "And to
spare you time, I will tell you that I read everything I
could find online related to Arielle's sudden death. I
never met her sister, Eve, but it sounded like she was
the guardian for her the baby?"

"Micah," Sierra corrected him, sounding oddly protective. "And yes, that's true. But Eve Martin was hos-
pitalized with heart problems of her own until recently,
and it was deemed best for Micah to remain in the
care of Camilla Wentworth—Cammie—the woman
who found him."

Colt felt ill at the thought of a total stranger acting
as stand-in parent to an infant that might share Colt's
blood.

"I need to see him." His hand tightened into a fist
where it lay on the wrought iron. "My God, the boy
deserves a home—"

"And he will find his rightful one." Sierra stabbed
her finger against the bench to make the point. "But
Cammie and Eve have trusted me to take on this search

for Micah's father, allowing me to use Arielle's diary for any clues. So I would appreciate you sharing how you knew Arielle. I went out on a limb connecting the dots from her diary to suggest you could be the father."

"You didn't sound like you were making casual guesses in your text." He sat back to look at her.

Her lips compressed into a line before she spoke. "I did what needed to be done to find answers. Yet even after flying all the way here, you don't seem inclined to share how you knew Arielle."

Colt pressed a thumb to his temple. He didn't owe this woman the intimate details. He could simply walk away and find Cammie Wentworth on his own. Yet if there was anything to what Sierra said about her having the trust of the baby's guardian, perhaps it would be wisest to hash through this here with her before he got distracted meeting a child that might be his heir.

"Our time together was brief," he explained finally. "We met right before I left for France. I was devastated over the death of my grandfather and eager to begin work on a dream that was dear to him—opening a winery. I realize my grief is a poor excuse for being so careless as not to contact her afterward." He studied Sierra in the patchy sunlight that filtered through the tree overhead. "Do you know if anyone else made a claim for the—for Micah?"

"No one has," she admitted, sliding out of her slippers to tuck her feet under her. "But since Arielle's diary never mentioned you, I was basing my sleuthing work on really limited evidence."

Colt considered this. The ache of regret in his chest had expanded to a throbbing of urgency in his temples, blotting out the resentment he felt for Sierra's blunt insertion of herself into the drama. He needed to find out for certain if Micah was his son, and if Sierra could help him do that, so be it.

The news still staggered him.

His life would have to change drastically, starting immediately. Yet one thing was clear.

"In that case, I owe you a great debt for finding me, Sierra." He could set his personal feelings aside long enough to acknowledge that. "One I don't know how I'll ever repay."

Sierra stared into Colt Black's serious blue eyes, trying to get a feel for him.

Could she trust his account of meeting Arielle? DNA tests wouldn't lie, of course. And if he were the father, she'd obviously back off to allow the baby to reunite with his daddy. But until that was proven, Sierra felt obligated to run interference so that Cammie wasn't wasting her time playing host to a local rancher who might not be connected to Micah at all. And Eve had basically given up, thinking the father would never be found. She'd been working extra hard on her physical therapy, assuming she'd be raising Micah.

For now, Sierra planned to stick to Colt. Find out if he was a good person. A trustworthy person. The kind of man who would give Micah a good home.

Because it wasn't enough to be attractive. And she couldn't deny Colt was that. Her awareness of the fact came as a surprise, considering she had thought she'd successfully shut down that part of herself to focus on her career and forget about…other things.

Sure, Colt was tall and muscular. Imposing, almost, but that had more to do with his serious, intense de-

meanor. She understood logically that he was a very
good-looking man. His tailored blue jacket and gray
flannel pants broadcast his wealth as clearly as the vintage silver watch on his wrist. But the shadows under
his eyes and the slight rumple of his freshly trimmed
dark hair gave away how little he'd slept since learning the news. Those hints of his distress pulled at her
more than his outward appearance since they might
suggest he cared.

And then, Sierra found herself drawn to the determination in his expression. The need to make things right.

After the months of worrying about Micah's future,
she found Colt's concern appealing.

The thought reminded her of his remark. That he
felt indebted to her.

"You don't owe me anything." She swiped away a
dried leaf from the bench. "It will be reward enough
if I can see Micah returned to family."

Although then she'd need to dig into her other mis-
sion in Royal. To write a book about the history of
the Texas Cattleman's Club. Professionally, the project appealed to her. Personally, she couldn't help but
take a deeper interest in Baby Micah. As much as she
wanted to bring Micah together with his father, Sierra
would miss her frequent visits to the child who'd found
a spot in her heart.

"If Arielle never mentioned me in the diary, how
did you end up finding out about me?" Colt swiped a
hand through his hair.

"Arielle had jotted the name of the Colt Room in
the margins of the diary," she explained, referencing
the luxe bar inside the Texas Cattleman's Club that one
of Colt's ancestors had founded and Colt himself had

recently paid to renovate. "One of the references had a heart next to the name, so at first I thought she met the father of her child there."

Colt frowned, a line between his heavy, dark eyebrows. "That's not much to go on."

"But there was more. Micah's middle initial is C. No name, just a C. I thought all along it could be a nod to his father." Sierra had gone over and over that diary searching for clues, the mystery obsessing her for days on end.

"It's amazing you found me at all," he muttered darkly, rubbing a hand over his face. "I was so absorbed with the winery, needing to make it a success for my grandfather. And all the while I should have been here, making sure Arielle had everything she needed."

Sierra heard the despair and self-recrimination in his words. She wished she had a way to distract him since neither of those things would help the situation.

"You're here now though. And I have to admit, you moved quickly once I put my cards on the table." She slumped more deeply against the bench, drawing her knees to her chest to hug them to her. And maybe to add a barrier between her and the compelling man sitting beside her. "Once I researched more about the Colt Room and your involvement, combined with the fact that you left the country soon after Arielle became pregnant, I thought you could be the father."

"Your earlier messages were full of questions without coming right out and asking. Or conjecturing." He shook his head at the memory. "I glanced at a few, but after I looked you up online, I figured you were just digging for an inside track on the Texas Cattleman's Club for one of your stories."

That stung.

"And ignored me accordingly." She felt a self-deprecating smile twitch her lips. "I see you subscribe to the view that reporters are vultures."

"What was I supposed to think? It sure as hell never crossed my mind you were writing to tell me I was— that I *might* be—a father." He shoved to his feet. "I should go. See the child for myself. Find out how to get tested."

She rose as well, feeling more off-kilter than she should have now that a potential daddy candidate for baby Micah was in town and seemed ready to take responsibility for the boy. The possible end of her involvement with the drama made her anxious. "Wait." She scrambled to stand, shoving her feet back into her worn slippers. "You can get DNA tests at Royal Memorial, although to expedite them is extremely expensive. But first, I should go with you to see Micah."

Colt studied her with those serious blue eyes. She felt weighed and measured, somehow, as if he were sizing up every last thing he knew about her. As a reporter, she should be used to the scrutiny. Instead, she felt suddenly aware that she wore only a thin pair of pajama pants and a sleep shirt.

"I'm definitely paying for the expedited tests. I'll stop by the hospital after I see Micah. And while it's generous of you to offer to go with me, Sierra, I can't ask you to do any more." He had a clipped way of speaking, articulating each word clearly. She wondered if it came from his time abroad. "I'm already deeply in your debt no matter how you view it."

"I haven't even told Cammie I was contacting you," she hedged, feeling in her bones that she needed to be a part of the meeting. To see Micah's journey through to the end. "And we should let Micah's aunt, Eve, know that you're in town, too." There were so many people in Royal who'd rallied around Micah these last few months, people who'd helped piece together the mystery baby's story. "But if you want to meet Micah today, I'd prefer to be there with you. Cammie and Micah are staying with her fiancé, Drake Rhodes, a local rancher who has a house in town."

While he seemed to weigh this, she found herself wondering how he would do with the transition to caring for a six-month-old if he proved to be the father. Would it bring him any happiness, or only worry? Anxiety for Micah stirred again, her concern for the baby very real whether or not it made sense.

Finally, Colt nodded. "In that case, thank you."

"Great." She hurried toward the house. "It'll take me ten minutes to change and call Cammie. I'll fill her in and let her know we're coming. Then we'll go. I can drive."

She was halfway through the kitchen when Colt's voice behind her made her pause.

"Sierra. Can I ask you one more thing?"

She glanced back at him as he stood silhouetted in the doorway, his broad shoulders filling the entryway.

"Sure. Shoot." Leaning a hip on the stove, she tried to picture him cradling a baby. The answering image that splashed across her mind made her mourn her missing ovaries.

Reminding her sharply why she'd avoided relationships.

"Does he look like me at all?" Colt asked in that intense way of his, blue eyes boring right through her.

With that one simple question, she was toast. It was all she could do not to clutch her midsection where her reproductive organs should have been, her every maternal instinct touched.

And yet tormented.

She had to swallow back a hurt she hadn't allowed herself to indulge in years to consider the question.

"Actually, I think he does," she answered softly before spinning away. She beat a swift retreat to her room upstairs to regroup.

Get a grip.

Because she needed to keep an eye on Colt Black until she could be certain he was Micah's father. And even then, who was to say Colt could take good care of a baby? She would stick like glue to him through the transition until she knew for sure.

Two

In the passenger seat of Sierra's compact car, Colt couldn't stretch his legs in any way that didn't jam his knees into the glove box. Still, he appreciated the ride to Drake and Cammie's home in town where Micah was being fostered. More importantly, Colt was grateful for the escort Sierra provided now that it had become clear to him she'd played an integral role in the search for Micah's father.

Having Sierra at his side would speed things along at the Rhodes' home, assuring him the audience he needed. If Micah's aunt had trusted Sierra to use Arielle's diary to discreetly look into the identity of the baby's father, clearly Eve Martin had faith in her.

After the call to Cammie, Sierra said she called Eve Martin and updated her about Colt, his arrival in the U.S., and his desire to have a DNA test. Eve wasn't in town today, but she would meet with him tomorrow to discuss the situation. Clearly Micah's aunt was invested in her nephew's life.

"Have you met Cammie before? Or Drake Rhodes?" Sierra asked over the blaring radio as they headed into a more residential section of town.

Colt set aside his phone as Sierra turned down the music, a country pop song that had been loud enough to rattle the speakers. She hadn't even seemed to notice the noise until she'd spoken.

"I don't recall meeting either of them, but I've had business with Cammie's father before." He hadn't much cared for Tobias Wentworth five years ago when Colt had visited his ranch about a horse he'd been interested in purchasing. But according to local gossips, the guy's disposition had improved after his last marriage. "I hope Cammie is good with kids?"

He resented having to ask the question since it only reminded him that he hadn't done his duty toward Arielle. That he may have failed his own flesh and blood, too. The thought was all the more devastating considering how much emphasis his own beloved grandfather had placed on family. Colt had spent the last year trying to honor his relative's legacy by making the Royal Black Winery a success. But what did that effort matter if Colt had overlooked his own son in the process?

"She's excellent with Micah," Sierra assured him, dragging her fingers through the blond strands that had escaped out a crack in the driver's side window. "I could see that on the very first day when she found him. I was first on the scene in the Royal Memorial Hospital parking lot after Cammie found him, you know. Cammie was totally smitten with the baby."

Would he be?

Colt's head throbbed at the reminder he had no idea what to do with an infant. He would need assistance. A nanny. But then again, he wouldn't allow himself to be the kind of father who delegated parenting.

After losing both parents in a small plane crash in early childhood, Colt had been raised by his grandfather. And while his granddad had been everything to him, Colt understood better than most people the way a kid craved family. Colt's life had been shaped by his parents' absence.

"Does she have help?" he wondered aloud, recognizing she must have adjusted her life a great deal to accommodate a new baby.

"Yes, that's part of the reason she moved in with Drake, so he could help out. Drake's stepsister is living there, and he has a housekeeper who watches Micah sometimes. Plus Eve and I visit often and babysit if they need time away."

Colt didn't miss the wistful note in her voice. And this time, instead of feeling suspicious about the reporter's motives, he tucked away the observation for the future. If he couldn't find a nanny in a timely fashion, perhaps Sierra would consider lending a hand temporarily.

His attention wandered back to her again as she drove, her fingers drumming on the steering wheel while she navigated through Royal as easily as if she were a native. She'd changed into black jeans and boots, a soft gray sweater falling loosely off of one shoulder. She was pretty—not that he was in the market—but he would be a fool not to notice, and he wasn't a fool.

He wanted to ask her about herself—only as a distraction—but a moment later she turned off the main road.

"Here we are." She pulled into a parking space outside a gracious two-story with a wide porch. She tugged her sunglasses from her nose before switching off the ignition. "Are you ready for this? You've been quiet."

"No stories today, right?" He needed to confirm this before moving forward. He remembered the reporters surrounding his house after his parents died, the media interest adding to the pain of an already harrowing time. "You said you wouldn't write anything else without the father's permission, but I'm well aware all of Royal wants to know who the father is. Gossip—even a whisper of information—travels fast."

He knew sooner or later he'd be tried in the court of public opinion, whether or not Sierra Morgan outed him in print. But today was too important to him, too personal, for him to worry about how a journalist would depict the moment.

"It's the *Royal Gazette*, not *TMZ*," she retorted as she shut off the engine. "And either way, I won't write anything about you and Micah unless you prove to be his father *and* you invite me to interview you."

Perhaps he shouldn't believe her. But as her green eyes met his—her expression restless and impatient—he found himself going with his gut and believing her anyway. Besides, he was too keyed up about the possibility of coming face-to-face with his maybe-son to worry about it any longer.

"Thank you." He gave a stiff nod before stepping from the cramped vehicle.

Sierra didn't wait for him. She was already out of

the car and halfway up the flagstone walkway, clearly at ease here. But then, she said she visited often.

Was it strange to form that kind of bond with a baby simply because she'd been on site when he'd been found? Swallowing down his trepidation and uncertainty, he dragged his attention from Sierra's feminine form, her hair swaying in the mild spring breeze behind her. Instead, Colt focused on his next steps.

Meeting the boy who could be his son.

Certain she had to be imagining the weight of Colt's gaze on her as she walked, Sierra climbed the three wide steps up to the house. She had messaged Cammie to warn her they were on their way. Still, she knew how hard it had to be for her friend to open the door to a man who might be Micah's father.

As much as Cammie wanted Micah to have a family, Sierra strongly suspected the other woman would have been only too glad to take in the baby permanently. Her stomach knotted over the thought of a potential tug-of-war—even one of emotions, if not literally.

Now, Sierra rang the bell and waited, very aware of Colt's warm presence behind her. He wasn't standing close to her, yet she felt acutely attuned to him. The hint of spice she occasionally breathed in that she knew belonged to him. The muted rasp of silk over cotton from the lining of his jacket against his button-down as he shifted positions. The warmth he emanated.

The door pulled open before her thoughts carried her any farther down that precipitous path.

Cammie Wentworth, with her tall, elegant figure and long red waves, stood framed in the doorway.

"Hello, Sierra." Her green eyes turned to Colt. "I'm Cammie Wentworth."

Taking her hand, Colt nodded. "Colt Black. Thank you so much for seeing us on short notice."

"Certainly." Cammie's smile was all cool politeness as she studied Colt. "If Sierra says there's a good chance you're Micah's father, then it only made sense to meet as soon as possible. Her investigative skills rival local law enforcement." She opened the door wider and stepped back to admit them. "Please come in."

Moments later, they were seated in the comfortable great room decorated in blues and grays, a painting of dramatic basalt columns in coastal Australia dominating the space. A nod to Drake's time abroad.

Sierra wanted to offer to retrieve the baby—partly because she loved any excuse to hold Micah, but also because she was eager to see if the boy truly did resemble Colt the way she thought he did. But she wasn't Micah's guardian, and this wasn't her home, so she tried to wait patiently while Cammie asked Colt some of the questions that Sierra had already discussed with him—where he'd been, why he hadn't been in the baby's life before now and how he'd met Arielle.

Sierra's eyes were on the hallway that led to Micah's room when she realized Colt was saying something she hadn't heard before.

"—we met after Arielle contacted me to ask for a meeting about some land I own on the outskirts of Royal. The old Fenwick land—"

"Violetta Ford's ranch," Sierra inserted quickly, wondering how much Colt knew about the local spinster rebel who'd posed as a man—Vincent Fenwick—so she could claim a place in the Texas Cattleman's Club.

The story was one of many gems she'd uncovered about the history of the club, and one of the most compelling reasons to write a book about that saga.

"You know about that?" Colt turned to her from his seat on a leather ottoman, surprise in his blue eyes. "Arielle told me the tale that night—the only night we were together. I wasn't aware of that story. I'd just bought the land as an investment."

Sierra's reporter brain clicked into high gear, wondering how she could gain access to that land. Emmalou Hillard, the ninety-nine-year-old Royal resident who'd once been a cowgirl on Violetta Ford's ranch had told Sierra that Violetta kept a diary. And that she thought it was buried on the ranch. Sierra would love to get her hands on it for the sake of the book she wanted to write.

Cammie leaned forward, her silver pendant swinging with the movement as she addressed Colt. "Did you know Sierra has taken up Arielle's work to uncover some of the TCC's lost past? Sierra already helped solve the mystery of Harmon Wentworth's birth mother."

Sierra smiled her thanks at Cammie, appreciating the way the other woman depicted her investigative efforts as helpful instead of intrusive. Sierra recalled plenty of times Cammie had tried to dodge her at first, convinced Sierra only wanted a scoop. But eventually, she'd won her over.

"That's kind of you, but Tate Wentworth was the one who finally put all the pieces together," she reminded Cammie. Sierra knew Cammie wasn't close with her second cousin, but the other woman surely knew that it was Tate who'd stolen pages from Arielle Martin's diary that led to the truth. Tate had then found out about Violetta Ford's long ago affair with Dean Wentworth, Harmon's father.

"But you weren't stopping until you had answers," Cammie shot back. "You lit a fire under all of us."

"Really?" Colt swiveled to look at Sierra. "I didn't even know Harmon was adopted."

Sierra folded her arms, uncomfortable with the spotlight on her. Especially when there was a new mystery to solve. One that tugged at Sierra's heart far more than Harmon's background.

"I haven't spent *all* my time in Royal hounding you," she admitted. "I'm collecting stories about the Texas Cattleman's Club for a book. That's one of the reasons I took a leave of absence from *America* magazine. The other was finding Micah's father."

Both Colt and Cammie looked like they might say more about the subject, so Sierra sprang to her feet. She needed to keep the meeting on track. Focused on what was most important.

"Cammie, do you feel comfortable letting Colt meet Micah?" Her natural drive and bluntness had carried her far as a reporter.

It hadn't done her many favors socially.

But Cammie didn't seem to take offense. She nodded slowly. Solemnly. "I feel very comfortable. While I haven't met Colt before, I ran into his grandfather often at the Texas Cattleman's Club." She turned to Colt, and her expression softened. "I'm so sorry for your loss. Clyde Black was a good man."

"Thank you." Colt's throat worked on a swallow before he continued. "I appreciate that."

Cammie moved toward the hallway. "I'll get Micah."

Something about the gravity of her tone made Sierra remember how hard this would be on her friend if she had to give up Micah. Sierra's heart squeezed in empathy while Cammie disappeared down the hall.

Colt's voice called her from her thoughts. "You've got better sleuthing skills than local law enforcement?"

She shrugged as she paced the great room to work off some of her nervous energy, unsure why she felt so keyed up.

"Investigative reporting involves far more research than actual writing," she explained, curious if he only asked to distract himself from the implications of the impending meeting with Micah. Was Colt nervous? "Most of my time is spent chasing down leads."

"And now you're writing a book." His blue eyes followed her as she circled the long sectional couch. "Will that keep you as busy as your last job?"

She guessed he was making small talk, and yet his attention—his interest— stirred something to life inside her that had been dormant for a long time. It had to be simple physical attraction, didn't it? She was just unaccustomed to the way a man's notice could heighten all the senses. Stuffing down the awareness, she tried to give the question consideration.

"I hope so." She would be the one in need of distraction once the mystery of baby Micah was solved. Cammie wouldn't be the only one with an empty space in her heart after the little boy departed from their lives. "I wouldn't have taken on the project if I didn't think there was a lot to uncover here."

Then again, Micah had been another reason that she'd justified remaining in Royal long after the gala celebrating the tenth anniversary of women in the TCC.

That may have been her impetus for coming to town, but she'd certainly been swept up in a bigger drama from day one.

She circled the room faster. Where was Cammie?

"And what do you think you'll be uncovering?" Colt came to his feet, stepping into her path before she passed the ottoman where he'd been sitting. "Secrets people would rather remain hidden? Scandals that will only hurt club members if they come to light?"

She drew back a step at the glittering accusation in his eyes. Also, the warmth of his nearness sent sensations skittering up her arms and over her shoulders. Down her back.

"So much for being forever in my debt for informing you about Micah," she muttered, cranking her neck to look up at him. "You're already convinced I'm going to do a hatchet job with the book and I haven't even started."

They stood too close to one another in wordless stand-off until Cammie's voice sounded from the entrance to the great room.

"Here he is, Colt. Meet Arielle's son, Micah."

For an instant, it felt like that moment on the playground as a kid when he'd fallen off the monkey bars and had the wind knocked out of him. Time stopped along with his breath, a frozen pause when he felt powerless to move. To think. To understand what was happening.

Logically, he could see Cammie Wentworth heading toward him with a dark-haired baby in her arms. The kid was a charmer, too, dark eyes wide and alert as he gripped the bare toes of one foot, a happy smile curving his lips as he seemed to bounce to unheard music. He wore a blue cotton one-piece outfit printed with dump trucks.

Was this even happening?

Colt still hadn't moved when Sierra laid a light hand on his arm.

"Oh, Colt, isn't he precious?" she murmured, her voice full of wonder. "He gets more adorable every time I see him, and I would have never thought that was possible."

Something about her fingers resting on his upper arm, a brief, feminine touch that glanced off him, nudged Colt back to life. She buzzed with so much restless energy all the time, maybe she'd shocked him out of the momentary stasis.

"May I hold him?" he asked, surprising himself.

He had no experience with kids, much less babies. But this was different.

Because he knew immediately this child belonged to him. With him. Except for the darker complexion of the child's skin and the deep brown of wide, curious eyes, the little boy could have been a mirror image of Colt's own babyhood.

And having been orphaned himself at an early age, he refused to let his son feel the painful loneliness that came with feeling abandoned. Colt had watched his grandfather step up to take on the parent role even though there was no way the old man had bargained for that much involvement in Colt's life. Now it was Colt's turn to step up. To fill a void where two parents should be and at least give the child one.

"Of course," Cammie agreed, stepping closer to make the exchange.

Sierra hovered close by, making soft cooing sounds at the infant, who rewarded her with a big, gummy smile, then kicked the foot he was holding.

"He's a wiggle worm." Sierra laughed delightedly at the boy's antics while Colt scooped him from Cammie's arms and into his own.

And if he'd thought the world had stopped when the baby arrived in the room, that incident was nothing compared to staring into the child's brown eyes for the first time.

"Hello, Micah," he said softly. Overcome as his world shifted.

Old priorities fell away as a new reality coalesced around this tiny life that he knew in his bones was his son. Micah C. was Micah Colt. No ifs, ands or buts about it.

Micah lifted one hand to his mouth, gently gnawing his fingers as he studied Colt.

He moved toward one of the large windows flanking the fireplace, wanting to study the baby's features more closely. Needing to memorize every line, every curve of the boy's face.

His. Son.

In his peripheral vision, Colt saw Sierra moved to one side of the room to speak quietly to Cammie. Discussing the possibility of his being Micah's father? Or letting Cammie know his plan to pay the fee for the expedited DNA test?

He'd called the hospital on the way here and learned that—for an exorbitant fee—results could be processed in twenty-four hours.

And as much as Colt wanted to spend more time with the tiny person in his arms, he knew he needed to get the wheels in motion to bring Micah home with him. Which meant the sooner he got to Royal Memorial Hospital, the sooner he could bring Micah home with him.

Where his son belonged.

"What do you think?" Sierra asked from just behind him, her fingers reaching around Micah to stroke a knuckle over the baby's round cheek.

Micah's eyes blinked heavily, as if the soft caress could put him to sleep.

"I think I need a ride to Royal Memorial," he informed her, shifting his gaze from Micah's face to hers. "But I'm happy to call for a car."

The enrapt expression he spied on her face brought home how much Sierra cared about the boy. She'd admitted as much, but Colt hadn't really appreciated the full extent of her feelings until he saw that unguarded, tender look in her eyes.

There wasn't a doubt in his mind that she would be an attentive sitter for the child if Colt needed help in the coming weeks.

But if he invited her into their lives—however briefly—could he trust her not to sniff out secrets and scandals for her book while he tried to rebuild his life here?

"The hospital is on the route to the B and B," she reminded him, green eyes lifting to his, her hand still cradled against the baby's cheek. "I can drop you off there on my way home."

He nodded as he moved toward Cammie to return the boy to her safekeeping. "That would be great. And thank you, Cammie. I appreciate you letting me see him."

Cammie shifted the boy to her opposite shoulder, tucking him against her with the practiced ease of any mother. "You're going to get the DNA test?"

"I am." Filled with new purpose, Colt realized he had a lot to plan. Starting with a call to his housekeeper in France to pack some of his things since he wouldn't be returning to the winery for at least a month or two. It looked like he'd be in Royal for the local Wine and Roses Festival after all. "If the test turns out the way I think it will, I'll speak to Arielle's sister and the social worker about taking over parenting duties immediately. With any luck, I can return tomorrow afternoon."

"So soon?" Cammie asked, her gaze darting to Sierra and then back to him.

But the timetable was fixed.

"It's not soon enough from my perspective," he reminded the baby's foster parent, hoping she understood his need to establish an overdue relationship with the boy. "I can't thank you enough for taking such good care of Micah. I know I'll never get back the months I've already lost not knowing about him. So if the test proves I'm his father, I will be back as soon as possible to start a new life with my son."

Three

Pacing her room at the Cimarron Rose, Sierra wondered how many more laps it would take to wear a hole right through the braided rug. Surely not that many, given that she'd been practically sprinting circles around the small space while waiting for a text from Colt.

Or a phone call.

Heck, she would have settled for smoke signals at this point.

She just wanted to know what had happened with the DNA test.

Would Colt ignore her now that she'd pointed him in Micah's direction? Maybe in his eyes, she'd served her purpose in informing him about the baby, and now she was out of the picture. In theory, she understood that the results of the DNA test were his personal business.

He had no obligation to inform her, even though she'd been totally invested in finding Micah's father from the moment she'd seen the baby carrier on the trunk of Cammie Wentworth's Mercedes that day in the Royal Memorial Hospital parking lot.

But damn it. She at least deserved to know if he *wasn't* the boy's father so she could continue her search. She braked to a halt in front of the window overlooking the tree and courtyard where she'd sat with Colt just the day before, navigating an awkward conversation about his relationship with Arielle. He'd filled her thoughts nearly every moment since then. Only because of his connection to Micah, she told herself. Not because Colt intrigued her with his caring eyes and broad shoulders. Gently, Sierra pounded her fist on the wooden sill, willing her phone to ring. For Colt to give her answers.

More than twenty-four hours had passed since she'd dropped Colt in front of the hospital doors the day before.

Surely he'd heard something about the DNA test results by now?

Abandoning her short-lived attempt to be patient, Sierra resumed her pacing. She lifted her phone to look at the messages she'd sent to Colt over the past week, scanning the notes until she came to the most recent one that had finally spurred him to get on a plane.

Please respond, it began, before dropping the bombshell baby news. Of course, he hadn't responded. At least not by text. She'd been stunned to see him at her door a day later and hadn't thought to make sure he let her know his next step.

Now her thumbs got to work.

Could you let me know what you learn about a potential family connection to Micah either way? I want to be sure I find his father, and if it's not you, I must return to the drawing board.

Rereading it, she hit Send before she could second-guess the wording. With a sigh, she tossed the device onto the middle of the four-poster bed, where it landed with a soft plunk.

Would Colt answer? He couldn't possibly understand how much the search for Micah's dad meant to her after growing up without knowing the identity of her own birth parents. But Sierra recognized the trail would go cold if she didn't press for answers now. That's what had happened to her as an abandoned infant. Her adoptive parents hadn't started a search in earnest until Sierra turned twelve, after she convinced them that it was important to her. Twelve years had been too long.

Beep. Beep.

The electronic chime of her phone made the mattress vibrate underneath the device.

Sierra dove on it, snatching up the cell. The notification was for a call, not a text. And, to her surprise, Colt's name displayed across the top of her screen. Stabbing the button, she answered as quickly as possible.

"Colt? How did it go?" She hadn't realized until this moment how worried she was that the baby might *not* be his. Would he be disappointed? Relieved?

Her stomach knotted at either scenario.

"The DNA is a match," he said quietly, his tone unreadable.

Her throat went tight with tension, her gut churning. A thousand reactions spun through her. Was he calling solely as a courtesy? Would he allow her to see Micah anymore? How did Cammie and Eve take the news? She sank to the edge of the mattress, knowing she needed to proceed carefully with Colt if she wanted to continue to spend time with the precious baby she'd grown to care for deeply.

And she did. Her heart couldn't bear the thought of being shut out of Micah's life.

"You knew it would be," she reminded him, thinking how confident he'd seemed the day before when they left Drake's house. "Congratulations, Colt. Micah is lucky to have you for a father."

She'd seen the determination to be a good father in his eyes when he'd looked at Micah. Still, the fast shift in Colt's life had to leave his head spinning.

"Thank you," he replied, his voice still unnaturally low. "Although I'm not sure Micah would agree with you. He cried the whole way from Cammie's house to the ranch."

Her heart clutched to envision baby tears.

"Aw. How hard for you both. Babies cry though, Colt, and Micah is going through a big change right now." She tried to reassure him, even as she yearned to check on Micah for herself. See with her own eyes that the sweet little boy was okay. "Is he better now?"

"He fell asleep moments ago," Colt explained, the cause of his near whisper immediately becoming clear. "And even though Cammie and Eve gave me four pages of schedules and instructions to ensure I do the right things, I'm man enough to admit I'm staring at the crib in pure terror for the moment he wakes up again."

A smile tugged at her lips to imagine the big, strong rancher at the utter mercy of his infant son.

"I'd love to see him if you'd like some moral support for your first day of fatherhood." She would like to think she only offered in order to assure herself Micah was in good hands. That Colt had all he needed to care for the little boy.

But she couldn't deny that Colt had been in her thoughts ever since she'd dropped him off at the hospital. He'd stirred something inside her.

There was a spark between them.

"You'd do that?" He sounded more suspicious than grateful.

Raising every one of Sierra's hackles. Spark or no spark, that frustrated her.

"Why does that seem so hard to believe? Just because I'm a journalist doesn't mean I'm immune to the universal appeal of babies. Even reporters have hearts, you know. And maternal instincts." She realized she'd snapped too hard as soon as the last bit tumbled out of her mouth.

But then, she was mighty defensive of her inability to have babies. Not that Colt had any way of knowing.

"You're right," he acknowledged, then let out a gusty sigh. "I guess I'm so preoccupied about what to do next with a baby, it's hard for me to remember that not everyone views this as scary."

Sierra stared at her toes resting on the bright braided rug in her room at the B and B, waiting for Colt's verdict on if he wanted her there or not. Her gaze went to the antique globe on the oak desk, where the side of the world with France was visible from her search to find the man on the other end of the phone.

Was it any wonder he was overwhelmed by parenting when just three days ago he was walking among his grapevines in his small town north of Toulouse, completely oblivious that he'd fathered a son on the other side of the world?

"Are you still there?" he asked when she—uncharacteristically—hadn't rushed to fill the silence.

"I am. But I won't plead my case when I've already offered help. I can't make you trust me." She understood that, even as it ruffled her feathers.

With an idle finger, she spun the globe, shoving away the sight of Colt's other home.

"It's not a matter of trust."

"No? Because I've been in Royal for five months, earning other people's faith in me. But you don't know me. I get it." She'd had an uphill battle from the first day she'd arrived in Royal. With Cammie. With the cop, Haley Lopez, who'd responded to the call about an abandoned child. With Harmon Wentworth, who hadn't known who his biological mother was. Arielle Martin had started the search, and Sierra got the conclusion for Harmon.

Sierra had liked to think she'd helped them all in some small way or another. Yet as far as Colt was concerned, she was just another journalist pariah digging for dirt on other people.

"Sierra, you told me you weren't writing a story, and I believe you." He sounded sincere.

"Then what's keeping you from accepting my help when you know Micah is unsettled from the change?" she pushed, exasperated. "Clearly you're feeling out of your element today. Imagine how Micah feels?"

"I am out of my element." He paused. "But I'm also attracted to you."

The surprise admission bowled her over. She gripped the corner of the duvet like a lifeline, waiting to feel steady again.

"Oh. I—" She reached for words but found she didn't have any. Because even though she'd felt the spark between them, too, she'd never imagined Colt would confront it head-on.

"That makes the time we spend together more problematic. But I can assure you that I won't act on it." The grim determination in his voice was hardly flattering, but she understood his reticence.

Respected it even, considering all that he had on his plate right now. Although a little part of her might have felt disappointed, too. Which made no sense when she was committed to avoiding romantic entanglements. She didn't need relationships in her life that would only necessitate telling someone else why she couldn't have children.

"Okay then," she continued carefully, her senses all attuned to his every breath and nuance of sound over the phone. "I understand. And my offer still stands."

She could hear the relief in the long breath he let out.

"Thank you so much, Sierra. Micah and I are staying at the old Fenwick ranch house. I'd be grateful for help anytime you can make it over here."

She hadn't forgotten about his connection to the Fenwick house. At the mention of it now, Sierra's brain started running in high speed again. That's where Violetta's diary was rumored to be hidden. Not that she would go searching for it today when Colt needed her help with Micah. And she hated the idea that looking for the diary would somehow confirm Colt's worst opinions about her. But she would figure out how to deal with it later. She wouldn't turn down this chance to spend time with Micah. Reassure the baby with her presence.

"I'll be there within the hour," she promised, hurrying to her closet to find something to wear besides pajama pants.

And yes, call her contrary, but she searched for something both feminine and pretty.

Even if they weren't *acting* on the mutual attraction, she couldn't pretend it didn't exist. Being around Colt made her feel hyperaware, all her senses heightened. It had been four years since she'd ended her last relationship to focus on her career. To ignore the conflicted feelings she had about her body and motherhood. Four long years without a romantic relationship hadn't seemed like a chore at that time, but right now, with the promise of spending time with Colt looming, she felt every one of those years without a man's touch.

As long as she continued to ignore the sparks between them, she'd be okay. Because if she wanted an invitation to the Fenwick house in the future to search for the diary, she needed to maintain a good relationship with Colt Black.

Staring down into his son's portable crib in the middle of the living room floor, Colt let the magnitude of the moment wash over him.

He stood alone in the rambling old Fenwick ranch house with his *son*.

How many times would he have to think it and say it in order for the news to sink in? The idea that he had fathered a child still felt surreal, as did this entire trip to Royal.

His hand flexed on one padded bar of the porta-crib as he wondered what his grandfather would say if Clyde Black could see Colt now. Colt had briefly con-sidered bringing Micah to the house Colt had grown up in before dismissing the idea. The home at Black Ranch still felt too empty without his grandfather's presence, even though it had been over a year since Granddad's death. The Fenwick place was smaller, but Colt had hired a crew to oversee renovation work while he'd been abroad. Now, most of the indoor changes were complete with a renovated kitchen, living areas and three bedrooms. There was an in-law suite that still needed work, and some exterior updates. But Colt ap-preciated that the space felt scrubbed clean, like a fresh start for him and Micah.

A soft tapping at the front of the house called his attention from his musing.

Shoving to his feet from the end of a chaise lounge, Colt strode to the front door. He caught a glimpse of Sierra's petite figure through one of the sidelights, and his anticipation ratcheted up a few notches. Which was all wrong, damn it.

He hadn't come to terms with the hurt he'd brought to Arielle's and Micah's lives by not checking in with her after their night together. So he had no business feeling an attraction to Sierra now, when the thought of Arielle pregnant and alone still haunted him.

Steeling himself against the inevitable tug of desire he was powerless to halt, Colt opened the door.

Sierra stood on the deep porch in a denim skirt and boots, the sheer hem of a turquoise-colored beaded blouse blowing in the spring breeze as she smiled up at him. She clutched a reusable shopping bag in one arm, a baguette peeking out of the top.

"I'm so glad you heard me knocking. I didn't want to ring the bell if Micah was still napping, and even tapping at the door felt risky." Her green gaze darted past him to peer into the house. "Is he still asleep?"

A long, piercing wail answered the question.

Colt's chest ached at the sound, but before he could formulate a response, Sierra was stepping inside the house.

"May I go to him?" she asked, settling the grocery sack on a plank table in the foyer, her eyes already on the portable crib in the living room.

"Sure. I'd be grateful. And I'm certain he'll be glad to see a familiar face." He stepped out of her way, feeling helpless. "I need a crash course in infant care," he explained, wondering if there was such a thing. "I have Cammie on speed dial, but if I spend some time watching you with him, I'll have a better feel for how to respond tomorrow."

Colt doubted if she heard a single word he said, however. As soon as he'd given her the green light, she dashed past him in a blur of turquoise, cooing soft sounds of empathy for Micah's unhappiness. Colt closed the door behind her and followed her inside.

"My goodness, so much sadness," she prattled softly to the boy, plucking him from the crib to hold him against her shoulder. "It's all okay," she soothed, rubbing a hand along his back. "You're going to love your new house with your daddy."

Daddy.

Another word to send Colt reeling.

He met his son's gaze in time to see a tear roll down the chubby cheek. The child had stopped making any sounds though, perhaps startled into silence to listen to Sierra, the baby whisperer.

Unable to resist the urge to wipe away the boy's tear, Colt smoothed a knuckle under one brown eye while Micah arched back in an attempt to see Sierra's face. Using his arms to push at her shoulder, Micah's fingers wound into her hair until he clutched a handful of her flaxen-colored hair.

"Is he hurting you?" Colt asked, steadying the tiny fist, and wondering if he should try to pry it open and free her hair.

Sierra glanced up at him over her shoulder, their three heads all close together. He'd never been this near her, in fact. And he became aware of several things at once.

Her hair was silky soft. Strands tickled over the back of his hand as he tried to prevent Micah from pulling any, and the feel of it made him long to spear his own fingers through the long mass.

Then there was her scent. She smelled like orange blossoms, a fragrance that suited her perfectly—sweet with a zing that tingled in his nose.

Finally, he noticed that Sierra's lips were soft and full, a shade of deep, rosy red that made him ache for a taste.

It would have been difficult enough if he'd been cataloging all those things about her on his own. But she didn't look away from him either. Almost as if she were as compelled by this pull between them as he felt.

"Um." She made a small hum of sound that went right through him. "I should probably change him. Where—"

"I know how to do that much," Colt assured her, grateful to her for breaking the moment with something so practical. "I had Cammie show me before I left her house. She and Eve Martin gave me a rundown of the basics before they gave the green light for me to take him." Reaching for Micah, he tried to be careful not to touch Sierra.

Much.

"I don't mind—" she began, her breath hitching as his forearm grazed her breast.

Colt ground his teeth against the heat that sizzled through him from the feel of her.

"I've got it. Diapers are upstairs," he explained too brusquely, heading for the staircase with quick, determined steps.

She might have said something about the groceries, or dinner, but Colt was too busy making his abrupt exit to answer.

He should be focused on his son, after all. Not the unexpectedly appealing reporter who'd united him with Micah. Or how soft she would feel against him.

"Don't worry, big guy," he said to Micah, who gnawed on his forefinger while staring at Colt. "We're going to get through this, I promise."

Did the baby recognize Colt's lack of training?

As they entered the room Colt had designated as a nursery, Micah's brown gaze appeared thoughtful. Questioning. As if he wondered why Colt had intercepted him from the arms of the sweetly scented, tender woman who'd held him earlier.

"She's only temporary, buddy," he informed the boy as he laid him on the changing table. Colt had spent the night before shopping online for the most important pieces of baby furniture. The cherrywood nursery set and other baby equipment had been delivered that morning. "So don't get too attached."

Micah frowned, slapping the thick white changing pad with one hand as if to protest the news while Colt passed him a rattle and got to work on the task at hand.

"I hear you. And I empathize," he assured him. "I'm not in any hurry for her to leave either."

And not because he was attracted to her. Far from it. Asking her to help temporarily with Micah would be easier if he didn't feel this pull toward her every time they were in the same room.

But Micah deserved a familiar face around while he got used to Colt, didn't he? That was the least Colt could do for his son after the way he'd failed the boy by not being with him from the beginning.

"Ba-boo," Micah announced, his brown eyes still serious while Colt finished cleaning him up. "Ba-boo!" he said again, more urgently.

Colt knew a six-month-old wasn't really giving him advice. But the child's face was so serious.

Like mine.

How many times had people told Colt he was too serious? His grandfather for one, and Clyde Black had been one of the few people in the world whose opinion mattered to Colt.

The connection gave Colt a pang as he taped the clean diaper into place and tugged a fresh white onesie covered with elephants over Micah's wiggly limbs.

Colt couldn't deny that he'd always taken a practical, methodical approach to life.

Son, you need to live a little. Find what brings you joy.

He could hear Granddad's voice in his head even now. That advice had driven Colt to move to France to fulfill his grandfather's dream of owning a winery. And while he took pride and satisfaction in that accomplishment, it hadn't necessarily brought Colt *joy* since it hadn't been *his* dream.

What if Micah was already genetically predisposed to be as solemn as his father? The idea troubled Colt in a way the characteristic had never bothered him in himself.

From the doorway came a sudden squeaky sound, making both Micah and Colt turn to see a blue stuffed bunny rabbit with tall, fluffy ears. Slowly, the bunny lowered to reveal Sierra's face, making Micah giggle.

Had there ever been a sound so sweet?

As baby laughter filled the room, Colt acknowledged that—while Sierra Morgan might have a serious side—she sure knew how to turn that off around Micah. She was fun, playful and kind. Exactly the right personality to help Micah transition into his new home.

The fact that she was also smart, thoughtful and sexy as hell shouldn't matter.

"How did it go?" Sierra asked as she walked deeper into the room, passing the stuffed bunny to Micah. "He sounds happy."

Colt's eyes wandered over her even as he wondered how he would handle having her around more often if he was fortunate enough to talk her into helping him with Micah.

"That had more to do with you than me," Colt acknowledged, lifting Micah in his arms, cradling the precious weight against his chest. "Which is why I'm hoping you'll consider a more formal arrangement for spending some time with him as he transitions into living with me."

Her pale eyebrows scrunched together. "What kind of arrangement?"

"I know you're working on a book about the Texas Cattleman's Club. But I wondered if, temporarily, you might be persuaded to work on it from here. While spending more time with Micah." The boy wriggled, and Colt tried to shift his hold on him, but Sierra lifted him into her arms.

Bringing her scent and softness enticingly close for a moment. Scrambling his thoughts.

"Like a nanny?" She shook her head even as she said the word. "I'm happy to babysit anytime, Colt. I did that to help out Cammie, too. He knows me, so that would keep him from having to get used to another stranger."

He winced at the idea of himself as a stranger. But he had to acknowledge it was true. He was a stranger to his own son.

"I need far more help than Cammie. At least for the next couple of weeks." Extending his arms, he gestured to the house around them. "I'm still trying to set up the house to be sure it's babyproof. And you can see I have a lot to learn about caring for an infant."

"You're doing really well, especially for being tossed into parenthood with so little time to prepare," she interjected, moving around the room to keep Micah engaged, showing him the mobile over the bassinet one moment, and then moving to look out the upstairs window with him the next.

"You'd be well-compensated, of course," he pressed, recognizing that he didn't need just anyone to help with Micah. He wanted *her*. She was good with his son. Micah already knew her. And her playful spirit would make this difficult transition easier for the more reserved Black males. "And there are plenty of rooms here. The Fenwick house is a historic Royal property."

Sierra's head swiveled toward him. "You want me to move in?"

Something about the way she said it sent awareness tripping up his spine. Briefly, he recalled his reservations about getting close to her because of her work. But the truth would come out about his parentage of Micah either way. He had nothing to hide.

"At least for a couple of weeks. A month, perhaps." He hoped he wasn't imposing. But as he stared at her slender arms wrapped around his son, her pretty face deep in thought even as Micah tugged on a few strands of her hair, Colt was prepared to meet any demand to keep her here. Micah needed her with him. "Just until I find a rhythm with caregiving, and then you can help me carefully vet a nanny."

When her green eyes met his, there was a hint of conflict in them. Reservation.

"You said it yourself, Sierra," he pressed, reminding her of what she'd told him about the unfamiliar surroundings for a baby. "Micah knows you. It will help him if you're around while we make this transition."

Her expression softened. Whatever concerns she'd had about the arrangement privately, she seemed to have set them aside at the idea of the baby needing her.

"In that case, Colt, how can I say no?" A smile lifted one side of her full lips.

Relieved to have secured her help with his son, Colt tucked away his own reservations. Though briefly he wondered if they mirrored whatever Sierra's concerns had been.

One way or another, they'd avoid the attraction for the sake of the child.

Yet as he followed Sierra out of the nursery into the dim lights of the hall, where his gaze was drawn to the sway of her curved hips, Colt recognized the next month together wouldn't be easy.

Four

Was there a better scent than a freshly bathed baby?

After dressing Micah, Sierra breathed in the fragrant baby shampoo as she kissed the top of his still-damp head where dark hair already curled after a splash-filled bath time. Colt had helped her with the chore to ready his son for bed, and they'd both ended up wet.

Which was how she'd ended up wearing one of Colt's T-shirts, the soft cotton containing her other favorite new scent—the pine and sandalwood notes of Colt.

Her temporary housemate.

Sierra had accepted the dry shirt, although Colt had bolted right afterward, insisting he should finish making their dinner. No doubt he'd been feeling the full impact of complicated awareness, too. She could hardly beg off the meal now since she'd been the one to bring

over fresh bread and a few groceries, just in case he
needed a hand with dinner. When she'd first arrived,
she'd assumed she'd have to talk Colt into letting her
see Micah again.

She'd been unprepared for his offer—no, his *urg-
ing*—for her to take on a nanny role for the next few
weeks. The idea thrilled her, of course, because she
already loved Colt's son. But it made her realize how
difficult it would be to separate from the boy once Colt
found a replacement caregiver.

By then, she'd be that much more attached to Micah.

As if that wasn't complicated enough, there was the
matter of an attraction that Colt had freely admitted to
her. An attraction strong enough to have him bolting
from the bathroom after they'd shared laughter, bump-
ing elbows, and wet clothes.

Sierra hugged Micah closer at the memory, hoping
the baby would distract her from the unfamiliar ache
for Colt's touch. If only Micah would be there with
them all evening to act as the perfect baby barrier. But
Colt had specifically timed this meal for after they put
Micah to bed.

Which meant she was already twitchy with the
thought of so much alone time with Micah's hot daddy.

"We'd better go check on him," she told Micah, nuz-
zling against his temple in a way that made the boy
giggle a little. He was already sleepy, his hold on the
stuffed bunny she'd brought for him getting looser.

Leaving the nursery that Colt had apparently outfit-
ted overnight, Sierra carried Micah through the rambling old farmhouse and down the stairs toward the
kitchen. The Fenwick ranch had been renovated in the
last months. The paint colors—muted blues and yel-

lows—made for inviting rooms. The open floor plan downstairs had to have been reimagined, since that certainly hadn't been the architectural preference when Violetta Ford had the house built. Sierra tried to imagine where the walls had once been, yet couldn't envision the layout any other way.

Now, a fire had been laid in the hearth that flanked the dining area, where a sturdy farmhouse table had been set with simple white dishes. Two pink azalea branches in a bud vase served as a centerpiece, while in the kitchen beyond, Colt slid a ladle into a red stoneware pot.

When had a man last cooked for her? A long ago boyfriend had warmed up soup from a can once when she'd had a cold. At the time, she'd been touched. But that experience hadn't come close to the way it made her feel to see Colt's efforts for her now.

Efforts he made only because he was grateful she'd agreed to help him with Micah, she reminded herself. There wasn't anything remotely romantic about it. It was just an exceptionally nice thank-you.

"Whatever you're making smells amazing." She breathed in the aromatic scents, trying to identify the meal.

Colt laid a towel over his shoulder and shut off the burner under the pot still on the stove. "Coq au vin is one of the few French dishes I learned to make while I lived overseas, but I figured with that in my cooking repertoire, how much else do I need?"

Turning toward her, he held out his hands to take Micah.

Sierra moved closer to pass the baby, their arms

brushing. Awareness hummed through her, even as she tried to focus on Colt's words and not his touch.

"It sounds impressive, but I will confess I know nothing about cooking beyond hitting the microwave button for the time listed on the back of a frozen meal." Back in Houston, she'd purposely distanced herself from all things domestic, convinced she could be happy making her work the focal point of her life.

Colt chuckled as he stepped back, securing Micah easily in one arm.

"I'm suddenly feeling all the more confident in my cooking prowess." His blue eyes met hers as they stood under one of the industrial pendant lamps. "But is it time to eat yet? Should we lay him in his crib first? Cammie gave me a schedule. I can check."

"It's okay. We've got this. We might as well try. I brought him down so we could put him to bed together." Her gaze moved to Micah as the boy laid his head on Colt's shoulder, as if he were too tired to hold it up any longer. With their faces so close to one another, Sierra could see the resemblance all the more. The shape of the eyes. The hairline around their temples. "Aw, look at him. He looks like he could doze off any minute."

"What do you think, big guy?" Colt asked, laying his cheek against his son's head. "Want to give the new crib a test run?"

Micah squeezed the ear of his bunny and gave the animal a shake, his eyelids drooping.

Sierra's heart turned over to see the two of them look comfortable together for the moment. "That looks like a yes to me."

Together, they ascended the stairs to the nursery.

Sierra tried not to think about the intimacy of the act. And her gaze definitely didn't search the hallway for the door that might lead to Colt's room. She still couldn't believe she was going to move in with him for a few weeks. A tingle shot through her at the thought of more nights together like this.

"Are you sure he's okay in a room by himself?" Colt asked as they entered the nursery. "I read conflicting things online."

The room had been painted a mellow shade of blue. Pale gray curtains and wall art depicting line drawings of the Fenwick ranch gave the room a more adult appeal, but the cherrywood furniture and abundant toys showed that Colt had tried his best to make it kid-friendly in the last twenty-four hours.

"Cammie just transitioned him to his own room, so I think he'll be fine. But if he's too fretful, we can move him to the portable crib, and he can sleep with one of us." The thought of inviting herself over for the night made her cheeks warm. "I mean, not that I'm spending tonight here. But other nights, he can sleep in my room if that works best."

If he noticed that she was flustered, she couldn't tell. His expression had turned serious again.

"The sooner you can move in the better, as far as I'm concerned, but I understand you might not be ready to stay with us tonight."

Sierra's mouth went dry at the thought of time spent under the same roof as this magnetic man who wanted to cook for her and who respected what she had to offer as a caregiver to a child. All the years that she'd been ignoring the lure of domestic comforts came back to bite her now.

"Let's see how he's doing once we've finished our dinner, and we can decide from there," she suggested, needing to make this night about Micah and not about the waves of awareness rolling over her.

Threatening to pull her under a tide of longing.

"Sounds like a plan." Colt turned from her to face the crib. "Now, how do I go about putting him down? Is there rocking involved?"

"If he needed soothing, I would say yes to the rocking. But he looks content to me, so maybe just lay him down gently on his back and see what happens?" She was no expert. But she'd read a lot before babysitting Micah in an effort to make sure she gleaned as much as possible about caring for an infant. "And the bunny can't go in the crib with him."

She took the stuffed toy from Micah's hand and set it aside.

Colt shifted his son closer to the crib before turning to her again. "Should we dim the lights? Wind the mobile?"

"I'm on it." She couldn't quite stifle a smile at the thought he put into the bedtime routine.

Then again, if she'd been able to have children, she probably would have been the same way. A tightness knotted in her chest as she reached over the crib to wind a mobile of brightly colored horses. By the time the device started playing a comforting lullaby tune, Sierra was already halfway across the room to turn down the overhead lights.

"There you go, buddy," Colt told him. With a kiss on the baby's forehead, he leaned broad shoulders over the crib and lowered the boy onto the thick mattress. "Sleep well."

Sierra's heart melted a little to watch them together. She dialed down the brightness on the switch, casting the nursery in a soft glow. Making the room feel more intimate.

Her nerves pinged with awareness.

"Do you have the baby monitor set up?" she asked, reminding herself to get used to this.

But sharing a bedtime routine with a decidedly hot rancher was going to test her commitment to avoiding romantic entanglements. Especially when getting entangled with Colt Black had a definite appeal.

"I do." Colt frowned down at Micah, who seemed content to kick his foot, his diaper crinkling under his onesie with every move. "I read that no one uses a blanket on infants anymore, but it seems strange to lay him down without one."

She was grateful for Colt's focus on his son, which kept him from reading the runaway thoughts in her expression. Bracing herself to get closer to him again, she kept her attention on the crib as she returned to his side.

"I know, right?" Sierra stared down at Micah, who had just caught sight of the mobile overhead. "Who would have guessed we were all lucky to survive childhood with the menace of blankets hanging over us?"

He turned to meet her gaze. "Best to be safe though."

"Of course," she agreed, thinking he might have missed the teasing note in her voice. But then, Colt didn't seem like the sort of man who'd ever made time for laughter and teasing.

For a moment, she had a frivolous hope that she could bring those things into his life over the next few weeks. Then she reminded herself that Colt wasn't her focus here.

She'd only agreed to take the temporary gig for Micah.

"Is it overly optimistic of me to think he's going to sleep?" Colt asked, reaching for the horse mobile to wind it again.

And why were his strong arms so distracting?

"Not at all." She turned away to flip on the baby monitor she'd spotted on a windowsill, then picked up the receiver to pass to Colt.

Only to find him still staring down into the crib.

"I can't believe I'm a father." Colt raked a restless hand through his hair. "It's incredible, and scary as hell at the same time."

Envy for his simple path to parenthood knotted inside her. Robbing her of breath for a moment. She would give anything for the chance to carry a child.

Still, she tried to reassure him. "I'll bet every first-time parent is a little terrified. And you've had less time than most people to get used to the idea."

"We will be okay." He gripped the crib rail tightly, as if he could make the words true by force of will. "I just feel bad that Micah will have so little family between me being an only child, my parents being gone, and Arielle's passing."

His jaw flexed as he spoke, the tension—the sadness—in his words making her wonder for the first time what might have happened between Colt and Arielle if Micah's mother had lived. The thought that Colt might have worked out a relationship with her for the sake of his child made Sierra feel all the more like an interloper in his world.

"But you're his father. And you're here with him." She laid her hand over his where it rested on the crib rail. "And he'll always have Eve, and his foster family."

Friendly. Comforting.

Or so she thought until Colt's gaze turned to hers in the dim light. Heat sparked and leaped in his eyes.

Her lips parted in surprise at his expression, her breath huffing in and out too quickly at the shifting, invisible current between them.

Did he feel it, too?

"Are you ready for dinner?" he asked, breaking the tension. His words rumbled along her senses, the quiet intimacy feeling like a caress.

She licked her suddenly dry lips.

"Sounds good," she managed, scavenging a polite smile all the while stuffing down the urge to flee the house and the attraction she had no idea how to handle.

This is for Micah.

Colt reminded himself of this over and over during the dinner he shared with Sierra. He'd invited the smart, sexy woman across the dining table into his life strictly for Micah's sake. He knew she was right about keeping a familiar face around his son during this time of tremendous transition. Kids needed that. His son *deserved* that.

But knowing he'd done the right thing in asking Sierra to stay with him didn't make it any easier to adjust to the way she lit up his insides anytime they were in the same room.

Even as he thought it, the fire he'd laid in the hearth snapped and popped, as if the heat he felt for Sierra only added to the blaze near the sturdy farmhouse table he'd set for their meal.

"This is delicious." Sierra sighed happily, seeming wholly occupied with the coq au vin. "And if the meal is an indication of how you cook on a regular basis, feel free to compensate me in dinners any time."

"I'll keep that in mind." He appreciated the way she'd dug into the food and kept the conversation light after the tension that had thrummed between them in the nursery earlier. "But I only learned a couple of dishes from the cook I hired at the Royal Black Winery."

"A French chef taught you how to make this?" She took a sip of the burgundy he'd served with the meal, the firelight casting a warm glow over her skin and her fair hair.

She really was lovely. The pink glow in her cheeks—whether from the warmth of the fire or the wine—made her green eyes even brighter.

"Tastings have an important role in developing a winery's reputation," he explained, toying with the stem of his crystal glass. "And food pairings drive more people to the tastings. So it made sense to hire a professional to handle that part of the business."

"Is this a vintage you serve with the meal at the winery?" She lifted her glass, the burgundy a deep, rich purple. "I know nothing about wine. Although I hope to learn more at the Royal Wine and Roses Festival later this month."

"I saw a flyer for that event," he mused aloud. "It must be something new. And as for this vintage, it's not one of mine. We serve our own Royal Black Malbec with the dish, but I didn't have time to ship a case over." He hadn't taken the time to pack much of anything. The trip had been a blur of sleeplessness and anxiety.

Hell, he was still reeling from the news that he had a son.

"What was it like taking on your grandfather's dream of a winery? Did you know much about it? Did you do a lot of research?" She speared a bite of chicken on her fork before turning her eyes back to him, appearing fully attentive to his answer.

He wondered if she ever turned off that quick mind of hers.

"I had to research a great deal, but I also knew quite a bit from Granddad." He let the memories come, realizing that he was grateful to share them with someone. Grateful to talk about someone who'd meant so much to him. "Back at the Black Ranch house, my grandfather had a room full of black-and-white prints of French wineries. They were photos he'd taken himself as a young man when he'd toured France."

"So you saw those images your whole life," Sierra added, reporter-like as she seemed to shape a story in her mind. "You always knew that was his dream?"

Colt nodded, his chest aching with the old pain that he hadn't pushed his grandfather to leave Royal and make the dream happen. "I knew that Granddad had put off the winery in order to raise his son here in Royal. But once my dad was managing Black Ranch successfully, when I was five years old, my grandfather decided it was time for his second act. He had already made the travel arrangements when he got the news—" Colt paused to clear his throat. "My parents died in a small plane crash. Granddad scrapped the winery plan to raise me."

"Oh, Colt. I'm so sorry." Sierra's hand slid across the table to rest on his, her empathy obvious in her tone. Her touch. "How heartbreaking for you."

He closed his eyes for a moment to sift through the

feelings her touch stirred, needing to suppress some of them. Wanting to soak up the others.

"Thank you. They've been gone a long time, and I made peace with their absence. But the grief of losing Granddad—before he had the chance to see the winery I was in the process of buying for him—that still hurts." Which was why he allowed himself to feel the weight of Sierra's cool fingers along the backs of his.

Why he took comfort from her.

"Did he know?" Sierra asked, a blond eyebrow lifting with the question. Her fingers stirred on his, the smallest grazing of her skin over his.

Colt shook his head, wishing he could shake off his regrets as easily. "Unfortunately, no. It was going to be a surprise." He felt her hand squeeze his. Heard her quick intake of breath that no doubt heralded another expression of sympathy that he shouldn't want. "But as much as that hurt, it taught me not to waste time with loved ones."

Sierra's hand slid away from his, and he missed her touch immediately. But her lips curved in a half smile as she seemed to follow his train of thought.

"Clearly you learned the lesson well. You didn't waste a minute once you knew Arielle had a child. You were here less than twenty-four hours later, ready to meet your son." She set aside her fork, her plate cleaned.

In the silence that followed, the fire crackled again. The baby monitor hummed with the sound of Micah making a soft baby sigh. And with Sierra seated across from him, her clear green gaze empathetic and accepting, Colt had a taste of what it might be like to have a woman in his life.

The idea rattled him to his core.

Especially since he had no business thinking about anything like that when he'd already failed his son by indulging his own selfish interests. He'd put his needs ahead of protecting Arielle and Micah.

So he sure as hell didn't trust his judgment where women were concerned.

"I arrived as soon as I could," Colt acknowledged belatedly, his brusque tone chasing the warmth from Sierra's green eyes. "But I'm not sure how long I'll be staying."

He needed to resurrect barriers with this woman. Starting now.

"What do you mean? In the Fenwick house?" Sierra's brow furrowed.

"I mean I won't be staying in the U.S. for long," he explained, certain the impending physical distance would help them maintain an emotional one. "Once Micah has adjusted to me, I'll be taking him back to France. To my home."

Five

Sierra tried not to react outwardly to the bombshell Colt had just launched.

She'd had a lifetime to grapple with the consequences of being an impulsive person, so she recognized that blurting out *hell, no!* would be uncalled for. Unwelcome.

And yet…how could Colt consider plucking Micah out of Royal, Texas, when the town had rallied around the baby all these months?

Gripping her fork with tense fingers, she felt the formerly delicious meal stir uneasily in her belly as she tried to craft an appropriate response to his news.

"I hope you'll reconsider that idea," she said finally, setting aside the fork and pushing her chair further from the table. "Micah has experienced a lot of upheaval in his life between losing his mother and then being taken away from the home and people he's known for the last five months."

"He's my son," Colt reminded her, an edge in his voice as he stood to clear their plates. "He belongs with me."

Sierra hurried to help him, not wanting to alienate Colt now when it might only hasten his departure from Royal. She'd never anticipated that he might wish to leave town with Micah.

"And no one is arguing that. Micah does belong with you." She carried the leftovers to the polished mesquite countertop that looked original to the farmhouse. "But I'm sure you appreciate that a sense of security is tremendously important for a child."

When he didn't answer at first, continuing to clean up after their meal, Sierra pressed, "I'm just suggesting you think about it for a while. Take the time to see how well-loved your son is in this town before you make any more changes in his life. You have to admit he's had a lot of upheaval."

"Understood." Colt's shoulders tightened as he bent forward over the wide, apron-front sink to rinse dishes. "But I also have to make the decision that seems best for my son and me. If that means leaving town to continue building the Royal Black Winery, then that's what I'll do."

Sierra buzzed with unhappy retorts about that, but she stifled each and every one of them, telling herself that Colt was dealing with a lot right now. She'd tamp down her own feelings and return to the subject when she felt calmer.

Yet as she brought their empty wineglasses over to the sink, she couldn't resist asking one more question.

"Why do you like your life in France more than the one you had here?" She couldn't imagine being happy so far from where she'd grown up. She'd traveled around the U.S. to pursue stories for her magazine but had never experienced any great urge to see the world, let alone live far from her birthplace. "Doesn't every native Texan claim the state as home no matter how far they roam?"

She was only half joking.

And fortunately, her words made Colt crack a smile.

"You'll notice I did name the winery after my hometown, so I see your point," he conceded, switching off the hot water before drying his hands on a kitchen towel. He leaned a hip against the countertop. "It's not that I prefer the French countryside to my home. But I haven't finished my work there, and I still intend to make my grandfather's dream a success."

"I see," she forced herself to say, even though she didn't see at all. The news rattled her, making her too aware that her time with Micah had an expiration date. "Although you must admit, it will make things difficult for me as I care for him every day, knowing all the while I'll only have to say goodbye to him in the end."

How hard would it be to grow more and more attached before Colt moved away?

Colt frowned as he hung the dish towel on the handle to the dishwasher. "I hope you're not reconsidering our arrangement now that you know my plans."

"Of course not," she shot back, not quite managing to hide her frustration. It would certainly be easier to persuade him to stay if she lived here. She folded her arms, staring him down while the fire crackled in the hearth nearby. "I will follow through. In fact, I should probably go home now and organize some of my things to bring over. Should I start tomorrow?"

The relief scrawled across his features was so evident that Sierra felt a small measure of satisfaction that—at least for now—he needed her help. Wanted it.

"The sooner the better. Would you like me to drive you to the B and B? I could ask the ranch foreman's wife to come over for an hour in case Micah wakes while we're gone. I have a truck if you need me to move anything." Straightening from where he'd leaned against the counter, he suddenly seemed closer.

Loomed larger.

Her throat went dry. And how could he have such a potent effect on her when she was still actively upset with his decision to leave Royal?

"No, thank you. I travel lightly and don't have very much." She took a step back, needing some distance. Craving some space to come up with a game plan for dealing with this unwanted attraction.

"Will you come back tonight?" His blue eyes locked on hers, stirring an answering flutter in her chest. "I can show you where you'll be sleeping."

The thought of being in a bed under his roof shouldn't have felt so intimate. It was a simple arrangement for Micah's sake.

And yet...

Her cheeks went warm at the thought of having Colt show her to a bedroom.

She swallowed hard. "That won't be necessary. Micah sleeps through the night now, so you won't have to worry. I think I'll spend the night at the B and B to organize and regroup, then I'll come by in the morning with my things."

He studied her for a long moment before nodding. Then he turned to open a long drawer and withdrew a key tied with a piece of twine. He passed it to her.

"In that case, here's the key." His fingers brushed her hand. "I appreciate you agreeing to help me, Sierra."

"Of course." She clutched the cold metal into her palm, willing away the tingling sensations his touch had inspired. "I'm looking forward to spending more time with Micah."

She would take every possible moment she could with the little boy, all the while using her time with Colt to convince him to remain in Royal. She couldn't bear to part with Micah, for one thing. But for another? She knew it would be good for Micah to have the love and support of the family and community he had here.

As for the baby's compelling father? Sierra would have to work overtime to keep the boundaries between them despite living under the same roof.

Four days into his arrangement with Sierra as a temporary live-in nanny, Colt seriously questioned his sanity.

He'd stepped out of the calving barn at Black Ranch after checking on a new mother, only to see Sierra at the fence near an outdoor group pen with other pairs of cows and calves. She'd taken to bringing Micah over to see the animals ever since he'd told her the ranch was in calving season.

Which was sweet of her, he admitted. He wanted to see more of his child and also wanted his son to acquire a love of the land.

And clearly Micah enjoyed himself, trying to imitate the animal sounds from his seat in the stroller that Sierra pushed a mile each way from the Fenwick house. So Colt could hardly complain about the activity. Yet he'd taken to working in the barns this week just to breathe in air scented with fresh hay instead of Sierra's orange blossom fragrance.

Having her under his roof was proving far more of a temptation than he'd ever imagined. She stood in his son's darkened room with him at night to put the boy to bed, her hair sometimes brushing Colt's shoulder as she leaned into the crib at the same time as him. She was in his kitchen in the mornings, looking sexy and slightly rumpled in the oversized shirts and shorts she slept in, her hair piled on her head and glasses perched on her nose. She didn't cook, but she bought exotic brands of coffee, making them brews that had more notes than his wines.

Just this morning, she'd informed him that they were drinking something with molasses undertones, and he'd gotten so caught up in listening to the slight rasp of her morning voice that he hadn't heard half of what she'd said. He'd been too busy thinking about waking up beside her.

Which, in turn, sent him running for a day in the barns.

Only to find her here, laughing at something Micah did, her head tipped back as the throaty chuckle escaped. Everything tightened inside him at the sound. Or was it the sight of her, dressed in dark yoga pants that hugged her curves and a loose green tee knotted at her narrow waist? Blond tendrils escaped the ponytail she wore, teasing her cheek in a warm breeze.

Seized by the days of frustration that came from

ignoring his personal hungers, Colt strode toward her as if drawn by a magnet.

Green eyes lifted to his as he neared. Her whole body went still, like a wild creature caught out in the open and unsure of its next move. He wanted to answer that uncertainty with the hot persuasion of his touch. His kiss.

But he only jammed his hands in his pockets as he tried not to scowl at her.

"Are we interrupting?" she asked, hugging Micah closer.

The baby played with a loose strand of her hair, watching his chubby fingers wind through the silky piece.

Colt wished he had the right to touch her.

"Of course not." He couldn't help his brusque tone, even knowing how he sounded. Clearing his throat, he tried again. "I appreciate you taking Micah out for some fresh air."

He dragged a boot through the grass near the calving pen, the soft green shoots smelling like spring. Then, realizing she was still holding his son in her arms, Colt reached to take the boy, being careful to untwine Sierra's hair from the baby's fingers first.

The interaction brought them close together and gave Colt a chance to smooth his fingers over that silken strand for himself, even though that hadn't been his objective. Or at least not his main one.

"How's your newest calf doing today?" she asked once Colt had straightened. She shaded her eyes with one hand against the afternoon sunlight. "Did the dam end up accepting her?"

He'd been worried about the heifer even before the

difficult birth and he'd shared the story with Sierra over breakfast the day before to avoid thinking about the appealing quality of her morning voice.

"All went well," he assured her, recognizing the soft spot she seemed to have for any abandoned baby—human or otherwise. Harmon Wentworth and Micah weren't the only ones who drew her maternal interest. "We had one of our most knowledgeable ranch hands on duty this morning, and he convinced the mama to lick her calf by pouring some of her feed on the baby. Now the two of them are bonded, and the mama's nursing like a pro."

"I'm glad to hear it." A sunny smile lit her face. "I probably shouldn't have made the walk over here so close to Micah's nap time, but I kept thinking about the calf being rejected."

"We take good care of the animals at Black Ranch." He was a little surprised that the story had lingered with her. "There's not a single ranch hand on staff that doesn't enjoy the springtime with the animals."

"I can see why," she told him softly, her attention shifting back to the new calves and mothers in the group pen. Two of the calves closest to them were running and jumping, demonstrating good social behaviors that meant they'd be ready to join the larger herd soon. "They're so fun to watch."

"Maybe you missed your calling as a rancher," he teased. "You could spend whole days out here." Colt watched her as one of the older cows moved toward the fence, clearly interested in Sierra. "You can pet her if you'd like. She's a veteran mother, not skittish or aggressive."

"Is that what makes a good mother?" she asked, her

tonesounding a bit strained as she scratched the cow's neck. "Firsthand experience?"

Colt followed Sierra toward the fence, careful to keep his body between Micah and the animal, no matter how much he trusted her.

"In a cow, it certainly helps." He wanted to see her face to try and read her expression, but she tipped her forehead into the animal's neck, remaining hidden for a long moment.

Had he missed something?

He stayed alert to her until she straightened again, her face cleared. Neutral. But sadder, somehow. The earlier laughter and sunny smile were gone.

"I should be getting Micah back home." Moving away from the fence, she headed toward the stroller. "Would you mind buckling him in for me?"

He followed behind her with the baby. "Is everything all right? Did I say something—"

"Everything's fine," she said in a voice that seemed too bright. Leaning over the stroller, she cleared aside the straps to give Colt a clear path for his son. "I'd just better hurry before Micah gets hungry for his afternoon bottle. I lost track of the time."

"Why don't I drive you both home?" he suggested gently, sensing something was off with Sierra even if she didn't want to admit it. "My truck's right over there. There's already a car seat in the back."

He pointed to the heavy-duty model he kept at Black Ranch for work. He'd taken it out of storage earlier in the week to supervise operations as long as he was home.

Her green eyes clouded as she hesitated. For a moment she appeared so troubled that Colt was tempted to do something foolish like pull her against him and demand to know what was wrong. What had upset her?

Micah patted his shoulder with his tiny hands, the fingers clenching and unclenching rhythmically against Colt's T-shirt.

"I could use a few minutes to myself, actually," she finally said. "Would you mind bringing Micah back while I—take a little time?"

She looked so vulnerable in that instant that he had no choice but to ignore the tug of his own curiosity. He would have done whatever she asked.

"Of course I will." He knew she'd shouldered more of the baby care this week than he had, in part because he'd been running hard and fast from his attraction to her. Had he inadvertently asked too much of her? Guilt pinched him. "Take whatever time you need. I can load up Micah and give him his next bottle."

"Thank you." Her voice was rough. The rasp was back, and not in the way that had driven him out of his mind with desire this morning. Now she sounded rattled, and it gutted him to think he could be at fault.

"Sierra, I'm sorry if I've been leaving too much to you—"

But she'd already spun on the heel of her tennis shoe to hurry away up the dirt road that acted as a shortcut between the Fenwick and Black lands.

Damn it.

"Should we check on her?" he asked aloud to Micah. His temple throbbed with the sudden knowledge that he might have pushed the limits of what a transplanted reporter was ready to handle as a nanny this week.

"Moo," Micah told him, his little face serious as he

stared back at the enclosed pasture full of calves and cows. "Moo moo."

Colt's chest filled with pride at the sound that may have been just lucky timing but felt more like a stroke of baby genius.

"That's right, big guy. The cows say moo." Colt hugged the boy tighter to him, planting a kiss on his downy-soft forehead.

"Moo moo," Micah seemed to correct him as he laid his dark curls on Colt's shoulder.

"You know best," Colt conceded, pushing the stroller toward his truck with one hand while he kept Micah secured in the other. "I admire that you stand your ground like that."

With one last glance over his shoulder to where Sierra had vanished into the woods separating the properties, Colt lifted the stroller into his truck bed before opening the rear door to settle Micah in the baby car seat.

"Moo moo?" the boy asked, sitting up straighter when it would have been helpful for buckling purposes to have him relax into the seat.

Micah's dark eyes were wide. Curious.

"We've got to leave them now, buddy," Colt soothed his son, guiding one leg through a seat strap. "We're going to head home now."

He was anxious to talk to Sierra once Micah was settled in for a nap. Find out what was troubling her. Maybe it had something to do with her work. The book she was writing on the Texas Cattleman's Club or a story she was tracking down. He hadn't asked her anything about her work since she'd moved into his house, his focus on Micah and—of course—avoiding the attraction to Sierra.

"Moo moo!" Micah's word became an adamant demand. An argument, really. His body was stiff. Unrelenting.

And very, very difficult to buckle into a car seat.

"We'll see them tomorrow," Colt consoled, wondering how a tiny body could exert so much force straightening itself out when Colt needed him to bend a little. Micah's body was like a plank. "But right now we're going back to the house to make sure Sierra is okay."

Dark eyes turned toward him. There was a momentary loss of focus on straining away from the car seat straps.

"You want to see Sierra?" Colt asked, wondering if the boy could possibly recognize her name. But then, hadn't Micah just shown some baby genius tendencies a minute ago? "I wouldn't blame you, you know. I need to see her, too."

Seeming to sigh with resignation, Micah relaxed into the soft cotton fabric of the car seat. Colt channeled his old calf-roping skills to weave the straps into their proper places, snapping, tucking and buckling in record time. He wasn't taking any chances that his son was going to repeat the planking routine.

Moments later, Colt was on the road back to the Fenwick house. He wouldn't take the pickup over the old dirt road that was a shortcut for two reasons. The ride would be less bumpy for Micah on pavement. Plus, Colt wasn't about to creep up on Sierra when he'd promised her some space.

He would return to the house, feed Micah and then think about what he could do to give Sierra a break.

He could cook dinner tonight of course. So far she'd joined him for evening meals.

Lately they'd used those dinners as a way to discuss Micah. Colt had been absorbing all she knew about babies, including all she knew about Micah. Over the last few days he'd been able to hear the full story of the hunt for first Micah's mother and then—when they'd discovered Arielle's death and Eve Martin's heart condition that had briefly incapacitated her—the search for him.

But Colt was caught up now. He'd made peace with his feelings about Arielle, because even if he'd been upset that she hadn't contacted him initially about their child, he couldn't be more grateful for the amazing kid she'd brought into the world. He had a better sense of how to care for his son than he had earlier in the week. Tonight, he was turning his attention to Sierra and whatever was troubling her today. Maybe he could help her find a way to relax. He had an idea for something she might like, too.

Because even though he had no intention of acting on the attraction between them, he realized that he absolutely didn't want to see her upset. He'd been serious about owing her more than he could ever repay. She'd made the connection between him and Micah that no one else had caught. If not for her, he wouldn't have known he had a son in the world.

His gaze went to the rearview mirror. Micah's dark eyes were already half-closed, his round cheeks pink from the outdoor air. A wave of tenderness rolled over him along with that ever-present guilt that he hadn't known about the boy just one week ago.

So yes, he'd do anything in his power to make things right for Sierra again.

Six

"I can't believe I'm going fishing," Sierra mused aloud as she stared out of Colt's pickup truck window toward the Brazos River meandering lazily in front of them.

Just two hours had passed since she'd had to leave the calving barn after a fit of emotions had overcome her. Colt would never guess how his comment about mothering in cows had tweaked Sierra's frustrated maternal feelings. She certainly didn't blame him for upsetting her. She'd just needed some space after an exhausting week of working on her book while Micah slept.

By the time she'd returned to the farmhouse, she'd felt a little steadier. Ready to continue with her baby caretaking duties. But Colt had surprised her with an impromptu fishing outing and picnic instead, having already arranged for Eve Martin and Rafael Wentworth to babysit Micah for a few hours since he was familiar with them.

"I know you mentioned needing some time to yourself," Colt explained as he switched off the truck and withdrew the keys. He turned toward her from his spot in the driver's seat. "But it occurred to me that fishing is the perfect way to have a mental and emotional retreat even when you're with other people. It's one of the reasons I renew my fishing license every year. I enjoy the quiet."

She tore her gaze from the winding strip of blue that babbled quietly between hills. "I'm game. Even if your idea of quiet and mine are probably worlds apart."

"Afraid I'll make too much noise?" he asked as he opened the driver's side door.

She couldn't help but laugh. Especially as she considered that had been the whole reason he'd said it. He'd wanted to make her smile. And as the more vocal of the two of them, Sierra didn't mind being called out about her voice.

"Maybe. But I'm sure you'll try your best to keep it down." Still grinning, she followed him out of the vehicle and around to the cargo bed, where Colt was already lifting a picnic basket and blanket from the back. "How can I help?"

Colt picked up a tackle box and carried the silver container in his free hand. "No need. Why don't you pick a spot for us to spread out the blanket?"

Frowning, she searched the truck bed with her gaze. "I can at least carry the fishing poles."

She gripped them in one hand before raising the rods free of the lift gate.

"How about here?" Colt called, setting down the hamper and denting the tall grass as he gestured toward a spot under a river birch.

She breathed in the fresh air and clean scent of spring, the leaves newly green in the trees all around them. The banks were softly rolling, not high, but not flat either. It was a pretty piece of countryside, well off the county route. There were no other cars around, or houses for that matter, although down below them, she could see two kayakers paddling silently downriver.

"Is this spot close enough to the water?" She set down the poles against the birch's narrow trunk, shading her eyes from the late day sun reflecting off the water. "I don't have any experience casting from a bank. I've only been fishing one other time, and that was from a canoe."

She couldn't help watching him spread out the faded blue quilt, the muscles in his broad back shifting with his movements beneath the close-fitting black Henley shirt. He'd showered after his work in the barns, and his hair had still been damp when they'd started their drive to the Brazos River. Now the dark strands lifted in the breeze off the water, making her wonder what it would feel like to comb her fingers through them.

"We'll be fine. I've got full spools and light lines on the rods, so a nice long cast won't be a problem." He waved her closer. "Come and have a seat."

For a moment, she hesitated. Everything about Colt Black and this afternoon trip enticed her. Hadn't she wanted to avoid one-on-one time with him just because she found him so appealing? Yet she'd accepted the invitation, seizing on the chance to forget the unexpected hurt she'd grappled with back at the calving shed. She'd been glad for the chance to redirect her thoughts and escape the muddle of her emotions.

Even if it meant throwing herself into a picnic that felt sort of like a date. She ambled closer to the quilt and dropped down to sit on one side.

"Your answer makes me think you must know a few things about fishing," she observed, tipping her head back to enjoy the feel of the spring sunshine on her face while he carried the fishing poles over to the blanket. "Is there anything you can't do? Cooking, winemaking, ranching, fishing—"

"Whoa. To say I've got more than casual cooking skills is an affront to any seasoned homemaker." He lowered himself to sit beside her, dragging the tackle box to rest between them. "And as for winemaking, I employ people who know what they're doing while I try to educate myself."

Head bent to the task of choosing lures, Colt seemed lighter out here. As if he were genuinely enjoying himself in a way that she hadn't observed before today. Prior to this afternoon, she'd had the impression he'd been avoiding her whenever she was alone. He was always ready, eager even, to help with Micah. Or to talk over issues related to his son. But Colt had never lingered in her presence when the baby wasn't with them.

Until now. Was there any chance he was enjoying Royal more? Any chance he would consider staying in town instead of taking Micah halfway around the world to live in a French winery? It was in her best interests to ensure Colt remembered the things he enjoyed best about his birthplace. All the more reason to stay right here, where he seemed at home.

"If you learn winemaking as quickly as you've taken

to baby care, then I'm sure you're doing well." She traced the shape of the rod and reel, observing for herself the full spool while the sound of a backfiring truck engine sounded from the county route in the distance.

Colt lifted his head from his task, his blue eyes lasering in on hers. "Thank you, Sierra. That means a lot to me. Well, *Micah* means everything to me," he amended. "So it only follows that I'd want to figure out how to be the best possible parent. I appreciate you helping me."

His honesty appealed to her as much as his love for his son. Colt Black hid a tender heart for his child underneath his very serious and driven exterior.

"I'm glad I could do this," she admitted, hoping this time together would help her convince him to remain in Royal. She couldn't imagine parting with Micah. "It worked out well that I took a break from the magazine to write a book. I wouldn't have been able to stay otherwise."

"Your commitment to Micah is obvious." He returned to his work, tying the end of one line around the lure he'd chosen before passing her the rod. "Do you feel comfortable casting on your own?"

"I'd need instructions." She peered over at him. "I wouldn't want to impale anyone on a fishhook."

"Of course." He shifted closer to her on the quilt, putting them almost shoulder to shoulder. "Take your pole, and I'll demonstrate on mine first."

Lifting the smaller pole, she followed his motions as he let out a few feet of line. The lure—a skinny fake fish of some kind—dragged against her ankle where her three-quarter-length jeans didn't cover the skin above her tennis shoes.

"Now what?" she asked, checking the length of his line compared to hers.

"Then press here, like you're holding a trigger. That's going to allow the line to unspool when you cast." He demonstrated this, too.

And although her attention should have been on his hands, her focus snagged on his lightly bristled jaw, and the strong column of his throat that disappeared into the collar of his shirt.

"Okay," she nodded absently, thinking she could watch him all day. "I'm ready."

Maybe something in her tone gave away her careful perusal of him, because he glanced over at her again, his blue eyes darkening as they met hers.

Sparks leaped. Her breath caught.

Yet Colt returned his attention the river below the bank.

"Now, we're ready to let it fly." Rising to his feet, he swung the fishing rod back over one shoulder before flinging it effortlessly toward the current. The line spun out, a shiny white filament that caught the sunlight for a moment before the lure splashed down into the middle of the water.

"Nice job," she murmured as she stood.

She didn't allow her gaze to return to the man beside her. Taking a deep breath, she cocked back the rod, remembering the way he'd flicked it forward to cast. For a moment, she watched the way the line unspooled, free and unfettered. The same as she'd been these last years since finding out her condition wouldn't allow her to have children.

But was she really free when her sadness about that weighted her down? When the hurt returned to twist her gut like it had earlier today at the barn when Colt mentioned what made for a good mother?

Colt whistled low and long. "Like a pro."

It took her a moment to realize he'd been admiring the cast while she'd been grappling with her demons. Demons that had started to make her feel more alone— lonely—than free.

After planting his fishing rod into the soft earth in front of the blanket so he didn't have to hold it, Colt took hers and repeated the action with the second pole. All the while, her eyes followed him hungrily.

Did he sense her stare? Her preoccupation with him? At least a dozen times a day she thought about him telling her that he was attracted to her. Wondered what might happen between them if they weren't trying to avoid the complications of acting on it.

Being with him reminded her of the months— years—she'd gone without a man's touch. A man's kiss. Funny that she had scarcely missed that intimacy until Colt strode into her life.

"Now we wait," he announced, settling back onto the quilt while she sat beside him. Not quite as close as before, but still near enough to make her aware of his warmth.

His strength.

Especially when he propped himself on one elbow, his whole body reclining as he tipped his face to the sun.

He propped an eyelid open after a moment, catching her staring at him. "Are you going to tell me what's on your mind, Sierra?"

His low voice rumbled through her. She felt it like a chord reverberating through her belly, humming long afterward. She didn't want to talk about what was bothering her. So she made herself more comfortable on the quilt, imitating his posture and propping herself on one elbow. Facing him.

"Right now?" She lowered her eyes to admire the shape of his mouth, appealingly close to hers. "Only one thing."

She felt his sharp intake of breath along her lips. A phantom kiss she longed to capture. Taste.

But instead of his mouth, she felt his knuckle under her chin, tipping her face so she had to meet his gaze. The heat simmering in those blue depths made her heartbeat quicken.

"Tell me." The words, though softly spoken, were a demand.

Would anything less have coaxed the truth from her?

She scavenged up her courage.

"I need you to kiss me, Colt. Right now. For as long as possible."

He didn't think twice.

Hell, he didn't even think one time.

Colt heard what she wanted—no, *needed*—and drew her closer to provide it. Releasing her chin, he slid his hand around to the small of her back and tucked her against him.

She stared at him with wide green eyes right up until the moment he grazed her lower lip with his. Then he watched her long lashes flutter and fall closed, her hand lifting to rest lightly on his chest.

She must have felt his heart thundering like a herd released to a fresh pasture. Must have known the effect she was having on him. He'd tried his best to lock it down. But today he'd seen a different side of her. A vulnerable one. Between that and her admission of the same attraction that had been eating at him night and day ever since they'd met, Colt couldn't possibly deny what they both craved.

Especially with her mouth so soft, so giving against his. He wanted to take his time. Feast on her. But her whole body responded to the kiss, a shiver tripping up her spine that he could feel where he touched her. Her hips rocked toward him, and he was pretty sure he saw fireworks behind his eyelids.

The need to roll her to her back, to cover her and feel every inch of her against him, was a new fire in his blood. It flared hot and greedy, which made it all the more imperative that he took no more than the kiss.

But damn, he would have his way with her sweet, sexy mouth.

Slanting his lips over hers, he licked his way inside. She tasted better than any world-class vintage he'd ever rolled around his palate. Sierra was more nuanced. Complex. One moment, her head tipped against the quilt to give him full access, submitting to the play of his tongue over hers. And the next, she raked her fingers through his hair to anchor herself to him, demanding more, answering each lick with one of her own.

He broke apart to give them air. To allow a cooling breath to tame the heat rising between them.

"Sierra." He growled her name against her damp mouth, unable to move any farther away from her than a fraction of an inch. "I'm doing my damnedest to keep this just a kiss."

Her breath huffed warm against his cheek. They

were so close that her breasts pressed his chest with every inhale. The need to wrap his arms around her and seal their bodies together had his hands twitching. The rest of him aching.

"And you're doing an excellent job of it." She curved her palm around his jaw, her fingers stroking along his cheekbone, her thumb sliding over his lower lip. "I can't remember the last time I had a kiss this good."

Her green eyes were passion-dazed, her focus returning to his mouth. Logically, he guessed she was hiding from something that upset her by acting on this attraction now. But he saw the appeal. How much would he rather lose himself in a kiss than face his real problems?

His unworthiness to be a father, for example, since he hadn't been around for Micah for the first six months of his son's life?

"Uh-oh." Sierra went still beneath him. "What's wrong?"

He closed his eyes for a moment, regretting that he'd allowed the thoughts to show on his face.

"I'm sorry." He eased away, putting space between them even though he would have preferred to dive back into the heat and connection between them. "Sometimes the realization of what I've done—putting a continent between me and my son during half of one of the most formative years of his life—"

He broke off, unable to complete the thought. Sitting up, he stared out at the Brazos River and the two motionless fishing poles standing sentinel on either side of their quilt.

"You're off to an amazing start at being a good dad, Colt." Sierra's voice beside him made him aware she'd straightened, too. She stared out at the water with him, her arms looping around knees drawn up to her chin. "You know how I know?"

Her blond hair blew onto his shoulder in the light breeze, a barely there touch.

Still, he couldn't answer. Wasn't sure he could grapple with this now when the anger at himself kept him awake at night. What if Sierra hadn't found him?

"I was abandoned as a child," she said finally, continuing even though he hadn't spoken.

Her words stunned him. His head whipped around to gauge her expression. Her face was set in unfamiliar lines, an old pain scrawled in her features somehow.

"I'm sorry—" he began, but she waved off the words with a shake of her head.

"It was a long time ago. But my story isn't all that different from Micah's. Except instead of showing up on the trunk of a car, I was found on a church doorstep in Houston's Third Ward when I was three weeks old." She turned to face him, tilting her temple onto her knee as she spoke. "I didn't tell anyone in Royal about that. But that's why I got so involved in Micah's life."

Her vigilance. Her relentless pursuit of the truth. Her quests to connect parents to children that— according to Cammie Wentworth—had been more effective than efforts by the police—made all the more sense.

"No wonder you bonded with my son." Then a pang ripped through his chest. "Although I can't stand the idea that Micah will tell that same story one day. That he was found abandoned and alone."

She lifted her head again, giving it an emphatic shake as it to refute his point though.

"He won't. And that's my whole point in telling you

my story now. I never had a reunion with my parents.
They never claimed me. And believe me, I searched for
them as hard as I searched for you." Her jaw tensed,
lips pursing. But then she seemed to huff out the tension, her shoulders easing a fraction and her voice soft-
ening as she continued. "The difference is they truly
did abandon me. Whereas you came as soon as you
knew there was even a chance that you had a child.
And *no one* can fault you for that."

He wouldn't have dared to argue with her. Not with
that fierceness in her tone, or that flashing of challenge in her eyes. He released a long breath of his own,
feeling some of the anger at himself fade. Not all. But
some.

"Thank you for that." He smoothed a wrinkle in the
quilt between them, wishing it were as easy to smooth
away the obstacles between them. To return to the sim-
plicity of kissing on a warm spring day. "I know you
only shared the story for my sake, but I can't help wondering how things went for you after you were found
as an infant. Were you adopted?"

"I was. It happened within a few weeks, too, and
my adoptive parents are kick-ass. They were older, and
I was their only child, so they made me the center of
their world." A smile pulled her lips up. "They still do."

"I'm glad." He wanted to stroke a hand over her
hair, smooth the strands and pull her against him at
the same time. But he knew that falling back into the
kiss was a bad idea.

Not only because he wasn't ready for any relationship. Also because she'd never told him what had upset
her earlier, back at the calving barn. Would she share
it with him now?

She remained quiet beside him, so he ventured, "Can I ask you one more thing?"

Her left eyebrow raised in question as she turned to look at him again. "I thought I was the reporter? Are you going to repay me in kind and let me ask you questions afterward?"

He refused to be deterred, however. Not when it seemed important.

"What happened at the calving shed earlier today? I keep going over it, and I'm still not sure what went wrong."

Her gaze shuttered. Expression closed off.

He knew right away that she wasn't going to answer him.

Lifting her chin, she turned toward the water again. Only to grip his knee a moment later.

"Colt!" She pointed at her fishing pole, eyes wide. "I think I got a bite."

Seven

A week after her fishing trip with Colt, Sierra continued to replay the kiss they'd shared. Even now as she sat working alone in the living room of the renovated Fenwick house—long after she'd tucked Micah in bed for the night—she couldn't concentrate on her notes regarding Violetta Ford for thinking about Colt.

How he'd tasted. How he'd touched her. How kind he'd been to plan an outing for her when she'd been feeling overwhelmed.

Tipping her head back into the leather couch cushion, she sat in front of a fire she'd started after Micah had gone to bed. A rainstorm had brought cooler temperatures for the past two days, and Sierra welcomed the warmth of the blaze as she closed her eyes to relive the kiss once more. At least, she hoped it was just once more, since she recognized that she had to stop thinking about her temporary employer that way.

She'd successfully avoided romantic relationships for four years to keep her fertility woes on lockdown, unwilling to weigh someone else down with a disappointment that was all her own. Yes, she could adopt. And maybe one day she would. But for now, she was all about her work.

Or she had been, until one kiss from Colt got her thinking about the joys of being with a man. And wow, she'd forgotten how good it could be to be wrapped in someone's arms and kissed like there was no tomorrow. Then again, maybe she hadn't missed a man's kiss all that much because no one had ever made her feel quite as delicious as Colt had last week.

Behind her, the front door to the house opened, startling her eyes open as the sound of a sharp gust whistled through the foyer.

She had a clear view of the entryway, where the man she'd been thinking about stepped onto the welcome mat, his black Stetson and oilskin duster still sluicing rain onto the floor. Her insides clutched at the sight of him, his wide shoulders angling away from her as he slid off the wet coat and hung it on a hook above a waterproof floor mat. His hat went on another hook before he toed off his boots.

With his hat gone, she could see his profile more clearly. The strong jaw. The slash of brows and prominent cheekbones. The lips that had molded so tenderly to her own.

"You must be glad to be out of the rain," she observed softly, suspecting he hadn't noticed her yet.

His head whipped around, taking her in. Expression turning troubled?

Something in his face made her wonder if he'd been avoiding her again. But then, she understood the impulse well enough. It was easier not to act on an attraction if they were never alone together.

"I'm sorry. I didn't see you there," he explained, swiping his forearm across his face, no doubt to dry off the lingering damp. His gray work shirt and jeans appeared dry, however. "How did things go with Micah today?"

She wrenched her gaze up from where his jeans hugged strong thighs. Colt still participated in as much of Micah's care as he could, but Sierra knew he had work to attend as well. Continuing renovations around the Fenwick ranch kept him busy some of the time, but he also had regular online meetings with his staff at the winery and duties on Black Ranch. She suspected the latter had kept him out in the rain this afternoon instead of putting Micah to bed with her.

"He was a little less fussy today. I called the pediatrician about all the drooling, and she thinks he's just teething again." She set her laptop computer on the low cocktail table so she could turn more fully toward Colt. "I put a couple of teething rings in the fridge, and he really liked gnawing on them."

She'd felt so relieved when he gummed the cold toy, his frustrated cries ceasing for what seemed like the first time in hours.

"Thank you for doing that." Colt strode deeper into the room, his steps silent in sock-clad feet. "And I appreciate you starting a fire. It's a miserable night out there."

He took a seat on the opposite end of the couch from her, the leather creaking as he stretched his feet toward the hearth. She cleared away the notebook and pen from the cushion between them, stacking them on her laptop. It wasn't until she tucked her legs under her and faced him that she realized how domestic the moment felt, sharing the couch at the end of a long workday.

Or maybe it was the way she couldn't keep her eyes off him that kindled the sense of them as a couple. Butterflies fluttered in her stomach.

"I thought you would have been back long ago. Especially because of the rain." She picked at a loose thread at the cuff of a favorite white fisherman's sweater. She hadn't brought many warm clothes to Royal, but today she'd been glad for this.

"I was sorry to miss putting Micah to bed, but we discovered a problem with the irrigation system when we couldn't shut it off." He shook his head, his expression dejected. "One of the hay fields flooded, but at least we found the problem."

"No wonder you're glad for the fire." She shivered just thinking about standing in muddy fields in the downpour. "And bedtime went well. I think Micah was tired out from the teething, and he settled down pretty quickly."

"If it wore him out, I bet it was draining for you, too," he observed, then nodded toward her notes. "I'm surprised you had enough energy to work on your book afterward. I apologize if I've asked too much of you."

The butterflies that had been flitting inside her slowed down. She'd been dreading talking about her project, aware that Colt still viewed her work with skepticism. She wanted to search the Fenwick house and grounds for Violetta's old diary that the woman's ranch hand, Emmalou Hilliard, had assured her was hidden there. She hadn't told Colt that she had checked over some of the outbuildings when she took Micah out for walks in the stroller.

Her gaze darted to the notebook, but she hadn't made any notations about the diary there. Beside her papers, the nursery monitor sat, switched on but silent.

"Sometimes I get a second wind when I start working," she said carefully, uncertain how much to share. Even more unsure how to tell him that she hoped the Fenwick property would yield the final key to Violetta's story. "And I've really enjoyed finding out as much as I can about Violetta's life. I can't imagine how much courage it took for her to deceive the world as a man just so she could claim a spot in the Texas Cattleman's Club."

The formerly men-only club had refused membership to Violetta, even though she'd run a successful ranch single-handedly in Royal. So Violetta "sold" the ranch to Vincent Fenwick and then disappeared. Vincent was admitted to the TCC almost immediately after moving into the place, a fact that must have made Violetta feel both proud and yet frustrated that she couldn't have achieved the feat on her own merits.

"I didn't know anything about the story when I met with Arielle," Colt mused, surprising her with the direction of his thoughts.

"In all of the drama that came with your arrival in Royal, I almost forgot that's how the two of you met." She propped an elbow on the low back of the leather sofa, warming to the subject. "No one would have unearthed Violetta's story without Arielle's help. Her notes directed Tate Wentworth to letters about Violetta and Dean Wentworth, and how their secret affair led to Harmon Wentworth's birth."

Harmon had seemed relieved to finally know the story of his birth mother. Sierra's role had been small enough, but she had helped drive things forward with her determination to unearth the secret by talking to everyone in town. She felt pleased that she'd been able to provide closure on the mystery that Arielle's diary had first revealed. For Sierra, it felt like a debt paid, considering how much joy she had in being a part of Micah's life.

"Arielle would have liked you." Colt stared into the flames still burning high and bright. "She was passionate about small-town tales, and although she was looking into a career as a photojournalist, it wasn't just the photos that captivated her. She liked the stories behind them."

For a moment, Sierra's gut cinched with a pang of jealousy for Arielle and what she'd shared with Colt. But she forced away the feeling immediately, angry at herself for coveting anything from a woman who'd died far too soon. Sierra knew Arielle would have traded anything for the chance to see her son grow up.

"I'm going to dedicate my book on Violetta and the TCC to Arielle," she confided, glad she would have some public way to acknowledge the contributions of the other woman.

Colt turned to her, the warmth of his blue gaze sending a shower of sparks through her as he extended his arm across the back of the couch, close to hers. "That's a great idea. And it's a coincidence that you mentioned this, because I was thinking when I finish the renovations on the Fenwick barns, I might ask Carson Wentworth if he'd like to name the stables in honor of Violetta and Dean."

She clapped a hand over Colt's wrist in her enthusiasm.

"You should," she insisted, knowing Carson would be gratified by the gesture, as would Carson's one-hundred-year-old great-grandfather, Harmon. "What a nice way to remember them."

As soon as she touched him, the companionable mood shifted subtly. Heat zinged up her fingers and into her arm. She made a move to draw back, but Colt flipped his wrist over so that he could capture her palm in his.

Surprised at the contact, she glanced down to where their hands joined, her heart racing. Butterflies returned in full force. A butterfly army.

"Sierra." Her name was a gravelly plea, the deep tone of his voice making her breath catch. "I've tried to give you space since…the day we went fishing."

She swallowed hard, not sure she was ready to talk about that kiss. Or why she hadn't been willing to answer his question regarding what had upset her the day she'd visited the calving shed with Micah.

"Thank you," she murmured, even though she wasn't certain she wanted space from him when memories of Colt's mouth on hers set fire to her every time she recalled it.

Even now, her pulse throbbed beneath the place where his hand rested, his long fingers lightly circling her wrist.

"But I'd be lying if I said I didn't enjoy that time with you." He paused the gentle circling to stroke one fingertip down the center of her forearm. "Not only the kiss, although that was a definite highlight. I liked just being with you."

She shivered from that simple touch, a wave of longing crashing through her while the wind and rain howled outside. Being with Colt made her feel...so many things. Too many things.

It was easiest to concentrate on the physical part since that kind of attraction was the simplest to walk away from afterward. Wasn't it? She feared she'd been so far out of the dating loop that she had no idea how to navigate romantic emotions anymore. Nothing about her attraction to Colt felt simple.

"I enjoyed it, too," she confessed, since he must feel her response to him anyhow. "But I remember that first night you asked me to be Micah's temporary nanny, you mentioned—"

"I recall," he interrupted, his tone grim as he withdrew his hand from where it held hers. "I assured you I wouldn't be acting on the attraction I felt for you. I shouldn't have—"

She retrieved his hand, squeezing.

"But you didn't," she rushed to remind him, unwilling for him to shoulder any burden for the turn things had taken on the bank of the Brazos River.

He went still at her touch, listening even though the corners of his mouth turned down.

"*I* asked *you* for the kiss, so if anyone is to blame, it's me," she explained, remembering all too well how they'd ended up in a lip-lock that day. "Only afterward did I let myself think about how you'd drawn that line between us from the start and I hate to think I blurred the boundaries by acting on the...er..." She gestured back and forth between them. "Chemistry."

His expression softened. He leaned closer, bringing the scent of rain and pine trees with him as his voice lowered. "You didn't hear me complaining. I wanted you then. I want you now."

Her heart leaped into her throat. Stayed there. Why did Colt have this potent effect on her? She didn't know what to say, could only stare back at him in a kind of rapt fascination.

"Talk to me, Sierra. What do you want to happen between us?" He slid his free hand around her neck, fingers sifting through the hair while his thumb stroked her cheek.

Could she claim a night for herself with him? The idea had smoked around the edges of her thoughts for days, tempting her. Teasing her.

"I don't want to risk my chance to spend time with Micah," she found herself saying, before she'd even realized that had been a concern from deep within.

"I would never do that to him. Or you." The sincerity in his voice rang true. "You've been a constant in his life."

She wanted to remind him that if Micah stayed in the U.S., he'd have more constants, but she didn't think it was the right time to drag out that argument. For now, she appreciated hearing that Colt saw her that way. That he respected the bond she'd developed to his son.

"Thank you. He means a lot to me." Leaning into Colt's touch, she allowed herself the pleasure of his strong hands on her. Her pulse quickened, heat stirring inside her.

Was she really considering this?

"So we agree you are an important person to Micah." Colt's thumb lowered from her cheek toward her mouth. Gently, he grazed the pad over her lips. "But you still haven't answered my question."

Sierra might have scooted closer to him on the couch. The space between their bodies seemed to shrink, the air in the room thick with longing. Colt was a good man. She trusted him with her body. And more than that? He didn't want a relationship any more than she did. His time with Arielle had left him reeling.

Surely they could enjoy each other this once without worrying about what tomorrow would bring.

"Remind me." Her voice sounded like someone else's. Scratchy with need. "What was the question again?"

All she could think about was closing the rest of the distance between them. Seeing if Colt's kiss felt as good as she remembered.

He tipped his forehead to hers. Their breath mingled. Chests heaving like they'd been running.

"What do you want to happen next, Sierra? It's one hundred percent your call."

Colt didn't trust himself to make the right decision. Not when he needed her this badly. Not when he'd thought about her night and day ever since that kiss had knocked him for a loop a week ago.

Better to let her direct what happened next.

Or maybe he just hoped for a replay of that time at the river when she'd ordered him to kiss her for as long as possible. He would enjoy a command like that. Hell, he craved it. Because telling himself she was off-limits hadn't worked. Reminding himself he'd screwed up in the worst imaginable way with Arielle hadn't been enough to squelch the desire for Sierra either, and he'd tried his damnedest to keep that failing in mind.

Still, he wanted her.

But until he knew that Sierra returned the feeling, he took pleasure from his fingers in the hair tucked behind her ear, his thumb stretched to trace the plump fullness of her gorgeous lips.

He was more worked up just *talking* to her than he'd been for women he'd taken to his bed. Even now, he dragged in deep breaths to catch her scent, the orange blossom fragrance of her skin an aphrodisiac that made him desperate to taste her. She looked so beautiful tonight, her pale hair limned by the firelight, the white cable knit sweater and leggings she wore not doing anything to hide feminine curves.

Finding her in his living room after a hellish day had felt like a reward he didn't deserve. He hoped she wanted him even half as much as he yearned to touch her. All of her.

Before Sierra spoke, she edged back to look him in the eyes, her hands coming to rest on his shoulders.

"I've had a whole week to think about what I want to happen next." Her green gaze never wavered from his as her fingers clenched the fabric of his work shirt. "And now that you've asked, I have a long list."

Heat streaked through him, turning him hard as steel. Sweat popped along his shoulders. His mouth went dry.

"Tell me. Everything." His fingers cupped the base of her neck, massaging lightly.

"I want no space between us." Her words were urgent. "Zero."

Before she finished, he had her in his lap, her legs straddling his thighs. He gripped her hips, pulling her to him where he needed her most. Through the thin cotton of her leggings, he could feel her warmth.

She gasped while he groaned at how good it felt to have her there. Still clutching his shirt, she twisted the fabric a little, grip tightening.

"What else?" he pressed, his fingertips straying under her sweater just enough to feel silky bare skin above the waistband of her tights.

Her head tipped closer as she gazed down at him, her hair falling forward to frame her face.

"I might need my sweater off for the next part—" she began, only to have her words lost in the muffling of cable knit as he dragged it up her body and off.

High, round breasts wrapped in peach-colored lace were the sexiest thing he'd ever seen.

"Please say you want my mouth here." He canted toward her, breathing the words through the lace so he could see the nipples strain against the fabric.

She arched in answer. "Yes. Kiss me there."

Colt took the request seriously, learning the shape of her with his tongue, teasing her through the material until the lace was wet enough not to matter. Then he peeled it away from her to kiss and lick each breast in turn, his hands returning to her hips so he could keep her fitted against him.

The damp heat of her through the leggings was enough to make him lose it if he let himself go, but he had every intention of seeing this list of hers through to the end.

"Now what, Sierra?" he asked once her hips rode

him in an unrelenting rhythm, her fingers now tunneled under his shirt to clutch his bare shoulders.

Her nails lightly scored him with a sting he relished if only to keep him from stripping her naked right here in the middle of the living room.

She paused the rocking to catch her breath, her teeth sinking into her lower lip for a long moment before she spoke again.

"Now take me upstairs and make me forget my own name."

Eight

Colt didn't presume. He didn't press. But once given the green light, he delivered everything Sierra longed for and more.

Already, they were upstairs in the master suite, and she hardly remembered how it had happened with him kissing her the whole way, his hands roaming her body. He'd brought the nursery monitor with him though, the device stowed safely in the back pocket of his jeans.

Heat stole through her middle, a blaze that he stoked higher with every touch, every glide of his tongue over hers. He broke away only to close the door behind them and settle the nursery monitor on the nightstand, while she tried to gain her bearings.

Her gaze darted around the renovated main suite with soothing gray paint except for the one accent wall in reclaimed shiplap behind the quilted headboard of a king-size bed. The dark plank floors and cathedral ceiling kept the focus on the bed, everything else in the room receding compared to that simple focal point with its cream-colored duvet and rows of down pillows. The scents of pine and cedar hung in the air, as if the room were more recently revamped, lit by a single sconce near the entrance to an attached bath.

And then Colt returned, hands wrapping around her waist, lifting her against him so he could resume the drugging kiss. Their bodies meshed, lips molding until she moaned against him, desperate for more.

This time, when he edged back, he didn't release her. He looked into her eyes, his lips brushing hers as he spoke. "I can't believe you're here with me after how many nights I've dreamed of you in this bed."

Pleasure curled through her like a teasing caress.

"We must be having the same dreams." She remembered vividly how many times she'd awoken with an ache that had Colt's name all over it. "Because I've been one room over thinking the same thing."

She reached between them, fidgeting with one of his shirt buttons in an effort to free it. A job he took over with smooth efficiency.

"How am I doing on that list of yours?" He made quick work of the buttons, momentarily robbing her of speech as he revealed his chest.

Oh. Wow.

Muscles rippled in his shoulders and arms. Ridges created shadows in his abs. Sierra didn't think she could ever look her fill, his body calling to her fingertips to touch and stroke. Trace and lick.

"I'm ready for you to go off script." Light-headed at the promise of what awaited her, she reached for his shoulders to steady herself. "It's been so long for me, I'm not sure I remember what to ask for next."

Even in the dim light of the room, she could see his eyes go a shade darker, the pupils widening.

"Then you can trust I'm going to do everything in my power to give you what you need." His hands skimmed under her sweater to band around her waist, the warmth of his fingers sending a jolt of desire to places that hadn't known a man's touch in years.

She raked her palms down his bare chest, wanting to feel more of him.

"I do trust you," she whispered, surprised to realize how true it was. And it was a trust that extended beyond the bedroom.

She recognized his sense of honor. His need to follow a moral code.

Perhaps he heard the feeling in her voice, the emotion she hadn't intended to show, because his gaze locked with hers for a long moment. But she wasn't ready to examine the emotions stirring inside her. The heat was safer. She lifted higher on her toes to kiss him again, letting her fingers drag lower on his abs until they reached his jeans.

His skin was hot beneath the clothes, her knuckles grazing along the flexing play of muscle. She unfastened the top button and slowly lowered the zipper, careful of the erection straining the denim.

"Sierra." He growled the word in her ear, his hand clamping over hers. Stilling her.

"Mmm?" She swayed against him, hips pressing nearer, pinning their hands between them.

"It's been quite a while for me, too. So this first time might be more of a wild ride."

"First time? I like knowing there will be more than one." She kissed her way along his bristled jaw while she shoved his unbuttoned shirt off his shoulders. "We can call this a practice round."

"I think it's going to feel a whole lot better than practice."

His blue gaze dipped to her breasts spilling out of her peach lace bra, the tight points aching even more under his scrutiny. Unable to wait any longer, she reached for the fastening to remove it, but he caught her fingers to take over the task.

"Let me." He nudged one strap off her shoulder before leaning closer to kiss the place he'd bared. "I want to unwrap you."

She could hardly argue with that. Especially with the way his mouth descended to her nipple, raising gooseflesh in his wake and sending ribbons of pleasure through her nerve endings. She was used to being in control. To asserting herself to get what she wanted in life.

But maybe right now, with Colt, she could relinquish that need. Surrender to a pleasure he seemed intent on giving her.

Sighing into his kiss, she let her body go limp, certain he would hold her. A thrill went through her as his arms banded tighter around her, lifting her up before settling her in the middle of the massive bed.

She kept her eyes on him, mesmerized by the way he moved over her, shoulders flexing, arms bracketed to keep his weight off her. Only his lips touched her, returning to her breasts. Then his tongue. Then his teeth, dragging the lacy bra cup lower.

Need for him sizzled through her. She arched her

back, pressing against him. He answered her by hooking a finger in the waistband of her leggings, hauling them down and off her legs, taking her peach lace panties with them.

She hadn't been naked with anyone in so long. For an instant, she felt a pang of self-consciousness, an awareness of her every imperfection. But the way his hot gaze roamed over her soothed away any concern and brought her back to the moment.

Stroking along his shoulders, she wound her fingers into the hair at his neck and whispered, "I'm ready for my wild ride now."

"You said you were going to trust me." He slid a hand between her knees, one palm spanning her thigh as he edged higher.

The touch robbed her of speech, all her focus on the breath-stealing caress while her heart raced. She clenched his shoulders, steadying herself against the onslaught of sensation when he reached the apex of her thighs and slid a finger over the slick heat there.

"Colt, please," she murmured, her eyes clamping shut to concentrate on the way he made her feel. The way he circled and pressed, stroked and teased her sex.

Her legs were already shaking when he kneed them further apart, planting a kiss where she needed him most. His tongue found the tight, hungry center of her and flicked back and forth, calling forth an orgasm that unraveled her.

Wave after wave of sweetness pummeled her, the pleasure so thick she thought she'd drown in it. By the time the contractions slowed, she felt light-headed. Thoroughly sated and yet very ready for more at the same time. She blinked her eyes open, wanting to articulate how good she felt.

But Colt was already rolling a condom into place, knowing what they both needed. She arched up off the bed, wrapping her arms around him and holding him close while his heart thundered against her ear. The sound reminded her that he'd been generous with her pleasure. She longed to return the favor. To make him feel as good as she did.

Wrapping her hand around his rigid length, she stared up into his eyes. "Now it's your turn to trust me."

Colt was hanging by a string.

His every protective, possessive impulse urged him to make Sierra feel good all over again. To ensure she reached that pinnacle of pleasure once more, this time with him inside her.

But with those liquid green eyes fixed on him, and her fingers gliding up and down his shaft in a rhythm that damn near had his eyes crossing, he could deny her nothing.

Not trusting himself to speak, he answered her by rolling her on top of him. She straddled him, her hair falling forward while she stroked him through the condom. He'd never been so glad for an extra layer there since he wasn't sure he could have withstood those silky touches and her fascinated gaze on him otherwise. Not when he hadn't been with another woman since Arielle over a year ago.

He was grateful as hell when she guided him between her legs. He braced himself for the slick heat, but that wasn't enough to prepare him for how good she felt. How right.

A groan tore from his throat, raw and hungry. He lifted his hips, unable to stop himself from sliding deeper. Sierra's soft gasp filled his ears, and he stroked her hips, steadying her. Hell, maybe it was him that needed steadying. She looked so beautiful, her hair tousled and a little wild from his fingers, her cheeks flushed pink, and bee-stung lips swollen from his kiss. The sight of her made him want to wrap her in his arms for days. Keep her in his bed. Pleasure her so thoroughly she never wanted to leave.

Never? His brain whispered the word back at him. Questioning.

He sank his fingers deeper into the soft curve of her ass, needing to shut out the query he wasn't ready for.

When she began to move again, a slow and gentle rocking of her hips, Colt was all too glad to lose himself in her. He liked the way she gave herself up to the moment, her hands pressing into his skin, imprinting herself on him somehow.

She leaned over him, her blond hair tickling against his collarbone as she kissed his cheek toward his ear. "Get ready. I'm taking my wild ride now."

He didn't have time to chuckle over her impatience or the determined way she approached sex. Because a moment later, her hips bounced and rolled, swayed and bucked. Fireworks blasted across the backs of his eyelids, the feel of her too good for praise. Sweat heated along his shoulders, an inferno building inside him as she moved.

At the last second, he remembered that he should touch her, that he wanted to bring her to that sensual peak once more tonight. Reaching between them, he found the swollen nub he sought and plucked it gently, a movement that had her back arching and her lips gasping his name.

Damn, but he liked how that sounded. Liked the way she spasmed against him so quickly, as if his touch overwhelmed her the same way hers did him.

With her feminine muscles squeezing him tightly, Colt didn't stand a chance of lasting another minute. He gave himself over to the exquisite pressure of her body teasing his, and he was lost to the rush of his own release.

His hoarse shout echoed in the room, his arms banding around her to keep her close while he found completion.

Holy. Hell.

The lush feel of her body had him lost for long minutes. When at last the spasms came to an end, he pulled her down to the bed to lie beside him. He stroked her hair. Kissed her temple. Wondered how to recover from something that felt earth-shattering.

He told himself that was just the side effect of incredible sex. But he wasn't sure he bought it, because he couldn't remember ever feeling this way before. Like he wanted a commitment from her to repeat the experience every night for the rest of time.

Had to be the endorphins, right?

Beside him, Sierra blew a blond strand out of her eyes. "If that was practice, I'm not sure I'm ready for the real thing."

A smile tugged at the corner of his lips. He should be grateful to her for keeping things light.

"I'll take that as a personal challenge. Wait until I get some food in me."

Laughing, she shook her head. "That definitely

wasn't meant as a challenge. It might take twenty-four hours for my toes to uncurl."

The warmth that bloomed in his chest felt like more than the effects of a sweet compliment. But damn it, that must be the endorphins, too.

He scrubbed a hand through his hair, wondering how to navigate his next steps without wading any deeper into a relationship that he wasn't ready for. He hadn't thought things through long enough to consider the aftermath of intimacy.

But then the nursery monitor crackled to life. First with the sounds of Micah's restless shifting.

Then with a full-blown, ear-splitting wail.

"I'll get him," Colt assured her, knowing she'd already had a long day with the baby.

Levering himself off the mattress, he found his boxers and dragged them on with a T-shirt before bolting for the nursery to check on his son.

And while he wanted to believe his haste was spurred by being a good father, Colt knew in the back of his mind that his rush wasn't just about running to his son. Without question, he was running from Sierra and the line they'd crossed tonight.

Sierra told herself not to take it personally.

After all, how many new mothers would love to have a partner who sprinted to care for their child at the baby's first cry? Not that she was even the mother of the infant in this case.

And maybe the fact that her brain went there, inserting herself into this household in a maternal capacity, was the only fact she should be concerned with here. Because no matter how much she told herself she was doing a good thing to help Colt bond with Micah—and vice versa—maybe what she was really doing was breaking her own heart. She got more attached to Micah with each passing day. And now she feared she was getting attached to Colt, too.

Sliding out of the big bed in the main suite, she searched for her clothes to make her retreat. She didn't know what was next for her and Colt after what had happened tonight, but the situation required serious thought and reflection. It made no difference that Colt couldn't leave fast enough when he'd heard Micah cry, because she didn't want a romantic relationship with Colt in the first place.

She jammed one foot into her leggings and then the other, remembering how much more fun it had been taking them off. Her whole body was over sensitized after being with Colt, so it was no wonder her emotions were prickly, too. Her face tingled with beard abrasion. Her thighs trembled from using muscles that hadn't been tested in years.

The scent of them lingered in the sheets, tempting her to fall back into the bed. See what would happen when he returned. But those were dangerous thoughts. She couldn't let tonight mean anything more than a momentary pleasure.

After refastening her bra, she retrieved her sweater and slipped it back on. Opening the door that led into the hall, she prepared to return to her own room.

Until Colt's voice sounded over the nursery monitor.

"Hey, big guy. Is it your teeth again? Are they giving you trouble?" The gentleness in his tone made Sierra pause on the threshold.

She glanced over at the monitor still switched on

where it rested on the nightstand, listening to the rustling noises of Colt moving around the nursery to soothe his son.

Micah let out another wail that clutched at her heart, making her wonder if she should go help, or at least offer moral support. After her long day of caring for the boy, she knew how exhausting it could be to cope with teething pain.

"I know, little man," Colt continued, his footsteps sounding as he crossed the floor. "It's no fun. Maybe we should check out that teething ring Sierra left in the refrigerator and see if it helps."

The tender, patient way he spoke to his son through the boy's crying was enough to melt her heart. She forgot that she was eavesdropping on a private moment until she heard the nursery door open just two rooms away. And damn if seeing him there, holding Micah in the dim light of the corridor, the baby's face tracked with tears, didn't override all her best intentions to retreat for the night.

"I can get the teething ring for you," she suggested, keeping her gaze on Colt's face instead of his strong thighs. Mostly. "That way you can keep him in the nursery and maybe rock him a little."

"Are you sure?" Colt strode closer, securing Micah in one arm. "I know you've already put your time in."

She bristled a little at the idea that Micah was only a job to her. He was so much more than that. But maybe she shouldn't think that way if Colt was going to take his son to France one day soon, leaving her alone.

"I'll sleep better knowing Micah isn't hurting," she replied a bit stiffly. "It's no trouble."

With that, she spun on her heel and headed for the

stairs. If Colt said anything else, she didn't hear it in her rush to retrieve the teether. Was she crazy to have taken this job where she was bound to fall for a dark-eyed baby boy that wasn't hers? Even crazier to let herself get close to the child's compelling father?

Yes. And double yes.

In the kitchen, she made quick work of finding the blue silicone toy in the stainless steel refrigerator. Padding across the hardwood floor in her bare feet, she told herself she would simply pass over the ring and go to bed for the night.

Try to put the intimacy behind her and start fresh in the morning. Focus on her search for the diary around Fenwick Ranch.

Yet as she climbed the stairs to the nursery, Sierra found the idea didn't fill her with the same old enthusiasm it had in the past. As much as she wanted to tell Violetta's story, she wondered how the other woman had done it. How had she parted with her own child to be raised by someone else, just so she could continue to live as Vincent Fenwick, forsaking marriage and motherhood to carve out a successful ranch and a life on her own terms?

Maybe if she found Violetta's diary, she would have the answer. She needed the answer. Because as Sierra walked into the nursery to see Colt and Micah settled in the wooden rocking chair, the baby clutching his toes in one hand while his dark eyes gazed up at his daddy, she couldn't imagine walking away from a life like this. Violetta had done it even though her child had her DNA.

Sierra, on the other hand, had no biological tie to

the sweet child in Colt's arms. Yet walking away from Micah would feel like having her heart removed.

To say nothing of Colt.

"Here you go," she said softly, passing over the teething toy and then backing toward the door. "Call me if you have any trouble getting him back to sleep."

He glanced up at her, a flash of something in his blue eyes before he masked it. "I'm sure we'll be fine. And thank you."

Once more, she keenly felt her position as a hired helper.

A temporary nanny, and no more.

Swallowing down a disappointment she had no business feeling, she forced her steps toward the door, not even pausing to wish him a good night. Tomorrow, she'd return to her search for the diary while she watched Micah so that by the time Colt replaced her with a new nanny, Sierra would have the information she needed for her book.

She just wished the task that once excited her professionally didn't feel so damned hollow now.

Nine

The next day, Colt walked a pasture perimeter between the Fenwick place and Black Ranch, looking for a break in the fence. A neighbor had phoned him about a Red Angus cow bearing the Black Ranch brand found wandering around his property, and Colt had sent one of the ranch hands to retrieve the runaway heifer while Colt started the search for a weak spot in the split rail barrier.

The weather was clear and cooler after the intense rains the night before, the fields still damp. Colt appreciated the dose of fresh air after the night with Sierra that had rattled him to the core.

Ducking under a low branch of one of the live oaks that grew along the property line, Colt tugged on a random fence post near a tree root to test its sturdiness.

Still solid. Unlike his personal foundations this morning.

Colt had suspected that he'd said or done the wrong thing when Sierra walked out of the nursery last night, but no matter how many times he reviewed their brief exchanges—both in bed and afterward—he couldn't come up with any idea of what might have offended her. He'd wanted to respond to Micah's cry quickly, knowing she'd had a long day with the baby already. And yet she'd seemed off when she left the nursery.

Too quiet. Hesitant.

Qualities that were completely unlike the Sierra he knew. A far cry from the way she'd been with him in bed. Assertive sometimes and vulnerable others, but he'd never doubted for an instant that she was on board with every single moment they'd shared. Right up until he'd left to check on Micah.

What had happened then? Had the time he'd been gone been enough for her to have cold feet? Morning-after regrets hours ahead of schedule?

Nearing the end of the fence line, Colt paused to lift his Stetson and swipe his hand along his forehead, allowing the cool spring breeze beneath the brim. He approached an old pole barn no longer in use on the Fenwick side of the property line, only to slow his step when he heard Sierra's voice lifted in song coming from the opposite side of the barn.

What was she doing out here on this deserted end of the Fenwick lands?

"...down came the rain and washed the spider out." Her tune made him smile in spite of the mixed messages of the night before. She seemed to take joy in the time spent with his son, and every time Colt witnessed

the two of them together, he was more convinced they
had a special bond.

He envied her ease with the boy, probably because
it reminded him that she'd been with Micah for most
of the baby's life while Colt had been unaware of the
child he'd left behind. The memory of how he'd failed
his son still stung.

Now he paused to listen for a moment before round-
ing the building. Micah burst into baby giggles after the
spider got washed from the rainspout, a sure sign Sierra had done something animated to illustrate the fact.

Then, as she finished her tune, the two of them
laughed softly in unison. And as much as Colt wanted
to simply enjoy the moment, he couldn't help but remember how much he would be disrupting Micah and
Sierra's bond when he took his son with him overseas.

Was it a mistake to consider it? Sierra certainly
thought so.

Walking along the side of the brick pole barn that
must have been built about the same time as the original house, Colt turned the corner to see Sierra seated
on a hay bale facing Micah, who was still strapped in
his stroller. Sierra wore a pair of faded jeans that fit
her like a glove, tucked into scuffed cowboy boots. A
long pink windbreaker covered her top half, a blond
braid resting on one shoulder.

"Good morning," he called as soon as he came into
their view, not wishing to startle either of them. "I hear
there's a spider problem out here?"

Any doubts that he'd harbored about the mood of
their parting last night were only underscored by the
troubled expression he glimpsed before she masked it
with a polite smile.

"My singing voice is the only trouble we're having," she retorted dryly before turning her attention back to his son. She passed the baby a set of brightly colored toy keys that Micah promptly gummed. "Although Micah is too much of a gentleman to comment on it."

"From what I could hear, he thoroughly enjoyed the performance." He couldn't take his eyes off her, his brain filled with memories of the night before.

Her urgent kisses. Her fingertips moving over him, undressing him. Her orange blossom scent.

Maybe she read his thoughts in his eyes, because she jolted up and off the hay bale to stand. She raised the zipper on her jacket, readying herself to leave.

"I should get Micah back to the house," she announced, swiping bits of hay from her jeans and carefully not meeting his gaze.

"Please don't go on my account." He stepped closer, needing to talk to her. Wanting to set things right.

Or, if nothing else, at least get a better read on what had sent her running in the first place. Last night hadn't been the only time she'd shut down on him inexplicably. There'd been the day they went fishing when she'd dodged his questions. He wouldn't be so quick to back down today.

"I'm not," she insisted, moving to stand behind the stroller, already gripping the handle bar. "Micah and I have a long walk back to the house."

For a moment, he wondered what had brought her all the way out here to the old, unused outbuilding, but he shoved aside the thought in an effort to keep her there.

"Sierra, please. We need to talk." He covered her hand with his. Entreating. "I've been going over last night in my mind, and I'm not sure where things went wrong."

A barn swallow swooped out from under the eaves to sit on an oak tree limb, chirping happily with a big group of them.

Sierra stared after them before turning back to him.

"Nothing went wrong." She slid her hand out from under his and tucked it in the pocket of her windbreaker. "I just got caught up in my thoughts afterward, I guess."

Her teeth caught her lower lip, stopping whatever else she might have said. He recognized the gesture, remembering the way she'd shut down their conversation the last time he'd tried to confront her about something that bothered her.

"All the more reason we should talk about what happened." He glanced down at his son to see Micah happily shaking the plastic keys Sierra had given him, his eyelids drooping. Colt leaned closer to adjust the back of the stroller so the baby reclined more. "Micah looks ready to nod off any second, so we have time."

"But there isn't anything to say." She spread her arms wide, voice frustrated. "We knew going into last night that you're not even planning to stay in Royal and you'll be replacing me soon. I'm temporary in every way for you, and I understand that. It's fine."

His stomach burned with acid to think that was what she'd taken away from their night together. A night that had meant something more to him. Perhaps if he'd been a better communicator with Arielle, he would have known about his son sooner. He needed to learn how to press for answers. How to convey concern without pushing people away.

"It's not fine. And I sure as hell never meant to give you the impression that *you* were temporary—only the nanny position, since I know you have other work commitments." He wished he could read her better, but even after their amazing night together, he still couldn't gauge her. "Just because I have business overseas—"

"Business important enough to bring Micah. Indefinitely." She folded her arms, her chin lifting. "Don't minimize it."

"Okay. Just because I have obligations to the winery doesn't mean you're a temporary part of my life. Or Micah's." Although he knew from her expression that sounded hypocritical when he'd told her weeks ago that he didn't want to get involved for that very reason. "Last night took us by surprise. We haven't had time to figure out what it means or what happens next. But we *should*."

She shook her head, blond hair swishing softly against the pink windbreaker. "Last night didn't change anything. I know that, and so do you. I'm not looking for a relationship any more than you are. You're focused on Micah. I need to focus on my book."

He wanted to argue with her, not liking the vision of himself as someone who indulged personal desires in a way that could hurt others. But hadn't he done just that? Not only with Sierra, but with Arielle, too? Except, damn it, no matter how much he screwed things up with this lovely, strong, determined woman, he wouldn't risk the bond she shared with his son.

He paced away from her, trying to pull his thoughts together so he didn't alienate her further.

"First of all, you're not a temporary part of Micah's life if you don't want to be." Turning on his heel, he faced her again in time to see her lower the shade on the stroller to shield more of Micah from the sun.

"You're so good to him. And it's obvious he adores you. I want him to be happy."

She blinked fast, not looking at him. When she spoke, her voice sounded thin. Thready. "Thank you."

Something was obviously wrong. Something he still wasn't understanding. He moved closer to her as she bent to gently pry the toy keys out of Micah's hand now that the boy had fallen asleep.

"What is it?" He laid a hand on her shoulder, only to discover she was shaking. "What's the matter?"

"I'm sorry," she sniffed through unshed tears, exhaling a long, unsteady breath. "You know I've gotten attached to Micah, and it's been so fun to be with him." She closed her eyes for a moment before turning toward him. Meeting his gaze. "But occasionally it stirs a personal regret for me since I can't have children of my own."

Sierra had never shared that with another soul.

Not even her adopted mother knew the secret pain she carried, the reason she hadn't dated in years. Sierra had always thought it better to lock down her condition and not speak about it, refusing to be damaged goods in anyone's eyes.

Yet no matter how carefully she guarded her prognosis, protecting herself from anyone else's unwanted opinions or sympathy, she couldn't change the fact that she *felt* damaged.

Logically, she knew that was ridiculously unfair to herself. She would never view someone else as lacking because of a medical condition. The very idea was abhorrent to her. And yet, deep inside, logic didn't apply to her sense of self, where she still felt the lack of normal biological function like a giant void. The loss of her dreams for a husband and family one day.

She thought all of that in the moment after her confession. In that smallest slice of time where Colt processed her words.

To his credit, she saw only concern and empathy in his blue eyes in the moment before he wrapped her in his arms.

"Honey, I'm so damned sorry." He spoke the words against her hair while he hugged her tight, his hands rubbing over her back in a way that really did comfort her.

A soft sob bubbled free, but it was more a cry of relief to have shared the burden. She hadn't realized how much weight she'd given it by keeping it locked inside for so long.

"Thank you." She burrowed deeper into his shoulder, grateful for his warmth. His strength. His compassion that didn't feel like pity. "I'm not normally such a mess about it. I thought I'd made peace with it—"

She cut herself off, knowing how far from the truth that was. She'd done some counseling that her doctor had recommended after her diagnosis, but the therapist had warned her the emotional toll of infertility could return in a myriad of ways throughout her life. Just because she'd found a way to cope these last few years didn't mean the ache was gone.

He kissed the top of her head, still stroking his hands along her back. "Thank you for telling me. For trusting me with that."

She closed her eyes for a long moment, still soaking up the feel of him. The scent of pine and sandalwood closed around her, the canvas of his jacket enveloping her along with his arms. But then, remembering that she was trying to resurrect boundaries after their night together, she forced herself to straighten.

"I appreciate you listening without judgment." She swiped her hand across her eyes before tipping her head back to look up into the tree full of tiny chirping birds. "Half the reason I've never told anyone about the infertility is a fear that someone will try and cheer me up about it with a platitude or offer advice."

She'd heard stories like that in one of the counseling group sessions. Exhausted women on their third round of IVF would confide that "well-meaning" friends told them it would help if they "relaxed more" during sex. Sierra knew herself well enough to know she ran the risk of decking someone who made a comment like that to her, so in the interest of all parties, she'd never shared the truth.

"You've never told anyone?" Colt repeated her words back to her, making her aware she'd unwittingly revealed even more than she'd planned.

Making her aware how much she'd come to trust him in spite of herself. How much she genuinely liked him as a person, above and beyond the physical attraction. Dragging in a deep breath, she turned to face him again.

His Stetson cast his face half in shadow, but she felt the intensity of that blue gaze just the same.

"It's very personal," she explained, not wanting to dwell on the whys and wherefores when she'd already shared too much. "I've never had cause to tell anyone else—outside of a counseling group. But I thought it only fair that you know since I occasionally wrestle with the emotional aspects of infertility. Like when I play with Micah or—like last week—when I hear you talk about what makes a good mother. Even when the mother in question is a cow."

She managed a wry smile at the admission, recognizing how sensitive it sounded.

Colt didn't smile though. He shook his head, blowing out a frustrated breath as he scraped a hand along his jaw. "I wish I'd known. I don't remember what I said, but I have no business passing judgment on what makes for a good parent. I do know you've been here for Micah when I haven't been, and that makes you far better equipped than me to be a caregiver."

His heartfelt words slid right past the barriers she'd tried to resurrect this morning. A tenderness welled inside her for his kindness. His recognition that she had good maternal instincts even though the baby she'd cared for wasn't her own.

Perhaps that shouldn't mean so much to her. Yet considering he was Micah's father, the man she'd searched for relentlessly for months, she hugged the words close and let them be a balm for the ragged parts of her soul.

But she knew that was all they could ever be. No matter how nice it felt to have Colt's acknowledgment of her role in Micah's life, she had to steel herself for losing them both soon. And maybe that was for the best since she'd given up on the idea of a family long ago. She shouldn't let herself get lulled into the idea that she could be a part of Colt's life.

"Thank you, Colt." She moved toward the stroller, knowing she needed to make a fast exit. Her feelings were too all over the place. Too close to the surface. "That means a lot to me."

"I can drive you and Micah back to the house," he

offered, scuffing a boot through the dried straw on the ground outside the pole barn. "My truck is about a quarter of a mile back that way."

Gesturing with his thumb, he indicated the opposite direction of the Fenwick homestead.

"That's all right." She didn't dare spend any more time alone with him. It was too risky when she remembered how good it felt to be in his arms. "My walks with Micah are my main source of exercise lately, and it's gorgeous out today."

His brow furrowed, and she knew that he debated pressing the issue. But thankfully, he only nodded.

"All right. Don't forget we have two nanny candidates interviewing this evening. I'm hoping you and Micah will be there to help me decide." He withdrew his phone from the back pocket of his jeans, the screen alight as it buzzed. "Sorry. This is my winery office in Cahors."

"Of course, please do take it." She welcomed the opportunity for escape, needing to collect herself and her thoughts before the nanny interviews that would put her one step closer to being out of Micah's life.

And Colt's.

"Wait, Sierra." Colt held up a hand to stop her, swiping aside the incoming call in a way that made the device quit vibrating. "I can call them back later." Returning the phone to his pocket, he continued, "I just wanted to make sure they're shipping over some Royal Black wines for the local Wine and Roses Festival. But I'm more interested in knowing what made you two come out to the pole barn? It's a rough walk with the stroller."

Her heart pounded harder at the question, knowing she needed to talk to Colt about her search for Violetta Ford's diary. Would he think it a fool's errand? Or would he somehow see her interest in Violetta as undermining her caregiving role for Micah?

She'd like to think he knew her better than that. But she couldn't forget how quickly he'd dismissed her journalism efforts when they'd first met.

I figured you were just digging for an inside track on the Texas Cattleman's Club for one of your stories... His words echoed in her head now.

"Just looking for new sights to see," she told him. A half truth, certainly. But she'd shared enough for one day. "How about you? What are you doing out this way?"

"A cow broke out of this pasture last night during the storm. I'm trying to find where she got through the fence." He gestured toward the Black Ranch side of the split rails.

Guilt pinched that she hadn't told him the real reason she was surveying the Fenwick property. But she would have time enough once she narrowed her search. Or found the diary.

"Good luck, then." Tucking her hair behind one ear, she turned to leave him, pushing the stroller over the dirt path that was definitely a bit lumpy. Especially after the rain. "I'll see you for the interviews later," she called over her shoulder.

Colt lifted a hand to wave, and she hurried away. Too bad her guilty conscience kept her company the whole way home.

Ten

Seated at the dining room table that evening, Colt stared unseeing at the printed résumé in front of him. The young woman currently interviewing for the position of Micah's nanny seemed supremely qualified on paper. That didn't mean Colt wanted to hire her.

How could he even consider replacing Sierra?

His fingers flexed underneath the table while Sierra exchanged small talk with the woman. Katie? Kaitlyn? It didn't matter since he didn't want to employ this candidate or the other one they'd met with over the course of the evening.

Because while—he focused on the résumé paper until the name came into view—Katie-Lynn might be accomplished enough to bathe, feed and care for a six-month-old, she sure as hell could never take the place of Sierra Morgan.

Micah loved Sierra.

As for Colt? He didn't know how to label the relationship he shared with Sierra, especially after their night together. But he appreciated how happy she made his son, and he respected that she'd been relentless in her search for Colt after Micah had been left orphaned. Now that he was aware of her personal journey with infertility, her selflessness with regard to Micah seemed all the more admirable. How tough must it be for her to get close to the boy, knowing Colt would take him overseas soon?

Frustration kicked harder.

"Thank you for stopping by," Colt announced abruptly, coming to his feet to call an end to the interview.

The startled expression on Sierra's face, though fleeting, told him he'd been rude. But then, he hadn't really been listening to the exchange in the first place. Damn it.

Still, Sierra covered for him, assuring Katie-Lynn they'd be in touch with all of the candidates within the next few days and thanking her again with more warmth than Colt had managed. Both women took a moment to admire Micah in his deluxe baby swing, banging the tray with a toy rattle while his happy grin showed off two tiny bottom teeth.

As soon as the young woman was out the door, however, Sierra spun on Colt.

"What was that all about?" Hands on hips, she glared at him. "If you want a good relationship with a new nanny, you shouldn't begin it by chasing her off. I thought she seemed ideal."

"She's far from ideal," he retorted, brushing past her

to wind the baby swing. Then, lowering himself until he was eye level with his son, he tickled the boy's toes through mint-green footie pajamas.

Micah kicked gleefully and tossed the rattle in his excitement. The kid couldn't be any cuter. And he deserved better than just some random job applicant with a background in early childhood education.

"Care to share what you could have possibly found lacking in her?" Sierra asked, retrieving the rattle and laying it on the coffee table instead of passing it back to Micah.

Colt had noticed how diligent she was about washing toys that the baby dropped before returning them to him. One of a million ways she took care of Micah better than someone else might. Did Katie-Lynn know Micah's favorite nursery rhymes or how quickly the boy could kick off a pair of socks if they weren't a special brand?

"She's just not the right person." Standing, he faced her, knowing he didn't have a good reason for the stubborn stance. "It's not about what's on a résumé. It's a gut feeling that I have about her." He extended his arms wide, a gesture of surrender. "Whether it makes sense or not, I'm going to follow my instincts. Micah's my son, and I only just found him, so I'm not trusting his care with just anyone."

Her shoulders sagged, hands falling away from her narrow hips.

"You're right." She nodded, her blond ponytail swinging as she moved around the living area, tidying a few papers and toys that had ended up strewn around the room during the interview sessions. "You have to feel one hundred percent at ease with whoever you hire to care for your son."

Was he right? He almost regretted that she'd agreed so readily, his unsettled nerves all too prepared to argue the point, even if he didn't fully understand the reasons.

Because he needed to supplant Sierra in the first place? Because Colt would be returning to France as soon as Micah seemed more comfortable with him? Damned if he knew.

"You're better with him than anyone else," he found himself saying, his attention remaining fixed on the swing, where Micah's head tipped to one side of the blue padded seat. It was easier than wrestling with his feelings for the woman in front of him, her green eyes seeing too much. "I'm trying not to infringe on your time any more than I already have. But is there any way you can continue helping out with him until I'm ready to—"

She made a soft sound, a hum of protest maybe. Or resignation?

"Colt. Don't ask me to do that." Her voice cracked. "You know I'm very attached to him already. The more time I spend with him, the harder it's going to be to say goodbye when you leave."

Emotion lay heavy in her tone, and he whipped around to see her face. Gauge her expression. Was it only Micah who would tug at her heart when he left? Or would she miss him sometimes, too?

Even as he thought it, however, he dismissed the idea. She'd been very clear about not wanting a relationship. And from the way she'd drawn boundaries between them, he believed her. Besides, who could blame her for feeling a special tenderness toward Micah after what she'd confided in Colt today?

He berated himself for being ten kinds of selfish bastard for thinking about himself after what Sierra had shared with him earlier. Of course she was only thinking of Micah.

"I have no right to ask anything more from you," he agreed, recognizing that he needed to buck up and hire someone else so that Sierra could establish whatever relationship she felt most comfortable having with Micah. Perhaps it would be easier for her to separate a little at a time. "You've been far more generous to me than I've deserved, and I appreciate how much of your personal time you've devoted to Micah. And me, too."

She lifted a brow at him. Indignant. "I wasn't on the clock with you."

He shook his head with impatience. "I don't mean that, obviously. But you've taken time to teach me how to be a better father. You didn't have to explain childcare to me as you tended Micah, but you always do." He recalled how she'd helped him shop online for toys that would help with the boy's coordination, not just items that were cute. And whenever she discovered things Micah liked, games or songs or a new twist on a bedtime ritual, she shared the discovery with Colt. "I'm more confident with him now because of that."

"Oh. You've done plenty of kindnesses for me, too." She shifted her weight from foot to foot, seeming uneasy. "I've appreciated the chance to stay here. My room at the B and B was beginning to feel a little claustrophobic after a five-month residency. So you've more than paid me back for anything I've taught you about babies."

For a moment, they locked eyes in the room gone quiet except for the ticking of the swing as the motion slowed down again. Sierra glanced away first, her cheeks slightly pink as she looked down at the baby. Micah had fallen asleep, his Cupid's bow mouth blowing a tiny, drooly bubble as he exhaled.

"Where will you go—" Colt began, not sure how to frame the question in a way that wouldn't set them at odds again. "If I hire someone to take your place? Back to the Cimarron Rose?"

"Most likely." She'd changed into a black knit dress for the interviews, the outfit both more formal and subdued than her usual clothes. The simple lines outlined her trim curves without drawing attention to itself.

Yet Colt found it difficult to look away from her.

"How much longer do you think you'll stay in Royal to research the book on Violetta and the Texas Cattleman's Club?" He regretted not asking her more about the project before now, but he'd had his hands full with figuring out fatherhood.

Not to mention the efforts he'd put into checking on Black Ranch, overseeing renovations on the Fenwick house, and making preparations for the Royal Black Winery to participate in the Wine and Roses Festival at the end of the month. The fact that a local wine event existed in Royal in the first place had got him thinking about the possibility of one day opening a local branch of the Royal Black brand. There were plenty of Central Texas wineries that had met with success.

"It's difficult to say." She ran a hand along her ponytail, settling it along her shoulder in a way that stirred her fragrance. "I'm still tracking source material," she said vaguely before bending toward the swing. "I should put Micah to bed."

Had the question made her uncomfortable? Or was their proximity stirring awareness for her the way it did for him?

"Please. Allow me to take over the task tonight." Colt's hand landed on the small of her back, the warmth of her skin evident through the knit dress.

He told himself to move his hand away from her, but his fingers only flexed and clenched against the soft fabric while he struggled with the need to touch more of her.

Straightening, Sierra's green eyes flashed to his. Awareness pinged between them like an electric charge, buzzing up his arm. Settling in his gut.

But before he could act on it, her expression shuttered again, and she darted away.

"Thank you, Colt. I'm grateful for the extra time to work." Pausing beside an end table, she scooped up her tablet and a legal pad with some notes on it. "Good night."

Of all the lies that Sierra had told herself in the weeks since she'd met Colt Black, the most egregious was that she would *work* tonight when all she could think of was the way his blue eyes had burned into her earlier.

The way his broad palm had spanned her back, the fingers raking lightly against the material of her dress.

Two hours later, she sat alone in the recently remodeled upstairs den, staring blankly at the screen of her tablet while she remembered snippets from the night she'd spent in Colt's bed. How quickly his brief touch tonight had stirred those memories.

The way he'd kissed her as if he couldn't get enough. The way he'd teased a response from her long slumbering libido, awakening hungers she'd believed she had conquered.

How was she going to resurrect the boundary between them when his touch was so magnetic? When the man himself compelled her like no one else?

The diary, she reminded herself harshly, straightening in one of the low barrel chairs to refocus on the tablet in her lap. Work had always been her way to keep herself from thinking about her old dreams of a family, and she would trust that it could be all-absorbing once again if she allowed herself to get immersed in it.

"If I were Violetta," she asked herself aloud, using two fingers to expand the map of the Fenwick property currently on her screen, "where would I hide a diary?"

She'd searched most of the outbuildings already, including the pole barn where she'd run into Colt. The only structures left to search were the old cellar underneath the house itself—a task she'd put off since the work crew in charge of renovations frequently passed through the basement—and a couple of ruins on the property that hadn't been cleared. One was the remnants of an old windmill with a limestone base, the other a fallen chicken coop.

Tomorrow, she'd tackle at least one of those spots. The cellar might have to wait until the weekend when the work crew took a day off. For now, she enlarged a photo of the windmill, turning the screen this way and that to see if she could find a likely place to start looking. She couldn't dig up the whole property, but she might bring a shovel to explore likely areas. Sierra assumed that Violetta would have tried to hide her diary somewhere that would be protected from too much water or sun. Somewhere safe from paper-loving rodents.

Tapping the screen twice, she brought up a different angle of the windmill, noting a few crevices in the remaining limestone. Could a diary fit in one of them?

She felt some of the old enthusiasm for the project returning. Violetta Ford really was an interesting character with her refusal to accept the proscribed outlines of what a woman's life was supposed to be. She'd lived on her own terms.

Not even a baby had slowed Violetta down. She'd ensured the child was raised by his dad. Dean was the one who could take the best care of him.

Had that been Sierra's mother's thinking when she'd left Sierra on the church doorstep? Someone better suited for caring? She hoped so.

Thoughtfully, Sierra switched off the tablet and stood, the baby thoughts reminding her she hadn't gone in to kiss Micah good-night. Not that the little boy would know since Colt had put him to sleep hours ago.

But she could hover over his crib for a moment and enjoy the sight of his sweet face in slumber before she sought her own bed. Once Colt hired another nanny, she wouldn't be able to share this ritual with the baby anymore.

Quietly, she left the den and walked down the hallway toward the nursery, pushing open the door already left slightly ajar. She didn't want to wake Micah, of course. But she also didn't want Colt to hear her on the other end of the baby monitor.

Moonlight streamed in through one of the partially closed blinds, the dull blue beams enough to illuminate the room she knew well by now with its sky-blue walls and cherrywood furnishings. The scent of the baby's laundry detergent and shampoo stirred in the slowly turning ceiling fan. As she stepped deeper into the room, her gaze went to the crib tucked in the far corner.

Only to spot the tall, imposing shadow of Colt leaning over the side rail.

Her breath caught in her throat, and she stifled a gasp of surprise to see him there. One elbow leaned on the cherrywood crib rail while, with his other hand, he stroked the dark, wispy curls off his son's forehead.

And then it wasn't just a gasp but a sudden lump in her throat at the tender display, especially coming from a man who'd struck her as coolly serious. Reserved. She'd tried so hard to keep some distance between them since their night together. To keep in perspective that what they'd shared wouldn't last. Yet seeing him here, now, stirred all of her feelings for him, never far from the surface.

Biting her lip, she stood motionless in the center of the room, hating to interrupt the moment. But before she could decide what to do next, Colt's voice rasped softly.

"I know you think it's a mistake for me to leave Royal with him." His words weren't at all what she'd expected. He didn't look up at her as he continued to smooth his fingers through the child's hair. "But it seems more important than ever that I provide him the best possible legacy. He deserves that. It doesn't mean I'm cutting him off from his mom's side. His aunt Eve will always have a place in his life, as will Cammie, and you."

Still she hesitated, feeling like an interloper at a private, family time. Or maybe she was just more sensitive to it because she'd been so careful not to let herself feel like a part of this family. Even when the temptation weighed heavily on her.

And yet, Colt deserved an answer. Clearly, he'd put a lot of thought into carving out a future for his son.

"It's only natural to want to do everything in the world for your child." She closed the distance between them, drawn to the spot beside Colt near the crib. For the man? Or for the chance to see Micah?

The warmth of Colt's nearness permeated her thin sleep T-shirt and pajama pants, the comfy clothes she'd changed into for working on her book research. She kept her gaze on Micah, knowing the sexy single dad was too much of a draw at any time of day, but especially here, alone, in the dark.

"I never would have guessed how much everything in my world would change in an instant." Colt straightened from the crib, standing at his full height as he shifted to face her. "And in spite of what you think, Sierra, I'm trying to do the right thing for him."

Her pulse quickened as his attention fell fully on her, and her eyes sought his despite the dark. There was enough moonlight for her to see his shadowed jaw, her fingers itching to test the texture of it. She'd liked feeling the slight burn from it on her neck. Her breasts and thighs.

"I know you are," she acknowledged, wishing she didn't sound so breathless and hungry. "But I can't help offering a different perspective for you to consider. Maybe it's too much in my nature to stir things up."

"I'm glad you do." His voice sent a pleasurable shiver up her spine. "You push me to weigh and consider my next move. Now that there's a baby involved, I can't afford to take solely myself into account."

It wasn't the first kind thing he'd said to her today. Earlier, after the nanny interviews, he'd intimated that she was the best person for the job because she loved Micah. Part of her relished the privileged role she had here. Another part of her feared she wouldn't be able to walk away from the draw of the man and his adorable son.

Except what choice would she have when he left?

And what if he accused her of using her position here to further her career ambitions once he discovered she was searching for Violetta's diary? No question, she should tell him about her search for that last missing piece of the woman's life in Royal.

Licking suddenly dry lips, Sierra laid a hand on his arm to begin.

Just as Colt's arms banded around her, his mouth descending on hers in a slow, claiming kiss.

Heat stirred inside her. Like banked coals being flipped and prodded into new life, all the emotions she'd struggled to tamp down now flared to brightness. The attraction to Colt. The love for his child. The private heartbreak she'd tried so hard to ignore these last few years. All the feelings made the kiss that much more potent.

Made her desperate to get lost in it when none of this would last much longer.

Colt was leaving. He'd take Micah with him. A new

nanny would get them through their last days before they returned to France. And as for Sierra, it felt like this might be her last chance to explore the big, powerful emotions of a life that would never belong to her.

The life of a mother.

And, she couldn't help imagining for a moment, a cherished wife. Would anyone blame her if she wanted to experience how that dream might have felt for just one more night?

Eleven

Had he read the moment correctly?

Colt had felt the attraction streak through him like a lightning bolt the instant Sierra stepped into the nursery, but he'd forced himself to move slowly, making sure they were on the same page after their awkward parting the night before. Now, with her slender arms twining around his neck and her body pressed tightly to his, he had his answer.

She still wanted him, too.

If her urgent kisses were any indication, she needed him every bit as desperately as he craved her. Even now, her hands tunneled under his shirt, fingers deftly traveling over his abs to trace the waistband of his jeans.

He felt every dip and hollow through the thin sleep shirt she wore. Her breasts molded to his chest, her curves all the softer without the barrier of undergarments. She wore nothing beneath the sleep shirt and cotton pajama pants, the feel of her body making him ready to back her against the nearest door to be inside her.

Except they needed to take this somewhere else. Now.

With an effort, he broke the kiss enough to speak against her lips.

"Let me take you to my bed," he urged, stroking over her shoulders and down her back, pressing her against him.

"Yes, please," she agreed, her slight nod moving her lips up and down against his.

Need thrummed heavier with every beat of his heart, and he wasted no time lifting her against him to carry her where he wanted her. He paused just long enough to grab the baby monitor off a small stand by the rocking chair so they could bring it with them. Then, a moment later, they were out of the nursery and in the hallway that led to the master suite.

Every step he took rocked their bodies together. Every step made his blood burn hotter for this woman who'd gotten so deep under his skin he didn't know how he'd ever dig her out.

Or if he even wanted to.

Inside his room, he tossed the monitor on a dresser and kicked the door shut behind them. And then, he really did back her up against it, giving her another slow, thorough kiss that had them both breathing hard.

Sierra arched against him, her thighs scissoring against one of his while she strained closer. His lifted her higher, guiding her hips more firmly to his. If not for the clothes they still wore, he'd be inside her.

As it was, the heat of her sex branded him through his jeans, the damp warmth evident through the seam of her pajamas.

"Hurry," she murmured against his mouth, the sound of their breathing harsh in the otherwise quiet room. "Please, hurry."

Were they experiencing this over-the-top need because they'd been interrupted the night before? Because they hadn't been able to take their time with one another the way he'd wanted to? Or would it always be like this between them, a hunger that felt like he'd been starving for her?

He couldn't afford to think about that now when she'd made her wishes clear. Releasing her from where he'd pinned her to the door, he carried her in his arms to the edge of the king-size bed. He settled her there long enough for him to retrieve a box of condoms from the nightstand.

And in that minute, she'd already unbuttoned the lower half of his shirt to sweep aside enough for her to kiss and lick her way along his abs.

A growl rolled up his throat, but he stifled the sound, spearing his fingers into her silky hair instead. The gesture must have encouraged her, because she went to work on his fly, opening it enough to free him.

Then, tugging his cotton boxers lower with one hand, she wrapped the rigid length of him in the other, gliding up and down before she bent her head to kiss and lick him there.

This time, he didn't have a chance in hell of suppressing a growl of pleasure. Of need.

"Sierra." He said her name like a warning, but he didn't know what from. He only knew he could get lost in her if he allowed himself. "Tonight, you're not leaving until after the sun rises."

She peeped up at him through lowered lashes, green eyes scorching him before she swirled her tongue around him, driving him clear out of his mind for her.

"I'll take that as a yes." He tore off his shirt the rest of the way, then turned his attention to hers, skimming it up her back and over her shoulders before he laid her down on the mattress.

Staring up at him, Sierra followed his movements, her cheeks flushed pink and her lips swollen. He couldn't get enough of her, a surge of possessiveness gaining momentum as he skimmed off her pajama bottoms and made room for himself between her thighs.

But then she cupped his cheek in her hand, her thumb smoothing along his bottom lip, the gesture checking his hunger enough to kiss her thoroughly all over again.

While he lost himself in the give-and-take of her lips and tongue, she palmed a condom and tore it open. Her fingers maneuvered a little awkwardly as she rolled the latex into place, her tentative touch making him feel protective of her even as his hips rocked toward her.

The soft sound she made in response shredded the last of his restraint. Knowing that she wanted this as much as he did urged him on. Had him gripping her hips to guide her where he needed her.

Her fingernails bit lightly into his shoulders as he eased inside her. He welcomed the sting, a counterpoint to how incredible she felt all around him. Looking down into her eyes, he sank deeper. A connection to her sliding into place.

He would have sworn she experienced it, too, because he thought he saw an answering light in her green gaze. The beginnings of something bigger than either of them had planned for. A bond that might weather time apart or even being on different continents.

But then, closing her eyes, Sierra wrapped her legs around his waist. Colt forgot everything but the sensation of her body squeezing his, molding and giving all around him.

Had he dreamed that moment when there'd been something more?

Sierra had never clung to a man before.

Not figuratively. Not even physically.

But she couldn't deny a serious amount of clinging going on right now with Colt. She couldn't let go of him. Couldn't get enough. She needed more. Deeper. Faster.

Or maybe she just told herself that she needed those things. Because for a second she could have sworn she'd looked into Colt's eyes and thought she wanted forever. A tenderness had welled up inside her, so soft and warm that she feared it would swallow her whole. So like a coward, she shut it down fast and concentrated on just this one moment.

The lush completion she felt at being in his arms and in his bed. And oh God, she didn't want to think about how hard it would be to walk away after this night with him. Why had she ever thought it would help to know how good it would feel to live the fantasy that could never be hers?

For now, she locked her ankles behind his hips, keeping him close. The hard planes of his body flexed and shifted, muscles rippling as he worked deeper and then withdrew, creating a rhythm that stole her breath. Made her whimper.

She realized she'd allowed her nails to sink into his shoulders, so she smoothed the crescent moon marks with her fingertips, trying to recover some control of herself. Finding it so much tougher than she'd ever imagined.

With her emotions raw and her body clamoring for more of him, Sierra had never felt so exposed. Like another stroke might shatter her. She couldn't untwine herself from him, though. Couldn't stop herself from following these addictive sensations through to their natural conclusion.

Her breath came faster, heart slamming against her rib cage like it might really break free.

"Colt." She said his name over and over, wearing it out, not caring how lost she sounded. Because right now, she was.

Lost.

And Colt felt like her only anchor.

"Sierra. Look at me," he whispered, voice ragged with his own harsh breathing. He paused his thrusts, going still on top of her as he stared down at her in the moonlight.

She swallowed hard and lifted her lashes, taking in the intensity of his blue eyes turned dark. Only when their gazes locked did he touch her, the pads of his fingers circling the aching bud of her sex before he sank into her again. Slowly.

His touch unraveled her.

An orgasm blindsided her, the release coming hard and fast as sensations rocked her. Her eyes fell closed again so she could soak in all the delectable ways he made her body feel.

When at last the shuddering subsided, Colt kissed her temple lightly before pushing deeper inside again. The pressure spurred more flutters of her feminine muscles, like a sensual reminder of what he could do to her.

Then he built a new rhythm all over again. Harder. Faster. A rhythm more for him, except that she loved it just as much. She wanted him to feel as incredible as she had. Needed for him to remember this night the way she would. They couldn't have a future together. But they could have a taste of how amazing it might have been if things had been different.

So when at last his thrusts were enough to even make the whole bed shudder, Sierra let them carry her away with him. Her body, already so sensitive from his touches, seized in another orgasm. The release spurred his own a moment later, his hips punching forward one last time to fill her completely. Their groans of completion mingled with their breath, hearts pounding madly.

In the long moments of stillness afterward, there was no sound except for the windy exhales growing more and more quiet. Even that rhythm synched up, until their chests seemed to rise and fall together.

Colt rolled to his side, taking her with him, so they lay there facing one another in the moonlight fading as the night deepened. She closed her eyes when he stroked her hair from her eyes, not sure she could hide the tenderness she felt.

Knowing neither of them was ready for those emotions.

He was leaving.

She was committed to her work for a good reason.

Sierra breathed the reminders in and out along with her slowed respirations, the mantra she needed to keep her heart in one piece after this night together. Would the affirmations work?

Tucking her head against Colt's chest, she shut down the question and simply hoped for the best. Because she cared about this man deeply. Maybe even loved him. Perhaps that was why she needed for him to be happy, even if it meant being apart.

She'd given up her dreams of family long ago, so she'd never try to tie him to her. But for the first time, she understood that letting him go would cost her far more than she'd ever imagined.

The doorbell rang at noontime the next day, right on schedule for Micah's lunch date. Sierra tightened her ponytail as she hurried to answer it, peeking briefly out the front window to be sure the guests were the ones she'd been expecting. She welcomed the distraction since she wasn't ready to think about the explosive encounter with Colt last night or what it meant.

Haley Lopez was the police officer who'd been the first to respond to the call of Micah being found abandoned in the Royal Memorial Hospital parking lot, and she'd continued to track Micah's story with as much interest as Sierra had. And sure enough, tall, gorgeous Haley stood on the welcome mat, her long dark hair blowing lightly around her face as she leaned into her real estate developer boyfriend, Jackson Michaels.

"Hello!" Sierra greeted them both warmly as she

opened the front door, waving them inside. "I'm so glad it worked out for you to visit Micah today."

"I've been dying to see him," Haley enthused, stepping over the threshold as her eyes went straight to the baby blanket on the floor of the living room where Micah was having tummy time. "Oh, look at him! He's grown so much in just the last month."

Haley had messaged her a few times about getting together so she could see Micah, but the timing hadn't worked out until today. Behind Haley, Jackson stepped inside and shut the door behind him, nodding a greeting to Sierra while Haley moved toward the baby.

"Is Colt home?" Jackson asked, glancing around the house. "I see his work crew is doing a nice job on the renovations."

Sierra swallowed a moment's discomfort at the question since she'd been the tiniest bit relieved when Colt was called away an hour ago.

"Colt couldn't be here. He went to the Texas Cattleman's Club a little while ago," she explained as they followed Haley into the living area. "The coordinator for the Wine and Roses Festival messaged him about a problem with the shipment of Royal Black wines for the event, so he went to help straighten things out."

After she'd assured him she'd be fine on her own for the rest of the day. Yes, their night together had been perfect, and she'd awakened to the scent of breakfast cooking for her. But she wasn't sure how long she could hide how wrecked she felt about their time together coming to an end. If Colt had sensed that she wrestled with morning-after jitters, he hadn't acknowledged it. He'd served her eggs and pancakes as if it were the most natural thing in the world to share the first meal of the day together.

But Sierra had needed a chance to pull herself together after the intensity of the night they'd shared. She knew the longer they continued to see one another, the greater the stakes would be for a breakup. For Micah especially. She needed to get this right.

"Well, we're only too happy to offer some babysitting relief," Haley assured her from her spot on the floor where she already lay across from Micah. She shook the soft bunny rattle, encouraging him to reach for the toy. "Jackson and I can stay for a couple of hours, so whatever you need to do, don't mind us. I'll be in baby heaven playing with this little guy."

Sierra smiled, appreciating how easygoing Haley didn't mind playing on the floor.

"Actually, I do have a few errands outside the house as long as you're here." Sierra shouldn't feel guilty about that, since she'd put in far more hours caring for Micah than duty called for since she hardly viewed her time with the baby as a job.

But given that she wanted to search the windmill for Violetta's diary today, she couldn't help a twinge of conscience since she hadn't spoken to Colt about it yet. She'd only promised not to write any more stories on Micah, so why should he mind about her research into Violetta's past for her book? Yet some instinct warned her he wouldn't be thrilled that she was conducting her search on his property.

In her work as an investigative journalist, she was accustomed to asking forgiveness instead of permission to obtain information. But with Colt, it would be different.

"Absolutely," Haley assured her, waving to Jackson to join her on the floor even as she kept her dark eyes focused on Sierra. "Just let me know when and if I need to feed him or put him down for a nap?"

"He's already eaten, so he should be happy to play until I return, but if he starts fussing, feel free to see if he wants to lie in his crib."

Arrangements made, Sierra slipped out of the front door a few minutes later. She wore a pair of work boots since the old windmill was a ruin and on a part of the Fenwick property that obviously hadn't been maintained in a long time. At this point, finding a buried diary on this huge property felt like coming up with a needle in a haystack, but she planned to at least try the final structures on her list.

Maybe the reason she hadn't shared the search with Colt was that she didn't really believe she'd find the diary in the first place, even though Emmalou Hilliard had sworn it existed. But still, Sierra hoped. Now more than ever, she wanted to understand Violetta's choices. Her own life had paralleled the woman's in some ways. Maybe whatever the diary had to say about Violetta's decision to live by herself—on her own terms—would help Sierra figure out her next move with Colt.

She unzipped her jacket after the first ten minutes of walking had warmed her up. Using her phone's GPS to ensure she stayed on track as she hiked through an overgrown section of a creek bank, Sierra spotted the stones of the crumbling windmill and hurried the rest of the way to reach it.

Patches of sunlight filtered through the leaves of small scrub trees growing on a hill behind the fallen mill. She had to pick her way over some of the loose limestone blocks now covered with dirt and moss. Yet somehow, the stone base still held the blades in place. Even now, they turned slowly in the breeze while small birds darted back and forth to their nests in two of the hollowed-out spots where stones were missing.

The spot was picturesque despite the decay, new life taking root in the old. Even though the presence of nests made it that much more difficult for her to search those crevices for a diary.

Sighing, she went around to the back of the windmill, looking for the bigger crack she'd seen in the limestone in the pictures she'd viewed online. Sure enough, there it was, centered down the back of the post, the separation larger than it had appeared in the photo.

Still, it remained narrow enough that no bird had tried to nest there, making it easier for Sierra to start her search there. She slipped a pair of thin work gloves from her pocket and slid them on, unwilling to stick her hands into dark places without at least some layer of protection.

"Here goes nothing," she muttered, bracing herself for whatever might be within the stone.

Did snakes nest in rocks like this?

Her nerve almost failed her. But she closed her eyes and reached between the parted limestone blocks. Tapping. Rubbing.

Feeling.

Mostly, there were little bits of crumbled stone and dead leaves. A few sticks, almost as if a bird had tried to build there unsuccessfully. She reached deeper.

And her fingers collided with a straight edge.

Like a tool of some sort, maybe? Or was it just a

windmill part? It was definitely a lighter metal and not stone.

Excitement made her stand taller on her toes so she could reach farther into the crevice. Awkwardly, she tried sliding the object toward her with her fingertips. Her gloves slipped off it twice before shifting it a little the third time.

Then, finally, she could edge her thumb beneath it to lift the piece.

The object didn't feel like a book. It felt like a case. But could it contain the diary?

With some twisting and wriggling, she managed to bring out a dusty gray tin—larger than a recipe box, but smaller than a bread box—into the light. The container was rusted in places, but it had been painted at one time. Flecks of red and yellow were still visible around the sides of the lid.

Could this be it?

Sierra kept her gloves on to pry off the top. A piece of rust bit into her finger anyhow, but she ignored the small sting to open the container.

Inside, a dust-covered, warped leather book nestled in dirty cloth that might have once served as a wrapping. A piece of twine held the book shut. But the cover was all that Sierra needed to see. Because even through the collected dust and deteriorated rags, she could read what someone had carefully inscribed with leatherworking tools.

Between two sunflowers, the name Violetta filled her with wonder at the discovery.

She knew that the answers to Violetta's story would be inside this volume, and at last, Sierra's search for answers about the spinster rebel would come to a close.

But even as she looked forward to writing the ending to Violetta's tale, Sierra knew that it was the ending to her own, too. With this discovery, she couldn't afford to remain at the Fenwick house anymore.

In order to protect her heart—and ensure she didn't hurt Micah with an even more painful breakup down the road—she needed to leave.

Twelve

After finishing up his meeting with the Wine and Roses Festival coordinator at the Texas Cattleman's Clubhouse that afternoon, Colt strode out of the private meeting room and into the dining hall. Thank goodness Sierra had convinced him to attend to the business in person.

He'd missed this place.

From the oversized leather furniture to the hunting trophies and historical artifacts that decorated the walls, everything about the Texas Cattleman's Club reminded him of home. A member couldn't walk through the place without seeing half a dozen friends. It sure made Colt wonder how his grandfather could have longed for a winery on the other side of the world when Clyde Black had the TCC in his backyard.

Like now, for instance. At the bar, Colt spotted Carson Wentworth sharing a drink with Drake Rhodes. As much as Colt looked forward to returning home to be with Sierra—she'd seemed distracted over breakfast, and he wanted to be certain that didn't have anything to do with their night together—he needed to speak to Carson in person. Sierra had helped him see how important his renovation of the Fenwick property was to a lot of people in Royal. There was a history there, and a lot of it was tied to the Wentworth family. He wanted a way to acknowledge that to Carson.

Heading in the other man's direction, Colt hadn't even reached his side when Carson lifted his beer in salute.

"I'd heard you were back in Royal," Carson greeted him as Colt drew nearer. "Welcome home."

"Thank you." Colt shook hands with both of them before turning his attention to Carson. "And congratulations on your new title. I hear you beat out some stiff competition in your run for TCC president."

Carson had been in a close contest for the president's seat against Lana Langley, the same woman he'd proposed to after the race was over. The other men both laughed, but Carson's green eyes took on a fond light—the half-dazed expression of a man newly in love—before he answered. "Lucky for me, the real prize came later."

Beside Colt, Drake clapped Carson on the shoulder before standing.

"Good to see you, Colt," Drake said as he retrieved his black Stetson from a nearby stool. "And I'm sorry to run, but I promised Cammie I'd join her for a fundraising event she's chairing this afternoon. This one is a fun run and not a gala, so at least I'll be wearing sneakers instead of a tux."

"Give her my best," Colt said as he flagged the bartender to gesture for a beer of his own. "And let her know Micah is growing bigger by the minute."

Drake nodded. "Sierra has been great about visits, texting us updates and sharing photos of Micah. It's really helped Cammie ease away from the big role she played in his life the last few months."

Colt owed Sierra a staggering debt for what she'd done for him. He'd told her as much from the beginning for her role in reuniting him with Micah. But now that he knew her well, he appreciated all she'd done for him even more.

Colt barely managed to stifle a wince at the gut punch of remembering how far he had fallen short in his duties as a father. Even now that he'd assumed responsibility for his son, Sierra was still helping him more than he'd realized, maintaining the connections that Micah's arrival in Royal had forged. Her big heart and caring nature were evident in everything she did. And she sure as hell deserved a family of her own one day.

Was he keeping her from finding that happiness when he wasn't sure how to make a relationship between them work? He hated that idea even as it killed him to think of her with anyone else.

As Drake left them, Colt refocused on Carson. Lowering himself into the seat Drake had vacated, Colt accepted a longneck bottle the bartender handed him. He needed to get home soon and figure things out with Sierra. But first, he wanted to follow through on an offer to the Wentworth family.

"I've been meaning to speak with you, Carson." Colt took a swig of the locally brewed craft beer. "You know I've done extensive renovations on the old Fenwick house."

Carson gave a wave to another rancher taking a seat at the other end of the bar before speaking. "I'd heard as much. Now that we know about Violetta's connection to our family, I'm glad her ranch is being well-maintained."

"Sierra is writing a book about Violetta and the history of the Texas Cattleman's Club. I have the feeling the project will bring about more interest in the ranch." He'd considered the idea of selling the property once he'd renovated the rest, but now he wasn't so sure. Sierra's interest in the Fenwick place—and Violetta—had given him a new appreciation of the ranch's local significance. "Which is why I've been meaning to speak to you."

Carson raised an eyebrow, pausing as he picked up his glass. "I'm listening."

"I hoped you might name the stables once I have them finished. I would take care of the signage and a plaque to honor the history of the place. But I'd like to leave the naming to you, so you could recognize Violetta and Dean or the Wentworths in general?"

Carson set his beer back on the coaster, never having taken a sip. He scrubbed a hand along his jaw, seeming to take in the request. After a moment, he exhaled a long breath.

"That would be much appreciated, Colt." He pushed aside his empty glass. "I'd be honored to name the stables, though I'd like to consult with Harmon first.

I know he'll be as pleased as I am that you want to do this."

"It seems only right." The matter settled, Colt caught up on a few other pieces of news from around the TCC, including the lowdown on the other vendors participating in the Wine and Roses event next weekend.

But in the back of his mind, he thought about Sierra and how much of an effect she'd had on his life since he'd returned to Royal. Connecting him with Micah had been huge, of course. But there'd been so many other ways she'd made an indelible mark on his life. Without her, would anyone even know about Violetta Ford? Sierra had jumped into Arielle Martin's work with both feet, picking up where Arielle had left off and doing a lot of good for Royal.

And what had the town given her in return?

He felt a moment's regret that he hadn't talked to her about doing a final story on Micah for the local paper, where she still freelanced. He'd been so convinced she was only in town to dredge up scandal, but he couldn't have been more wrong. She'd done so much for him. He couldn't help thinking he hadn't been an equal partner. He needed to make things right between them before he left Royal.

So, finishing his beer, he shook hands with Carson and headed for the door. He needed to return home and see Sierra. He'd find out the reason for her distracted air over breakfast, and then do whatever he could to fix it. Because he wanted her to remain in his life for as long as he was in town.

And maybe even after he returned.

Sierra had made him see that he and Micah belonged in Royal. So his upcoming trip to France didn't need to be permanent. He could finish his work at the winery there, then bring Micah home to start a branch of the Royal Black Winery here.

For the first time in a long time, he felt the stirrings of hope. And he couldn't wait to share that with her.

Pulling clothes off the hangers and folding them in her bedroom at the Fenwick house, Sierra heard Colt's foot on the staircase.

Her stomach cramped at the sound. Just days ago, she would have felt a thrill at the prospect of seeing him, even if she hadn't wanted to admit it to herself.

Now, after knowing how deeply she'd begun to care for him and how much damage that could do to her relationship with Micah, Sierra felt only anxiety. Dread. A sickness at what she was about to do.

Because she knew, without a doubt, he wouldn't understand her decision.

Clearing out the middle drawer of a built-in bureau inside the massive walk-in closet, she didn't bother folding her night clothes or active wear. She just chucked the untidy pile into the suitcase on top of the few dress clothes she'd brought with her.

That's how Colt found her when he walked into the room, her hands smoothing out the pile enough so she could fasten the elastic strap to hold the clothes in place inside her luggage. She sensed his presence behind her even before she turned around.

The air shifted somehow, all her nerve endings attuned to this man who'd grown to mean a great deal to her in a short span of time.

"Sierra?"

Biting her lip, she didn't need to turn and see his expression to read into his tone of voice. Surprise. Wariness. Cautious concern.

She heard all of that and more in the space of a single word.

"How was your meeting at the TCC?" she asked carefully, trying to keep her own voice neutral. The last thing she wanted was to fall apart in front of him. It wouldn't make any difference in the outcome of their talk anyhow. "Did you straighten out the wine shipments?"

"It went well. The Royal Black wines will arrive in time for the festival. Is Micah still sleeping?" He walked closer, the soft sound of his footfalls on the hardwood floor making her realize that he'd removed his boots when he'd entered the house.

Such an unremarkable detail to notice when things were about to crumble between them. But she couldn't help thinking of the intimacy they shared that went beyond the bedroom. There were a hundred details she'd learned about Colt by living with him these last weeks. The way he liked his coffee in the morning. That he woke up without an alarm when the sun rose. That he moved with athletic grace for someone his size, his step almost silent as he came up beside her now. She would miss all those things, and so much more.

"He is out like a light. Haley and Jackson visited with him today, and he's all tired out from playing." She closed the lid of her soft-sided suitcase, her fingers shaking a little as she reached for the zipper. "I'm glad you were able to settle things at the Texas Cattleman's Club."

"Sierra, what's going on?" He covered her hand with

his, halting her before she could close the case. "Why are you packing?"

The warmth of his touch slid right past her defenses, reminding her how easy it would be to lean into his strength. To let their attraction burn away all the difficult parts of their relationship. But for how long?

Even if she allowed that to happen, they'd be right back to this point tomorrow.

Taking a deep breath, she moved away from him. Not just because his touch was so potent, she told herself. She also wanted to show him the diary.

Retrieving the leather volume from the low mahogany desk near the guest bed that had been hers the last two weeks, she passed it to him. His blue eyes were full of concern as he looked at her, and she wished she could capture the moment since she suspected he wouldn't be so pleased with her when he found out she'd been searching for the diary all along.

"I found this hidden in the old windmill today," she explained after his gaze shifted down to the object in his hands. "It's Violetta Ford's diary."

His brow furrowed as he turned it over, examining the worn book. Her attention narrowed to his hands. She was going to miss his touch so much. The sound of his voice. Why hadn't she considered that more before she let herself get so attached to him?

"I don't understand. What were you doing at the windmill? The property is in shambles over there." He lifted his eyes to her face again, and for a moment, the concern lingered. "I'm not sure it's a safe place for walking the baby—"

All at once, his expression cleared, the confusion

morphing into understanding briefly before suspicion took its place.

"You went there looking for this," he said flatly, his grip tightening around the leather. His left jaw muscle ticked. "It only makes sense since you're researching a book on Violetta that you would welcome the chance to search the property for clues about her. Cammie did tell me that you didn't stop until you had answers."

"I think Violetta's story is worth documenting. Both as a woman and as a TCC member," she rushed to explain, feeling defensive. She'd had more time to consider the local spinster rebel, and the more Sierra thought about her, the more she found to admire. "She refused to compromise the kind of life she wanted for the sake of social norms. She was a frontier maverick, a woman unafraid to take chances."

Colt's face had turned stony. "She also abandoned her baby," he reminded her.

Did he dare to imply Sierra was abandoning Micah, too? Whether or not that had been his intention, he certainly knew the topic would be sensitive for her. His words struck her every last frustrated maternal nerve.

"In those days, she knew her child would be labeled illegitimate, and that would limit his chances in life," she found herself arguing, having read some of the diary already. She couldn't help herself, even though she knew the book was technically Colt's property now since it had been discovered on his land. "She loved him too much for that. Instead, she gave him up to be raised in a life of luxury by his dad, Dean Wentworth."

Slowly, Colt placed the diary on top of Sierra's suitcase, setting the luggage aside.

"So you've been searching for the diary the whole

time." His blue eyes sparked with fire as he met her gaze again. "It doesn't feel good to think that might have been your real reason for being here. Would you have even said yes to the nanny position if it hadn't been for the chance to explore the Fenwick land?"

She hesitated, knowing there was some truth to what he said. But it was only a small part of her reason.

"You can't possibly question how much I love Micah," she flashed back at him. "I wanted to spend time with him, and I'm fortunate you gave me the chance to do that. This has nothing to do with him."

"And yet I noticed you're packing your bags the moment the diary came to light." He made a sweeping gesture around the guest room, where some of Sierra's belongings were still scattered. "That tells me you were more interested in your professional search for answers than you were in Micah." He paused a moment before adding, more quietly, "Or me."

The fact she might have hurt him by leaving hadn't occurred to her. Something twisted in her chest. Her instinct was to reach out to him. Touch him. But hadn't he made it clear that they didn't have a future? She stuffed her hands in the pockets of her jeans.

"You've said all along you don't want a relationship. You told me from the beginning that you're returning to France and taking Micah with you." A thready panic loosed inside her. Had she misread the situation?

Had there been a time when he'd thought about something more between them, and she'd missed the chance to explore these tumultuous feelings?

But that was foolish to think. He'd been on a collision course with his destiny at Royal Black Winery since they met.

"So you gladly made your time here about work instead of…whatever we shared." He didn't budge an inch, keeping his distance from her.

She bristled, immediately defensive. So much for letting her guard down.

"That's not fair. I heard you tell Micah that very first day not to get too attached to me. That I was temporary." She remembered overhearing those words before she stepped into the nursery to check on him. "And I understand that, Colt. Your first obligation is your son, and it makes sense that you want to protect him. That's why I'm leaving. It's easier to end things now before we get even more attached. I don't want to hurt Micah more down the road."

"So your answer is to run?" His voice lowered. He stretched his strong arms wide in disbelief. "How can you think that's a good plan after everything you said about Micah needing to be around people he's bonded with? You came here so he'd have someone familiar around him. Doesn't that matter anymore?"

Was she making a mistake?

The confusion in his voice, the indignation at her decision, made her question herself. But he'd been so quick to jump to conclusions about her search for the diary, not giving her the benefit of the doubt. How could she be with someone who just assumed the worst of her? If she didn't stick to her path—maintaining her focus on her career—she'd only run into the same hurts that had almost leveled her four years ago when she discovered she wouldn't have children. It was one thing for her to make peace with not having kids. But she couldn't be responsible for someone else grappling with the reality of that.

"*You* are familiar to Micah now," she reminded him, blinking past the burning feeling in her eyes. "You've read him bedtime stories and kissed him good-night. Fed him and changed him and rocked him in your arms at night." Her voice faltered at the memory of Colt staring down into the crib the night before, awed at the responsibility of raising his son. "Micah has you."

Reminded how tough it would be to walk out of this house today, Sierra picked up another duffel bag and brought it over to the desk to pack her work things.

"You're just scared," Colt accused a moment later, his voice cool now. Dispassionate.

Of course he was right.

She was terrified of losing Micah. And yes, Colt, too. But the longer she stayed, the worse it would hurt. Dragging in a breath, she waited to speak until she trusted her voice to remain even.

"Says the man who's moving to France." She zipped the second bag shut and hefted the weight onto her shoulder, adjusting the strap. "I guess that makes two of us."

For a moment, Colt looked like he was wrestling with what to say next. Part of her wished he would tell her differently. That she had it all wrong. That he wasn't moving, and that he wanted to try out a life together with her.

Or maybe she just wanted to hear that it was okay she couldn't have children, whispered a tiny piece of her heart that she chose to ignore.

But when Colt spoke again, he was all business.

"I'm not going to let you carry your own bags," he said finally, lifting the wide strap of the duffel off of her shoulder.

His knuckles brushed her arm as he took the weight, sending an unwanted shiver through her. Memories of so many other touches taunted her. But his face was a cool mask now, all hint of concern long gone.

Not trusting herself to speak, she simply nodded while he set aside the forgotten diary and lifted her suitcase from the bed.

Her attention remained fixed on the leather volume for a long moment. Even while her heart broke, she couldn't help but give some thought to Violetta, the woman whose unconventional journey had inspired Sierra over the last five months.

"What will you do with the diary?" she asked. "I'm sure Harmon would like to hear Violetta loved him. It's an artifact that would be of interest to any local historian."

He looked at her long and hard, his eyes grown cool as the gulf between them widened.

"You're the one writing the book on Violetta and the TCC. It's probably of most interest to you." Standing on the threshold of the guest room door with her bags, he turned to look back at her. "Take it. But when you're finished, the diary should probably go to Harmon. Let him decide what to do with it next. Family is what really matters, after all."

She felt raw inside, like he'd raked over all her feelings and found her wanting. Family mattered to her, too. But she had never been a part of his, even if some days it had felt like she belonged here, with him and with Micah. Swallowing back the bitterness of the hurt, she tried to focus on the gift he'd offered her.

If her work was all she had, at least the diary would make it easier to write her book.

"Thank you," she said softly, picking up the slim volume, mindful of its age.

But Colt was already gone, his footfalls heavier on the stairs now that he carried her bags than when he'd first arrived in her room. Not that she was surprised that her baggage was weighty. Unwieldy.

Following him out, she clutched the diary to her chest, wishing the historic book was enough of a prize to soothe her broken heart.

Thirteen

The weather for the Wine and Roses Festival proved ideal, with clear skies and sunshine that showcased the local gardens at their best. Everyone commented on it as they stopped by Colt's wine tasting booth in the gardens outside of the Texas Cattleman's Club. Colt knew he should be celebrating the successful event.

But no amount of sunny weather could dissipate the dark cloud that still hung stubbornly over his head a week after Sierra had left him. He'd swung from hurt to angry at first. But as the days ticked by, he realized that underneath that, he was just plain devastated.

He nodded at Nathan and Amanda Battle as the couple walked by, though Colt kept moving to minimize conversation when he knew he wasn't at his best. Today was a triumph for Royal Black Winery, with orders piling up from local tasters. People didn't just ask for a bottle. They bought by the case. The show of support from Royal was overwhelming, and Colt knew he should be thrilled. Certainly he was happy for his grandfather's sake that so many people remembered him well and were excited to be a part of Clyde's dream. And yet without Sierra at his side, sharing this with him, the day still felt empty.

He glanced back at the clubhouse building, grateful he hadn't needed to bring Micah to the day care facility. He'd ended up hiring Katie-Lynn, the nanny candidate Sierra had liked best for Micah, and the woman had been more than competent.

Colt supposed he should have been happy that he'd found someone trustworthy who Micah liked. But that proved tough when he missed everything about Sierra, including the way she was with his son.

Now, with a country band playing a lively zydeco waltz on the opposite end of the pool from his booth, Colt tried to scavenge up his game face as more people filtered into the event. He recognized Carson Wentworth's fiancée, Lana Langley, and Lana's sister-in-law, Abigail Langley Price, as the women stopped in front of his display. They examined the wine bottles on the table and read the six-foot banner about the French winery with the Royal name. The event company he'd hired to help him design a presence for Royal Black had done a good job for his debut on U.S. soil.

The Wine and Roses Festival lasted all day at different venues around town, including the Cimarron Rose B and B where he happened to know Sierra was once again staying. Not that he'd driven past it a few times this week like a lovestruck kid, hoping to see her. Needing to figure out how the hell things had gone so wrong between them. Wishing he could wind back time and somehow fix things.

Abigail faced Colt now that she and Lana had finished browsing the display. Her long red hair fell forward as she bent to choose one of the tasting cups on the table, her expression thoughtful as she selected a vintage to sip. Beside her, dark-haired Lana worked more methodically, trying the three available wines in order. The contrast in their styles made Colt think of him and Sierra—Colt quietly cautious, Sierra charging forward.

Was there anything that *didn't* make him think of her lately?

"Wow. This is fantastic, Colt," Abigail declared a moment later as she lifted the vineyard's signature bottle, the Malbec, examining the label before meeting his eyes. "Your grandfather would be so proud of you."

"Thank you, Abby. Granddad would have loved the winery." He told himself that he should discuss the wine. That was his job today, after all. But after a week without Sierra, he found he didn't have the heart for small talk when Abby might know something about the woman he'd been missing for days. "Did I, uh, hear right that Sierra will be speaking tonight?"

He'd heard that she planned to share snippets from Violetta Ford's diary in relation to the TCC. The club's Women's Association had organized a reading during the Roses Under the Stars dinner that capped the Wine and Roses Festival since Violetta had become something of a cult hero to the female membership. In her guise as Vincent Fenwick, Violetta had been the first woman member, technically ousting Abigail for that honor.

There must have been something peculiar about his tone of voice, because Lana's ears seemed to prick up, and she moved closer to join their discussion. Abby's reaction was subtler, but there was no mistaking the curiosity in her blue eyes.

"Sierra is scheduled to say a few words about Violetta's diary for the Women's Association tonight," Abby informed him before passing her credit card to one of his booth assistants, indicating that she wanted two cases of the Malbec. "I imagine she'll be here soon. When Lana and I saw her at the Cimarron Rose, she had just come into the rose garden. And she was already dressed for dinner."

Anticipation fired through him. Colt remembered his first meeting with her in that rose garden, sharing a bench with her as she tried to explain to how she'd connected Arielle's diary to him. He'd been upset, jetlagged, and beside himself about leaving a child on the opposite side of the Atlantic from him. Yet even then, he'd felt the pull toward Sierra, the dynamo who hadn't let an obstacle like an ocean get in the way of her quest for answers.

Damn it, he missed her so much. Every second of every day and night, he wanted her by his side.

As he was jostled from behind, he recognized he'd never answered Abby when Lana edged closer still to add, "Sierra told us how you let her borrow Violetta's diary for research purposes. That was very kind of you, Colt, since we're all eager to learn more about one of Royal's feisty females."

His throat burned with regret to think Sierra had

been speaking so well of him, crediting him with the diary somehow when he'd done nothing but give her a hard time about searching for it. Even though he'd known all along it was her job to dig for answers.

Her special gift as a person.

Why had he insisted on seeing that skill as negative? Not all investigative reporters were out to raise scandal for the fun of it.

It's the Royal Gazette, *not* TMZ, she'd told him when they first met, back when he'd been convinced she wanted to write a story about how he'd left Arielle Martin pregnant and alone while he founded a French winery. But she'd never done anything of the sort. His view of the media had been skewed a long time ago, after his parents' deaths, and he'd never bothered trying to see a member of the press in a different light. That was on him.

"Sierra did all the leg work," he admitted finally, realizing his preoccupation amounted to rudeness to two important local ladies who were trying to support his business. With an effort, he tried to shake off the dark cloud over his head for the hundredth time that day. "She searched the property for the diary with Micah while taking care of him during the day, then worked on her book at night."

Abby and Lana exchanged a look before Lana smiled at him.

"Multitasking is sort of a feminine superpower." She mimed shining her nails on the label of her red dress styled like a long men's jacket. "In fact, Sierra said something about her work slowing down since she stopped taking care of Micah. I'll bet she misses him."

He wondered if she felt half as hollow inside as he

did this week. But he understood maybe that was his perfect excuse to speak to her. Surely she wanted to arrange a visit with Micah in the upcoming days? She hadn't seen him for a whole week. Already he found himself searching the festival crowd for any sign of Sierra's blond hair.

Abigail signed the receipt for her wine and took possession of her credit card again before saying, "Sierra also told us you were returning to France soon."

His head whipped around to meet Abby's gaze. He wanted to ask her for every detail that Sierra had shared, he was so starved for news of her. Instead, he explained, "I haven't firmed up my plans yet. I still have a lot to settle here."

And how strange that was since he'd been so eager to return home. Now he was dragging his feet, his plans on idle since his breakup. He'd wanted to make things right with her a whole week ago—after he'd come home from his talk with Carson Wentworth. Even then, he'd wanted to talk to her about getting together again once he returned to Royal. But his plans had gone up in smoke when he'd come home that day and found her packing her things.

Just the sight of her with a suitcase in her hand had sent his thoughts off the rails. And then he'd jumped on the first cause for blame he could find. Her search for the diary.

"Well, I can't help but hope that once you settle things here, you'll realize how much you'll miss Royal if you leave us again." Abby tucked her receipt in her red leather purse and closed the clasp on her bag. "The Blacks are a Royal family."

Lana tapped one of his wine bottles with a long pink

fingernail. "It says so right on the label. And Micah is kind of a native son after the way the town rallied around him." A smile curved her lips. "Do you know how many of us were ready to adopt him? I would have stood in line myself to be a volunteer mama, except I don't think I could take on Cammie Wentworth."

For the first time since he'd returned to Royal, he didn't feel the same twinge of guilt that he usually experienced about abandoning his child by not having followed up after the brief affair. Hearing Lana talk about how Royal embraced Micah helped Colt see how quickly his hometown had been ready to come to the boy's rescue. How many places could boast the small-town feel that Royal had always possessed? He would offer to stay here if that made a difference to Sierra. Because Royal was a place to call home.

As the gardens and pool area outside the TCC filled with people tasting local wines and dancing to the country band, Colt still scanned the grounds, hoping for a sight of Sierra. He needed to try one more time to fix things.

To be a better man for her.

"Micah is a charmer," Colt acknowledged, seized with a new sense of purpose now. The dark cloud over his head hadn't left, but maybe there was still a chance he could salvage something from the ruins of his relationship with Sierra. "And I'll always be grateful to everyone who was ready to help Micah. But there's only one reason I would stay in Royal, and I'm not sure if she still wants me."

Abby Langley Price seemed to be fighting to hide a smile as she said, "You'll have to ask her." Then she nodded toward someone behind him.

Pivoting fast, he caught sight of Sierra entering the garden area from the clubhouse, a fitted black dress skimming her curves. The high neck and long length were demure, but a high slit at the thigh and slashes in the fabric along her shoulders made the dress sexy.

No. It was the woman inside the gown that did that part.

"Sierra?" His voice rasped as if the word was unfamiliar to him.

She wasn't close enough to hear him, yet somehow she must have sensed his notice, because she turned toward him suddenly, green eyes meeting his from twenty yards away.

He hoped Abby and Lana weren't offended, but he couldn't take his eyes off Sierra. He needed to speak to her. "Ladies, I hope you'll excuse me."

Fueled with a new determination, he charged toward Sierra. Because he couldn't move on with his life until he told her how much he missed her. How much he loved her.

He hadn't wanted to admit it, even to himself, for fear he'd mess up his life plan and the commitment he'd made to his grandfather's memory. But in his heart, he knew his grandfather would never want him to sacrifice his future for the sake of a winery.

He just hoped it wasn't too late to make Sierra see that they were meant for each other. Because he loved her more than he could have imagined possible.

And he hoped like hell she felt the same.

Why did she have to turn and meet Colt Black's eyes the moment she stepped out into the gardens behind the Texas Cattleman's Club? There must have been two hundred people out there, milling around the booths and listening to the country band.

Two hundred people, and Sierra just happened to lock eyes with Colt. It made no sense that something could feel so improbable and yet inevitable at the same time.

Of course, she'd torn her attention away as fast as possible, but even that had been like slow motion since she'd missed the sight of him. Now she gathered her skirt in her hands and headed in the opposite direction, hardly seeing where she was going until she reached an archway of pink roses that ended in a small bench tucked off to one side. There was no exit. And no people, either, to help her make an escape or at least pretend to exchange small talk as a buffer.

She must have walked beyond the festival area without really seeing. But then, turning on one black peau de soie heel to backtrack, she all but ran into a wall masquerading as a man's chest.

"Oof." She made an inelegant noise as she half bounced off the muscular wall. A pair of strong masculine hands reached to steady her.

The scent of pine and sandalwood told her who she'd run into even before she picked her chin up to meet a familiar pair of cobalt-blue eyes. Her breath hitched in her throat. All the loneliness of the past week without him came swelling back to the fore, the ache, the regret.

But he was here. Now. He looked so handsome in his evening wear. The Roses Under the Stars dinner didn't call for a tux, but his black suit was almost as formal. Clean-shaven and hair freshly trimmed, Colt appeared ready for the next phase of the evening.

Did he have a date? The possibility made her stomach hurt and her heart break all over again.

"I'm sorry, Sierra." Colt's words wrapped around her even as his hands fell away from her shoulders. "I didn't mean to startle you. I was trying to get your attention."

Had he called to her? Her thoughts had been so full of trying to escape attention that she might not have heard. Now she could hear the country band switching to a slower waltz. Fairy lights began to come on around the gardens, a reminder that her presentation would start shortly. Still, the evening was so lovely, she was in no rush to retreat indoors.

"It's fine." She stretched her lips in what she hoped passed for a polite smile, still thinking about the possibility of him bringing a date to the evening festivities. "I'm all right. What do you need? Is Micah all right?"

"Micah's fine," he reassured her quickly, then cupped her arm gently in his broad, strong hand. "Can I talk to you for a few minutes? I know you have an obligation to speak soon, but we still have a little time." He pointed to his watch even though she was well aware of the hour.

"I came out here to keep from getting nervous about, uh, presenting about Violetta's diary," she blurted, unsure how he would feel about her presenting to the group about the small volume she'd found. Had he forgiven her for searching for it? "I thought the fresh air would help."

"Then do you mind if we sit for a while?" He gestured toward the wooden bench under the arbor. "I'll help you keep track of the hour."

Her heart thundered. She could have sworn it felt

like an incoming storm inside her chest with all the rumbling. He didn't look angry at all. Could he have rethought his position on the diary?

On the two of them?

But if so, why hadn't he so much as called her this week? In order to have closure, she needed the answer to that, either way.

"I suppose that would be all right," she agreed finally, giving a jerky nod and allowing him to lead her toward the bench.

She'd forgotten how nice it felt to have his hands on her. Just the smallest brush of his fingertips on her lower back made her feel weak.

A burst of laughter from the festival area reminded Sierra that other people were still mingling close by even though their corner nook among the roses felt very private. The scent would forever remind her of this moment with Colt.

Lowering herself onto the wooden bench, she tried to keep a reasonable amount of space between them without looking like she was avoiding him. But the thought of him touching her again made her hyper-conscious of her body. She couldn't afford to melt at his feet.

"I've missed you," he began without preamble, surprising her with his directness. "More than I can say."

What? Had she misheard? For a moment, she wondered if the heady scent of the roses had somehow made her light-headed, because heaven help her, she'd missed him more than she could have imagined possible. She hadn't known it was possible to care so much for one person. To love one person so much.

"I—" She stalled, unsure how to respond to his

statement—the very last thing she would have expected him to say. She'd been prepared for his anger. Not this. Backtracking, she couldn't help but ask, "You do?"

He shook his head his voice sounding strained. "That you'd doubt it for a minute lets me know how much I've failed you."

Out of her depth, she allowed herself to study him more carefully. She hadn't noticed the dark smudges beneath his eyes earlier when they'd locked gazes. But even in the shadowed nook, she could see them now. Had sleep eluded him, too?

Had their argument kept him awake all night the way it had her this whole week?

"I don't understand." She licked her lips, telling herself to keep her hopes in check. Just because he said he missed her didn't mean that anything else had changed. "I've missed you, too, but I know that you're still leaving Royal. And I know that I will remain focused on my career while I try and make peace with my…fertility problems."

That old hurt hadn't gone away. She wasn't ready to share it with anyone else. Especially after what happened between her and Colt.

He picked up her hand from where it rested on the bench. He layered it carefully between both of his. What was it about him that made her feel so cherished? So special? Her eyes burned at the knowledge that she might never feel this way with anyone else ever again.

"If you've missed me the way I've missed you, I think we can work things out. Because we care about one another deeply." He squeezed her palm.

"I care about you. So much. But—"

"No buts. Let's think through this, because I know

I would compromise a whole lot to be together again." His voice was strong, sure. Though she could see the vulnerability in his eyes. "For starters, I don't need to go to France unless you want to go with me. I'll let you make the call."

She straightened in her seat, wondering how else he might surprise her. "I'd go to France in a heartbeat and write travel articles if you wanted me there, but that doesn't change the bigger issue."

She felt nervous now, sensing the next topic up for discussion. She wasn't sure she could have remained seated if he hadn't been holding on to her hand and looking in her eyes the way he might gentle a scared horse.

"There's nothing to discuss," she reminded him, trying to keep her voice steady. "Mine isn't a problem that anyone can fix."

"Then maybe you shouldn't look at it as a problem that needs fixing, Sierra." He curled her palm inside his and lifted his other hand to her face, stroking her cheek with his thumb. "I love you. Every single thing about you, I love. And there's no part of you that I'd change, because then you wouldn't be the uniquely incredible woman that you are."

A half sob escaped her throat midway through his words. She had to cover her lips to keep in the rest of the emotion ready to burst free.

"You have to know you're incredible and I, uh, care for you so very much," she confessed, a tear spilling from one eye. "But how can you be sure you love me?"

"Love defies logic. There's no way I can prove my feelings for you, except with time," he protested, thumbing away the tear. "But make no mistake, it's the truth. I couldn't even function this week without you in my life. I just had a conversation with two women at my booth who wanted to buy wine, but I couldn't even dredge up a single interesting thing to say about the Malbec when I only wanted to ask them questions about you."

A small laugh escaped her. How easy would it be to fall into his arms and absorb all that love shining from his words, from his eyes?

"I haven't thought of anything but you and Micah either." She tipped her face into his hand, savoring the feeling of his fingertips on her temple after not being near him all week. She drew in a deep breath and shared the words she'd sworn she would never utter to another person again. "I love you, too, with my whole heart. And because I love you, I don't want you to be hurt. How can you know how you'll feel about a life with no more children in ten years from now? What if you regret—"

Softly, he kissed her lips, quieting her question. Then, while fireflies danced behind her eyelids, he spoke against her lips.

"Please give me credit for knowing my own heart." He kissed her once more, and she opened her eyes to meet his steady blue gaze. "For knowing what I want. You're it for me, Sierra. If I can't have you, there will be no more children ten years from now anyway, because I will have missed out on the only woman I want to be Micah's mother."

There was something so unflinching in the way he said it that allowed her to feel how much he meant it. That helped her see how much he loved her.

The sob in her throat this time was all happy. And

she did fling herself right into his arms. Wrapped him up tight.

"I love you so much, Colt. You're it for me, too. Always."

She clung to him shamelessly, not caring if her outfit wrinkled, if her mascara smeared, or if her hair ended up in a tangled mess. Soon she'd have to speak to the Texas Cattleman's Club, and she'd surely look like a hot mess. But the residents of Royal, Texas, already knew she cared more about a good story than looking like a beauty queen.

And her story just got an ending better than she could have ever imagined with the man of her dreams.

* * * * *

COMING SOON!

We really hope you enjoyed reading this book.
If you're looking for more romance, be sure to
head to the shops when new books are
available on

Thursday 14th April

To see which titles are coming soon, please visit

millsandboon.co.uk/nextmonth

MILLS & BOON

MILLS & BOON

THE HEART OF ROMANCE

A ROMANCE FOR EVERY READER

MODERN

Prepare to be swept off your feet by sophisticated, sexy and seductive heroes, in some of the world's most glamourous and romantic locations, where power and passion collide.

HISTORICAL

Escape with historical heroes from time gone by. Whether your passion is for wicked Regency Rakes, muscled Vikings or rugged Highlanders, awaken the romance of the past.

MEDICAL

Set your pulse racing with dedicated, delectable doctors in the high-pressure world of medicine, where emotions run high and passion, comfort and love are the best medicine.

True Love

Celebrate true love with tender stories of heartfelt romance, from the rush of falling in love to the joy a new baby can bring, and a focus on the emotional heart of a relationship.

Desire

Indulge in secrets and scandal, intense drama and plenty of sizzling hot action with powerful and passionate heroes who have it all: wealth, status, good looks…everything but the right woman.

HEROES

Experience all the excitement of a gripping thriller, with an intense romance at its heart. Resourceful, true-to-life women and strong, fearless men face danger and desire - a killer combination!

To see which titles are coming soon, please visit

millsandboon.co.uk/nextmonth

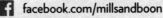

JOIN US ON SOCIAL MEDIA!

Stay up to date with our latest releases, author news and gossip, special offers and discounts, and all the behind-the-scenes action from Mills & Boon...

 millsandboon

 millsandboonuk

 millsandboon

It might just be true love...

MILLS & BOON
MODERN
Power and Passion

Prepare to be swept off your feet by sophisticated, sexy and seductive heroes, in some of the world's most glamourous and romantic locations, where power and passion collide.

MILLS & BOON
MEDICAL
Pulse-Racing Passion

Set your pulse racing with dedicated, delectable doctors in the high-pressure world of medicine, where emotions run high and passion, comfort and love are the best medicine.

MILLS & BOON
True Love
Romance from the Heart

Celebrate true love with tender stories of heartfelt romance, from the rush of falling in love to the joy a new baby can bring, and a focus on the emotional heart of a relationship.